I, DEMIGOD

JOHN DUFFY

To Rob,

Hope you enjoy!

John

2/2/2020

Published by John Duffy

Copyright © 2019 John Duffy

All rights reserved.

This is a work of fiction. Names, characters, places, and incidents are products of the author's imagination or are used fictitiously and should not be construed as real. Any resemblance to actual events, locales, organisations or persons, living or dead, is entirely coincidental.

Other Books by John Duffy

Freak Show
Purple Cane

ACKNOWLEDGMENTS

A few words of thanks firstly to the usual suspects.

My fantastic wife Amelia of course, who remains a legend beyond compare.

And our beautiful daughter Annabel, who gets more beautiful and talented with every passing day.

And Jacqueline (Yia Yia!), whose unflinching faith in the merit of my work is a constant source of motivation.

Also – and as always – the weird and wonderful cast of famous and infamous characters that grace the pages of this bizarre little tome as it barrels along. This particular work in fact, more than either of its' predecessors, takes a significant degree of 'licence' as it were, vis-à-vis what the characters may or may not have been thinking or saying at a given time or place.

It's all total nonsense of course, and never happened at all in actual 'real life'.

That said however – and in the interests as ever of covering my arse – I would like to apologise to all of them MOST PROFUSELY whether they be living or dead, for my blithesome approach to what *might* have been their innermost thoughts.

Here they are anyway; the motley supporting cast!

Guns 'n' Roses, Freddie Mercury, Queen, Benny Hill, James Joyce, Samuel Beckett, U2, Alexander Pope, Brian May, Jimi Hendrix, Neil Diamond, Moses, David Bowie, Phil Collins, Roger Taylor, John Deacon, Metallica, James Hetfield, Joe Elliott, Robert Plant, Tony Iommi, Mick Ronson, Tom Waits, Rod Stewart, The Rolling Stones, Coco Schwab, Annie Lennox, Extreme, John Bonham, Paul McCartney, Reeves Gabrels, Paddy McAloon, Prefab Sprout, Neil Conti, Thomas Dolby, Mike Garson, Woody Woodmansey, Trevor Bolder, Keith Richard, Lindsay Kemp, Dick Cavett, Elton John, Axl Rose, Slash, The Edge, Nat

King Cole, Led Zeppelin, Larry Grayson, Bob Geldof, Bono, Eamon Dunphy, Willie Dixon, Scott Walker, Grace Slick, Jefferson Airplane, Jimmy Page, The Yardbirds, Roy Wood, Jeff Lynne, Ozzy Osbourne, Leo Sayer, Vanilla Fudge, Van Halen, Bon Jovi, Bette Midler, George Michael, John Fogarty, Moby Grape, Anthony Newley, Peter Gabriel, Genesis, Lord Henry Mountcharles, Noël Coward, Duff McKagan, Bob Dylan, Robert Fripp, Thin Lizzy, The Sex Pistols, Cary Grant, Gary Moore, The Grateful Dead, Jerry Garcia, David Niven, Kate Bush, James Bond, Tom Petty, Elvis Presley, Cole Porter, Fred Astaire, Glenn Hoddle, Francois Mitterrand, Christy Dignam, Adam Clayton, Larry Mullen, Derek Rowan, Gavin Friday, Mohandas Gandhi, Yoko Ono, The New York Dolls, Mr. Magoo, Lesley Dowdall, Paul Brady, Midge Ure, Leonardo De Vinci, Richie Sambora, Pete Townshend, Mephistopheles, Martin Luther King, Ronald Reagan, H.G. Wells, Benjamin Disraeli, Sting, Adolf Hitler, Mohammad Ali, Charles Darwin, Phil Lynott, Gay Byrne, Colette Farmer, Peter Ustinov, Scott Gorham, Philomena Lynott, Pink Floyd, Philly Grimes, Peter Hamill, Brian Robertson, Brian Downey, John Sykes, Bruce Springsteen, Paul McGuinness, Tony DeFries, Charles Haughey, Gerry Adams, Hugh Leonard, Joe Public, John Lennon, George Harrison, Stuart Sutcliffe, Pete Best, Ken Dodd, The Queen Mother, Philip Larkin, Pete Shotton, Astrid Kirchherr, Helen Shapiro, Denny Laine, Jimmy McCulloch, Josef Stalin, Marty Whelan, Oliver Reed, Ossie Kilkenny, Prince, Roger Waters, Kenny Rogers, Willie Nelson, Michael Johnson, Bob Geldof Senior, Zenon Geldof, Michael Buerk, Mark Ellen, The Cars, Harvey Goldsmith, Enid Blyton, The Boomtown Rats, Lionel Richie, Mott the Hoople, Van Morrison, Ronnie Ross, Geoff Emerick, George Martin, Del Palmer, The Grim Reaper, Buddha, ZZ Top, Robin Williams, BB King, Johnny Rogan, John Lydon, Frank Zappa, Lee Trevino, Lord Dorchester, The Princess Sophia, King George the 3rd, Isambard Kingdom Brunel, William Makepeace Thackeray, Anthony Trollope, Mary Scott Hogarth, Charles Dickens, Johnny 'Freak Show' Fortune.

Last but not least I would like to remember our wonderful mother Vera, who died on October 27th 2018. Our loss is compensated only by the knowledge that we were so very, very fortunate to have been able to call her our Mam.

John Duffy
July 2019

For my dear old pal Matt

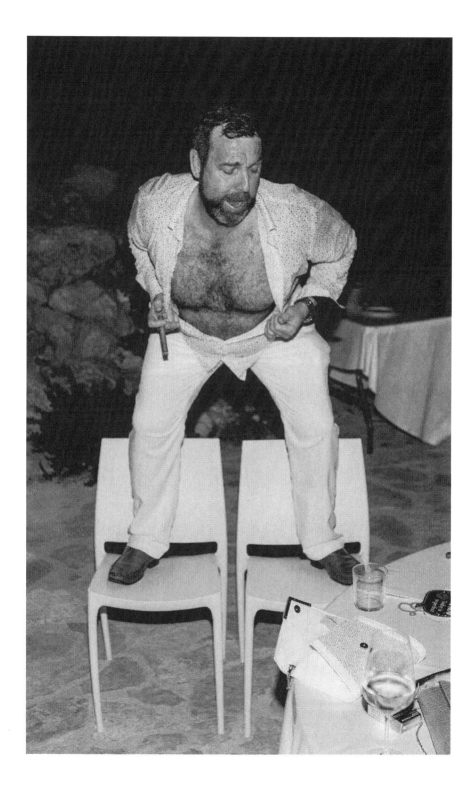

I, DEMIGOD

CHAPTER 1

The year was 1992 and the future was bright.

Politicians were gathering in Holland to sort us all out – BUT FUCK THEM!

They couldn't dampen our spirits.

We were moshing man!

MOSHING TO GUNS 'N' FUCKING ROSES!

'Things' however *as* ever would deteriorate; with life soon enough returning to its more habitual state of embarrassment and calamity.

The entire debacle had started some weeks earlier - on April 20th to be exact - in London.

Suffice it to say that my meeting with Belinda, although undeniably pleasant at first, turned out in the end to be anything but.

This chance encounter - chance, *seemingly* innocuous encounter - culminated eventually in disaster, and would mark the beginning of my ultimate transformation into, in no time at all, an entirely different beast.

Today however, on Saturday May 16th 1992, in Slane, County Meath, it was all about being fucked.

Fucked AND stoned as a matter of fact.

And on Acid too, which, for me, was an entirely radical departure.

Axl Rose had sorted that shit out for us in London, with 'that' being - being brutally honest about it - the exact point where I believe you can mark the origin of my decline.

Gargle is one thing but tripping on Acid?

A totally different ball game.

Yes indeedy.

A quarter of a tab here and a half tab there, and before you know it you're bolloxed for pretty much most of the time.

And when you're not you're wishing that you are.

But ho hum - c'est la vie, right?

I was probably over thinking it.

Before however, I elaborate further on the events that followed, let me start where I always do.

At the beginning.

April 20th 1992 as I was mentioning there before.

Belinda.

BE LINDA!

I mean, what sort of a handle is that?

Why not just 'LINDA'?

Pretty superfluous to my mind - that old additional 'BE'.

Encouraging you to be what you already are?

Her parents had quite clearly been drunk or something, all those years before, when appraising available and apparently appropriate appellation for their newly arrived bundle of joy.

But then again with a surname like Carruthers - which was what theirs was – their penchant for dubious designation was hardly remarkable.

Belinda Carruthers.

It was a tough start.

She was a Killiney girl also, with a silver spoon to match.

Looking for a 'bit of rough' on the day in question she was too; with the 'bit of rough' that she latched on to in the end, being me.

I had presented myself anyway at the Rose and Crown in Union Street, SE1; which was my usual port of frequency when returned.

Stick to what you know I say; and they know me well enough in there as well.

There was no need at all so, for the reasons outlined above, to deviate from what was in all respects a tried and trusted blueprint.

I had left London in 1989 - as you may recall from previous accounts - having tired of its capacity to ravage the soul.

Every now and again though, over the past number of years since I had left, I'd wander on back for the odd weekend here and there; for a bit of an old gander kind of thing, and to see if anything of significance had changed.

I had scored tickets also for that Freddie Mercury tribute concert thingamajig in Wembley, off some dude that I half knew from the Neptune Bar in Lower Abbey Street, D1; and whereas Freddie Mercury and all things 'Queen' related are unquestionably reprehensible, the fucker as you may know, had fallen off his perch just the year before, in 1991, so was unlikely at any point in the near to medium term future, to be heard whining anywhere about needing somebody to love, or substantiating also, yawn-festingly, to anybody in his midst, his desire to break free from wherever it was that the bollocks wanted to break free.

And although there would almost certainly be other jerk members of the virulent band on the stage on said day – which was pretty unavoidable to be fair - we could be rest assured at least that the 'singing' aspect of the programme would be executed by, no matter who they were, individuals that were considerably less vexatious than the moustached jabberer under present review.

But that's just, like, my opinion.

You may, of course, disagree.

Perhaps you like Queen?

'Bismillah, NOOO!' etc.,?

No offence intended so, if any taken.

Facial hair of such a contemptible nature however, is, you must surely concur, unforgiveable under any circumstances.

Let us, however, move on.

Brain dead, half deaf fuckwits are entitled to their view also, I always say.

I had positioned myself anyway at the bar in the Rosie, and was getting stuck into, with some degree of brio, gargle number one.

My old pal Marcus would be joining me 'at some point' he had said, but for now it was just 'yours truly' and the scoop.

The news had just come through on the tube in the corner that the great Benny Hill had died sometime earlier that day.

A comic genius I had always thought myself, but those on the bulletin were a good deal less laudatory.

Censorious if anything.

A 'slapstick has-been' they intimated.

'With a less than impressive penchant for the inane'.

The Brits are like that though.

Peculiar, you know?

Happy to 'put down success' kind of thing?

Begrudging.

We're quite like that ourselves in fact.

Us Irish.

Oh yes.

Particularly if the 'success' in question is not overly *high-brow*.

Joyce and Beckett however?

'Knock yourself out', say the intelligentsia.

Even if most of it is incomprehensible.

'Not I' for example.

Drivel really.

'Looking aimlessly for cowslips'?

Please.

A probing light in the dark of a theatre Samuel, will not render bolloxology of such a denomination any more endurable.

The Eurovision song contest though?

A 'free for all' of abuse.

And U2?

Wankers, of course.

And it's our job to let them know it!

But with the latter, fair enough, of course.

How can any sane individual feasibly disagree?

'In the Name of Love?'

'In the name of GOD, WILL YOU EVER SHUT THE FUCK UP, YOU INSUFFERABLE SHORT-ARSED PRICK'!

Hill had been a roaring success in the US anyway, which in 1992, and before that indeed, had been a notoriously difficult market for comics from this side of the pond to surmount.

Oddly enough however, his 'cheeky chappy' dirty old man routine had struck a chord with the yanks, with the slightly tubby and old fashioned, semi-vaudeville phenomenon, against all odds, becoming a household name stateside, practically overnight.

Today however in SE1, no-one appeared to be overly concerned with what I believed personally to be the saddest of news regarding his demise.

To the extent even that as soon as the headline broke, and for at least a half an hour afterwards, the crowd in attendance were happy merely to just dash around the pub like drunken idiots, whilst at the same time singing the music from the closing credits of the eponymous programme in question; and also, whether the injured parties were happy about it or not, slapping all bald or balding people in the vicinity on the back of their heads, smartly and in quick succession, à la as Hill himself had done on so many occasions before, to his perennially set upon and hairless sidekick from the show.

Various young ladies that were in situ also – ladies that were without doubt a good deal more worse for wear on the gargle than was befitting - appeared happy as well to disrobe into their undergarments and allow one of their group - a male - of whom they all agreed in their opinion was the most 'pervy' looking of *all* of the males that were in attendance on the day - to chase them around the pub in the exact same manner as had been perpetrated on the broadcast all those years before.

As a general scene so, it was not hugely edifying.

Although in their defence it *was* quite humorous.

And any day that you can cop an eyeful of nubile young fillies in a state of near undress is a pretty decent day as far as I'm concerned.

"As a general scene, this is not hugely edifying, is it dude?" remarked Marcus, as he slapped me several times on the back of the head in double quick succession.

"Marco, you old bollocks!" I remonstrated loudly, as I turned to face my newly arrived comrade in arms.

"Welcome to the land of the blight!" I continued, happy to see him of course, although not best pleased with the slaps.

"And yes, I must agree with you, my old pal" wincing slightly as he slapped me again, but holding out my hand to him anyway, by way of a welcome.

4

"The scene is less than agreeable!"

Marcus, my old buddy, was in the house.

He'd phoned me in Dublin just the week before, to say that he'd be accompanying me to the pestilent concert in question, having acquired tickets to it himself from that same dude in the Nep.

This had been very satisfactory news to me at the time, I'm not going to deny it; as being a handsome enough chap – and perhaps even more so when examined adjacent to my good self – Marcus attending said event was a development that almost certainly determined that any potential 'scoring' of the 'ladies' would be improved considerably, potentially, as a result of this ostensibly extraneous but incontestably positive progression.

Very fickle, you see; that old 'fairer sex' lot.

Capricious, I might even go as far as to say.

They'd be wetting themselves anyway as soon as they copped an eyeful of young Marco.

His chiselled jaw had proven on many occasions in the past, to be all that was required to transform delicate damsels into swoon-like states.

He would take the boat from Dublin anyway he had said, as he couldn't afford the flight - my old man worked for Aer Fungus, so air travel was next to nothing usually for myself - so would be arriving a few hours after me, having taken the over-night ferry from Holyhead in Wales the evening before.

I'd flown into the capital myself earlier that morning and made it by tube to London Bridge from Heathrow, before strolling across the river from there to Southwark.

And here we were now.

Ready to rock and roll, as they say!

Some randomer came up to me then and by the look on his face had a general administering of slaps to the back of my head on his mind.

The glance of stern rebuke from me to him then though, shortly after his arrival, left him in no doubt as to the outcome of such an action if he was to dispense with personal sagacity and succumb to his yearning to follow through with said perpetration.

Slaps would be ensuing alright.

But from me to him rather than from him to me.

Fortuitously for him anyway he recognised, astutely enough I suppose you might say, that such was the case.

He moved on swiftly so, to the next punter along.

A wise move.

A VERY wise move.

And besides which also, I wasn't bald.

So what the fuck was his problem?

5

"A tasty scoop, young man?" asked Marcus then, which, considering the nature of how things had degenerated in the pub so speedily, was a solid enough idea all round.

If you can't beat 'em, join 'em kind of thing, you know?

"Fuckin' suredin!" I answered quickly, draining my first, after which he nodded to Dermot the barman for two of the best.

Stella, of course.

We started to lash them back then, with our collective mood very soon becoming a good deal more carefree.

We talked of this and of that and in general just caught up.

The ongoing shenanigans in the pub however and subsequent ridiculousness that ensued, was showing very little sign of decline.

Oddly enough also - and almost certainly without intention - what had commenced as a semi good-natured if slightly disparaging 'piss take' of Benny Hill, was now, as time passed by, almost perfectly apt and fitting for the occasion.

If he had been there himself in fact at the time, or had been looking down on it indeed, from whatever dimension he may or may not have been residing now anew, he would almost certainly I believe, have given the current scenario a more than robust 'thumbs up' and congratulatory seal of approval.

The mayhem had escalated quite significantly now to the extent that some-body from somewhere - we were unsure who initially - had managed to unearth the 'end of show' theme music in question, and had found also - we weren't sure how exactly either, but would find out soon enough – a way of transforming it into a state of public amplification.

As in beforehand it was being sung, merely, and was in our heads also - it was hard to dispel it from there to be fair, once it had wormed its way in.

As things stood now however, it was, believe it or believe it not, emanating from the speakers that were attached at a height to the walls on either side of the bar.

This was all pretty surreal at the time if I'm being honest, but as with most things in life when reviewed afterwards in the clear light of day, perfectly reasonable explanations for weird stuff that's going on are identified easily enough usually in less rose-tinted hindsight.

And so it was on the day in question.

Dermot the barman was, unbeknownst to us at the time, an ardent fan of the comedic maestro in question, so actually had a copy of the theme tune in his collection of CD's.

When he saw so how things had been developing in the pub over the last little while, he just popped it into the CD player behind the bar and stuck it on to a loop.

He had spotted it on some stall apparently in Camden Market several years before, and relieved the vendor at the time, for the princely sum of £1.50, of the item in his stockpile that he no doubt believed he would never be relieved.

So although disagreeable at first, the scene before us was quickly metamorphosing into a jubilant and joyous celebration.

Dermot's idea to give the theme music a whirl had elevated events to an entirely new level.

His main inspiration for doing so of course may have been to keep the punters there for just that little bit longer, and as a result of this turn a faster buck.

His superficially commercial motives however, in the end, had significantly more momentous and farther-reaching ramifications.

Suffice it to say that as time went by the atmosphere became a good deal more uplifting and high-spirited.

The easy-going timbre of the music in question, in addition to the liberal quantities of alcohol that were being consumed, assured that over a relatively short period of time the general mind-set of those in attendance was becoming increasingly uninhibited.

More modest females who to date had foregone this general 'dismissal of garments' ethic that others of their assemblage had been happy to welcome into their lives, were throwing caution to the wind now and joining in with the melee.

A conga started also, with a long stream of semi-clad and in some cases, semi *semi*-clad honeys – quarter-clad you might term it - becoming interspersed soon enough with chaps every four or five persons along.

Chaps who by the looks on their faces as the conga weaved in and out of the tables and chairs in the establishment, could quite honestly not believe their luck.

Marcus looked at me then, and I looked at him, with our determined and focused countenances saying all that was needed to be said.

Telepathic.

Inaudible.

Intangible almost, you might say.

We would be joining the conga.

"Cha cha, cha cha, cha, CHAH!" opined a girl directly before me, as I regarded her svelte lower back and naked waist in the grasp of my hands.

"ARIBA!!" cried another to my rear, who was grasping, similarly, mine own.

It was all good.

Excellent, in fact.

The conga snaked through the establishment erratically, whereupon I met Marcus again at the apex and nadir of a brace of serpentine loops.

One of the more drunken girls stumbled at the front then, which gave us a moment to converse.

"Is this not what life is all about, young Marco?" I imparted breathlessly to my wide-eyed and ecstatic friend.

"It is" he answered, correspondingly convulsed.

"As scenarios go in fact, my old pal, I can think of none before that have been more gratifying".

"Largely unanticipated of course" he continued.

"But exceptional nonetheless".

"*Blessed is he who expects nothing*'" he wittered on.

"*For he shall never be disappointed*'"

"Pope" he said, by way of clarification, I supposed, for the incongruous elucidation.

"The poet" he explained further, confusing me obviously, with a person for whom a quote of this nature might hold some semblance of fascination or interest.

He should have known of course, that this would, nor could, ever be the case.

'Pope' is not, nor has ever been, my 'thing'.

And Marcus also (if we are to assume that it was to himself he was referring) was hardly *expecting nothing*; to go back to the quote.

As in, aren't we all always expecting 'something'?

His citation so - in addition to its inarguably suspect appositeness - was pretty spurious too.

That was Marcus's problem you see.

I believe that I may have recounted this before?

Chisel-jawed though he may have been, he more often not, for no other reason bar self-obsessed obsequiousness, inserted his big size nines into 'situations' where calm reticence and mature reflection before offering an opinion of any inclination, might at the time have been a notably superior selection.

But he couldn't help himself.

It was part of his nature.

I believe that the apropos expression is 'smartarse'?

And so it would be today.

Fatigued by our exertions we made our way back to our pints, with the idea being that a tasty cold beverage whilst resting our elbows on the bar, would be a decidedly more favourable way for us to be taking in the view.

"What the fuck was that shit you were banging on about over there!?" enquired the girl from the front of the conga who had fallen over before.

The girl who not long after we had left the conga ourselves, had done so also, and was stationed before us now.

"Was that you pal?" she went on, with her hands on her hips.

"With the fucking *poetry* or whatever the fuck it was?!"

8

These were the first words that I would hear spoken by the young lady referred to in the narrative already as Belinda Carruthers.

And although her initial dialogue was out there for both of us to consider, I do have to admit that it was directed at Marcus mainly rather than myself.

This was not surprising.

As I have alluded to before, the ladies tend usually to opt for Marcus; certainly in the early stages anyway.

As ever though, he proceeded to wade straight in and snatch inglorious defeat - not for the first time I might add - from the jaws of almost certain victory.

"If it is to me you address" he answered, turning to face her.

"Then yes. It was I that expounded same. 'Pope', don't you know, in a letter to a pal - although he may, I believe, have purloined it from a beatitude? That, however, as a fact, is wholly unproven. You are familiar anyway, I suppose, with the poesy under scrutiny? Perhaps so, *if* so, we might reach an understanding? Ladies that are keen on the verse, are, as I'm sure you are aware, a veritable scarcity".

Not a particularly zippy opening so.

Belinda was definitely looking at him like he had two heads.

Unwisely enough then, he made a decision to proceed in a similar vein.

"You are scantily clad, young lady" be continued, as he looked her up and down.

"Which although unconventional, is a sound approach nevertheless. Vis-à-vis the 'positive nature of the development for the male spectator' kind of thing?"

Notwithstanding Marcus's verbosity, Belinda could scarcely deny the pronouncement.

In keeping with how things had panned out in the Rosie over the last little while, she had *indeed* removed a significant proportion of her clothing; to the extent now in fact, that the only garments that she was donning were a flimsy red G string type affair on the bottom half of her anatomy, and at the top, a decidedly revealing red and black leather and lace basque type thingamajig, which as a device for pushing ample breasts upwards to a point where they were very nearly departing the entire set up, could never in any way be declared as a device that was inadequate.

The events that took place over the course of the following few minutes anyway - to elaborate further - did nothing to dissuade me from a view that I already held.

That is, that when compared to all other cities in the world at any other time over history, London really was in the early to mid-1990's one hell of a debauched cesspit to behold.

Marcus had ordered a Kir Royale mere moments before Belinda had dragged me away, and when I tell you now that in the time it took for the barman to prepare the pertinent ingredients for said tipple and place it before my old friend at the bar, Belinda and I had not only visited the ladies lavatory and engaged in messy and incontestably unimpressive coitus, but had returned to the bar also, and were getting stuck into our drinks again with gusto, you'll no doubt I imagine, understand from where I am coming.

As I was taking her from behind in the grotty cubicle, not ten seconds after we had begun our journey across the pub - and without yet also, at this point, having spoken any *actual* words to her, or her to me directly - I marvelled at our decadence.

Graffiti on the wall before me also, corroborated my view that this really was a scene that was not unlike, probably, what one might have encountered during the headier days of the Borgias whilst they were still in their pomp.

"I LOVE IT WHEN MY BOYFRIEND STICKS HIS BIG FAT COCK UP MY ARSE!' the words conveyed, etched there in penknife by a promiscuous libertine of the opposite sex who had obviously visited said convenience before. A libertine that deemed it important to let the world at large know of her happiness regarding the size of her partner's phallus, and the fact also, that when he inserted it into her anus, whenever he was encouraged to do so, that she liked that as well, very much indeed.

"Not the arse!" panted Belinda, who, having probably noticed the inscription herself as she leaned forward with her hands grasping the porcelain cistern before her, left me in no doubt as to her own feelings on the matter - if I happened to take it upon myself that is, to remove a certain thing from a certain place and insert it into another place that was located further north.

That option now, was not an option.

How and ever, it was all good.

I had little to be complaining about.

As in, it usually took a considerably greater degree of effort for me to get to this juncture, and more often than not, generally, involved some degree of prior dialogue.

Talking of dialogue, Marcus enquired as to our recent absence.

"Where the fuck did you pair go?" he said, as we stood before him now, a couple of minutes later, all flush-faced and breathless.

"I didn't get yiz a drink anyway - yiz weren't here, so, you know, toughskie shitskie and all that, as they say in St. Petersburg…"

"A tasty beverage now however?" he asked further, as he pointed back and forth to the both of us with his index finger.

Belinda had a drink already though; the glass of which - the upper rim in fact - was clasped now between her teeth as she endeavoured to climb back into her jeans.

She had picked them up on the way back from the loo, along with some other accoutrements from where she had discarded them earlier on, next to where her friends were gathered on the other side of the pub.

She succeeded in getting the jeans back on anyway, eventually, before casually throwing an 'off the shoulder' tee shirt on then, and slipping her feet into a pair of threadbare old flip flops that had definitely seen better days.

Within an instant so, she went from being a burlesque and lusty lady of the night to a twenty something art student to whom you wouldn't give a second glance if she passed you on the street.

She bundled her black and red tinted tresses up with her hands then, before clasping a giant hair clip around them to just about hold the unruly mess together.

The transformation was complete and stark.

If you had seen her moments earlier and then eyed her up now, having turned away for just a moment, you'd have every reason to believe that a semi-similar imposter had surreptitiously come along while nobody was looking, and taken her place.

Her actions anyway, appeared to encourage everyone around the place to do similarly, with the hitherto raucous and semi-naked debauchery that had been abroad for the previous short while, desisting now considerably, with everything, give or take, returning to normal before long.

Clothes were donned once more, as people returned to their drinks.

Dermot turned the music down also which gave us time to think.

"Some introductions?" said Belinda, as she warmly held out her hand.

"You're Irish too obviously, yeah?" she went on.

"I'm Belinda".

I grabbed her hand and shook it; which, considering the nature of the bodily contact that had taken place between us already seemed a tad absurd.

"Johnny Fortune" I said.

"'Freak Show' to me pals" I blathered on.

"A series of fairly gruesome facial 'aberrations' shall we say, in my youth?" I elaborated further, by way of an explanation for the moniker.

I'd had a torrid time of it in that regard when I was younger.

A lunar landscape on the old boat race if I'm being totally honest; but things had cleared up well enough since then, thankfully, with a pin prick pock mark here and there the only remaining evidence of prior calamity.

"And this is Marcus, me old pal" I continued, gesturing in his direction, to which she barely registered interest and looked the other way.

He didn't look that interested himself either, in fairness to him, and just got back to his drink.

His opening monologue, it appeared, had been more romance-deadening than if he'd elbowed her in the face.

Love would not be blossoming here.

"Yiz are off to the concert so, yeah?" she said, turning back to me, assuming correctly.

"We are" I answered cheerfully.

"Although as I'm sure you agree, it is expected to be a pretty grim affair. But at least there'll be gargle there, right? Which will numb our senses enough hopefully, to drown out the band".

She looked at *me* now like I had two heads.

As in, she was not impressed.

"Brian May is a fucking GOD!" she responded icily, after which I began to wonder if my initial evaluation of her - that is, that she seemed to be a kindly enough soul, albeit a tad fruity - had been correct.

First impressions can be like that sometimes. An otherwise excellent initial meeting can very often deteriorate badly as you familiarise yourself further with the subject.

This announcement regarding her apparent appreciation for the abominable axe man in question was an acutely alarming advancement.

"You like Brian May?" I asked, straining hard to keep the look of incredulity from my face.

"I do" she retorted defiantly.

"And why wouldn't I?" she expanded further.

"Well, there's the ridiculous barnet for starters" I responded, as any sane person might.

But she was no longer listening.

Some dude from across the way had waved a double G and T at her, so off she tootled on her merry little way.

"For fuck sake dude, I was in there!" spouted Marcus.

And if ever an evaluation of a situation and the *actual* reality of a situation were to be compared and then following on from that, derided, then this was that situation, right here, right now.

"Why did you have to take the piss out of Brian May?!"

"Firstly pal" I retorted,

"IN YOUR FUCKING DREAMS!"

"And secondly, Brian May is an Astro Physics loving BOLLOCKS! Plain and simple. You DO know this dude!"

"And if she was into anyone also, it was me" I went on.

"Sure didn't I get the fucking ride off her in the jacks?!"

He had the look of a person who thinks that you're bullshitting.

But I was not bullshitting.

"You might want to consider shutting the fuck up in the future also!" I continued.

"Or failing that; bringing a fucking interpreter! This has been mentioned to you before also, by the way. So, you know, following on from that, you might want think about taking a fucking hint at some point?!"

"No chance dude!" Marcus responded, obstinately.

"If the womenfolk can't deal with Marcus and his ostentatious articulation, then the womenfolk can go and fuck themselves!"

It would appear so, going forward, that the womenfolk would be fucking themselves.

This was a impetuous enough approach by Marcus I believed, but telling him about it there and then would have been an exercise in frivolity.

I made a decision so – wisely I believe - to move on.

I looked back over towards Belinda and her pals, and saw that they were making preparations to leave.

Having gathered their bits and bobs together eventually, they moved as a marauding mass towards the exit, before boisterously departing the establishment.

Belinda coquettishly blew me a kiss on her way out, and that was that.

She had disappeared into the London afternoon, never, I assumed, to be seen again.

"Fuck her!" said Marcus dismissively, as he took another sip out of his girly drink.

"Plenty more fish in the sea. Dispel her from your thoughts, my old friend" he continued.

He was right.

There *were* plenty more fish in the sea.

Billions really.

But none that looked like Belinda.

Or were that promiscuous.

Certainly not so expeditiously anyway.

Although I *have* heard rumours about the blowfish?

What the fuck was I banging on about?

She was gone.

I felt sick to the stomach.

We had shared a connection.

Beyond, that is, one that was merely physical.

I could feel it.

"Down it Marco" I said, with purpose.

"We need to go after them!"

"Ahh for fuck sake dude!" he answered, visibly pissed off at my latest proclamation.

"What about my Kir Royale?!"

Which, as a statement, when considered soberly and then ruminated upon for a moment or two afterwards, is about as gay a statement as has ever been uttered, either before or since.

Kir Royale!

I ask you!

What the actual fuck?!

I retorted, naturally, with a considerable degree of righteous indignation.

"Will you for once in your life Marcus, get your head out of your arse? Your girly drink, as things stand now, is of zero importance. Grab your jacket and come on will ye, te fuck?"

To his credit he did, and put a sock in it also, thankfully.

We bundled ourselves through the exit a couple of moments later and scanned the horizon for our recent émigrés.

Sadly however, they were nowhere to be seen.

"Fuck it anyway!" I spat out angrily.

"Why the fuck didn't we leave with them?" I went on.

"The tube station!" said Marcus.

"They're bound to be there dude. If we run, we're sure to catch up with them!"

He was right.

What a shout!

They had to get to Wembley Stadium as well, so surely the mode of transport that Marcus had suggested would be the obvious mode of transport of choice?

Off we dashed so in the general direction of London Bridge.

If we put a step on it, we were bound to make ground on them, before they had gone too far.

CHAPTER 2

We made it to the station soon enough and having purchased our tickets from the teller - two singles to Wembley – we stopped at a wall map in the main ticket hall to work out our route.

The journey looked relatively straightforward, and required us to just head to the Jubilee line platform and then take a westbound train from there to Wembley Park. It was just fifteen stops in total, so not that difficult a trek really, and no changes either, which was good.

Arriving at the designated platform a few minutes later, I was disappointed to find that Belinda and her crew were nowhere to be seen.

'Fuck it anyway!' I was thinking.

'We'll never find them now!'

I was well pissed off.

"Put it out of your mind, good sir" Marcus opined, noticing my disappointment.

"What was that I was saying there before about fish?" he went on.

And although his previous analogy regarding fish and how many there were in the sea was indubitably correct, it still didn't take away from the fact that I believed, strongly and as I mentioned before, that Belinda and I had developed a connection and that ergo, we should be together.

And where else also, was I going to find a girl that was happy - nay, that *encouraged* one even - to have sex with her within no more than a minute or two of our very first encounter?

It was a certainty to me so, following on from these reflections, that for the remainder of the day, and from the instant that I arrived at the gig, I'd be scanning the crowd anxiously in my quest to locate her again.

Our journey was swift so within no more than a half hour we had disembarked from the tube and were making our way up the escalator to the exit.

Upon reaching fresh air outside we got stuck into the old Harry Rags immediately, before following the rest of the punters that were streaming up Olympic Way in the general direction of the stadium.

And what a crowd it was!

A vast collection of denim-clad unkempt drunkards, who by and large appeared to have no concept at all as to the fact that mullets, under any circumstances, are not an acceptable state in which to have your coiffure, ever.

If that is you are considering at any juncture the notion of venturing outside from your homestead, into what might be considered in most circles to be a generally public space.

Some of these dudes appeared to have girlfriends as well, which as a situation to behold at the time, was almost entirely inconceivable.

A parallel universe really.

Marcus and I had dabbled in long haired-ness in our youth also; don't get me wrong.

But the individuals that were congregated here today were grown men.

Adults, you know?

It just goes to show you so that no matter how desperate or pathetic you look - or indeed *are* - at a particular time or place, that every loser at some point has some possibility at least, however slight, of scoring a chick.

If the circumstances that are prevailing that is, are in your favour at the time.

The female fraternity here for example - and some of them were very cute indeed – had decidedly unambitious aspirations.

And the same in many respects also- when we arrived there ten minutes or thereabouts hence and reviewed the scene before us - could be said to apply to the young ones that were gathered at the venue.

It was hard to countenance really. As in some of the birds that were congregated here were absolute stunners, with the dudes that they were latched on to in most cases, quite ludicrously put together by comparison.

Thousands upon thousands of fuzzy-mopped losers we're talking about here, who at any other time in history up until that moment, would have been derided upon vigorously - and quite justifiably too - by whomever they encountered during the general course of their daily comings and goings.

Leather strides folks.

Leather strides!

Not acceptable, I'm sure you concur, under any circumstances, ever.

A word anyway about the day.

Weather wise, that is.

And the 'set-up' generally.

Aside from the dodgy looking dudes with the hair, all else for now appeared to be kosher.

The sun was splitting the trees and a general air of alcohol-fuelled bonhomie was ubiquitous throughout.

All present were fairly 'well on' also, so when you pair that at any time with a festival that's imbued with anything remotely akin to agreeable climatic conditions, the prevailing atmosphere more often than not is benign.

At least in the early stages of the day anyway.

Mine and Marcus's moods were as carefree as you can imagine, and with moderately priced gargle available from the various vendors that were dotted throughout the stadium, here and there, within and without, you could be forgiven for thinking that little if anything could dampen our mood.

You would, however, if you thought that, be wrong.

Very, VERY wrong.

Assuming - quite rightly, of course - that Marcus was as keen to get stuck into the scoops as myself; I pointed my finger in the general direction of a tented booze dispensary of sorts that was situated towards the rear of the field.

We had entered the main stadium pitch-side at around the half way line, so it wasn't too far to get to the back where the stalls and tents that were vending such wares were positioned.

It was difficult to be heard over the sound of the crowd now though, with a new and distressing downside to our situation menacingly emergent.

This being the fact that the great unwashed now, were 'en masse' singing along to the grisliness that is popularly known as 'Radio Ga Ga'.

The abhorrent number was blaring relentlessly from the PA system next to the stage, and another one also, halfway down the pitch adjacent to where we were at present ensconced.

It was difficult to fathom the veneration of this ghastly tune to be honest, and even more so with a crowd such as this.

It was similar almost I believed, to a comparable gathering, perhaps twenty-five or so years earlier on, watching Jimi Hendrix set fire to his guitar on the stage following a spectacular rendition of 'Purple Haze', and then five minutes later, when he returned for an encore, the crowd being similarly effusive when he made efforts to encourage them to join him in a sing-along to the abominable Neil Diamond tune 'Sweet Caroline'.

Hardly Rock 'n' Roll, you know?

All in all so this was another reason why gargle, and a subsequent numbing of the senses as a result of the expeditious ingestion of said elixir, was such a capital idea at the time.

"Quick Marco!" I grunted, before grabbing him by the wrist and pulling him towards the tents.

"Scoops, post haste!" I went on.

"This putridness is far too much for any poor young soul to bear!"

He regarded me gravely and by the look on his face it was clear that he was similarly unnerved.

"Agreed dude" he answered with a wince.

"Gargle is unquestionably exigent!"

Off we tootled so, in the general direction of the sauce.

Upon arriving at the first of the tents that sold said imbibes, we were disappointed to note that the queue was as lengthy as you can imagine.

Which for a duo that was thirsty to a point of near desperation, was not an ideal development at all.

"FUCK IT ANYWAY!" I spat out, with my hands on my hips in exasperation as I perused the line.

"How are we gonna deaden the pain now dude?" I asked Marcus, referring of course to the odious number that was blaring still from the stadium's auditory equipage.

"I don't know dude" responded Marcus sullenly.

"But you're right" he continued.

"Our situation is grave. And what if they play 'Flash Gordon'? Or, God forbid, and JESUS CHRIST, 'I Want to Break Free'? We need scoops badly, my friend; and we need them NOW!"

Weighing up our situation so, and assessing how best to gain any form of advantage vis-à-vis reaching the top of the queue more speedily than it appeared we might be able to under present circumstances, a plan began to formulate in my mind.

It made perfect sense to me at the time, so putting it into effect was the work of no more than a moment.

I was so convinced that it would work in fact that I didn't even canvas Marcus for his views on whether he believed that it might be a runner himself.

I just fucking went for it.

"THEY'RE COMING ON!" I shouted out fervidly to all in our midst.

"I DON'T FUCKING BELIEVE IT GUYS!!" I continued, waving my hands about in mock consternation.

"THE BAND ARE ONLY COMING ON!"

Marcus got in on the act too, fair play to him, and became similarly animated for the purpose of the ruse.

He may have even jumped up and down a few times if I recall it correctly, and emitted a girly squeal here and there also, to illustrate his ersatz excitement.

"WOOOOO!!!" he shouted.

"WOOOOO!!!" he shouted again.

Lo and behold and believe it or believe it not, our plan appeared to be working.

A general air of excitement and inherent alarm became apparent as the fake news permeated along the line.

Panic stricken long haired weirdo's, some laden down with more beers than they could handle and all in a state of extreme array, started rushing about erratically, with most eventually making a beeline for the stage.

A gap in the queue opened up so, à la Moses in Exodus, after which we sauntered on unobstructed towards the largely by now, empty bar.

"Two of your finest beverages, my good man" I said, as I arrived there a few moments later.

"Stella" I elucidated further.

"You showah treecoh?!" enquired the middle-aged and portly purveyor of pints.

"Ya do naow vat the bandz star'in, yeah?"

"Incorrect dude" I answered as I delved around in my wallet for some wedge.

"A mere subterfuge to clear the masses. Which has worked too incidentally. There's no accounting for stupidity, right?" I went on.

He looked at me like I had two heads.

Relieving me then of the fairly exorbitant, in retrospect, sum of £6 for the order, he plonked the two pints down on to the makeshift bar before us.

"Naow oideer wotchur sayin' moy saan" he remarked to us cheerily; happy it would seem to not understand in any way anything that I was saying.

"Barinjouy the beeyahs anywaiy, wintcha!"

"Will do guvnor!" I responded chummily, and then having handed Marcus his scoop, made designs to get out of there pronto.

The recently dispersed crowd would be returning eventually no doubt, as soon as they realised that they'd been hoodwinked into giving up their spot in the queue by what they would know soon enough, was fairly spurious information delivered to them, sneakily, several minutes earlier, by yours truly and his partner in crime.

"OI!!!" blasted a voice behind me, which when I turned to face from where the noise was emanating, appeared to be from the larynx of a straggly haired, bedraggled looking dude, who was wearing also, a quite unforgivably gaudy purple paisley shirt.

"YOU FACKING SPOOFT US YOU DID, YOU FACKING CANT!" he continued.

"VE BAND AIN'T STAR-IN FER FACKING AARS YETSS!! YOU'RE GERRIN A SMACK NAA, MOY SAAN! TOO ROIGHT YOU BLUMMIN' ARE! YOU'LL WISH YOU ADDINT MEDDOWED WIV MAY!"

"EHHH, COME AGAIN, TRACY" I responded aggressively – and by utilising said name I was referring of course, uncompromisingly, to the quite unnecessarily lengthy nature of the hair on his head.

And, of course, fight fire with fire also.

Always.

"SPEAK UP PAL!" I went on.

"I CAN'T HEAR YOU OVER THE BLOUSE!"

He was not best pleased anyway, despite the reprehensible nature of his chemise.

"YORR 'AVIN IT NAAA MOY SAAN!" he indicated aggressively, before moving swiftly and purposefully in my general direction.

Several of his cohorts - all of whom were similarly attired - that is, ridiculously - made moves towards us also.

There were five of them at least, so regardless of the fact that they were dressed like girls, we were at a serious disadvantage nevertheless, when it came to overall numbers vis-à-vis 'FOR' and 'AGAINST'.

We were in the soup alright.

There were no two ways about it.

Reviewing the situation as it was so, it was patently obvious to anyone that might be looking on, that actions of a zippy enough nature were very urgently required.

Glancing at Marcus, and then almost telepathically you might say, coming to the same resolution, we put our non-verbalised plan into action.

Not that it was much of a plan mind, but in a crowd such as this, it was unquestionably effective and as simplistic as you like.

Flinging the contents of both of our pints - mine over my immediate adversary and Marcus over some other dude, the next one along, we turned on our heels then, immediately, and made like gazelles through the tumultuous throng.

Darting in and out of the combat jacket, desert boot festooned mob, and jumping over dudes and dudettes that were smoking dope, heavy petting or whatever, we lost our pursuers in no time at all.

We had relinquished our drinks, yes.

That was a definite negative.

But it was infinitely preferable to being taken out by the festering mob that was on our tail.

"Phew!" said Marcus breathlessly as we arrived on the other side of the field.

"That was a close one! They could have strangled us with their putrid tresses dude if they'd wanted to!"

"Agreed young Marco" I agreed, wheezing similarly.

"It would have been an odious capture indeed. Make no bones about it! A lesson learnt, my friend".

"How so?" asked Marcus.

"Obvious enough dude, no?" I answered.

"As in, we must cultivate patience in the future. For the sake of a few minutes of waiting in a queue that wasn't *actually* that long in the first place, we are now 'sans boissons' in the middle of a field, with close to half a dozen hairy-assed hippies on our tail. Let's wait next time, ok?"

"Oh yeah" Marcus responded, getting it now.

"You're right, of course. And on that note, let's find another drinks tent. And on this occasion ideally, one that is NOT full to brim of any more of those hairy-assed hippy types!"

He was right on the first count undoubtedly; but if he imagined that we could move anywhere in this particular jurisdiction without being no more than few feet away from the specimen referred to in the second instalment of his commentary, he was very much inaccurately informed.

The place was teeming with the fuckers.

Moving on to more important matters however - namely the acquisition of further gargle - we left our present travails behind us and went in search of same.

Spotting another tent at the back but on the opposite side at the stadium, we made our way, quite naturally, in that general direction.

And ridiculous as it might seem, I kept an eye out for Belinda for every step of the way.

It might have been unlikely for me to come across her of course, in a crowd of over seventy thousand people or more, but not impossible either, I reasoned at the time.

Our initial meeting had been a chance enough affair, so why not the second?

It was not unfathomable so, I reasoned – albeit unrealistic, perhaps.

We made it to the beer tent then, and although the queue was definitely as long as the first one that we had encountered on the other side of the park - if not more so - it appeared to be moving along swiftly enough.

Rather than attempt any other diversionary deception so, as we had before, we just joined the back of the line and waited for it to clear like the rest of the populace there that were lined up like schmucks.

Disaster however, struck once again.

Gauging that because we had no drinks left as a result of the fact that we had fucked our previous pints over them, the hairy-assed hippies made an assumption - and in fairness to them, it was a pretty logical course of action to follow - that we'd probably be heading towards one of the other beer tents in the establishment.

And given the fact that the one that was closest to the first one was on the opposite side of the stadium, as we ourselves had noticed also, they made an obvious enough choice to make their way there and attempt to nab us by surprise.

And so it came to pass.

Within a matter of no more than milliseconds we were horizontal, with ogreish brutes - ogreish brutes who by the way, had never, it would appear, considered the notion of 'ablutions' as an exercise that was worth bothering over that much - pinning us down and in an undeniable position of ascendancy.

The funk was unbearable - so much so in fact that I considered at the time, the idea of any future personal decontamination to be a wistful and barely realistic proposition.

As a collective, their odour was almost inconceivably vile.

Which was as a result of bad hygiene of course, and the beer that had been added to their hitherto unwashed ensembles also, following our aggressive counter-attack just a couple of minutes before.

"WE 'AVE YOU NAAA, YOU AARISH FACKING CANT" spouted the key protagonist into my ear.

And if Halitosis is to be measured in terms of who has suffered the affliction most, ever, over the grand expanse of time, even when the staple diets of the average man many hundreds or thousands of years ago even, consisted no doubt of decidedly less healthy foodstuffs than they do today, you'd be hard pressed to come up with a dude that had worse breath than the dude that was hovering over me now.

"Ahh Jaysus man, give us a fucking break wha'?!" I spluttered, as the fucker's knee squeezed down squarely upon my, by now, very badly set upon bollocks.

"Sure we were only takin' the piss, yeah?" I went on.

"A mere stratagem to get to the top of the queue before the rest o' yiz? Sure wouldn't you do the same yourselves under similar circumstances?"

"NAOW WE FACKING WOULDN'T, YOU MICK PRICK!!" answered the dude, bizarrely happy to debate the point.

"AND WE WUDDENA FROAWN FACKING BEER OVA YOU NEEVA!" he went on.

I toyed with the idea of telling him that he sounded like a bit of a fucking bell end, but thought better of it then under the circumstances.

I left the issue of the double negative to the side also - although that for me was a decidedly more difficult undertaking.

"AS PUNISHMENT AS WOW!" he continued aggressively,

"YORR GONNA BUY PINTS FOR EVREE WAN OF US EEYAH, JOOEER - OR ELSE WEER GONNA DO YOU!"

This was not a positive development.

As in a choice between the two of us buying pints for these greasy bozo's or having the shit kicked out of us as an alternative?

Neither option sounded like a particularly welcoming proposition.

As ever anyway, I let the fucker - perhaps unwisely - have a piece of my mind.

"FUCK YOU PAL!" I iterated defiantly.

"YOU CAN STICK IT UP YOUR BLEEDIN' HOLE!"

Not very edifying discourse I know, but he had his knee on my bollocks!

More high-brow patois was the last thing on my mind.

"And another thing, fuckface!" I carried on, not quite as loudly as before, but determined in spirit nevertheless.

"Might I suggest to you that if substance of a liquefied nature is your immediate desire, that you consider a foregoing of this beer option that you've brought to the fore in recent times and opt instead for good old H20? And then, when you have made said choice - perhaps the wisest you have *ever* made - that rather than drink said liquid, you utilise it instead for the purposes of general toilet? You have to admit dude, seriously, that such a course of action is required as a matter of the most extreme urgency. Yes? Do you get me? As in, am I making any sense to you at this particular juncture in time?"

I was back in the game.

"FACK YOU ON ABAAT!" he asked.

An air of general confusion had settled about his personage which was transformed even more, some moments later into further bewilderment, when, from where I wasn't sure at the time, a large bottle appeared over his crown and made heavy contact with it in what you might term as a decidedly corrective capacity.

Yes indeedy.

He definitely looked perplexed.

As in 'What the fuck happened there?'

His crusty pals were set upon similarly at the same time by whomever it was that was doing the setting upon, so were also, thankfully for us, in a similar state of disarray.

Our situation so – a situation that mere moments ago had appeared irretrievably grim – was showing signs now, of being, once again, very much back on track.

"IF YOU TOUCH 'EM AGAIN!" growled Belinda, into the main protagonist's blood-stained visage as she grabbed him by the scruff of the neck.

"YOU'LL HAVE FUCKING ME TO DEAL WITH!"

Belinda and her pals so, had been passing as we were being accosted by the hairy trolls, with the apparent new love in Belinda's heart encouraging her to throw caution to the wind and weigh in in my defence.

Or perhaps she was just a bit mad and liked aggro?

Realistically it was probably the latter, but it didn't stop me from fooling myself all the same; just the same as so many other fools have fooled themselves on so many other occasions before.

"What the fuck are you doing mixing it with *that* shower?" she hissed at me as she dragged me away by the arm.

And fair play to her crew also, for their efficiency.

It had taken them no time at all to take the greasy bozos down.

"Those fuckers are seriously fucking dodge dude!" she went on, as we rushed away.

"Yiz were in for a serious battering if we hadn't shown up. I've seen them bastards before at other gigs and seriously dude, they do NOT fuck around!"

Marcus had been led away by some of her pals also, and we were heading off now in what appeared to be the general direction of the stage.

"I hear ya Belinda" I answered.

"And I honestly appreciate your weighing in" I went on.

"I can't help but notice however" I continued seriously.

"That we appear to be moving in the general direction of the stage; which although bad enough, when you consider the general nature of what is likely to follow very soon from an aural perspective, is also very much away from the business end of proceedings vis-à-vis accoutrements for the altering of the mind?"

As happens often, she looked at me like I had two heads once again.

"The gargle, Belinda?" I went on, by way of explanation.

"To numb the pain? The pain potentially, of having to have to sit through, for any period of time at all, 'Who Wants to Live for Fucking Ever'?"

"The fuck you on about?" she responded defiantly.

"That's a great fucking tune!"

It was clear to me then that she was quite clearly insane.

As in she had heard quite clearly every utterance that I had emitted, but remained on course for the stage nonetheless.

I was beginning to second guess now, this dalliance with my evidently unstable new acquaintance.

She and her pals had rescued us from a pounding, yes; that much was true.

But I've said it before, and I'll say it again.

Anyone that is into 'Queen' in any way must have some sort of screw loose somewhere.

"Don't worry!" she shouted back, as we continued steadfastly towards the front, with Marcus and the others following closely behind.

"I have a plan!" she continued, as we wove our way through the progressively fractious crowd.

I was beginning to think though that unless her plan was related in some way to the shooting of the dude that was in present control of the sounds - as a matter indeed, of the most EXTREME imperativeness - that it couldn't have been, under present circumstances, that much of a plan at all.

The 'music' had degenerated to such a gruesome extent now you see that it was hard to imagine the situation deteriorating any further.

The 'song' that was playing at the time in fact, was rescued only, marginally, by the Thin White Duke himself, as the turgid screeches of Freddie Mercury's voice rained down relentlessly on all that were here.

'Under Pressure' folks.

I kid you not.

'Under fucking Pressure!'

And when it gets to that part where the great man himself, in his attempts, as I indicated, to rescue this heinousness from the depths of hell where it at the time, and indeed *has always* resided, he must surely have been thinking in his head during the performance, that the following words, rather than the *actual* words that made it onto the eventual recording, would have been an appreciably more precise lyrical alternative.

"It's the terror of knowing what this world is about; watching some WHINING BOLLOCKS screaming 'Let me out'!"

Let me out indeed.

LET ME OUT!!

Once again, it was difficult to conceive of the tune's popularity, but the crowd as things were were going absolutely fucking bananas for it.

I needed gargle so, and I needed gargle NOW!

"Not being funny Belinda" I emphasised further as I trundled along, nearly crying at this point if I'm being totally honest.

"But if we don't get gargle soon, I don't think that I'll be able to stick this, what you must surely agree, is total and utter BOLLOCKS, for very much longer".

I don't think that she heard me, but we arrived at our destination then anyway, after which she imparted to us her 'plan'.

"Alright dudes" she said to us, all 'up close and personal' like, as we were gathered there no more now than ten metres or so from the stage.

"Here's the plan".

Her own crew were not paying a whole lot of attention, so must have known already what she was about to impart.

Her delivery was directed more towards Marcus and me anyway, so we leaned in closer to hear better what she had to say over the raucous cacophony of the crowd.

"Ok men, listen up" she went on, as the restless throng around and about us jostled and harried.

"If you are lily-livered or pusillanimous in any way, I urge you to retreat from this place right now. Those of a craven disposition should at this stage in the proceedings, be reconsidering their association".

Lily-livered?

Pusillanimous?

Craven?

I was warming to her again.

And Marcus was impressed also.

You could tell.

Most of the girls that we knew didn't talk like this.

"Alright so gents, you are familiar with the notion of 'moshing', I assume?" she continued.

We were, and indicated such by a combined nodding of our heads.

"We are, Belinda" I added for good measure, in case she was unsure.

"Good" she said.

"Because the moshing that occurs at a Queen concert is a thing to behold. This is not a Genesis gig, my friends. Things can get rough".

I toyed with the idea of imparting to her the information that Queen fans in their entirety, were big girls' fucking blouses, and that as a result of this fact were considerably more likely than not to be sedentary.

Given what she had indicated to date however regarding her grá for the pasty rockers in question, I decided on this occasion to keep my thoughts to myself.

'But what was her plan?' I was thinking to myself.

As in how would moshing at a Queen concert bring us any closer to the acquisition of further scoops?

I indicated these misgivings to her so, with the following, I think, fairly uncompromising observation.

"Not being funny Belinda" I said.

"And don't get me wrong, I hear what you are saying. Jumping around like a bit a fucking space cadet at the front of a rock concert is never a bad thing. There is definite merit to it, particularly if you are off your head. Does it however, bring us any closer to the acquisition of further scoops? Am I wrong with this, what I believe to be, more than salient assessment of the facts?"

She could hardly deny it.

She explained her plan to us then, and although it was a tad complicated, and dependent also on other forces that were in a lot of respects out of our control, I had to admit that on the face of it it was a decent enough scheme.

"We need to get the front gents" she elaborated.

"And when I say the front, I don't mean near the front, I mean the VERY front? Are you hearing me?"

Being plain English that she spoke, we certainly understood her words.

Rummaging around through the contents of her bag then, she withdrew a small container of what looked to be a type of white powder.

"Talc" she said curtly, as she withdrew a fistful of said powder from its receptacle of transmittance.

"Hold out your hands" she muttered further, even more brusquely than before, to which Marcus and I duly did.

Pouring a liberal amount of the powder on to both of our palms, she instructed us to close said palms and make a fist.

"Hang on to this powder!" she said urgently.

"Do NOT lose the powder!" she went on.

She imparted to us the plan then, once again, which although sound enough as I was mentioning before, had elements of farce to it as well.

It had worked very well for her in the past though she said, so she saw no reason at all to assume that it wouldn't go well for us on this occasion also.

She would give us the nod she said, when it was time to engage, after which she was certain, she expounded further, that the wheeze would culminate in success.

We made our way towards the front so, and although it was hard enough to make it there through the increasingly sardined horde, we arrived at a steel barrier eventually that was located next to the stage.

Belinda's own crew had not made it through however, so for the moment, it was just us three.

The stage was still twenty feet away from us, but being that close to it and with no-one in front of us also, we could see and hear everything that was going on better than anyone else that was there.

Our timing was ok also, with the gruesome sounds that had been emanating from the PA system dissipating almost as soon as we arrived, and the remaining three members of Queen striding out on to the stage to address the by now bizarrely enthusiastic swarm.

Three middle aged dudes dressed like someone's oul fella?

For 'rockers' these geezers did not look cool.

'Phil Collins' uncool really, to be fair.

"Hello Wembley and the World!" said a corkscrew haired chap on the right.

Brian May, is it?

A nasally, tinny little voice he had anyway, which screamed mediocrity more than any other voice that I had ever heard, either before or since.

And then some other dude, a blonde chap, with an even higher pitched timbre than the first, warbling on mundanely about Freddie Mercury and Aids, and the fact that today, Wembley, 'We're gonna rock the world!'

Like, fucking YAWN dude!

Get on with the show if that's what you're gonna fucking do!

Last but not least anyway, the worst of the trio, on the left.

A pasty looking bloke wearing jeans, a sports jacket and a semi-concealed tee shirt that you just *knew* had something trendy or lefty on it, like 'Save the fucking Whale' or something similarly insipid.

Or vegan.

Something vegan actually, almost certainly.

'Give Peas a Chance' probably.

Tosser.

He didn't speak for long anyway, thankfully; and then, would you believe it, the situation improved in an instant, to a quite inconceivable degree.

Just when things had been showing all the signs of being a spectacularly grim day performance wise, the scenario altered suddenly, and became considerably more agreeable as a result of what came to pass next.

Rather than begin to play, which as I mentioned before was a prospect more galling than any other that was imaginable to me at the time, the pasty looking tee shirty fucker announced the band 'Metallica' to the stage instead, and then fucked off along with the other two geezers, somewhere off to the right.

What a result!

No Queen?

Metallica instead?

'Enter fucking Sandman'?

Fucking A!

All once more was right with the world.

Metallica were magnificent.

The drummer, whatever his name is, giving it absolute socks with his shirt off, and the singer, James Hetfield - I think that's his name - growling menacingly into his microphone about a dark and dreaded journey to 'Never Never Land'.

These dudes were the exact opposite of 'Queen' really, and not at all what I had been expecting.

I had no idea at all that Metallica would be playing, so this new turn of events was a very welcome surprise.

The crowd was getting into it in a big way also, so much so in fact, that I was beginning to question if my decision to accompany Belinda into the mosh pit had been that great an idea now that the in-breds in my general immediacy had found a new lease of life.

It was an extremely uncomfortable environment to be in as things progressed, with moving in any direction exponentially more difficult as time passed by.

'Sad But True' began then, which was just as good as the first number, and in actual fact probably better.

The uncomfortable nature of the heaving throng was put on hold so, as a result of this new euphoria, whilst I temporarily, also, lost myself in the grandeur of the song.

The ordinariness of the next tune however, brought me and everyone else back down to earth with a bang.

'Nothing Else Matters' which as a 'song' is practically Def Leppard by comparison.

Gauging then that now, for clear enough reasons, might be as good a time as any to put her elaborate plan into effect, Belinda went ahead and did just that.

"NOW!" she screamed into Marcus and mine ears.

"NOW" she screamed again, while at the same time rubbing her own fistful of powder over and across her forehead and face.

"RUB IT IN!" she went on, before going limp suddenly, but not falling, as the buoyancy of the crowd and those wedged tightly around her kept her upright.

I could see the angle that she was coming from alright, and could ascertain also how it might eventuate potentially in success.

Rubbing the powder into my own face so, and closing my eyes similarly, I affected limpness also, allowing, as Belinda had, the buoyancy of the crowd to keep me afloat.

Squinting ever so slightly through the sleeveen eyes of my sly subterfuge, I observed that Marcus had decided that he wouldn't be playing along.

He just stood there obstinately, realising of course what was going on, but disclining to engage in the ruse nevertheless.

Which was fair enough at the time, I was thinking.

His call.

I myself however was happy to give it a go.

It was a decent enough plan I believed, and what was the worst also that could actually happen?

Lo and behold anyway, it worked!

Spotting that both Belinda and I were in 'difficulty' some 'Good Samaritan' type that was nearby called a couple of the bouncers over to where we were, to bring our communally contrived 'condition' to their attention.

Spotting the cadaver-like pallor of our faces then, and our lifeless torsos also, it was the work of a mere moment for the two of them to reef the both of us up and out of the mob, and carry us then, away from the madding crowd.

And that was where, I suppose you might say, the lunacy of the day, and indeed all other subsequent lunacy from that point onwards, could be said to have begun.

Things, following on from these events, would never be the same again.

CHAPTER 3

I'm lonely.

I truly am.

And look at all of these Rock Star DemiGods that are milling about!

Blummin' loads of 'em there are.

And me here alone toying despondently with this bloody saxophone reed.

Robert Plant.

Tony Iommi.

Mick Ronson.

To name but a few.

He fucking HATES me that Ronno.

Fucking HATES me.

And rightly so as well to be fair, if you consider how badly I fucked him over in 1973.

I may be a Rock Star Demigod, perhaps the most famous alive today.

But that doesn't take away from the fact that I get lonely as well, every now and again.

Desperately, desperately lonely.

More lonely in fact than most ordinary people might think.

Lots of shifty hangers on here.

And other nobodies noodling nearby.

Toying with the idea of coming over, I expect.

To say hello.

I'd like to speak with them of course.

More than anything in the world.

But I have a persona to uphold.

The Thin White Duke must remain aloof at all times.

I am adrift.

Eternally lost, never to be found.

An astronaut, directionless; dancing out in space.

Hello Spaceman.

Do I not however breathe air, merely, just like everybody else?

Why so - if that IS the case - am I so revered?

I harvest song, alone.

Hardly a cure for cancer.

Staring at the ceiling in my hotel room this morning, I reminisce.
Claridges.
Companionless once again.
Ornate cornices.
A crack emerging there.
That needs to be filled.
Or plastered.
Otherwise dampness.
And then dry rot.
Possibly.
Faceless loiterers.
In numero, duo.
Outside my door.
Whisper, whisper.
Shwish, Shwish, Shwish.
"Oim 'avin' a glass, oi am" hisses the first.
"Wan varreez drank frum!"
"Searchin' for a pube me!" whispers a second, stifling a snigger.
"Vers baand to be wan somewayah in tha showah yeah? Be worf facking mooyins wan day, moy san!"

Fuck me.
Has it really come to this?
Bell boys congregating outside my hotel room contemplating the purloining of my pubes?

THAT wasn't mentioned 'pre-craving' for fame.
A lot wasn't mentioned actually, now that I come to think of it.
Oh, for anonymity once again.
To walk down a street and nobody follow.
To enter a place, ANY place, and the air not bristle.
To order a beer then, and just sit in a corner.
An alcove.
Undisturbed.
Snug.
Nobody knowing me.
Lambeth.
'57?
Can't remember.
Probably.
Possibly?
'58?
A derelict bomb site, thirteen years on.

Post war.
Some things never get fixed.
Jesus CHRIST will these fuckers outside my room ever fuck off?
Hide and seek.
Yes.
I remember it now.
1957.
Be elusive but don't walk far.
A game of footie.
They tell me that they want me.
They don't want me.
Last to be picked
Bastards.
I'll show them!
Silken skills!
I don't show them.
Well THAT went well!
They're just older children.
After all.
Long evenings.
Nobody cares.
Not really.
Just another young working class lad lost in his thoughts.
Kicking a can home, all the way to Brixton.
Endless summers.
Tea's ready.
Shepherd's pie, my lad!
And you'd best be thankful for it as well, Sonny Jim!
TV.
Black and white.
Tubby the Tuba.
Signature tune.
Off kilter.
I like that.
Please trip them gently.
After all.
Oh by jingo!
Tom Waits.
What's that tune?
Cemetery polka?
That's it.

GREAT lyrics.
Love Tom.
'And the tumour that's as big as an egg'.
Ha ha!
Like that too.
Wouldn't want one though.
A tumour, that is.
WOULD like an egg.
Hungry now.
Might get breakfast.
Brought to the room.
Nobody knows him.
Tom Waits, that is.
Not really.
Just another dude in a bar.
Do I ask for it?
I DO ask for it.
Attention.
Probably.
Relish it.
CRAVE it.
Pathetic really.
But I MUST be relevant.
NEVER irrelevant.
'Rod Stewart' irrelevant, as in.
Fucking jock sell out.
'Baby Jane' my arse.
Fuck me.
Is he serious?
Soho.
1964.
Bright eyed and bushy tailed.
The world being my oyster.
Long blonde hair.
Cock of the walk.
Swaggering around like I own the fucking place.
The Stones at 'The Marquee'.
I'll take a leaf from their book.
Oh yes.
Absolutely!
Fuck everybody!

A knock on the door.

"Breakfast, sweetheart?"

Coco.

Darling Coco.

Up already.

Where would I be without my darling Coco?

Although I WAS gonna knock one off.

Ahh well.

That'll have to wait.

"Those cretinous bell boys gone yet Coco?" I shout back, not wishing to share my pubic hairs with anybody, least of all them.

A short pause.

"There ain't nobody here but me darlin'!".

She probably thinks that I dreamed it.

"Perhaps you dreamed it?" she affirms.

I'll freak her out.

"Tell 'em that they can't have my pubes!" I shout out again.

She doesn't respond.

"I'll get coffee" she says eventually, before shimmying away.

That DEFINITELY freaked her out.

"Get breakfast too" I shout after her.

But she's already gone.

Dear Coco.

Has been with me forever.

Through thick and then.

Keeps me real.

On the straight and narrow.

"Rather than do Y" she will say with that persuasive Yankee lilt that I love so much.

"Should we not instead, do X?"

"We should Coco!" I respond always, which by my intonation and pause free delivery denotes humorous disagreement.

That makes her laugh.

I SHOULD, Coco!

And although persuasive and my right-hand woman, Coco sometimes – even Coco – doesn't get through.

My mind is made up and that's just the way it is.

That castle in Ireland for example.

My God, when was that?

'87?

'86?

No.

'87.

Near Dublin.

Five years ago, give or take.

That's ALL we got!

She DID say don't do it.

'You're in the wrong frame of mind' she declared.

"And you should listen to your audience".

She was right there.

Biggest mistake ever.

What was its name again?

The venue?

It's gone.

Mum was Irish.

Sort of.

Ergo me, I suppose.

But they must have thought... WHAAA'?!!

As a, you know, collective?

Slane!

That was it!

The crowd was not happy.

I DO remember that.

As in, are you fucking kidding us, Duke?

Definitely a low point career wise.

What was I thinking?

Perched on the gantry having strapped myself in.

God knows how many people were in attendance.

Fifty thousand?

Sixty?

More?

A lot anyway.

And my scarlet red suit.

And the red telephone - the one that I used for a microphone.

Fuck me!

Descending slowly on the chair lift from the back of the stage from fully fifty metres above the crowd, they slowly but surely see that I am there.

Swooping down on them like some sort of self-appointed deity.

Flabbergasted by the bombast, they play along, nevertheless.

Initially.

Unsurprisingly though, their mood soon enough becomes choleric.

BUT I AM A ROCK STAR DEMIGOD!

I CAN DO NO WRONG!

I COMMAND YOU TO WORSHIP ME!!

Some do, I suppose.

By and large however, the prevailing mood is sombre.

Sombre and flat.

A really good rendition of 'Fame' even, towards the end, can't save this damp squib of a show.

I happily pick up the dosh though even so, and sidle off insidiously into the night.

Back to the present.

This tribute concert thingamajig in Wembley Stadium.

I'm not really sure what it's all about, to be honest?

Annie Lennox asked me to do it so I thought that I would, just to please the good lady herself.

Annie's cool.

Flat as a board though.

Fried eggs.

Coco brought me some earlier.

Fried eggs, that is.

And coffee.

Not cocoa.

Good old Coco!

So this Freddie thing.

Aids or something?

Not sure.

Not that it matters.

"Oi David" shouts that Def Leppard Joe Elliot bloke from across the way.

He is standing next to the stage.

"You juss gorra see vis maite! Vis dudes' strides? Seriously maite, they are facking TRAGIC!"

I stand up and wander across.

Just to be nice.

"Hello Joe" I say to him as I arrive.

"What was it that you were saying to me just then?" I go on.

It's nice to be nice.

Even if you ARE David Bowie.

"Jussteez traazzahs treacoh!" Joe verifies.

"The voclist frum Extreme over theyah maite. WOTTS - a plonkah!!"

Regardless of the name of the band - which I believe is 'Extreme' - Joe has just verified this - it's hard to deny that he is not on the money.

The chap is bad.

Bad in the 'extreme' ha ha!

But one must be magnanimous at all times.

Outwardly in any case.

"Come, come, young Joe" I say, all conciliatory-like and master to the pupil.

He's hanging on my every word.

"He is doing his best, merely".

Which - it has to be conceded - is not that well at all.

'Keep yourself Alive' by Queen.

That's the number.

Which by anybody's standard is putrid enough to begin with.

This version however, is a considerably more turgid affair.

The singer also appears to be wearing a pair of baggy black legging type trouser things, which, regardless of the 'music' that he is attempting to convey, is not that wise a selection vis-à-vis clobber.

On the top half also he is sporting a skimpy, black, wife beater type thingama-jig.

All in all so, it's a pretty damnable combination.

"Well yeah" answers Joe, not convinced, but not going to argue the point with me either.

"But the strides maite" he continues, hoping against hope I suppose, that I might join him in his game.

I am not, however, for biting.

Joe also - as an aside - is sporting skin tight 'sock down the front' Union Jack trousies himself; so, you know, is hardly one to be pointing the old finger.

People in glass houses etc.,?

I let it go though.

Discord with me would be absolutely devastating for the chap.

I'm David fucking Bowie.

You know?

I smile instead benignly, as a kindly uncle might smile on a favourite nephew.

To my right, and looking pretty shifty, I spot two weirdos out of the corner of my eye.

Two very pasty looking weirdos, it has to stated.

They look like ghosts to be honest, and are staring at me furtively, with some agenda or other almost certainly in mind.

'Fuck this shit' I'm thinking.

I don't need this.

They look sick.

As in, you know - cadaverous hues?

I'll go back to speaking with Joe.

Pretend that I don't see them kind of thing.

"He's trying too hard Joe" I say as I ponder the stage, wincing at the cringe-worthiness of the 'Extreme' chap's performance.

"That's the main problem here".

It's true.

He's definitely trying too hard to impress.

Probably knows that I'm here actually, now that I come to think of it.

Hence his attempts to be the star of the show.

Jesus Christ though, he is failing miserably.

It's painful.

Pitiful even.

Somebody has to tell him.

Here comes the drummer.

The Def Leppard drummer?

Decent touch that, letting him stay on after he lost his arm?

I can't be slagging Joe off too much.

Although there's no way that I'd have kept him on myself.

No fucking way!

Sure didn't I fire the Spiders in '73 for no viable reason bar Mick Ronson's flatulence?

Def Leppard's drummer loses his arm in an accident however, and they let him continue on as their drummer even so?

That's loyalty for you.

"Hello Mr. Bowie" the drummer says jovially, and I reach out to shake his hand.

I realise too late of course that there isn't actually an arm there to be shaken.

I slap him on the shoulder so instead, never breaking stride once.

That's the key to it folks!

You may fuck up, of course.

It's probably inevitable.

But you must NEVER break stride.

It must appear at all times to anyone looking on, that you know exactly what you're doing; even though in your heart of hearts you know, and they know, that it's in actual fact a crock of steaming shit.

"Hello son" I say benignly, as a kindly uncle might to a favourite nephew.

"Nice suit" he says, and in fairness to him that's well spotted.

It IS a nice suit!

Light green – but not quite lime.

Lime would be mad.

They decided to set him up with foot pedals anyway after the accident, and told him to just get on with.

Which in deference to his ability to adapt, he took to like a duck takes to water.

Although it has to be attested also, that complicated fills are never going to be the prime constituents of any of their songs.

As in he's not, nor will ever be, the great Bonzo from Led Zep.

'Good Times, Bad Times'?

That ain't happening.

The ruefully attired chap on stage anyway, remains on course for the good ship implosion.

The odiousness that is known as 'I Want to Break Free' is now in full flow.

I offer an opinion so, through clenched teeth, and under my breath.

Which is not like me at all.

I usually maintain my council.

Remain aloof, you know?

"I know that ees 'armless and a good bloke, probably" I say anyway, directing my comments towards Joe.

"But how can he honestly be permitted to continue?"

"As in, if ever a dude was so obviously NOT in control of the required faculties to complete his duties as a performer, then surely this fucker is THAT fucker, right here, right now!"

Joe is not impressed.

And when you consider how alike the two words are, and indeed my propensity to drop h's from time to time as well; as a result of the fact that I hail from London and do so as a matter of linguistic course; you can probably see from where the confusion has been derived.

The drummer storms off anyway, which, with just one arm looks a bit weird.

For some reason, I don't know why, I have a vaguely surreal notion that he should be travelling in circles rather than going straight ahead.

A one legged duck, you know?

Swimming in a pond?

Joe grabs me by the lapels then and the confrontation is a shock.

The two pasty looking characters come to my aid though, thankfully, and along with some other security chaps that have arrived over to the fracas also, Joe is led away, kicking and screaming and being a bit of a nut job basically, when all is said and done.

"FACK YOU BAAWIE! WE STICK BY AAR MATES, MATE! NOT LOIKE YOU WIV THA SPIDERS! FACKING CANT! AND YER SUITS RIDICULOUS AS WEOW!"

Hmmph.

How can he say that about my suit?

The suit is the business.

I realise then, my faux pas.

As in 'harmless' being, in many ways - phonetically and phonemically, that is - quite if not VERY similar to 'armless'.

Bugger.

That was not my intention at all.

Me and my 'h's.

I'm actually pretty impressed that they kept him on.

Although I'd have definitely found some excuse to shaft him myself.

"Are you alright Mr. Bowie?" says the pasty looking girl.

Her similarly waxen boyfriend remains silent.

Star struck I expect.

Hardly surprising.

I AM David Bowie.

After all.

"I'm fine my love, thank you" I answer, before smoothing down my crumpled lapel and resuming my more usual hubristic persona.

I DO have a persona to uphold.

I've mentioned this before.

"Are YOU alright?" I say to the girl.

She looks even worse close up.

More ashen.

The dude too.

Mannequin like, kind of.

Is that powder on their faces?

"You look quite pale, you know?" I go on.

"Oh yeah, shit" she says.

"It's actually talcum powder, Mr. Bowie. A ruse to get us backstage if I'm being totally honest with you. We applied it to our faces in the mosh pit to make us look sick, and then, you know, let things take their course. And here we are. So it worked!"

Pretty clever, I'm thinking.

Hard to deny it.

MOST resourceful.

"But why are you here?" I ask, keen to know.

"To meet you of course!" she answers enthusiastically.

"And any other Rock Star Demigods that we see hanging about as well!" she goes on, as if it's the most natural thing in the world for a person to say.

Although she's hardly likely to find anyone here that's as big as me, fame wise.

Percy maybe.

But that's it.

And he's just a singer.

As in, not a swashbuckling multi-instrumentalist such as myself!

"We're groupies, don't you know?" she continues, to which her wan looking partner does a bit of a double take.

As in whatever about the revelation that his girlfriend is such, it's pretty obvious by the look on his face, that it isn't an avenue that he's particularly comfortable going down himself.

He looks uncomfortable.

"I'd be interested to know something actually, Mr. Duke" he pipes up.

She looks at him herself then, as if to say, 'Shut the fuck up dude! I'm doing fucking business here!'

But she'll never get with me.

Those days for me are gone.

I have a girlfriend.

I am in love.

With Iman.

Not A MAN!

Iman.

The supermodel, you know?

Tia Maria?

The pasty chap ignores her anyway and proceeds.

"What is it like" he asks,

"To have an audience this large - or any size in fact - in the palm of your hand?"

I look on him sympathetically as a kindly uncle might look on a favourite nephew.

If only he knew.

If only he knew!

"Actually, let me rephrase that" he says.

"What does one have to do" he goes on.

"To be as comfortable on stage as you are? That confidence, you know? The swagger?"

I know what he means.

I'm brilliant at that.

I kind of recognise this kid though.

As in, I've definitely seen him before.

"Have we met kid?" I say.

"Your face looks really familiar".

The kid looks at me and nods.

He remains ill at ease though as far as I can make out.

Still star struck I expect.

"I met you a few years ago in a cocktail bar on the Strand, TWD" he says.

"You were with some geezer in a dress?"

I remember him now!

The young lad that was with McCartney that day, in the wine bar by the river.

I was with Reeves.

I DO remember him, of course!

The young Irish barman!

Can't let on that I DO though.

That would be waaay too familiar.

I'll pretend that I forget.

"Don't remember that kid" I go on, pretty convincingly it has to be noted.

"When was that exactly?"

"'89 dude" answers the kid.

"I was with a 'badly fucked up on the scoops' Paul McCartney" he goes on.

"And you were with that bloke in the dress" he intimates to me once again.

I'll stick to my story.

"Seriously, I don't remember that kid" I say, scratching my head to denote perplexity.

"Although my guitarist – Reeves Gabrels, don't you know - does wear a kilt from time to time" I concede.

Reeves DOES wear a kilt from time to time.

That much I can admit.

Which, considering the fact that he is from America, and from his nomenclature also, you could never assume that there's lineage at all that might stretch back to Caledonia of old - he's not called Hamish McStravick for instance - you'd have to agree that said item of attire on the day in question - and many subsequent days since then in fact – was, and has been, a fairly dubious choice.

That was the day that we got into the row with that vegetable type character as well.

What's his name again?

Cabbage?

Turnip?

Sprout?

Sprout!

That's it.

Paddy something?

Prefab Sprout.

That's the band, I think?

A song about frogs?

This Paddy guy insinuated anyway on the day, that I had robbed his drummer, Neil something, for the Live Aid gig, but that never happened at all.

That was just Coco ringing around beforehand to see what session dudes might be available for the show.

That's how we got Thomas Dolby as well.

It might have been anybody, you know?

42

Nothing to do with me.

This Neil 'sprout' chap was obviously on some list or other and Coco just picked up the phone.

"It's pretty easy to be honest anyway kid" I say, referring back to his original question.

As in, you know; how do I hold audiences in the palm of my hand?

"First of all, it is an absolute imperative that you surround yourself with the best musicians that are available" I continue.

"And then ensure that you spend every waking hour trying to be better than they are. It's not easy of course, if you have the likes of Mike Garson and Ronno in your band, so from time to time, every now and again, you need a bit of a cull; if you, you know, detect that the audience is paying a little bit more attention to them than you. That's one of the reasons why I shafted the Spiders back in '73 to be honest, but when I think back on it now, poor old Woody and Trev got a raw enough deal out of it at the time. It was all about getting rid of Ronno though, you know? He was becoming waay too popular. And it was never supposed to be a duo."

"That's really interesting" says the kid.

I can tell that he's impressed.

Even though I'm, like, totally lying to him about Ronno.

I carry on.

"Delivery is critical also" I impart.

"As in that thousand yard stare? Pointing as well - you know, into the crowd? They love that. Pointing and smiling to a general area basically, but to no one in particular, as such. They all think that it's them, you see? And then, as a result of that, they almost always go absolutely fucking ape shit. Cool, right?"

"Great" says the kid.

'Ahh, kids' I think to myself, smiling inwardly.

Little scallies.

I remember being like that myself.

Trying anything to get into a gig, and then after that, attempting to sneak backstage?

And for what?

To see total legends like myself, that's what!

The Stones gig in The Marquee for example.

I mean they were as cool as fuck back then, but I've met them since and believe me when I tell you this, but they are total fucking arses now.

In every way imaginable.

Especially Mick.

Keith's a bit of a twat alright, but bloody hell, Mick is a right knob.

My old pal Lindsay introduced me to him back in '67, I think.

And talk about stuck up!
It works though.
Arrogance.
I've tried it myself often.
'73?
Check.
'75?
Check.
'76?
Even worse.
Messing with canes and shit on chat shows?
Dick Cavett?
And he was a nice chap actually, if I remember it correctly.
I felt guilty about that.
Pretending to be stoned?
It was all part of my 'creating the mystique'.
Incorrigible lemmings anyway, audiences, by and large.
Feed them enough bullshit with any degree of swagger and they'll swallow it up every time.
Hammy Odeon.
The last show.
THAT last show.
Did he fart?
He fucking did alright.
Right in the middle of the 'Moonage Daydream' solo.
Fucking Ronno!
You can take the man out of Hull, right?
My eyes are watering.
I'm smiling of course, but I ain't happy.
I ain't happy at all.
The crowd can't see that though.
Seriously though, I've had enough.
That is the moment.
THE moment.
People said afterwards that the decision was spontaneous; and I suppose to a degree that it was.
But for artistic reasons?
To reinvent myself and take myself, creatively, down some other road?
I don't bloody think so.
I'd just had enough of Ronno and his irritable bowels.
His irritable bowels and subsequent stench.

I knew then, right at that moment, when he farted during the 'Moonage' solo, that I could go on no longer.

I mean there's only so much that one man can take!

There's something wrong with the lad.

I'm sure of it.

Something poisonous living within.

Eating him up inside.

How can it not be so?

Such a rancid stench, foul and inhuman.

Borne out of no place nice.

I'll play with him today though, and all will be well.

I hope that he doesn't fart though.

Jesus Christ, they have got to be smelt to be believed!

I'll stay away from him.

Across on the other side of the stage.

He'll get the message I suppose.

A few cursory nods and smiles here and there and he'll be fine.

The crowd will lap that up as well.

Throw a dog a bone I always say.

"What's that, kid?" I say.

The kid is still here.

"Why the green suit?" he asks.

Ahh yes.

He is obviously impressed.

And why wouldn't he be?

The suit is the fucking business.

"In honour of you and all things Irish, my young Gaelic friend" I spout magnanimously, to which, I can tell, he is seriously pleased.

The 'Extreme' guy with the dodgy strides has finished finally – thankfully - and his crew and he are leaving the stage.

In deference to his professionalism, Joe from Def Leppard - a totally transformed Joe from Def Leppard - takes to the stage next on the other side, along with the rest of his band members, and launches into their set.

And pretty banal it is too.

"What say you to cock rock kid?" I ask the kid.

I'd be interested to hear his opinion.

He remains bashful but offers an opinion to me of sorts, nevertheless.

"Better than tonight dude" he suggests.

And he's right as well.

The bands so far have been woeful indeed; at least those that have performed to date.

And they probably won't get much better as the night wears on.

I'll be way better myself when it's my turn.

But surely Joe and his pals, armless or otherwise, can do a better job than 'Extreme'?

They were piss poor really.

Reprehensible.

'More than Words'.

That was their last number.

Like, 'What a Crock!?' as our brothers and sisters across the pond are wont to elucidate!?

How about 'Less than Words' in fact?

An auditory arrangement without any words at all?

Or sounds even?

That would be a far better arrangement.

The kid has fucked off with his girlfriend anyway, to hassle Robert Plant.

He won't give them the time of day though, that fucker.

He's one miserable bastard Percy.

Back to Joe anyway and his pals.

And their opening number.

The lyrics are not overly high-brow, it must be declared.

'And I want. And I need. And I know. Animal'.

Indeed.

Dire really.

I'm on my own again.

But I don't mind that TOO much now, now that I've had some chats.

People keeping their distance?

That suits me fine.

I'm not sure why however.

Although they're probably too nervous to come over.

Oh no!

It's Elton!

Must hide!

Must hide at all costs!

Too late.

Oiv bin RAAAAMBOOOLD!

That old Queen is unbearable.

Is there any bandwagon on which he won't straddle?

He's with that bloke in the kilt now as well.

Not Reeves.

The other dude.

What's his name?

Axle Grease?

Axle Grinder?

I can't remember.

And his pal with the funny hair?

The guitarist, is it?

The 'Edge'?

Not sure.

Although I don't think so.

He's a joke anyway.

As in, does he ever actually smoke that fag?

Talking of which, that'd be nice.

I'll have one now.

Ahh, there she is!

My little Angel.

There must be an Angel.

Playing with my heart.

"Annie, you old tart!" I shout out, after which the subject in question comes swishing across.

She loves me, does Annie.

"David, DAHHLING!" she effuses, as she arrives at my side.

"MWAH! MWAH!" she continues, air kissing me to the left and to the right.

Annie's mad.

But at least I have company.

Not for long though.

She makes up some excuse about needing to fix her face - and in fairness to her she does have a bit of a panda eyeliner thing going on - and tootles off in the general direction of the loo.

Despite the shit music that's abroad anyway, I remain, as ever, eternally optimistic.

Why would I not?

I'll nail my own set and the plaudits will ensue.

'Let's Get Rocked'.

Joe's next tune.

Which is a play on words, clearly, for 'Let's get fucked'.

'Let's go all the way'.

Hmmm.

These are the ACTUAL words that he is singing.

Which for a benefit about Aids and Aids awareness generally, seems somewhat insensitive to me.

I doubt however that he's made the connection.

Elton arrives, and pinches me on the bum.

Standard.

"Hello Davypoos!" he says, all mincy-like and weird.

"Fancy coming back to my dressing room for some fun?" he continues.

He has a dressing room?

How does Elton John have a dressing room and David Bowie NOT have a dressing room?

Has the world now all of a sudden gone fucking flat?

This is not right.

This is not right at fucking all!

"Hang on one second there Elton!" I remonstrate.

"How come you have a dressing room and I don't have a dressing room?"

"I really couldn't say dahhling!" responds Elton nonchalantly.

"A personality thing?"

I have no idea what he's on about there.

I have a great personality.

"DO come dahhling!" he pleads further, pawing at my sleeve.

I can see where he's coming from.

Wanting me to go?

He IS only human, after all.

"I have champers!" he continues.

"Well why didn't you say so, you old ponce!" I respond gushingly.

At last, a party!

Even if it is only with Elton and that funny looking chap in the kilt.

Who grunts something unintelligible when Elton asks him if he'd like to come with.

The guitarist has fucked off some place else.

I know not where.

Ahh well.

Off we pop.

Shabbah Dee Doo Dah Day, Shabba Dee DayyyeEEE!

SHABBADEEDOO!!

CHAPTER 4

You had to hand it to Belinda.

She was right on the money when it came to her plan.

It worked a charm.

No sooner had the bouncers deposited us backstage - having mere seconds earlier reefed us up from out of the crowd as a result of our sickly hue - they just left us there and went back to the task of ensuring that other more genuinely perturbed concert goers were afforded respite from the *actual* crushing they were experiencing at the front.

What a result!

We were exactly where we wanted to be in the hallowed sanctum behind the stage; the hallowed sanctum where mere mortals usually do not hang out.

Marcus would be well pissed off when I told him about it later on.

Of that I was sure.

But 'He who dares' right?

The miserable bollocks should have just grown a pair and given it a shot like ourselves.

Belinda and I, that is.

It was doubtful so as a result of these recent occurrences and Marcus's un-characteristic limp-wristedness, that I'd be seeing much if any of my buddy for the remainder of the day.

It would be just 'yours truly' and the new 'squeeze' from here on in.

I supposed at the time anyway that I might as well just get on with things.

Make the best of the situation, you know?

I'd miss my pal of course; don't get me wrong.

And girls are excellent too and uppermost in our minds usually for most of the time.

But they're not your pal!

Not even close!

I don't care what anybody says but the old 'fairer sex' just aren't the same as your old pal at all, especially when it's not *that* long since you've had your Nat King Cole!

But I'd get over Marcus's absence soon enough.

Belinda had redeeming 'qualities' shall we say as I have referred to already.

One of which as you have witnessed, was a penchant for wanton and gratuitously random intercourse at any old time that she had a 'passion for a lashin''.

There are upsides always you see, to every situation.

"Fuck me!" she squealed then suddenly with a start.

"There's David fucking Bowie!" she continued excitedly, like some sort of a fucking maniac.

"Just standing over there dude! Minding his own fucking business, for jaysus sake!?"

She was right too.

There he was indeed.

The legend himself.

Although dressed it has to be said, in what can best be described as the most disgustingly snot-green coloured suit that has actually ever been.

It was hideous.

Vile.

And so bad in fact that even a good-looking chap like Bowie couldn't render the ensemble – the TOTAL CAR CRASH of an ensemble - acceptable.

I'd always liked Bowie though; don't get me wrong.

Even if the one and only time that I'd seen him performing live up until that point, was at that Slane concert in Meath in 1987, when he had brought his incomparably ghastly 'Glass Spider' tour to town.

What a fiasco *that* show was!

Bombast at its most extreme.

A ludicrous display from start to finish, from a dude that had quite catastrophically lost his way.

I remember thinking at the time actually as he was being lowered down from a gantry fully fifty metres above the stage - whilst wearing a scarlet red suit and speaking/singing into an old-fashioned red telephone type thingamajig - that we were, without any doubt, in the presence of a dude that had finally lost the plot.

I'd met him after that also, briefly, some years later, in a considerably more informal setting.

I'd scored this temp job at a wine bar on the Strand in London during the summer of 1989, and in he had popped on the evening in question with some dude in a skirt.

I'd been keeping bar there for the evening, and happened to be attending at the time to the legendary (albeit mad) scouser himself, Paul McCartney, just as Bowie and his dubiously attired acquaintance made their illustrious entrance.

It all ended in tears though with Bowie and Macca having a right old go at each other towards the end.

No digs were exchanged, but it was a close-run thing.

Myself and one of the other barmen had to step in in fact, to ensure that no blood was shed.

McCartney was the main instigator of the fracas also, which was one hundred per cent as a result of the fact that he was, at the time, totally and utterly fucking plastered.

It petered out in the end anyway, with Macca and me heading off to some other bar elsewhere in London, where other even more reprehensible events came to pass.

But anyway; that was years ago – and here was Bowie before me now again. I wondered if he'd remember me.

"Let's go over and say hello" said Belinda, and even though I could take him or leave him either way as I mentioned before, I saw no reason why we shouldn't wander across to chew the fat with the old bollocks for a minute or two.

Perhaps he might know someone there even, I was thinking, that could line us up with some scoops?

A fight broke out then though, oddly enough, between himself and that Joe Elliott dude from Def Leppard, so we did the right thing of course and rushed across to lend him a hand.

A few of the bouncers ushered Joe away then, after which it all died down.

Handbags at dawn type of thing.

It was definitely embarrassing for Bowie though – that much was clear from his unsettled demeanour - so arriving at his side when we did, we made a conscious decision to say nothing at all about the recently terminated fracas.

Belinda's effusiveness though over the ensuing few minutes, was a good deal more over the top I felt myself, than was absolutely necessary at the time.

That was her way though, so I was content enough for the time being to just play along.

I remained insouciant myself though, throughout.

I mean he takes a dump just the same as I do, right?

So, like, you know - what's the big fucking deal?

"Are you alright Mr. Bowie?" she asked.

He definitely looked a bit shook.

"I'm fine my love, thank you" he answered distractedly as he smoothed down the suit lapels that had just been crumpled out of shape by Joe.

He *did* notice the talcum powder on our faces though, so perhaps he wasn't as up his own arse as I'd remembered him from our previous encounter.

"Are YOU alright?" he asked then of Belinda, with what appeared to be genuine concern.

"You look quite pale, you know?" he continued.

Belinda went on to explain that it was actually talcum powder that was giving us the look of the deceased, and that it had been applied deliberately also, earlier on, as a ruse to get us backstage to meet with mega famous Rock Star DemiGods such as his good self.

He had appeared initially to be showing concern, as I was mentioning there before; but something about his countenance now - I don't know – was screaming disinterest.

Feigning enthusiasm type of thing, but with a look that indicated that he *actually,* really, couldn't give a flying fuck.

If you were to get inside his head, that is, and read his mind.

"We're groupies, don't you know?" said Belinda, to which I must admit I did a bit of a double take.

I don't usually like to reveal my emotions to anyone publicly if I can help it at all, and this recent revelation on Belinda's part was unexpected in the extreme.

Whatever about her own inclination to curry favour with the more distinguished patrons in our present midst by putting herself out there as a hussy that might commit any act to ensure that her deepest desires might be actualised, I can *more* than categorically state that I myself, was not in ANY WAY of the same predilection.

I decided however to let it go.

It would take too long to explain and besides anyway, as I said before, Bowie didn't look that interested either way in what she was attempting to impart.

Spotting some dude then behind him on the stage, who was totally fucking bombing in every way that you can imagine, I decided to ask him what the secret was to his *own* success, vis-à-vis the successful commanding of an audience.

I was interested to know his thoughts on such a thing; and moving away from the whole 'groupie' related dialogue would be a good move as well.

I didn't want him to think that I was some sort of a steamer you know?

I'd heard stories about him before and whereas 'each to their own' and all that, it wasn't a road that I was keen to be travelling down myself anytime soon.

"I'd be interested to know something actually, Mr. Duke" I asked of him so.

"What is it like to have an audience this large - or any size in fact - in the palm of your hand?"

Belinda did not look happy.

As in, it was pretty clear that she didn't like at all, the thoughts of me hogging the conversation.

The look of condescension that Bowie threw out then however, was arrogant in the extreme.

As in 'Look at this pathetic young Irish fucking loser, asking me such a stupid fucking question'.

His eyes were raised to heaven and his lips were almost certainly bordering on a 'tut-tut'.

These were accompanied additionally, by an absolutely *certain* look of 'What the fuck did I do to deserve fucking this?'

Belinda I think was beginning to have second thoughts about her hero as well.

I considered referring to his 'Glass Spider' tour then, with a view to bringing him back down to earth; but decided against it for now.

He deigned to give me an answer then, but only after I had put the question to him again in another way.

"Actually, let me rephrase that" I said.

"What does one have to do" I went on.

"To be as comfortable on stage as you are? That confidence, you know? The swagger?"

It was his turn then to do a bit of a double take.

I'd been wondering if he'd recognise me.

We had 'previous' as I said.

"Have we met kid?" he asked.

"Your face looks really familiar" he continued.

"I met you a few years ago in a cocktail bar on the Strand, TWD" I answered.

"You were with some geezer in a dress?"

Belinda was looking at me now in a new light.

As in I believe that for the most fleeting of moments, I was *actually* more appealing to her than our illustrious companion.

A light of recognition was quite clearly evident in his demeanour now also, but being the bollocks that he is – I know this now – there was just no way in a *million fucking years* that he was going to admit to having met such a complete nobody as myself.

And so it came to pass.

"Don't remember that kid" he went on, pretty unconvincingly.

"When was that exactly?"

The fucker knew alright.

My response was acerbic.

"'89 dude" I replied.

"I was with a 'badly fucked up on the scoops' Paul McCartney."

"And you were with that bloke in the dress."

And I meant it to sting.

"Seriously, I don't remember that kid" he responded, scratching his head as if to indicate that he was at a loss.

"Although my guitarist – Reeves Gabrels, don't you know - does wear a kilt from time to time."

By way of an answer to my original question then, he warbled on about the standard of musicians in his band, and pointing at people in the crowd and stuff; but I had lost all interest by now in what the fucker had to say.

It didn't stop him from rabbiting fucking on though.

"That's really interesting" I said sardonically, but on he went even so.

"Great" I said after his next foray, hoping that my monosyllabic riposte might encourage the bollocks to put a sock in it.

Sadly, it did not.

He just stood there, staring into space, mumbling something under his breath about Mick Ronson's farts.

He was definitely losing it.

"Why the green suit?" I asked then, in an effort to bring him back into the present.

It was important, I decided, to put him on the spot re; his livery of choice.

I was so annoyed with him at this point basically, that taking the total mick out of him was the only course of action that I felt was appropriate for the time.

"In honour of you and all things Irish, my young Gaelic friend" he responded vaingloriously, which I really must say was the final straw.

Even Belinda was eyeing him with disdain.

It was hard to believe that just one person could talk such an unbelievable amount of shite over such a comparatively short period of time.

Def Leppard took to the stage then, and were exactly as you would expect Def Leppard to be.

As in, we're not talking rocket science here.

I could see that Bowie was unimpressed, but that he would have been that way anyway, despite his and Joe's recent contretemps.

Joe though, in fairness to him, was professionalism personified, with his recent fracas with the duke a thing of the past.

Perhaps the polished nature of his performance was what was pissing Bowie off so much?

"What say you to cock rock kid?" he asked of me then.

And much as I despise the genre and believe it to be a grotesquely sanitised version of the true tenets of rock and roll, I couldn't find it within myself to align my views to Bowie's as things stood right then.

And yes, I know.

He hadn't exactly said that he didn't like it himself.

I could tell however by the pursed nature of his features and general look of distaste that was evident across his face, that he was not a fan.

He was one to talk though!

When I cast my mind back to the grisly nature of the stadium rock/plastic reggae pugwash that was to be derived from his own gruesome offering from 1984, 'Tonight', I felt inordinately compelled to bring his attention to the fact that not all was kosher across his own canon of work, from his humble early beginnings to the present day.

As in, that is, that everybody has their low ebbs here and there.

"Better than 'Tonight' dude" I suggested so, to which, amazingly, he seemed quite pleased.

He had clearly not cottoned on to my inference.

I looked at Belinda then and she looked at me, with it being patently obvious to me then by the expression on her face that she, like me, had had enough.

Spotting Robert Plant so, nearby, we decided to leave Bowie to his own little world, and wander across to the Zeppelin front man instead.

Perhaps more lucid discourse might be elicited from *him*?

Reviewing his long golden tresses however as we arrived, and despite the fact that it was not 1972 his denim shirt being open down to the fifth button revealing his tanned and hairless chest, I was not overly confident of a successful outcome to my aforementioned desire for intelligent debate.

He pouted and preened to such an extent in fact, when we arrived across, that I was unsure as to whether before us was the lead singer/ Rock Star Demigod of one of the greatest, if not *THE* greatest rock and roll band of all time, Led Zeppelin, or Larry fucking Grayson!

Perhaps he could sort us out with some gargle though; which considering the exacting time that we had experienced since our arrival at the venue earlier that day - and of course the fact that as Belinda had mentioned before, there would be practical LAKES of the stuff floating around here backstage – backstage where it has to be said we had suffered much trial and tribulation in order for us to be just here - a zippier than usual expediting of the components required for liquid pleasuring, would, in my view at the time, have been a considerably more favourable outcome than not.

"Where can we get a gargle here Percy?" I asked of him tersely.

No need for pleasantries I was thinking.

I was as thirsty as fuck, so priorities to the fore etc.,

The last thing I wanted, or needed indeed, was another aimless interchange like the one we had just engaged in with TTWD.

Plant mentioned something then about Elton John and booze, so the situation all of a sudden began to look more promising.

Notwithstanding his reference to 'Elton John'.

That was a worry.

I'm not going to deny it.

Belinda though, for some unearthly reason, began to bang on about Plant's shirt; but, more specifically, questioning him as to why the buttons on it were opened down so unnecessarily close to his naval.

That's the trouble with the womenfolk you see.

When it comes to priorities, they just get it all wrong.

There we were, with no substance of any kind in our possession that could ever in any way be referred to as 'mind altering', and there *she* was, banging on about the fucker's shirt?

I mean what the actual fuck?

It was time to make my very strong feelings on the matter known to one and all.

"Look, are we getting this gargle or fucking what Percy?" I piped up.

"I'm losing the will to fucking live here"

Percy was his nickname.

Something I had heard before from somebody else.

A no-nonsense reference I believe to the unusually large nature of his appendage.

Belinda kept pressing him though, but rather than answer her at the time he just stared off into the distance, as if in some sort of fucking reverie or something, and talking to himself about Marrakech and some other 'rebirth' shit - fuck knows what - before coming out of his trance finally, and dragging us all off in the direction of what I imagined must be Elton John's dressing room and the booze.

Thank fuck for that!

Although when we arrived there some minutes later, my mood darkened once again.

Not only was Bowie there – I thought that we'd seen the last of *that* bozo – but the 'get up' of the dressing room had to be seen to be believed.

Pink and a sickly cream were the decorative hues of choice, with feather boas lying around the place also, fucking everywhere.

I threw a few of them off a stool to the floor anyway, and parked my arse down sullenly, waiting for Percy to make with the bubbly; if he could bother that is, to tear himself away from Bob Geldof for five fucking seconds and get fucking on with it!

Yes.

That's right.

You heard me right.

Bob Geldof.

Who I happen to think is a bit of a fucking legend to be honest, although the line of dialogue that he pursued as we arrived did not, I have to inform you, lighten my humour to any great degree.

I knew Bob 'kind of' from before you see, having encountered him several years previously in Dublin.

I had a vague recollection of meeting him again also in London some years later, although that rendezvous is hazy enough; and given how badly I was on the sauce at the time, it may not have even happened at all.

"Ahh Jaysus kid!" he opened cheerily.

"Don't tell me it's your bleedin' self again? What has you here?"

As ever, he was well on.

"I'm only after telling them your joke" he continued.

"You know; that Noddy gag that you told me and the Queen a few years back?"

I had a memory of one occasion when I had imparted to him the details of said yarn, but definitely didn't remember any QE2 being present at the time.

Just Bono and that football dude, Eamon Dunphy, so I supposed that there was a reasonable chance that when he mentioned the word 'Queen' he might, indeed, have been referring to either of those two gobshites, as opposed to the monarch that presided at present over the deservedly maligned and consistently contemptible perfidious Albion.

Percy was keen to know more about the gag.

"What's the joke Bob?" he asked.

"I love jokes me" he went on.

They greeted each other quickly – Bob somewhat insultingly it has to be said - referring in a quite derogatory fashion to Percy's unnecessarily bare paunch and asking him also, as to why he was here - I think they knew each other from before – before he threw out the old epigram then again for public review.

"Why does Noddy have a bell on the top of his hat" he asked, sniggering away to himself, to which Percy answered.

"I don't know Bob. Why DOES Noddy have a bell on the top of his hat?"

"Because he's a cunt!" answered Bob, to which all and sundry present whooped and hollered to denote general approval vis-à-vis the wheeze.

Elton John was a bit over the top though and way too excitable in my opinion as to be taken seriously.

There was definitely something not quite right with *that* old bollocks.

"Yeah, good one" I said to Bob, unimpressed and narky also, about the consistently 'non-champagne swigging' nature of our present predicament.

"Albeit old" I went on.

And I definitely meant for *that* to sting.

"Pass the champers David dahhling!" said Elton then to Bowie, and in an instant my mood towards him changed.

What a shout!

I was warming to the dude.

It turned out anyway that there was a crate of the stuff behind where Bowie was sitting, so he just grabbed a few bottles of the fizzy nectar in question and passed them around.

NOW we were sucking fucking diesel!

That Axl Rose dude from 'Guns 'n' Roses' was present as well.

I'd only just noticed him there, after my mood had improved.

I'm like that sometimes.

If I have a focus on something – and in this instance, it was my immediate pursuance of alcohol – then all else, usually, fades into insignificance.

Objects and persons become peripheral until such time as my needs are assuaged, after which a veil becomes lifted and other seemingly invisible things to me up until then, become apparent.

And so it was with Axl.

I like Axl.

And his music too.

Some of it is bland, indeed - don't get me wrong.

'November Rain' anyone?

I defy anyone however to argue the point that 'Welcome to the Jungle' is not an all-time fucking classic.

He was going down in my opinion now though, which was mainly as a result of his sickeningly sycophantic attitude towards Robert Plant, as soon as he had noticed that he was there.

I've never seen brown-nosing quite like it to be honest; and could tell clearly enough also, that Percy was similarly unimpressed.

Axl just wittered on inanely, while Percy waited for the fucker to finish.

It was painful.

"Like, it's omm, like, a really great fucking honour to be in, like, your fucking presence man!" he said.

The gushing was odious.

Percy had no idea who the fuck he was as well, which rendered the entire episode even more embarrassing than it already was.

And for some unknown reason also, he kept referring to Axl as 'Mr. Grease'.

I'm not sure what Percy was on exactly, but whatever it was, it was strong.

So strong in fact that for the next ten minutes or more, he regaled us with a story from one of Zep's US tours in the mid 70's, and to say that the anecdote was odd, would be a considerable misrepresentation of the facts.

A whole lot of rambling nonsense basically about some groupie getting molested by a fish, John Bonham doing wheelies in a hotel foyer, and Jimmy Page fucking a TV out of a window whilst dressed in a leopard skin leotard and blonde wig.

At what point it came to him that any of this shite might be of any interest to anybody, ever, was something that I mused upon considerably at the time.

Another thing that I considered also; as Percy continued to babble on about what was basically nothing at all; was how a more expedient fulfilment of the task at hand - that is, getting as wasted as possible as quickly as possible - might be achieved.

The champagne was fine, don't get me wrong.

An instantaneous high was very much required now however, as a matter of the most extreme urgency.

Glancing around me at the parties that were present, I made the fairly obvious call that Axl was the dude in attendance who was considerably more likely than not to have a substance about his person that was more 'high end', shall we say, than what was being offered to us as things stood.

Positioning was crucial however, so changing stools so that I was sitting next to the fucker was the work of a mere nanosecond for a seasoned sponger such as myself.

I bade my time though.

Nobody likes a bollocks that makes it *too* obvious.

Timing was everything.

Critical really.

And making it seem like it was his idea rather than mine was the best way to approach it as well.

Percy was starting to lose it now though even more than before.

For no apparent reason, he just stopped during the middle of his monologue to sing – yes, that's right, you heard me right - to SING - the eponymous last line from what is regarded arguably, as Zep's most famous number, 'Stairway to Heaven'.

"AND SHE'S BUY - EYE - ING THE STAIR - AIR - WAY - AY - TO ......HEAVAAN..."

He remained silent after his line, after which we all regarded him, gob smacked. What a douche!

I don't suppose that anybody there, looking at the faces of all that were present, in their lives up until that juncture, had ever come across a greater dick.

You could see it on their faces.

He went on with his story then anyway, but not before Geldof butted in to inform everybody of an ignominious episode involving 'yours truly', some years previously in Dublin, when I chanced a fart in a city centre nightclub that went very drastically wrong.

My ingestion of 'substances' on the day and night in question (co-incidentally enough, on the very same day in July 1987 that I had attended the concert that David Bowie, sitting directly opposite from me now, had performed in Slane Castle) AND the consumption of a curry that in any person's opinion, could never have been deemed to be *actual* curry in any way, shape or form, led my sorry arse to the unfortunate circumstances that prevailed upon it eventually, on the calamitous evening in question.

Bob *did* help me out on the night though; so fair dues to him for that.

Everybody else there however - including known friends and associates – were more than happy to stick the boot in in my hour of greatest need.

Bringing the matter up every time that we met though, did not endear me to Bob any further.

A legend he was (and is) of course – don't get me wrong.

But this spilling of the beans re; the humiliating events on the evening in question, was more than any person should ever be expected to bear.

Couldn't the fucker just let it lie?

As in, surely it was old enough material at this stage.

The answer was no.

He couldn't let it lie.

He proceeded to tell the entire story from beginning to end in fact, after which everybody present - particularly that bollocks Elton John - had a great old laugh at my expense.

As always however, I gave as good as I got.

I was fucked if I was going to let that Geldof beanpole get the better of me.

Yes he was a legend.

I've said that before.

But there was no way that I was putting up with fucking this!

He may have lent me some jeans at the time, but that didn't mean that he could shit on me forever.

"I do remember Bob" I answered, when he asked me if I did.

"Because every time I think back to the time in question!" I went on.

"My abiding memory is that the strides that you lent to me, given their length in the leg, must surely have belonged to the lankiest cunt that has ever lived, at any time, anywhere, during any age. Oh, they were yours, were they?! Right so".

That told him, the gangly git.

Fight fire with fire, you know?

Axl went on another little monologue then – a gushing little interlude that made me want to throw fucking up.

Had he no dignity?

Yes, OK.

You like Zeppelin 2.

Fair enough.

But does it mean that you have to suck Percy's dick as a result of the fact?

He was pissing me off major league now to be honest, so I decided that it was time to take him to the side while the rest of them were rabbiting on about some other shit, and have a word.

Elton John had just asked him to duet with him later that day as well, so my thinking was that I could probably advise him against that as well.

As in, 'if you want to retain any of your 'street cred' dude, *THAT* is not a road that you want to go down'.

"Please don't do it dude" I said to him, just to be clear.

Above all of this however and paramount in my mind at the time, was how to convince the dude to part with any substance at all that might render our present circumstances just that little bit more bearable.

On the sly so, after I put in my request – and with very little further induce-ment required on my part at all - he popped me a small white tablet while nobody was looking, after which I consumed said capsule in an instant, regardless of the fact that I had no idea at all as to what it was.

'Fuck it' I was thinking.

'What's the worst that can happen?'

Percy called me over to him then, so I wandered across.

It was an unsteady enough journey though; I'm not going to lie.

That shit that I had just popped, whatever the fuck it was, was already start-ing to take hold.

Percy anyway, fair fucks to him, had managed to locate a bottle of proper booze from somewhere - JD I think it was - so with that being the situation, he wasn't going to have to be calling me over fucking twice.

No sooner had I stood up though, and made my way over, Belinda, that fucking floozy, took my place immediately, and plonked herself down resolutely beside Axl.

He didn't appear to be that interested in her though – well initially anyway - so I don't know - maybe he was batting for the other side?

Not that I give a flying fuck about that!

Each to his own I say; as I've said indeed on many occasions before.

Nothing to do with fucking me!

Sitting next to Percy then anyway, and drinking his bourbon, I was thinking that I should probably be making some kind of an attempt at polite conversa-tion.

What to say though?

What to say?

"What happened with Jimmy and the telly dude?" I ventured.

It was the only thing that I could remember from the boring story that he'd been throwing out there before.

I was sorry that I asked though, as the answer that he gave me was pretty much interminable.

More shit about fuck all.

He had mentioned something to me about me 'singing' though, earlier on, so why not now, I was thinking?

It was as good a time as any was the way I saw it, and might go some way as well I was thinking, towards shutting the fucker up.

I launched into it so, with a considerable degree of verve.

Heartbreaker.

First song.

Side 2.

Zeppelin 2.

Why not indeed?

Sure hadn't Axl been banging on about it before?

I might as well keep it prescient I was thinking.

It felt good anyway.

It felt VERY good.

I was totally fucking nailing it which was definitely weird as I didn't remember ever being that great a singer before.

The drugs must have been giving my voice more clarity or something, I don't know.

Either way, it was fucked up.

But I didn't care.

I just fucking went for it.

I decided to go for a medley then, throwing out a few excerpts of 'What is And What Should Never Be' and 'Killing Floor' there also, for good measure.

You could tell that they were all impressed, so I continued on with 'You Shook Me' from Zep 1 – the old Willie Dixon number, you know?

I stopped for a breather then, with Axl Rose practically sucking my cock during the break.

"FUCKING WOW DUDE!" he piped up.

"WHERE THE FUCK YOU BEEN HIDIN'? YOU BELONG ON THE FUCKING STAGE MAN!"

I'd never thought of it before but maybe he was right?

Having met all of these present bozos tonight as well - and many others before indeed - there was certainly nothing about any of them that was in any way more special or talented than myself.

That bollocks Bowie was unimpressed though – jealous more like, the skinny fuck – and grouchily made a reference to the fact that I was 'no Scott Walker'.

Prick.

He launched into 'Sweet Thing' then from his 1974 offering 'Diamond Dogs', and even though it's an absolute classic - and up there, probably, in the top ten of any Bowie songs that a discerning fan or set of discerning fans might put together - there was still no way in hell that I was letting the fucker get away with stealing my thunder.

The song is a perfect vehicle also, for anyone with a wide register to show off their vocal prowess, and ability to reach both low and high notes; so as a choice of tune to impress, he could definitely not have picked a number that was any better.

I just took it over though, and with the drugs and JD combination at what appeared to be some sort of a nadir, I made the falsetto bit at the end of the first verse with absolutely no fucking issues at all.

I could tell that Bowie was livid now, so rather than just stop there, as I probably would have done if I hadn't seen his face, I decided to proceed further.

Grabbing the bottle of JD from Percy so, I stood up and launched into 'No Regrets' by The Walker Brothers, just to piss the snot-suited fucker off, using the bottle as a pretend microphone for, you know, effect.

It worked too, as I totally nailed that one as well.

I was feeling a good deal less than clever now however, with my recent ingestion of additional mind-altering substances finally taking their toll.

I did stand on a chair though; which in glorious hindsight after the event, was not the smartest move that I've ever made.

'Give me a P please Bob!' I was thinking, as I spotted an incredulous looking Percy and similar looking Bob Geldof out of the corner of my eye.

And then, finally - some might say at fucking last – after some other mumbled words thrown out there that I can't actually remember - I succumbed to the abyss.

CHAPTER 5

One more button?
Dare I risk it?
Risk it for a biscuit?
Yeahhhh!!
ONE MORE BUTTAAAAANNNN!
Doin' it to me, doin' it me!
Ah, Ahh, Ahhh, AHHHH!?
Shake for me girl!
I wanna be your back door man!
Oh!
Oh!
Oh!
Oh!
Oooh my, MY, MY!
Oooh my, MY, MY!
Ahh keepa cool yeah baby!
Ahh keepa cool yeah baby!
Right down to the naval?
Too much?
Fuck them!
NOT too much!
I'm Robert fucking Plant for fuck sake!
Right down to the naval it bloody is!
Who are these dudes?
Irish.
Don't they know who I am?
I'm Robert fucking Plant for fuck sake!
Like I said.
Preen.
Must preen.
Stomach out.
Washboard stomach.

Left foot, ten o'clock.
Right foot, steadfast at twelve.
Pictures at eleven.
Pouting.
Don't forget to pout!
Looking for a drink these kids.
I can get them a drink.
I think.
And if not, I can always purloin some of that old queen Elton John's champagne.
That lush fucker always has a champagne stash hidden somewhere.
Queen!
Fucking Queen!
Is there anything worse than fucking Queen?!
'Somebody to Love'.
Not theirs.
Grace's.
Jefferson Airplane.
Y'all dig?
That was the one.
The MOMENT.
Me blasting it out and Jimmy knowing that I'm the man.
Fucking Bowie!
He stole that off Jimmy too.
A Yardbirds number.
'I'm a man'.
Prick!
'Jean Genie', my arse.
Where was that again?
A college in Brum?
I think.
What a ghastly city!
Worse now.
The Bullring!
'We're going down the bullring to get a packet o' peas!'
Roy?
Jeff?
Ozzy?
How can such a dreadful place beget such greats?
A burning desire to get out, I'll warrant.
Not Wales.

My beautiful Wales.
Misty mountain hop.
Bron Yr Aur.
Leafy glades.
Sumptuous valleys.
A haar like mist covers all.
I look to the bottom from a lofty perch.
How far down?
Difficult to tell.
Ohh, the peace of it all!
Silence.
Heddwch.
A steadier climb.
Further up.
Have fashioned a stick.
Moss glistens in the distance.
Crackling underfoot.
Wood fractures under milky white soles.
A warbling brook.
After time, I descend.
Fatigued.
There she is.
In the gloaming.
Waiting.
My mystical refuge.
Glittering gold.
Log fire bosom.
Alas, she is gone.
Disappeared now.
The sands of time have secreted her away.
And John.
Beautiful, beautiful John.
Dreams of you in my head.
Hear the horses thunder, down in the valley below.
Waiting for the angels of Avalon, waiting for the Eastern glow.
Dear John.
Magician's rings.
Three fifths an Olympian.
Herculean.
I'll sing it now!!
YEAH!

Doin' it to me, doin' it to me!

Ahh, ahhh, AHHH, AAAHHH!

Why the fuck not?

"DON'T YOU WANT SOMEBODY TO LOVE? DON'T YOU NEED SOMEBODY TO LOVE?"

Shit.

They're not happy, that Queen shower.

That squeaky voiced drummery dude looks just about ready to burst!

Not THEIR 'Somebody to Love' you see.

But fuck him, the limp wristed fuck!

A midget with tennis elbow could hit a snare harder!

I'll sing what I fucking want!

Dear John.

Dear beautiful John.

'Do not go gentle into that good night,

Old age should burn and rave at close of day;

Rage, rage against the dying of the light.'

And what's with all that 'Radio Ga Ga' bollocks?

"Sorry kid?"

The kid has asked me a question.

The bloke kid that is.

The girl looks weird.

"Where can we get a gargle here Percy?" he says.

And when he says 'gargle', I'm assuming that he means a tiddly-wink of some ilk?

I can get him something.

He seems alright.

Better than those Queen dicks!

What is wrong with that guitarist's fucking hair?

Like, do NOT stand out in the rain dude!

The Leo Sayer 'look' IS NOT, and HAS NEVER BEEN, a good 'look'.

"A bit short back here to be honest kid, but if you follow me, I'll take you to Elton's dressing room. He ALWAYS has booze!"

The kid seems happy enough with that and the bird is made up too.

This could work out.

As in, I might even get a blowie.

Definitely seems up for it.

Must preen some more though.

And pout.

"Are you feeling ok?"

She's finally spoken, the girl.

Of COURSE I'm ok, I'm thinking.

I'm Robert fucking Plant for fuck sake!

"I'm fine darlin'" I answer.

"And you?"

It's nice to be nice.

Even to minions.

"Aren't you cold?" she continues, which seems to me to be an odd line of questioning, especially when you consider the fact that it's the middle of fucking April.

"As in", she goes on.

"Why on earth would you have your shirt buttons open down to what has to be admitted is seriously close to your naval?"

She obviously knows nothing about style this girl.

Otherwise why would she be asking me such a ridiculous question?

"Look, are we getting this gargle or fucking what Percy?" says the dude.

"I'm losing the will to fucking live here".

And in fairness to him, I can see where he's coming from.

That Def Leppard crew are on to their third number now, and it's just as putrid, if not more so, than the first.

The Queen guitarist with the stupid hair has joined them as well, so it's definitely time to depart.

"Seriously, are you feeling OK?" says the girl once again.

Well I am and I'm not, to be fair.

I like being here what with the adulation and all that, but I'd probably prefer to be somewhere else really, if I'm being totally honest.

And the shirt being open down so far is definitely making me feel a bit chilly too.

Not that I'd ever tell anyone that.

Or do the buttons up.

I have a persona to uphold.

A warmer clime though; for that I do yearn.

Where nobody knows me and I can be just me.

Marrakech.

My spike.

My revelation.

Music from within.

Gnawa.

A magical journey.

My future realised.

A new order.

I will re-immerse myself.

Realign.

A rebirth.

"Sorry, what's that?" says the girl.

Shit.

Thinking out loud there again.

I'm always at that.

"Nothing, nothing!" I answer hastily.

"Let's find Elton and that bubbly!"

They both look pleased with that so off we mooch in the general direction of the temporary dressing rooms that are situated further back.

Elton looks happy.

Although Elton ALWAYS looks happy.

The place looks grim though.

As in, what's with all the feather fucking boas?

Bowie's here too.

And that grumpy looking American singer in the kilt who keeps following me around.

And Geldof.

Fucking Mick do-gooder!

"Ahh Jaysus kid!" he says to my young Irish compadre.

"Don't tell me it's your bleedin' self again? What has you here?"

They appear to know each other.

"I'm only after telling them your joke. You know; that Noddy gag that you told me and the Queen a few years back?"

He's off his head as usual.

Although I would like to hear the joke, whatever it is.

I love jokes me.

"What's the joke Bob?" I ask.

"I love jokes me".

"Ahh jaysus, sure isn't it only yourself Robert Plant!" he answers chummily.

"With your shirt an' your belly 'n all! What the fock has you here pal?"

Ehh, like, WHAT?

I'm here to like, sing man!

Obviously?

I'm Robert fucking Plant for fuck sake!

"Here to sing dude" I answer tersely.

And I mean it to sting.

"But what's the joke dude?" I ask him again, getting impatient now and very seriously toying with the idea of just going the fuck home.

"Why does Noddy have a bell on the top of his hat?" he says, stifling a snigger as he speaks.

The joke obviously.

"I don't know Bob" I answer.

"Why DOES Noddy have a bell on the top of his hat?"

"Because he's a cunt!"

Excellent!

I do like that.

Elton does too.

As if he isn't happy enough.

"CAPITAL MY DEAR FELLOW!" he shrieks madly.

"CAPITAL!"

"A TRIUMPH!"

He slaps Bowie on the back good-naturedly, who appears to be amused also.

I thought that Bowie and he weren't talking though.

Something about Bowie calling him a Queen some years before?

Seriously though, like pot, kettle?

They appear to be reconciled now however.

"Yeah, good one" says the kid, unconvincingly.

"Albeit old" he continues, wincing somewhat.

I like this kid.

He has something, although I know not what.

Not in awe?

I think that's it.

Yeah.

That's DEFINITELY it.

We could be anybody.

As in not Rock Star DemiGods?

He doesn't give a fuck.

Elton is bleating on now about something else.

Champagne, I think.

"Pass the champers David dahhling!" he says.

Idiot.

As in, why is he so affected?

Talk like a normal fucking person, you blithering buffoon!

Not Danny la fucking Rue!

What was I on about there?

Let me get it back, let me get it back, let me get it back!

Oooh, yeah.

Ahh yes.

I remember now.

Elton's bullshit way of communicating.

I will devise a Sigul to take him away.

Away, away, in a puff of smoke.

Ha ha, a puff of smoke!

Appropriate actually that he be disappeared in such a fashion.

Ironic, as the Americans say.

Not that they even know what the word means.

Fuckers.

"Like, it's omm, like, a really great fucking honour to be in, like, your fucking presence man!" says the dude in the skirt.

What is his NAME again?

Axle Grease?

Axle Grinder?

Not sure.

He's a bit over the top anyways.

As in what's with the bandana?

If he puts weight on as well he'll be an absolute fucking RINGER for Benny Hill when he gets older.

Did I hear that he died?

A shame if so.

Loved that Claude Le Twit skit.

I'll tell them a story.

But in a really low voice so that they have to listen up.

Mysterious.

Esoteric.

That's me.

Whispering tales of gore.

An overlord.

"Good to hear Mr. Grease, good to hear" I say.

I've opted for Grease.

Not that it matters.

As in like, who the fuck cares?

Not me for one.

He looks confused.

"So there's like this bird right?" I continue, commencing my tale.

"And she's been making eyes at me ever since we arrived at the bar. You know the type, yeah?"

I nod knowingly with a smirk to everyone, including the girl, who DEFINITELY knows what I'm talking about.

They all do.

"Come closer and listen in" I continue, whispering now, so that they have to, really, if they like, you know, want to hear the yarn.

They all gather in.

Hanging on my every word.

How can they not?

I'm Robert fucking Plant for fuck sake!

Funny how it turns out anyway but my intended turn is pretty bland in the end.

Not esoteric at all.

Far from regaling them with a wild and wonderful histoire from the foothills of Eyjafjallajökull or some other cool place, I just throw out a bullshit story instead about that redhead in Seattle.

You know; the ginger groupie that got fucked by the fish?

"Woooaaah there, hold up there Percy!" says the Irish bird.

"A bit TMI there methinks?"

Fuck knows what her problem is.

Doesn't she know who I am?

I'm Rober...

Well, you know what I mean.

"Ok guys" I say.

"We're in the hotel, some dingy joint anyways, and we've like, left the bar and are back in the room after the gig. This ginger chick is like, really gagging for it still, but I'm like, 'get the fuck out of my face man, I'm tryin' to get fucking stoned here! Little Robert Anthony does NOT want to come and play!' She ain't listenin' though, so I nod to some handler dude nearby to take her the fuck away. He duly obliges of course – handlers are good that way - but rather than fuck her out the door, he just ushers her over to the other side of the room, next to where those Vanilla Fudge dudes are hanging out. I've like forgotten about her anyway, until a little while later, I'm not sure how long, one of the dudes is like, fucking her with a fish. You know like, shoving a snapper or something up her fanny?"

That's when the Irish chick butts in with her 'too much information' bullshit.

'Nothin' to do with me darlin', I'm thinking.

'I'm just tellin' the story.

As in 'Don't shoot the fucking messenger man!'

"It's pretty gross anyway" I go on.

"So I just, like, leave and push off to Jimmy's room to see what he's up to. I get there anyway and he's like, off his head as well. He's not fucking anybody with a fish though, so it's an improvement at least on my last encounter with a dude or dudes that are under the influence.

"'evenin' Percy" he says to me as I arrive, just like that.

Which wouldn't seem to be that unusual ecept for the fact that he's wearing a leopard-skin leotard and a blonde wig, and looks as if he's just about to fuck a TV out of the window. He grabbed it as soon as he heard me coming in, and has it now, balancing on the frame. One false move and it'll be hurtling downwards towards old terra firma, two floors below.

"Fuck me Jimmy" I say.

"What the fuck are you doing with the telly?"

I decide to ignore the whole leotard/wig subject.

Some things are better left unsaid.

He seems to do a bit of a double take then as if he doesn't know how he got to be in that position, but I'm thinking myself that he's probably just letting on that he's spaced. The telly hanging out of the window also, I'm thinking at the time, is probably a ruse in the same vein.

Anything to get out of telling me why he is attired as he is."

They're hanging on my every word now.

Especially Grease.

It's a bit like that bit at the end of 'Stairway to Heaven' - you know?

The last line?

That sheer anticipation of the audience, just waiting for me to sing the words.

I really am the greatest Rock Star Demigod that has like, ever lived?

I'll sing it now actually!

"AND SHE'S BUY - EYE - ING THE STAIR - AIR - WAY - AY - TO......
HEAVAAN..."

I remain silent after my line and they all regard me, gob smacked.

Open jaws all round.

Ohh yes!

Boom!

Job done.

They'll be telling their grand kids about this.

"So like" I go on, eager to finish the story.

"He only goes and drops the fucking telly! Out it tumbles, into the night sky. I can't believe it really, to be fair – we aren't that type of band really, despite what the papers say – and the look of shock on Jimmy's face is fucking priceless. He is SHITTING himself!!"

"HA, HA!!" pipes up Geldof.

What the fuck is that fucking do-gooder butting in for about now?

"That reminds me kid" he goes on, addressing his words to the young Irish dude.

The young dude who it has to be said looks none too pleased.

"Do you remember that time that you focking shit yourself in that noight clob back in Doblin and had to come back to my hotel room in the Clarence to borrow moy jeans?"

"I do remember Bob" the kid retorts, fierily, still visibly pissed off.

"Because every time I think back to the time in question, my abiding memory is that the strides that you lent to me, given their length in the leg, must surely have belonged to the lankiest cunt that has ever lived, at any time, anywhere, during

any age. Oh, they were yours, were they?! Right so".

I like this kid.

Like I was saying; he doesn't give a fuck.

We could be anybody.

Geldof has told the whole story now anyway, and the kid is not HP.

Whatever, anyways.

I couldn't give a fuck.

I'll sing some more.

"I'M IN THE MOOD FOR A MELODY, I'M IN THE MOOD FOR A MELODY, I'M IN THE MOO–OO–OO–OO-OO-OO-OOOD".

They're loving this.

Although how could they not?

On a highway.

Drifting.

No name.

Asphalt glistening lazily in the heat.

Driving me on.

Driving me down the road.

There is no turning back.

On the road.

A gas station.

Route 66.

Get your kicks.

Top down Cadillac.

And the coming of the night time.

"I was just ten dude" says Grease, through a cloud of smoke of his own making.

He flicks the butt to the floor whilst his other hand grapples with a half-spent bottle of something.

"When I first got turned on to 2. And what a fucking head fuck man! That goddamn stereo sound on my brother's Technics? The black number, you know? The three in fucking one? Fucking STEREO? More like fucking QUADRAFUCKINGPHONIC man, I mean like fucking WOW! How the fuck did you guys fucking DO that SHIT man? With the sound going from side to side and the whole goddamns? Fucking trippy man. Got stoned and wasted to that many fucking times my friend, MANY fucking times. Kudos man. BIG fucking kudos to you my man. There'd be no fucking Guns without you man, or Halen, or Jovi. You blazed a fucking trail man, upon which us rock and roll fucking disciples are honoured to follow in your fucking wake. We salute you man! You are a fucking GOD man! A fucking Rock Star DEMIGOD!"

Anyway, much as he appears to be babbling - which he quite obviously is - Grease definitely has a point.

I AM a fucking Rock Star Demigod.

Probably the biggest there is, as I was mentioning there before.

And although rambling and barely decipherable, he is, of course, referring to our totally awesome masterpiece from 1969, Led Zeppelin 2.

And 'Whole Lotta Love' also, the opening track, being the number that he means.

"But enough about me" I say, half-jokingly.

"Let's talk about you. What do you think of me?!"

That old Bette Midler gag works every time.

If self-effacement of an ostensible nature that is, is your immediate desire.

"Would you do me the most gracious honour Axl dahling" interjects Elton.

"Of accompanying me later this evening on 'Don't let the Sun go down On Me'? Georgie Porgy said that he'd do it, but the mischievous young macavity is nowhere to be found. You simply MUST do it dahling, I'll simply DIE if you don't!"

"Please don't do it dude" I'm thinking - as I am sure everybody else there is too.

But no.

Fate will not be that kind to us today.

Axl – apparently that's his name – not Grease - against all odds, agrees to weigh in.

"Sure man, it'll be a fucking honour" he responds.

Fuck me!

Maybe he likes cock.

If that guitarist dude of his anyway – what's his name again?

The Edge?

Well if he was alive today - which he may or may not be - he'd definitely be spinning in his grave.

"Please don't do it dude" says the kid, taking him to the side.

I LOVE this kid.

I smile at him a knowing smile.

He glances back and I can tell that he gets it.

We're kindred spirits.

A union of souls.

I'll take him under my wing.

Teach him the ropes.

I wonder if he can sing?

Let's find out.

"Pass us that bottle there Grease" I say, who duly obliges and makes with the booze.

I'll keep calling him Grease for the laugh.

"Sit over here kid" I say to the kid.

"We'll get drunk and sing some tunes, yeah?"

The kid seems happy enough with the suggestion and makes his way across.

The chick doesn't seem that bothered either way and looks to have eyes for Grease now, more than her beau.

Don't think that she'll get too far there though.

As in, based on how quickly he agreed to Elton's request just now, I'd say myself that it's 2 to 1 on, that he's batting for the other side.

"What happened with Jimmy and the telly dude?" the kid asks.

AND he listens as well!

The rest of them have moved on but the kid wants to hear the end of my story!

Not that it's much of an ending mind, but I tell him anyway, seeing as he's asked.

"So yeah, the story kid" I say, eager to get it over with at this stage and get stuck into the booze.

He's sure to be impressed though.

Of that I am certain.

"So Bonzo anyway was riding his Harley up and down the hotel corridors, and the hotel management were none too happy. None too happy at all. We were like, this close to getting fucked out man, like, seriously!"

I hold up my thumb and forefinger close together to denote how close.

"But then Bonzo wasn't that happy either" I go on...

"When as he was motoring his way through reception - doing a pretty impressive wheelie down the stairs in fact, if legend has it right - and then out through the front door, a giant 32 inch televisual box lands no more than two metres away from him as he's careering down the path. Seriously man, he was like, fucking LIVID, but when he saw Jimmy some minutes later, having ran up the stairs immediately afterwards, with a view to offering to the perpetrator or perpetrators a bunch of or several bunches of fives in quick succession, as deserved retribution for the heinous act in question, he didn't have the heart, when he copped how Jimmy was attired, to exact his previously desired revenge. As in, the dude quite obviously had some pretty serious issues that needed to be addressed, you know?"

Ok, so the kid is semi-ignoring me now and has broken into song.

Which would normally piss me off in a really big way when I'm holding court, but on this occasion, for reasons that I'll outline forthwith, it does not.

And besides - and even though I've moved on a bit with that whole story of Jimmy fucking the TV out the window in Seattle - I do 'kind of' remember suggesting something to him a few minutes earlier about he and I singing?

And what a voice!

Not only is he arrogant and giving the impression that he's above it all he has the voice also, of a fricking angel!

OK, well maybe not an angel but a Rock Star DemiGod definitely.

To a one we are open-mouthed.

He is unbelievable.

He launches into 'Heartbreaker' a capella.

'Hey fellas, have you heard the news' and the ground shakes.

He's fucking going for it, this kid.

That's the opening number to Zeppelin 2, Side 2, you may recall, and I fairly nailed it myself, all the way back in '69 when it was first released.

The kid's version is better even than mine though, and that's saying something.

A kind of a cross between John Fogarty and the dude from Moby Grape, only louder and less, oh I don't know, rough?

A more refined timbre – is that the word?

Timbre?

Not sure.

He breaks into 'What Is and What Should Never Be' next and his voice trans-forms into a high falsetto, which brings to mind a young Anthony Newley, or dare I say it, Bowie?

'Killing Floor' follows - the 'Squeeze me Baby' part - before he finishes it off right where it all began (well for me anyway) with Willie Dixon's 'You Shook Me', which I myself, as you probably know, laid down on our first Zep album as well.

You can hear a pin drop.

The kid has been singing for no more than a couple of minutes, but in that short time he has succeeded already in transforming our party hardened and semi-drunken attendees into a state of near ethereal catalepsy.

We are transfixed.

"What?" he says, as he realises now that all eyes are focused on him.

"FUCKING WOW DUDE!" pipes up Grease.

"WHERE THE FUCK YOU BEEN HIDIN'? YOU BELONG ON THE FUCKING STAGE MAN!"

The kid looks embarrassed now, but for the life of me I don't know why.

With a pompous demeanour such as the one of which he is in possession; and the voice of a Rock Star Demigod also, the Grease dude is right.

The kid DOES belong on the stage.

"Ahh I'm not sure pal" interjects Bowie, directing his comments to the Ameri-can in the skirt.

"I've heard better," he continues.

"Like for instance, Scott Walker? This kid is definitely no Scott Walker".

Bowie appears to be peeved that the kid is getting more attention than himself.

Believing so, as a result of this, that he is in danger of being ousted as the only singer of note in our little group (yes, I know – mad right – as in, I'M fucking here??) he proceeds to break into song himself.

I know the one that he starts off with as well, and to be fair to him, it's a fucking corker.

Say what you want about Bowie being a dick and all that, but his vocal range is unfuckingbelievable.

'Sweet Thing' from his 'Diamond Dogs' album in the mid 1970's.

I remember it because Jimmy turned me on to it in '75 when we were touring in North America.

I'd always thought of Bowie before that as being a glam artist - you know; an Alvin Stardust type character?

But this album was astounding; almost prog really in its weirdness.

I met Peter Gabriel on the same tour (we were in New Orleans for a few days in mid-January, before our own tour started in Illinois later that week, and Genesis were playing there at the time, so we all went along), and he said to me that he'd never heard anything himself personally, that was quite like it.

And to be fair to TWD, it really is an unfuckingbelievable album.

He launches into 'Sweet Thing' now anyway, as I said, as a riposte.

Just as he gets to the falsetto bit at the start of the third bar however, the kid takes over and like, totally fucking nails it again!

Bowie is fit to be tied.

Standing up then, the kid, using the near empty now bottle of JD as a faux microphone, launches into the most impressive version of the first verse of 'No Regrets' by the Walker Brothers that I, or anyone else for that matter, has ever heard.

He proceeds then to stand on a chair and inform one and all the following:

"Thank you very much fuckers and good night. Thaaaaaat's BLOCKBUSTERS!"

And then he collapses in a heap on the floor in front of us, stone cold out.

Grease rescues the bottle, which quite miraculously has stayed intact, before necking another few swigs of it greedily, and wiping his mouth with his sleeve.

"God DANG!" he says, shaking his head with disappointment.

"That kid has one motherfucking great voice dudes!" he goes on.

"But he SERIOUSLY cannot hold his fucking acid man, no fucking way!"

"Acid?" I say, not understanding him at all.

Although the penny drops soon enough.

The fucker must have meddled with the JD while nobody was looking, to the extent that it is now, basically, just one giant bottle shaped Mickey Finn.

Or failing that, he just gave the kid some pills.

"Sure man" he responds anyway, as if a statement like his last is the most natural thing in the world for a person to say.

"The chick is fucked as well now actually" he goes on, pointing to the girl who at this stage – and I'm only just noticing how bad she is when he points her out – is curled up in a ball on the floor.

Drool is dropping out of the side of her mouth and she cannot be confused at this point with an individual that is a picture of health and vitality.

"Where did they get the acid, Grease?" I ask, knowing in my heart of hearts that is was from him, but wanting to hear him admit to it anyway.

"Fucked if I know man" he answers, lying, after which I lean over and administrator to him a kiss of an exceedingly Glaswegian nature.

Shock envelops our little party then, but if I'm being totally honest, I couldn't give a flying fuck.

I'm well pissed off with Grease, if only as a result of the fact that I was really enjoying the young dude's voice.

Grease has ruined that for us all now, and I'm cognisant of the grisly fact also (as thoughts of my departure lead to what might be coming next) that as soon as I leave this place, I'll have Queen or some derivative of Queen and their mediocrity to contend with as well.

Still though, it's probably better, marginally, than staying here with these dicks.

I turn to leave so, and regardless of the general state of Grease's beak, as blood runs from it profusely as a result of my recent less than uncompromising intervention, you can tell even so, that he's devastated to see me go.

And why would he not be indeed?

I'm Robert fucking Plant for fuck sake!

CHAPTER 6

But before all of that.

You remember that I mentioned it to you about a million years ago?

The concert in Slane?

Guns 'n' Roses?

1992?

Moshing?

I talked about it at the top anyway don't you know, before I went rambling on about other shite as I very often do.

Axl had mentioned for us to drop by if we happened to be around, and even though backstage at concerts is fine and dandy and satisfactory for some, I prefer myself to get down and dirty with the homes, if an option to do one or the other is to be considered.

'Feeling it' you know?

The sweat?

The aggression?

I was off my face on Acid though, which as I was mentioning there before, Axl had turned me on to as well the bollocks!

Getting backstage now so, I was thinking, without Axl actually *being* there to chaperone us in (as would almost certainly be the case) would be a definite challenge, given my badly narcotised state.

It was a practical *certainty* also, that he'd be entertaining gobshites such as Bono, Lord Henry Mountcharles and the like, so having to deal with me too, especially in the state that I was in right now, was something that no fucker, least of all him, would be content to abide.

I was coming down now though, which was an entirely different scenario as to my predicament just an hour or two before.

I had been ALL OVER the shop!

It had been a strange enough experience as well; I'm not going to lie.

Quite different to the Wembley gig a few weeks earlier, which although badly ended was decidedly more positive than this second 'acid-laced' odyssey that I came to experience at Slane.

My recollection of the earlier part of the day was vague, but I *did* remember some.

Let me recount it to you so, in an 'as it transpired' way.

I am two hundred feet tall with the masses at my feet.

They can see me coming but there's nothing they can do.

Dipluran hexapods running this way and that.

Fee Fi Fo Fum, I hear the beating of a double bass drum.

I sweep them aside with my feet to the left and to the right, but the terrain is dense, too dense to break through.

Before long it is above my head; compressed foliage and trees, swaying in the breeze.

I cannot see.

Escape, I must.

Fast.

Impenetrable undergrowth this is; as far as the eye can see.

Welcome to the jungle!

I thrash before and behind me and to the sides with a scythe, before it clears suddenly, and a vast city becomes discernible in the distance.

An Emerald city.

A Paradise city.

I'll get you my pretties!

And your little dog too!

An army of savage orcs and flying beasts surround me, there for no other reason bar to obey my command.

They'll get me a beer!

"GET ME A BEER!" I roar, but my request is irritatingly ignored.

I make efforts again to sweep them to the side, but they are no longer miniscule and indeed are dipluran hexapods once more.

Lamentably also, they are fighting back.

"Get out of my face, you drunken fucking cretin!" says one, before would you believe, knocking me to the ground.

The tables are turning and not for the better.

These bugs can talk AND fight!

Dubious signs of insubordination.

They must be taught a LESSON!

I raise myself from off the ground so, and take off into the sky.

My wings expand outwards as I climb ever higher, before I swoop down to just above their heads, and unleash my fiery breath o'er them all.

They fall and flail as the power of my vengeance becomes apparent.

They'll not cross me again.

"Uuugh" says one.

"You're one disgusting pig!" says another.

Odd to think I think that they're not writhing in pain.

What gives?

And then I start to come down, and with that slink sheepishly away.

Some hours later, after waking in a pool of my own vomit, I considered the notion that it was SURELY time for a beer.

I stood up so - not too gingerly - and headed off in search of same.

What could be more agreeable than a beer?

Nothing in the world at all.

Marcus was here somewhere and Belinda too - although fuck knew where?

I headed to a beer tent so, and scanned the crowd for them there.

And lo and behold, I encountered them before long.

Additionally - and difficult as I know you might find it to believe - Marcus was ensuring, as ever, that the auditory 'experience' for anyone that was unfortunate enough to be within range of his delivery, was as exacting an ordeal as to be withstood.

Would he ever learn?

It was unlikely.

"The origin of the kilt, don't you know" he warbled on to a conspicuously beleaguered looking Belinda who was stationed by his side.

"Is many fold".

She did not look HP.

As in, that is, not in any way fascinated by the subject that was under present rumination.

"Its true origins are Norse in fact" he babbled on, whilst at the same time leaning his head to one side, with a pinky stationed at the corner of his mouth to denote that arrogant and condescending university lecturer type like superiority.

"But the garment is undeniably Caledonian".

There's the problem you see, right there.

With Marcus, you know?

Whereas all others in a similar situation would have called Scotland by its actual name – that is, fucking SCOTLAND – Marcus, instead, prefers to confuse the issue by referring to it by a name that it was known many centuries before.

Why, you may ask?

Well, because he's a dick, mainly.

"About time dude" said Belinda, before grabbing me by the arm and shoving me squarely between herself and himself.

To denote definitively and in 'no uncertain terms' as they say, that said action was to be a representation of an absolute and unequivocal termination of their recent communiqué.

I would be her buffer.

"Where the fuck have you been?" she remonstrated further.

82

"Look, I know that we agreed to attend this event as a trio Freakers" she continued.

"But did I not make it abundantly clear to you before we left that I am not in the least bit interested in spending any more time than is necessary in the company of your absurdly verbose friend? He's banging on about kilts Johnny. Fucking KILTS! And where the fuck they come from! Can't you get him to shut the fuck up? Please? Just for a minute or two? Until the pain in my head subsides?"

She was struggling alright.

That much was clear.

Marcus has that effect on people.

As in that old 'losing of the will to live'?

We'd arrived as a trio as she had quite rightly said, but as soon as I'd popped my tab I'd been pretty much lost to the world.

"Sorry Belinda" I responded meekly, being genuinely so.

"I popped the tab so, you know - kind of lost it. No idea where the fuck I was to be honest, and no idea how I've ended up here either, bar my inherent desire for a gargle and instinctive ability to be able to make my way to a beer tent no matter what my condition. Apologies again anyway. I'll take it easy for the rest of the day, I promise."

She grudgingly shrugged her shoulders and grunted moodily, as if to say 'Well OK for now, but I'm pretty sceptical as to the credibility of your recent pronouncement'.

Or to put it another way that she had a feeling that I might have been bull-shitting her to just keep the peace.

To which she was probably right, in fairness to her.

As you may recall from what I mentioned before anyway, Axl *had* invited us along, so believe it or believe it not, we were cast iron and bone fide invitees on the guest list for the day.

All we had to do to gain entrance into the hallowed sanctum behind the stage was to show our faces to security on either side of the mosh pit - it didn't matter which one - and be ushered through then as cool as you like, by the chappies in attendance, away from the great unwashed, or the proletariat, or the lower orders; whatever name for them indeed that takes your fancy; to partake in the fun and frivolity, and MOST importantly free gargle, that was sure to be available to us as soon as we crossed the line.

At least that's how easy it was supposed to be if we just asked for Axl at said location, as directed by the man himself.

The reality of the situation however, as it was meant to pan out, and the reality of the situation as it ultimately came to pass, ended up being two entirely different things.

'As directed' also by the way, meant exactly how he had put it to us himself, just before we took leave of each other some weeks earlier, at that Freddie Mercury concert debacle thingamajig in London.

But more of that in a second.

Shutting Marcus up eventually and thankfully (he had since moved on to the veritable merits, good or bad, of Clan Stewart tartan over Clan MacGregor) we made our way to the security cordon that was located to the right-hand side of the stage, with the by now pretty odious looking moss-pit stationed to our left and imposing west wing of the castle towering above us on our right.

Considering our entrance beyond this point to be little more than a two second formality, we arrived there with a significant degree of élan.

Perhaps in hindsight this was our problem.

We were dressed well enough as well, so looking like a trio of scobes was definitely NOT the primary reason for our eventual rebuttal.

In comparison to the *rest* of the concert going populace on the day in fact, we looked positively dandy.

Belinda looked as awesome as ever, with her purple streaked, henna-like hair accentuated perfectly by a buttoned down, navy sequined blouse and pristine white, figure-hugging jeans. Star spangled silver docs completed the look, and with her strikingly beautiful facial features a permanent fixture, she was unquestionably a sight to behold.

Marcus additionally - although consistently aggravating as referred to before - was in habitual resplendence as well.

His garments might not have been the garments that I'd have chosen myself for attendance at a rock concert in the middle of the bog during a typical Irish summer - where quite simply *any* weather might arrive at any time to accost you with its appositeness - but there could be no denial of the fact that he looked very dapper indeed.

An immaculate dark grey smoking jacket was complimented by a gleaming white linen shirt and silk paisley-patterned cravat. Burgundy slacks, with the seam ironed perfectly down the length of each leg, were finished off by an exceedingly comfortable looking, albeit totally inappropriate, pair of brand new blue suede moccasins.

There was no way so that Marcus should be mosh pitting it today; although in fairness to him we *had* said to him before our departure that our admittance backstage was 100% 'nailed on', and in all ways that you can imagine, an indisputable fait accompli.

I was dressed quite nattily myself too, even if I do say myself.

A leather bomber jacket, à la James Dean, accompanied by a cream cheese-cloth shirt, brand new stonewashed tight-fitting jeans, and brown ankle height crocodile-skin boot type thingamajigs to complete the look.

We looked sharp alright; there was no doubt about it.

Our recent hob-nobbing with Rock Star Demigods was definitely rubbing off.

There was an aloofness about us that was palpable.

Imagine our surprise so anyway, and indignation indeed, when the total bollocks at the barrier looked at us like we had six heads, when we informed him in our matter of fact way (and why not indeed - it was the truth) that Axl had asked us to come along.

"Yeah, like FUCKING RIGHT he did!" said the fucker.

"And I suppose Bono is on standby to wipe your feckin' arses as well, yeah?" he went on.

"You know" he continued.

"After yiz have yizzer shites later on after downin' yizzer caviar and yizzer champayen in the castle!"

What the fuck was the gobshite banging on about?

It was hard to be sure.

Upon regarding his gombeen looking disposition then, I came to the conclusion that it wasn't *that* odd really for him to be emitting such mindless drivel.

There remained however, toujours, the issue of entry.

And even though I wanted to take the fucker down a peg or two, I reasoned, quite logically I surmised at the time, that such a course of action would end in dismal failure only, vis-à-vis the successful completion of our communally desired assignation.

Or to put it another way, that we needed to be keeping the fucker onside.

I retorted cheerily enough so, despite his negative approach.

"Look pal" I said.

"I know that you're only doing your job, but regardless of whether you believe that we require anal hygiene assistance from painfully mundane and insufferable north Dublin bred rock star mouthpieces, our situation nevertheless, remains as it is. Axl Rose *did* invite us along today, hence our party's presentation to you here and now, with the three of us being 'ready to rock and roll' as it were. I mean seriously dude; do you honestly think that we'd be bedecked in clobber such as the clobber in which we are bedecked, if we weren't venturing backstage? Look at my buddy's shoes for fuck sake!" I continued, pointing at Marcus's moccasins.

Belinda piped up also, reaching over the railing simultaneously, before leading the dude a few feet off to the side by his elbow.

"Not meaning to be overly tactile here lover" she said, releasing his elbow then, and talking loud enough, just, for Marcus and I to overhear.

"But I have just *GOT* to get backstage. The bozos that I am with right now are driving me absolutely fucking bananas, and I'll do literally *ANYTHING* to get away from them. One of them just gave me a ten-minute monologue regarding

85

kilts. I kid you fucking not dude! Anyway, I'll make it worth your while" she went on, before grabbing him suggestively by the forearm and throwing out a practically impossible to resist 'come to bed' eye in his general direction.

The fucker was quite clearly made of stone however, with his silent and stony-faced response to her advances a clear indication that with regards to what she had just proposed, he was very much unavailable for selection.

Belinda's less than fair synopsis of the facts regarding Marcus and my behaviour to date also I felt, was a bit much.

Ok, so perhaps Marcus deserved some stick; but what had I done to piss her off so much, besides getting wasted?

Sure doesn't everybody get wasted at concerts?

The bouncer made it back to where we had encountered him initially anyway, before re-stationing himself there, implacably; arms folded now resolutely, with a stern look of rebuke plastered all over his moronic visage.

Marcus then, regrettably - but true to form also, to be fair to him - decided to impart to the dude one or two more than difficult to understand (even for him) home truths.

"The pathetic nature of your general existence, my good man" he commenced.

"Is evident for all to see. It really is a sad state of affairs. You can however, and *MUST* indeed, take heart. Redemption of the soul can be yours, if this be your ultimate desire.

'Turn away from your sins, because the Kingdom of heaven is near!'
"Matthew 4:17."

"You know it makes sense, my friend. And in doing so, your life will be fuller, with the people that you encounter and that despise you now – obviously - on a daily basis, despising you a good deal less. I'm not saying that they will stop hating you completely - I mean, let's be honest here, the world is not flat. But I *am* saying that they might, possibly - and I'm just saying *possibly* here - they might, *possibly,* learn to *just about* tolerate your despicable and deplorable fucking character at some point further on down the line."

And much as Marcus's next drastic action did absolutely nothing to determine that this turd in human form might at some point today be mending his hitherto reprehensible ways, I have to admit that it was all that I could do NOT to break into a robust and tumultuous bualadh bos, when no more than a couple of seconds later, my good friend perpetrated said offence.

Not only you see, was this gorilla unreasonably steadfast in his resolve regarding permitting us to pass beyond, he also believed, apparently - quite incorrectly as it turned out - that taking the piss out of Marcus's outfit was a thing today for which he would not endure rebuke.

That however, emphatically, was not the case.

"Look fucking Noël Coward" emitted the t in hf.

"You're not getting fucking past ok?"

I must confess that it was a big surprise to me at the time that the dude was familiar with the great English coxcomb himself.

An incongruous enlightenment indeed.

"Coward eh?" responded Marcus aggressively, before squaring up to the dude with no small degree of bravado.

"Coward, is it? Well NOT by nature my good man! NOT, I must inform you, quite vehemently, by fucking nature!" he continued, before planting a perfectly executed haymaker squarely on to the bollocks' lower left jaw.

Applause was the only response that was warranted here really after that, and even though we had to leg it ourselves for obvious enough reasons, there were definite cheers to be heard in our wake as we darted off in the opposite direction.

The fucker had DEFINITELY had it coming; a notion that all of those that were in close proximity to him had appreciated also.

I would have preferred to elucidate to him further however, the circumstances around how and why we happened to be there, and attempted to convince him also that Axl Rose had *indeed* invited us to join him backstage on the day in question.

I would have conveyed to him in further detail as well, our backstage antics at the Freddie Mercury concert some weeks earlier, and that this was why, unlikely though the scenario might appear to him, we were knocking on his door today with a view to getting past.

Alas, as a result of Marcus's recent drastic (albeit admittedly appropriate) actions, that ship had now, most emphatically, already sailed.

And it wasn't bullshit either.

Axl *had* invited us to come along.

I had a vague recollection of singing Led Zeppelin songs on the day, to the motley crew that were in attendance at the time in Elton John's burlesque boudoir themed Wembley dressing room backstage.

I had blacked out though, after the gargle and the acid, before coming around some hours later to witness Belinda astraddle of Axl in a plastic chair, with a fairly 'no holds barred' view of her bouncing up and down on his cock a physical and indeed *visual* authentication of exactly how I was feeling at the time.

I was fucked.

She's some brazzer though, Belinda, in fairness to her.

Will fuck anything, anytime, anywhere.

Sure didn't I ball her myself earlier that day as well in the Rose & Crown on Union Street?

I waited for them to finish anyway, but made sure to let them know at the same time that I was there, and awake too.

You know, by shuffling about that little bit more noisily than usual, and a good deal of harrumphing going on here and there as well.

Not that it made the blindest bit of difference.

They basically just finished what they were doing, with regard for me and what I was thinking about the situation at the time, not something that either of them gave it a second thought.

I might as well have not even been there in fact, for all the attention that they paid to me whilst in the throes of their tryst.

Although in fairness to them - and to paraphrase the great Billy Connolly when he was expanding on some other occasion on a subject of a similar aspect - 'There isn't a herd of WILD HORSES that will make my arse go in that direction at the point of ejaculation!'

That is - and as I'm sure you've guessed already - anywhere that's away from the business end of a similar rendezvous.

"Ace Doll" said Axl, before Belinda dismounted him and moved across to the next seat along.

She lit up a fag then and blew the smoke upwards noisily towards the ceiling.

"That's some mighty fine work right there!" he continued, before reefing the bandana/tee cloth type thingamajig that had been stationed on his head for the duration of the time he had been there, and using it to wipe off some of the excess ejaculate that remained on the end of his cock.

He threw it at Belinda's face then, jokingly; as if this was the most obvious thing in the world to do after having had sex with a girl that until a few hours earlier you had never met, and are looking for something to do or say afterwards when the whole shebang has become just that little bit weird.

Not a scene that a person would be eager to observe *every* day so, as I'm sure you no doubt concur.

Unusually enough though, Belinda, rather than being horrified as any normal person might, picked up said garment from off the floor and secreted it away down her cleavage.

Something to tell the girls about on some other occasion I imagined.

That's Belinda for ya!

I've said it before and I'll say it again.

She's one hell of a piece of fucking work.

"Hand me a smoke there, Sugar'" said Axl, as he leaned back contentedly into his seat.

Belinda took one from her pack, before lighting it off her own and handing it across.

I had made it to a seat beside Belinda now myself also, so bummed one off her as well while there was one going.

We sat in silence then, listening to the music that we could hear from outside.

"Hey!" said Axl, to nobody in particular.

"Is that like, your fucking dude, dudes? I ain't seen him here today but it sure as hell sounds like that fucking dweeb that's singing right there dudes. Like, seriously? That douche is fucking everywhere man, like, you know, even when he's goddamn not, ye know?!"

He was right too.

Fucking Bono!

Some fucking satellite feed from the US that we found out about later on.

What IS it with this guy?

Can't he shut the fuck up for like, even five minutes?

Apparently not.

"Fuck dudes, I'm up fucking next!" declared Axl then loudly, before gathering himself together and pulling up his fly.

"Somebody said that I was up after that fuckwit - I remember it fucking now!"

I liked Axl.

OK, so he definitely was a perpetrator of unconventional post-coital habits; that much was in no doubt.

But he was an exemplary judge of character at the same time.

Off he popped so; but not before unleashing one final salvo.

"Like, fuck dudes? What the fuck is wrong with that fucking guitarist? Did he like, you know - learn how to play the goddang thing yesterday?"

Belinda and I had a good old snigger at that.

As in as an acute observation regarding 'The Edge' and his ability, it was difficult to imagine any other that was more on the money.

"Oh and listen up kids" he went on.

"You know like, that big show that we're doing in Ireland in a few weeks' time? Slane, is it? Well, let's hang there, yeah? Slash and Duff would love to meet y'all"

"'specially you darlin'" with his last comments directed quite obviously towards Belinda.

"Just tell Security that I said it was OK" he finished,

"And I'll like, you know - see you there, dawgs!"

And with that he was gone, off to do his turn outside with the rest of the band.

Thinking back on it then - as the security dudes in Slane were hot on our tail after Marcus had delivered the straightener to the fucker that had most definitely been asking for it - it occurred to me in a moment of crystal clear clarity that at no time during our meeting had Axl ever asked me for my name, or Belinda, indeed, for hers.

So, you know, following on from that - how the fuck was he supposed to be leaving our names with security?

"Belinda?" I asked breathlessly, as we weaved in and out of the crusty looking concert goers in our path.

"Do you know that invite that Axl threw out to us there, back in Wembley?"

"Yeah, what about it?" she answered narkily, clearly pissed off I think, that I was picking this moment of all moments, to strike up a conversation about a subject that had to all intents and purposes given recent events, already run its course.

"Well" I went on.

"Does he like actually know your name? Because he certainly doesn't know mine. So, you know, I was just thinking like - how is he supposed to be leaving our names with security, if he doesn't know who the fuck we are?"

"You're right!" she said, stopping now in her tracks and turning to face me. Marcus who had been just ahead of us stopped also.

"So what the fuck are we *doing* here?" she continued.

"I mean Jesus fucking H man; how could we have been so fucking dumb?"

"Totally" said Marcus with his hands on his hips, interjecting into a conversation that at this stage had been nothing the fuck to do with him.

"Additionally, and like, WAAY more important dudes - my moccasins are like, fucking ruined!"

"Shut the fuck up dude!" I retorted, majorly pissed off with him for being such a dick.

"We have bigger problems to deal with here, than your inappropriate fucking footwear! Like for one, having to associate right now with what appears to be a collection of ginger-headed farm hands in our immediate range. This is significantly less cool I have to say than I had imagined our day would be turning out earlier on".

"Agreed dude" said Belinda, with her annoyance and exasperation readily apparent.

"Drastic measures are required" she went on, perking up then somewhat, from what I could see.

"And thankfully chaps, in that regard, I can deliver most excellently!"

Unsure where she was going with this line of conversation, I enquired further as to what she was alluding.

"The fuck you on about Belinders?" I asked, desirous to be made privy as to the inner workings of her odd little mind.

"What I am on about, young Freakers?" she responded mischievously, with a smirk on her face.

"Is related to a significantly positive development of which, you will concur I'll warrant, is most agreeable. You will no doubt be DELIGHTED to hear my friend that both yours and my convivial companion, Cousin Charlie, paid me an visit early this morning first thing, and that after very little deliberation - if any, in fact - I made an immediate and executive decision to bring said distant family cognate along for the ride to this ancestral Mountcharles country seat as per where we are situated right now. Cousin Charlie so, is at present nestled snugly into a small baggy at the nether end of my arse pocket, which, given the nature of recent developments, is a very welcome state of affairs. Charlie is of a mind also, I believe, to be making his presence known to us soon, and introduced into our little gathering forthwith as a matter of great imperativeness".

'Excellent' I was thinking.

This was *indeed* a positive development.

Although Belinda had quite clearly been hanging around with Marcus and myself for too long.

As in, that is, an inclination towards brevity was no longer a trait.

This was a hugely favourable change of fortune for us anyway, as I said.

Not only had we managed, finally, to lose the security dudes that had been on our tail since Marcus had decked one of their colleagues, Belinda also, had come up with a perfect antidote for all of our recent disappointments.

Yes indeedy.

It could not be disputed by anybody that our present predicament was sticky in the extreme, surrounded as we were in the mosh pit - which was, by the way, where we had eventually ended up after all of our zigging and zagging and bobbing and weaving - by what must surely go down in the annals as the least stylish concert-going crowd that has actually ever been.

And yes, we would probably end up slumming it with these fuckers for the rest of the day; but with Charlie in our corner we could at least now elevate our senses to the extent that none of the abovementioned bozos would be of consequence.

We'd be so off our heads on 'Charlie' basically, that any denim jacket-clad clodhoppers with cauliflower ears that we might encounter along the way and during the course of the festivities, would be so beneath us existentially, as to be pretty much immaterial.

Mere collateral beings they would be, neither here nor there one way or another, and certainly not subjects for us more rarefied individuals to be concerning ourselves with in any way.

"Not sure if I've told you this before Belinda" I said to her with great earnest.

"But are you aware that I, like, actually love you?"

She smiled back at me and looked very pleased with herself, generally.

And why wouldn't she, I was thinking?

What a shout!

"Horse it out so" I said, all 'business like' now and 'matter of fact' now that our initial platitudes and slaps on the back had been meted out and dispensed with.

There were minds to be altered!

Marcus was pretty happy about this new development also and just stood there, all Gollum-like, with his eyes bulging greedily and his palms a-rubbing together in covetous anticipation.

Gathering in a huddle so, to keep out the wind and prying eyes also, we snorted said stimulant post-haste and waited for the fun to begin.

Moving to the front with difficulty, but doing so anyway - why would we not - we found ourselves next the stage barrier before long - with the ginger lead singing bollocks that hands out backstage invitations like they're candy, and then ignores them summarily afterwards just because he can, there before us in all of his finery.

And when I say 'finery', I mean in actual fact, dressed in a skirt.

Or a 'kilt' as the Scots I believe call it?

It is however, a skirt.

A fucking skirt.

So anyway, yes indeedy, there he was.

The man himself, lashing out 'Knockin' on Heaven's Door' without a care in the world.

Axl Rose, our erstwhile pal, and former lover of our female companion of the moment.

Raising his booted left pin then to rest it on an amp, he very kindly exposed us to - well, anyone that was within eyeshot anyway - a fairly 'full on, no holds barred' view of his hairy cock and bollocks that were hanging down from beneath the tartan.

No joke.

No jocks.

No anything.

Not pleasant, people.

Not pleasant at all.

Although Belinda seemed pleased enough despite mine and Marcus's immediate urge to spew.

Which, moments later, we did.

Consider the irony so, the delicious irony, of being pulled out of the crowd and deposited backstage, when not long before this moment, we had been practically *begging* some arsewipe at the security gate to grant us entry to the exact same spot.

Sweet!

Although for the first ten minutes or so it was still decidedly hairy, particularly from a general health and well-being point of view.

Thankfully on this occasion however - unlike Wembley - all three of us had been dragged up; Marcus and I because we had been genuinely sick, and Belinda more by association really than anything else.

That is, because she had been standing next to us and raised up her arms, after which the security dudes that had already plucked Marcus and I out, just plucked her out as well.

There we were so, backstage at Slane Castle, just minding our own business.

Attempting to realign our badly set-upon and damaged dispositions however, was the key initial order of the day,

Between the acid and the pints and the coke now also, it had been an arduous enough day to date; certainly for me.

Seeing Axl's appendage as well, swinging from side to side over the PA system at the front of the stage just a few minutes earlier, had definitely been the straw that broke the camel's back.

I needed another drinky poo of some description, sharpish-like, to get me back on track.

Marcus was in agreement.

"Fuck me pal" he indicated forcibly with a grimace.

"Axl Rose's John Thomas?! Not good. I need a fairly significantly sized gargle to take *that* image the fuck away. Agreed?"

"Agreed most certainly dude" I answered.

"I thought it was ok!" piped up Belinda, which given her recent acquaintance with it, was hardly surprising.

"Well, considering the fact that you were bouncing up and down on it like a bucking fucking bronco less than two weeks ago Belinda, this is hardly an unprecedented revelation" I responded.

And I meant it to sting.

She didn't answer me anyway, and just threw me a dirty look.

"Hello?" said Marcus, spotting something over my shoulder out of the corner of his eye.

"I do believe" he continued.

"That I *may* have found the answer to our problems."

"Take a look over there."

I looked to where he was pointing, with the vision that greeted me being, I really must say, very much a sight for sore eyes.

Stationed there, not ten metres away, through a crowd of desperate and fairly pasty looking Z list celebrities and hangers on that were hovering about, was an untended keg of Guinness on a table, set up and ready to go; with another small incidental table to the right of it, with various snack based accoutrements and pint glasses upon it, and what appeared to be also, even more thrillingly, a crate of decidedly exclusive looking Irish whiskey on the floor directly underneath.

Things were looking up.

"Things are looking up fuckers!" said Belinda.

"Free fucking gargle! Well, what are yiz waiting for, soft cocks? A fucking invitation?!"

I went to answer her but she was already gone, with a pint glass in her lámh mere moments later as she stood next to the table, and a wave of her hand and surreptitiously mouthed 'will yiz come on te fuck' following on from that not long after.

It was hard to stay mad with Belinda for long.

We thought the same way basically, me and her.

As in, that is, that if the people that left this treasure trove of beer and whiskey unattended expected it to stay unliberated just because they believed that people at heart, essentially, were honest, and would, when push came to shove, do the right thing and look the other way; foregoing their very natural and reasonable desire to get twisted; then they quite honestly deserved what they fucking got!

Within seconds so, we had joined our female counterpart and were waiting, one and all, for humdrum brown to mysteriously darken.

As would our day soon alsoin fact, regrettably, as an arrival of fuckwits and dickwads momentarily, determined that such a vicissitude would be so.

CHAPTER 7

"AYE. AYE. AYE. AYE YEYE AYE!!"

God DAMN, this is SHIT man!

If Dylan was alive today, he'd be spinning in his grave dudes!

God DANG, what a crock!

"Mmmmmmmooooooohh, knock knock knockin' on HEAVEN'S doewoowoe!"

Yep.

It's shit alright.

Fucking SHIT!

But at least my bollocks ain't sore.

What a great idea to wear a fucking kilt?

David Bowie's axe man got me on to that.

Sheeat!

What a call, dude!

No under britches neither.

Fuck man, it's been life changing, is what its bin!

The fuck I bin doin' all these years, wearin' dem tight denims 'n leathers 'n shit?

Bein' a fuckin' dick, that's what!

Bowie's axe man though - like, he is one weird fucker man!

What's his goddamn name again?

Dunno.

And his axe sounds like goddamn fucking kittens being strangled!

Like Robert fricking Fripp or sometin' man, I dunno!

Anyways, I was a fit to be tied one time dudes, with a, like, sore bollocks and shit, and this dude, like, you know, just said straight out 'Why don't you, like, wear a fucking kilt man?'".

So, like, you know, I fucking did!

Well ok, as soon as I got some chick back in the office to sort that shit out, that is, ha ha!

And BOOM!

Here I am now, wearing a fucking kilt!

Although it's a skirt really.

Like let's not fucking kid ourselves here!

Anyhoo, this is one fucked up crowd man!

But at least they like, you know, like their rock 'n' roll!

GODDANG, though, I don't remember the last time I saw fuckers that were this pasty!

Or this fucking ginger!

Scotland maybe?

Ahh well.

Best get on with the toon.

"AYE. AYE. AYE. AYE YEYE AYE!"

Fuck me, this really IS shit.

Nothing I do will make it any better.

It's just fucking SHIT dudes!

I mean, how can you fuck around with a classic?

You're only gonna like, fuck it up, no matter what.

Which of course, we did.

And are.

Like, now?

You know?

I mean, like, nobody fucks around with 'Hound Dog', do they?

Goddamn frickin' right they don't!

Coz a classic is a fuckin' classic man, period!

Fuck me, there's that Irish chick again with that other dude.

The fuck they doin' here?

Some voice that dude has though - gotta admit that.

Unfuckinbelievable!

Should be on stage.

Thought I'd seen the last of them though, at that Freddie Mercury gig in England.

A nice screw though.

Yeah.

Fuckin' A.

The chick though.

Not the dude.

She don't hold back!

Ahh well.

At least they're down there and I'm up fucking here!

Think I'll have some fun with them actually, and like, show them my bollocks and shit?

They're close enough to the PA to see it, if I put my leg on it, and like, wiggle it about a bit.

And why the fuck would I not, goddammit!

I'm Axl fucking Rose, for fuck sake!

Are they hurlin'?

Fuck me, they ARE fuckin' hurlin'!

Better get 'em outta there.

I nod to the security dude and like, point them out.

'Hey security dude, can you like, get these sick kids up? They're, like, fucked man!'

He gets them outta there anyways, and like, that's the end of fucking them!

Bye bye fuckheads!

Better get on with the show.

Although we ARE nearly done as it goes.

I'll just pop over here for a minute, outta sight, and like, let the crowd whip themselves up into a frenzy or whatever the fuck that word is.

A quick swig of JD and a drag of a smoke and then back on out for the last toon.

Then party time dudes!

Fuckin' A.

I'm thinkin' Vegas.

Why not dudes?

When you have your own private frickin' jet, you can do whatever the frick you want!

Ok so.

Back to it.

'Paradise City' dudes.

That's some number as well dudes!

You're goddamn right to be, like, a whoopin' and a hollerin' and shit?!

More like PARASITE city though man, where I grew fuckin' up.

Scumbags freakin' everywhere dudes, had to do something to get out.

And here I am!

My ancestors are FROM here actually.

Fuckin' A!

And Scotland too.

Probably why I'm so pasty as well.

Not ginger though.

Strawberry blonde if anythin' man!

Gingers are frickin' FREAKS!

Mr. Brownstone makes me pasty though, I gotta admit that.

But that shit's in the past man, I'm a clean liver now.

Just booze and butts man; that's all I frickin' need.

So maybe the liver ain't so clean after all, ha ha!

BOOM!

Fuck it though dudes, you gotta have some vices, right?

A good move anyways.

Like, you know - leavin' Lafayette 'n shit?

A fuckin' one horse shit shack of a town man!

Although I WAS kinda run outta there too, truth be told.

But fuck me, what an upbringing!

Religion fuckin' EVERYWHERE man, goddamn OPPRESSIVE is what it was!

Was never gonna run with that, no frickin' way!

And I tell you what too man, I'd hate to see fuckin' hell if Bailey's vision of heaven is on the frickin' money!

My 'stepdad', you know?

Fucking douche!

And for a religious dude the frickin' opposite of a do-gooder.

Do fucking BADDER if anything!

Anyways, I got outta there and made my way to LA.

With the rest being frickin' history as the feller says.

Goddamn right!

Right, let's get back to it properly this time.

"Take me down to the Paradise City, where the grass is green and the girls are pretty. TAKE, TAKE me home!"

Jeez, these fuckers are pasty!

Phil Collins has a song called 'Take me Home' actually.

Not bad neither.

He gets bad press, Phil Collins.

Frickin' great drummer!

Not a lotta dudes know that.

Played on a Lizzy album too, so, like, you know; what the fuck is wrong with that?

Johnny the Fox, I think.

What a cut that is man!

I mean like 'Don't Believe a Word' is fuckin' A dudes, but frickin' 'Massacre' as well?

Like, what the fuck man, you know?

Two unfuckingbelievable numbers just, like, thrown out there, and like, no-one actually knows Lizzy that well, I mean, not really!

Not like they frickin' SHOULD be known anyways!

Take this number now for example.

'Paradise City'.

I mean it's not bad dudes, like, you know - don't get me wrong.

But it's not fucking 'Massacre'!

Ok, so like, I'm frickin' bored now.

I'll finish up and let these pasty fuckers go back to whatever it is the fuck they do.

Farming probably.

Like they gotta be farmers, right?

Or like, you know, be related to farmers?

Goddamn no way it can be any other way.

Enough of this shit anyhoo peeps!

I got partyin' to be doin'!

A quick wave to the throng and then off I will fuck.

Although someone said to me recently that the word 'party' is, like, a noun rather than a verb?

Was it Bowie at that London gig?

That Queen thing?

I think it frickin' was, you know.

But fuck him, I'll fucking 'party' if I want to man!

"You HAVE a party Grease" he said to me at the time, if I remember it right.

But I was fucked if I knew what the fuck he was goin' on about.

And why was he calling me Grease?

Maybe it's like, an English version of 'Slick' or sometin'?

Robert Plant was callin' me the exact same thing earlier that day actually, so like, yeah - that's gotta be it.

I AM fucking slick!

"Or you ATTEND a party" he went on.

"And sometimes you can be a party to the fact etc., as in, like, you know, a witness and stuff? But you can never 'PARTY' Grease? The locution is not a verb."

I ignored him anyway, and like, just got on with fucking things.

He may be one of the greatest Rock Star DemiGods to have ever graced a stage, but right there and then, while I was trying to like, 'party' and shit, he could go and fuck himself!

No idea what the fuck 'locution' means neither; although Slash did get a shock one time when he, like, stood on an iffy wire.

Maybe that's it?

Why are fuckers always using words that other people can't understand?

That really fuckin' bugs me man!

'The Man Who Sold the World' though, like, what a frickin' album!

And his voice on 'Saviour Machine'?

FUCK ME!

Frickin' awesome!

I'll party tonight anyways though, either way, whether David Bowie likes my frickin' grammar or not.

"LET'S GET THIS FUCKING PARTY STARTED!" I shout as I arrive back-stage.

One of the security-type handler dudes tries to convince me to go back out for another encore but, like, fuck that!

I'm done for the day.

Those pasty Irish fuckers can go and fuck themselves.

"Fuck them dude!" I say to him.

"The axe is done for the day and ready to get fucked!"

I light up another smoke and take a swig of JD.

YAYASS!

All good in the hood.

The security dude seems ok - he's wearing a Sex Pistols tee shirt so he like, HAS to be righteous.

Although he does look as if he's eaten his frickin' dinner off it!

I'll stop to have a quick chat with him though, to be like, you know, nice.

He's certain to be telling his grandkids, like, years from now, about the time that he was speaking to Axl Rose backstage at that gig in Dublin.

It IS Dublin, right?

Not sure.

Near Dublin anyway.

Maybe.

Although who gives a fuck?!

Not fuckin' me!

Looking at him again now though I dunno if this dude will actually make it to an age where he has grandkids to tell anything to.

As in - and I'm not kidding with you here - but he's like, as fat as fuck dudes!

Anyhoo, whatever.

I'll be nice to him today.

I'm in a good mood and to be honest I'm already half fucked!

I chat to him anyways about the general pastiness of the crowd, and like, my kilt too.

He's impressed alright, which is no surprise.

I mean, like, you know - I'm Axl fucking Rose for fuck sake!

I see the Irish chick out of the corner of my eye then as well, but like, don't let on that I do?

Always keep chicks guessing, right dudes?

Kind of a rule with me anyways.

"Hey, and guess what as well dude" I say to the fat dude, a bit louder than I like, have to, so that the chick hears.

What is her name again?

Fucked if I remember.

100

Lindsay, is it?

Maybe.

Not that it matters a goddamn!

Although she does love fucking cock man!

Better keep her onside.

As in, like, you know - maybe I'll get a blowie out of it later on, if there ain't nothin' better goin' down!

I keep talking to the dude anyways, who's like, just standin' there sayin' nothin'.

"I like, saw this chick that I boned in London a few weeks ago as well man, like, I mean, how fucked up is that? She must be like, you know, followin' me around and shit? Say, one of the security dudes picked her outta crowd too, actually - I wonder where she is now? Oh yeah, and I like, showed her and the dudes that she was with, my cock as well dude, like, that was a fuckin' blast man! This fucking skirt has many uses dude, like, you know, MANY uses. Say, is that a monkey up there? Far out dude!"

He nods at me to indicate that he's like, really interested in what I have to say.

No surprise there neither man.

I can tell that Lindsay's listening too, so I, like, just keep on truckin' on!

What was the other kid's name?

You know, the dude from the London gig who's with her again today?

The good singer?

Johnny?

I think that's it.

And he has, like, some weird frickin' nickname as well or sometin'!

Freak Show?

That's it!

How the fuck did I remember that?

Dunno.

He's a pretty cool customer anyway, this kid, I gotta admit it.

He's got style, like, you know?

And a great frickin' voice too!

There was another dude with them in the crowd too, who was like, dressed like he was goin' to a frickin' ball!

Think that's him with them too.

OK, so we'll see who blinks first.

You know, between me and the Lindsay chick?

She caves in in the end anyway, and like, shouts across to me that she's there - as if I don't frickin' know that already!

I'd better say sometin' to her, I suppose.

"Oh, hey doll" I say, not even missing a beat.

Right on.

"Never even saw you there darlin'. So, like, you know - how goes it 'n shit?"

I wander over to her anyway eventually, now that she, like, knows that I'm there and our pretendin' and shit is done.

Like all frickin' women though nothin' ain't ever that simple.

She just wanders off in a huff as I arrive.

I decide to hang there anyway though, to like, you know, have a chat with the dudes.

She'll be back soon enough.

If there's one thing that I've learnt about chicks over the years, is that if you treat them like shit, they'll come back to you for more every frickin' time.

Goddamn fuckin' guaranteed man!

I say sorry to the guys first though, for, you know, flashing my cock!

That can't have been too pleasant for them, I gotta admit it.

Unless they like dudes?

I don't think so though - they seem happy enough anyway, to like, you know, put it in the past.

I don't know this other dude though – you know, the one that's dressed like Cary frickin' Grant?

So I like, decide to ask him who the fuck he is.

"So, like, who the fuck are you dude?" I say to him.

"I don't remember seein' you in London?"

He answers me then, but seriously, like, fuck knows what the fucker is sayin'.

Like, a goddamn million words where one or two will do?

"Fuck you on about dude" I say, and then, like, offer him a swig of JD to, you know, shut him the fuck up.

Johnny anyway, the other dude, explains to me that that's just the way the other dude is.

Not that I give a fuck.

I've already moved on.

"Say man" I say.

"Was that like, that Bono fucking dweeb I saw earlier on? He is, like, one weird fucking dude, dudes!"

The Johnny dude confirms anyway, that it was him.

"And you dodged a bullet there most assuredly dude" he says.

"Marcus here gave him a couple of slaps - naturally enough - after which off he popped off with that Edge fucker, crying like a fucking baby with his tail between his legs"

'Fuck me, that's impressive' I'm thinking.

"Really dude" I say to the Marcus dude, viewing him now in a totally different light.

As in anybody that's prepared to kick the shit outta that bonehead Bono, at any time, on any day, is alfuckingright with fuckin' me!

"Right on dude!" I say.

"That fucker's been cruisin' for a bruisin' for frickin' years!"

I'd better tell them what that three-chord trick shit guitarist of theirs was saying to me earlier as well.

Like, you know, about the fact that that Bono dick is, like, using the lyrics of his songs, and ONLY the lyrics of his songs, to communicate with people?

I mean, like, what a fucking douchebag!

Alright, so they gave me beer and whiskey and shit so don't get me wrong - that was a pretty neat touch.

But it still doesn't take away from the fact that that whole 'talking with lyrics' thing man, is like, a total fuckin' crock!

Here comes that Lindsay chick again.

What the fuck did I tell you dudes?

Every fucking time!

I ask her if we're ok.

"We cool now sugar tits?" I say.

She says that we are, so that's good.

Coz I could do without the shit, you know?

The Johnny dude don't look happy though.

But fuck him!

Like I give a shit?

I don't fuckin' think so!

The Lindsay chick tells us anyway that this fucking Bono dick, was, like, using that lyrics crapola on her earlier in the day to, like, you know, make a pass at her and shit?

And like, fuck me man, he was doing the exact same thing to me before the show too!

"I'd sometin' similar sweetie!" I say to her.

"I asked him if he, like, wanted to grab a beer with me and Slash later on in the, like, you know, city and stuff, but all the fucker kept saying over and over again was 'All I Want is You'! I mean, like, fuckin' bogus or what dudes?"

They're like, hanging on my every word these kids - so I, like, you know, go on.

"So, like, then I said to him, like, NO FUCKIN' WAY MAN!" I say.

"Do you think I'm, like, some sort of fuckin' faggot or fuckin' sometin'?!"

The Lindsay chick nearly falls over laughing at my last line, and I'm thinkin', like, you know - hey, settle down doll!

It ain't that frickin' funny!

But she's probably just trying to like, you know, impress?

The over the top kid that's dressed like James frickin' Bond, has only gone and spilled Guinness all over his nice clean linen shirt.

Like, what a frickin' dufus.

"I always get chocolate stains on my pants!" shouts Gary Moore over to us from across the way, and I'm thinking to myself, like, fucking COME ON Gary Moore - not fucking you too?!'

That's a line from 'Dancin in the Moonlight' you know, so I'm thinking, like, don't tell me he's in that dick Bono's frickin' gang as well!

You know, the 'using lyrics for frickin' words' fucking gang!?

But then I get to thinking - HEY! IT'S GARY FRICKIN' MOORE MAN! HE CAN DO WHATEVER THE GODDAMN FUCK HE WANTS!

I think the others as well, from, you know, my body language and stuff, get that this is what I think.

And besides I wouldn't want to get into a fight with him.

Those scars on his face like, fucking scare me man!

He must be like, one hard fucking bastard.

But fuck it dudes.

It's like, time to move on!

Vegas is a good spot as I was saying there before and besides, The Grateful Dead are playing there tomorrow, and I'd like to see Jerry Garcia play before he, like, you know, falls off his frickin' perch!

That won't be too long now as well, that's for sure!

Not the way that dude frickin' drinks!

We got a few days to kill before our next show in Poland anyways, wherever the fuck THAT is.

Somewhere in Europe?

I dunno.

I just get the handlers to point me in the direction that I need to be going and sing my frickin' songs then when I get there!

And with a private jet lined up, fuelled, and ready to take me to wherever the fuck I wanna go, anywhere in the world, it'd be downright rude of me not to avail of an opportunity like that, right?

"Say kids!" I say to the kids, thinking that it might be nice to like, you know, invite them along.

"Do you, like, wanna go to fucking Vegas tonight? There's like, plenny a room on the jet if you'd, like, you know, like to come with?!"

The Johnny dude and Lindsay are on board big style judging by their reaction, but from the answer that the David Niven type dude gives, I'm not a hundred per cent sure if he's, like, in on the deal or out.

Some shit about frauleins and escapology, although what that's got to with anything I've no frickin' idea.

I'm second guessing inviting the fucker now.

So like, the chick and Johnny are in but if I, like, give them all a quiz or sometin', I can definitely find a way to, like, blow this other fucking bozo off.

Not in the biblical sense though, aweite?

I ain't that sorta dude!

Its frickin' chickin' lickin' all the freakin' way with Axl Love Mafuckingchine Rose!

It'll fuck with their heads too, which I, like, you know, like doin' to people?

"Favourite song dudes!?" I say, and I can see straight off that it's like, fucked up their mojo's.

Right on!

This should be fun!

"Street Fighting Man" shouts Johnny, straight off the bat, and woah, talk about frickin' nailing it!

I fuckin' LOVE that song man!

"AND WHAT CAN A POOR BOY DO!" I scream, practically delirious now that the toon has come into my head.

"'CEPT TO SING FOR A ROCK 'N' ROLL BAND! COZ THIS SLEEPY LONDON TOWN IS JUST NO PLACE FOR A STREET FIGHTIN' MAAAAAAAAAANNNNNNNNNOOOOOOOO!!"

What a call!

Johnny Freak Show is frickin' DEFINITELY on my night flight to Vegas!

"Cloudbusting!" says the Lindsay chick, and like, how can I argue with that?

Kate fuckin' rocks man - I'll fight any frickin' man that says that she don't!

Frickin' hot too, I don't mind sayin' it.

Way outta my league though.

Whores and groupies for frickin' Axl man!

I like, you know, doubt that Kate and me would have that much in common.

Then, best of all, that Mark dude – I think that's his name – the one that's like, dressed like frickin' James Bond - only shouts out frickin' 'Night and Day'!

I mean like, what a fuckin' song dudes!

God DAMN it to hell?!

The motherfucker has only gone and frickin' nailed it!

It's, like, I dunno, the dude has been readin' my mind or sometin'?

As in, like, I've been frickin' itchin' to waltz all goddamn day long to that, or something like that in any case!

Oh yeah, I frickin' love to waltz man.

Big surprise, huh?

I learned how to do it in Indy when I was a kid, like, you know, after Sunday school 'n' shit?

We'd have, like, classes and shit, and there was this old broad that took, like, a shine to me.

Mrs. Frobisham.

She was nice, like, an old spinster type doll, livin' on her own.

Nuthin' like rest of the fuckin' douchess there man, like you know - she was alright.

Taught me some good moves too dudes, I never forgot 'em.

She'd invite me round to her house after Sunday school, and, like, you know, put me through my paces.

Nuthin' sinister though dudes, all above board.

She reminded me a bit of like, one of those old sisters from 'The Waltons'; you know, the two old broads that used to still moonshine in their parlour, and then, like, let on it that it was for like, for medicinal purposes and shit?

The 'recipe' - that's what they called it.

Ha ha, a frickin' recipe for disaster if I ever got my fuckin' hands on it!

Anyways, like, what the fuck was I talkin' about?

Oh yeah, the song and the frickin' waltz.

That Mark dude has made a great call with 'Night and Day' anyways, so like, fuck it man!

As that Bowie dude says, let's frickin' dance!

I just grab him by the hand and go.

I know the moves well; it was one of old Frobisham's favourites.

I lead, obviously, with the Mark dude following, competently enough I reckon.

"NIGHT AND DAY!" I croon, as we circle the back of the stage, pretty impressively, it has to be said.

'Ha!' I'm thinking.

That's goddamn fucked up these fuckers looking on!

I sing on.

"YOU ARE THE ONE,
ONLY YOU 'NEATH THE MOON OR UNDER THE SUN
WHETHER NEAR TO ME OR FAR
IT'S NO MATTER, DARLING, WHERE YOU ARE
I THINK OF YOU DAY AND NIGHT"

Eager to impress I'd say, or sometin' like that probably, everybody else there decides to, like, join in.

Fuck yeah!

Now we partyin' dudes!

It IS a frickin' verb, David fucking Bowie!

I nod to Slash and Duff across the way, and they like, know exactly what the fuck to do.

Dropping what they're doin' - which I think is 'Horse' as it goes - they head off in the general direction of the stage.

They may have been just about to shoot up, but the music takes centre stage every time dudes.

Goddamn frickin' right!

They know it!

Even that Bono dick wants to get in on the act.

The monkey as well, from like, earlier on, swings down from the gantry and, like, attaches itself to him.

It must be his so, I'm thinking, which gets me thinkin', that like, you know, even though he's like a primate and shit, the monkey must be a bit of a dick as well!

As in, you know, why would you hang around with a fuckin' douchebag like that when you could be with anyone else?

Micky Dolenz for example.

He's a frickin' Monkee!

We all dancin' now anyway, so I like, lead everybody that's there out to the stage.

The boys have struck up the number now, big time, with Dizzy, Gilby and Matt on board now as well.

And it's a pretty cute arrangement too - kinda off kilter, you know?

I thought the fans woulda been gone by now too, but there are like, a few of them still hangin' around.

They slowly make their way back to the stage.

They must be wonderin' as well, like - what the fuck is goin' on man?

As in, like, you know - a number like this is not really our thing.

It sounds fuckin' A though - no fucker can deny fuckin' that!

The Bono dick is trying to make it to the mike though, the sneaky fuck, but the Johnny dude pulls his monkey's tail as he's, like, goin' by.

The monkey is goin' absolutely frickin' ape shit now as a result of this, and has like, started to punch Bono in the ears.

I'm thinking, like, right fuckin' on Bubbles!

Maybe you're catching on!

It looks a bit like one of those Japanese windy-up toys as well.

You know.

The one where the monkey crashes the cymbals and shit?

Anyways, whatever.

They've fucked off someplace else - Bono frickin' blubbering again as well I think - which the crowd quite rightly have given the fucker a rough time over - and the Johnny dude is making a move towards the mike.

I'd, like, usually stop a fucker from doin' that, on like, my patch, but having heard the dude sing before backstage in London just a few weeks ago, I'm thinkin' like, HEY!

Give the fucker a frickin' break!

He's moved out anyway, and like I thought that he would, he's frickin' nailing it big time!

I'm lovin' this now.
'Night and Day' and a bit of an old waltz?
What could be freakin' better?
Fuck me though, it's only that frickin' Bono dweeb again!
Like, can't the fucker get the freaking message?
The crowd are telling him to fuck off now as well, so that's something I suppose.
In a, like, chant?
"Fuck off Bono, you prick!" I think it is.
I love my freaking fans!
They know a fucking dick when they see a fucking dick.
He's fucked off again anyway, with his tail between his legs.
Good riddance dufus!
The Johnny dude is giving him the finger too, as he's, like, pushin' off.
Fuckin A as well, I'm thinkin'.
Like, you know?
BOOYAH!
That Bono dude has, like, had this coming for fucking ever!
Johnny goes back to the song anyway and I'm thinking, like, I might as well join in with him now.
I let go of the Mark dude so, and nod to Matt as well, to indicate to him that we might, like, you know, do another number?
I'm enjoyin' myself now, so like, you know, why the fuck not?
And Matt's the drummer too so, you know, rhythm wise, he pretty much decides what tune we gonna be doin' next.
"WE FUCKIN' ROCKIN TONIGHT DUBLIN!" I scream into the mike as I arrive to the front, which I can tell has really impressed the man of the hour.
Always mention the town that you're playin' in dudes.
The fans, like, freakin' love that shit every time!
Matt cuts in then, and I can tell like, straight off the bat that it's 'Massacre'.
Like fuckin' 'Massacre' dudes!
What a frickin' track!
Probably Lizzy's best, like I was sayin' before, and they got plenny o' awesome toons!
I let Johnny take the first verse anyway, which he frickin' nails, I gotta admit it, and then I take the second.
"Through the devil's canyon,
Across the battlefield,
Death has no companion,
The spirit is forced to yield"
We flyin' now and Johnny aces the third too.
The crowd is goin' absolutely frickin' mental!

Checkin' them out so, and, you know, judgin' the buzz to frickin' perfection, Matty takes us off in a completely different direction a couple of seconds later at the end of 'Massacre', with the next number, as final encores go, pretty much hittin' the nail on the freakin' head!

Fucking 'Gimme Shelter' dudes!

The Stones' best, for sure!

Or maybe 'Street Fightin' Man' like the Johnny dude was sayin' there earlier on.

"YEAH!" I scream, as l stomp back and forth and, like, you know - prowl the fucking stage.

My kilt is lookin' frickin' ace as well still – like, you know, flowin' really nicely and shit?

I gotta say dudes, I love my fucking kilt!

"YAAYASS!" I scream anyway, with the fans goin' fuckin' nuts again.

"Y'ALL READY FOR SOME FREAK SHOW?!" I go on, pointing at Johnny.

Like, why not?

Throw a dog a bone, right?

He probably doesn't even know that I, like, know his frickin' nickname and shit, so like, that's bound to weird him out!

As I said, that Lindsay chick told it to me before.

"I SAID!" I continue, waving my arms around a bit and like, pointing at him so that they know the fuck who I'm actually talkin' about here.

"ARE Y'ALL READY FOR SOME FREAK SHOW!?" I shout again.

The answer from the crowd is unanimous.

"YEAH!!" they say.

There's just no frickin' way that Johnny – or 'Freak Show' - will ever forget fucking this!

It's like, you know, that time when Tom Petty met Elvis as a kid, and like, knew that that's what he wanted to do with his life after such a life-changing meeting?

It'll be the same for Johnny when he thinks back to this, years from now.

Inspirational, he'll be thinking.

And that's all down to frickin' me!

I rock dudes!

OK so I'm gettin' tired now and thinkin', like, you know, enough is efuckingnough?

But Slash and Duff are, like, still freakin' rockin' it man!

Real rock 'n' roll dudes - takes me right back to my teens!

Beach life, you know?

Stick fires and pot and beer and chicks and nuthin' fuckin' else!

Right on!

LA though, not Indy.

Indy ain't nuthin' like that.

Just treelined suburbs, and like, sexually repressed God-fearing dweebs like fuckin' Bailey!

At least where I was raised anyhoo.

Lucky to get freaking out!

Anyways, like I said - 'Gimme frickin Shelter' dudes.

What a frickin' cut man!

Like, awesome.

If you wrote that and like, JUST that, over your entire career, you'd be happy right?

Its frickin' timeless man, is what it is.

We gettin' into it BIG TIME now anyway, like, vocally and shit?

Can you frickin' believe it though, but that Bono cat has only come back for more?

Like this is a frickin' metal crowd dude!

Nobody wants you here!

Can't you get the freakin' message?

Know your goddamn audience Bubba, and like, you know - this ain't it!

You've been told to fuck off twice already!

Fuck this anyway, I'm thinking, lookin' at the fucker as he's singing outta bar.

Like, enough is efuckingnough, you know?

I gotta make an example of him, to like, show that it ain't right.

Singing the words like, half a second later, just to make himself heard over everybody else?

Fuck that man!

Not on my frickin' watch!

I stride over to him so, with just one thing and one thing alone on my mind.

To push him into the frickin' crowd!

He's only a midget anyways, so like, puts up frickin' no resistance at all.

In he drops, and like, off he goes.

It looks like he's enjoyin' it though, as he like, drifts off, but, like, I know myself that that's just temporary.

I know my fans, and I know EXACTLY what they have in mind.

As they carry him further away, it's only a matter of time before they get rid of him for good.

Bye bye fuckhead!

See you in the next frickin' life dufus!

The last I see of him anyway is like, a dot in the distance, as one of my fans is givin' him a kick in the ass to send him on his freakin' way.

Right on!

No more than the dick deserves!
We gettin' to the end now anyways and I'm lookin' to get goin'.
Vegas man - I can't freakin' wait!
An open air asylum is what it is.
Which suits me just frickin' fine!
Bring it on dudes!
Bring it fucking on!

CHAPTER 8

"Hey, you lot! Get away from our feckin' gargle!"

'SHITE IN ANYWAY!' I was thinking.

That Evans bollocks again.

Or 'The Edge' as I believe he prefers to be called?

He ran over to us anyway like a little fucking girl, before standing there with his hands on his hips and a look of general indignation all over his handlebar-moustached visage.

"That's the gargle we, like, bought for the lads!" he wittered on.

"Like, you know - the band and stuff?"

"Nice hat Dave!" I answered offhandedly, referring to the ridiculous looking 'beanie' type chapeau thingamajig that he was modelling on his moronic crown.

"Nearly as cool as your bandana!" I went on; referring of course to the tea-cloth type garment that he had worn on his head a few years before.

We had history, Dave and I.

Although I doubted that he'd remember me from the time we'd met in the past.

A slight altercation shall we say, some years previously, in the Horseshoe Bar of the Shelbourne Hotel in St. Stephen's Green, Dublin 2.

Not unsurprisingly our disagreement at the time was related to the ridiculous millinery that he was sporting on that occasion too.

This 'bandana' indeed, as referred to before.

"It's all the style, I'll have you know!" he responded defensively; which as a riposte that was intended to deride, fell some way short of its target.

Decisively, you might say.

"Get away from our drink in anyway!" he went on.

"We bought that for Axl and the lads as a present. And they'll be here in a minute too, so yiz, like, better feck off before they come back!"

"Nothing to worry your pretty little festooned head about Davy boy" I responded smugly, as I swallowed the first slug of my recently settled stout.

"Axl and the boys know that we're here".

Belinda was impressed with me again.

As in that because of the fact that I knew this 'Edge' dude from some time in the past, I was apparently cooler and more interesting now, than she'd considered me to be before.

Although how knowing this complete *BELL END* could make anybody, anywhere, look anything other than a total fucking dick, was a notion that I really must say was very much beyond my comprehension.

"Are you not going to introduce us there Johnny?" she asked of me then before sidling up to him flirtatiously and giving him the old 'come to bed' eye.

'For fuck sake' I was thinking.

Why do chicks always want to meet jerks that are famous?

I'd met this bollocks before as I was saying; and believe me when I tell you that he has absolutely NO redeeming features.

Yet Belinda wanted to be introduced to the fucker even so, despite the patently obvious character flaws that were out there in the open for everybody to regard.

I decided to ignore her so, taking the view that by *not* introducing her to him now that she'd thank me down the line when she realised; quite soon I was of a mind; that he was a major league knobhead who was to be avoided at all costs.

Then as if things couldn't get any worse - and talking of knobheads - that fucking gobshite Bono showed up.

I had history with him as well, from that very same encounter with Evans in the Shelbourne.

He had backed up his cohort quite vehemently at the time, referring to him if I remember it correctly - quite unbelievably really - as a 'fashion icon'.

I mean, seriously?

These fuckers are definitely living on some other fucking planet.

He made an immediate beeline anyway towards Belinda.

"Let me be your lover tonight!" he said to her up close - all cringy-like and weird.

After which she definitely considered him with no small degree of contempt.

Whatever about 'The Edge' and her overall feelings towards him, it was an absolute certainty that Bono was not figuring high on her list of Rock Star DemiGods with whom she wanted to liaise.

"Ahh no, you're alright there pal!" she responded to him disdainfully, before returning her gaze to his partner in crime.

But if she thought that that was the end of it she had another thing coming.

She realised soon enough, to her annoyance; that he hadn't quite gone away.

He had a pet monkey by his side also, which he was holding by the hand.

This state of affairs so - in addition to giving the impression to anyone that he encountered that he wasn't *quite* all there - was doing very little for him also, in terms of his overall 'street cred'.

"Your usual tipple Bono?" asked a young waiter then, who had wandered over to where we were stationed, and was just standing there now, patiently, waiting for a response.

Of which there was none forthcoming.

The diminutive one just stood there with his monkey, silent; believing, I suppose, that being aloof and tranquil was a sign of enigmatic superiority.

When all that the waiter was desirous to know was what the fucker wanted to drink.

"As in a G & T?" the waiter enquired further, to which Bono in his infinite ignorance responded with what I imagine he believed at the time was an esoteric nod.

"Anything with that?" asked the waiter.

"Ice" Bono responded, deigning finally to speak.

"Anything else?" said the waiter, to which the stunted one responded.

"Lemon"

He really was some bollocks Bono, which was a point that Marcus, after the recent and fairly painful back and forth with the waiter had run its course, felt compelled to make known to him once and for all.

Wandering across to the fucker so, with his pint in his hand, Marcus stopped there for a brief moment after his arrival before poking Bono suddenly and aggressively in the chest a few times with his forefinger, as accompaniment for the first few syllables of his choice, but carefully chosen nonetheless, words.

"LISTEN HERE FUCK FACE!" he expounded aggressively, before stopping again briefly to take another quick mouthful of his scoop.

Resuming then a couple of moments later, he continued on with what has to be agreed was an excruciatingly damning harangue.

Laudatory it was not.

"We have history, you and I, you short-arsed goblin fuck! You may not recall it but I do. The Shelbourne Hotel in 1984? Well you were a bell end then dude, and you're a bell end now! Along with your dopey 'Mad Hatter' pal here! Don't you realise, either of you, what you have become? This poor lad here – the, like, you know, waiter type dude? - earning a crust, merely - enquiring as to your required tipple, and the best that you can do in response to said enquiry, is to offer up contemptible and monosyllabic grunting? Who the fuck do you think you are, you cretinous pustule of purulence? Are you aware that all that you *actually* do for a living is sing fucking songs? Hardly a cure for cancer dude!"

Bono just stood there holding his monkey's hand.

And responded then, sardonically - or so he believed.

It was a pretty damp squib of a retort though to be fair.

"Maybe you can educate my mind?" he said, with his intended sarcasm not at all reaching its target, but his pathetic whining conversely, being very much on the mark.

He looked around him then and behind; for a handler, presumably, to take his nattily bedecked antagonist away.

Sadly for him however, there were none to be found.

And when I say 'sadly for him' I mean as an outcome of the subsequent sequence of events that came to pass not long after.

Events that were initiated by a swift kick into his bollocks by Marcus - who was quite clearly today on a bit of a roll – and concluded by the resultant and inevitable trauma to his surely microscopic liathroidi, and his eventual capitulation to the dirt.

Standing there so, taking it all in, I had to concede that as entertainment goes generally, this really was stellar fare.

You'd like, you know, pay for it?

And then Bono started to cry.

Seriously.

Just kneeling there like an elfin oaf; having a good old sob because his bollocks were sore.

"Don't let it get away!" he wailed uncontrollably then, as the monkey let go of his hand and started up the tarpaulin-covered scaffolding to our left that led to the lighting rigs that were just above our heads.

"How high can he go?" asked Belinda; curious for some reason to know.

"High" Bono answered, whimpering still.

"Higher than the sun".

What on earth was the fucker prattling on about?

And Marcus wasn't finished either, with Bono's latest outburst aggravating him even more.

To the extent indeed that he made a further decision to deck him on the nose.

"OOOOOWWWWW!" cried Bono again, practically hysterical now as a steady stream of blood departed from his nostrils and deposited itself liberally about his person.

A St. John's ambulance dude arrived then, having heard the pitiful and girly screams that were emanating from behind the stage; and began - reluctantly enough, it seemed to me – to tend to the stricken sissy's injuries.

Asking him to hold his head back while he cleaned the blood from around and about his face, he asked Bono how he was feeling.

"How ya feeling Mr. Bono?" he asked, to which he received no response.

Bono just shook his head.

"Are you dizzy?" he asked further.

Still no response.

"Are you feeling anything at all?" he persisted, as he carefully examined the area around and about the dude's nose.

"Numb" was the terse response.

"Is it getting better?" Bono asked of him then, to which the medic responded that yes, it was.

Asking Bono then to pinch his nose at the bridge whilst he attempted to insert some cotton wool into one of his nostrils, Bono once again reverted to type and gave the poor bastard a piece of his mind.

"IT'S ALRIGHT" he cried out impatiently, as he pulled back and pushed the dude's hand away from him aggressively.

"IT'S ALRIGHT, ALRIGHT?!" he barked out again, as the medic made one more attempt to help the fucker out.

"Leave him alone pal" suggested Belinda to the volunteer.

"The short-arsed prick clearly doesn't want your help!"

The monkey was screeching wildly now from the top of the gantry, in time, quite admirably in fact, to the latest tune that was emanating from the stage - 'Paradise City' - but he was showing no signs of coming back down, as a result of which Bono was vexed even further.

"IS IT GETTING BETTER?" he moaned again to the first aider, who just shook his head impatiently and raised his eyes to heaven to the rest of us that were still there.

As in, the fucker's head was hardly falling off, you know?

"Just keep pinching the bridge of your nose" he said, as a parent might, soothingly, to placate a frightened child.

"And hold your head back also, to stem the flow of the blood"

Bono did as directed but remained a whimpering dick.

Belinda, feeling sorry for him I suppose, and perhaps displaying some of that old 'benevolent female instinct' of which us males, generally speaking, are not in possession, decided to wander across to him again, to check if he was ok.

"Look, are you ok Bono?" she asked of him softly, as she rested a kindly hand on his quivering torso.

He looked up then - a pathetic wimp of a specimen really - before intimating to her the following words.

"Anything at all" he said, with a saccharine-laced yet semi-tearful still smile accompanying his sleaze-laden delivery.

"I'd do it for you!"

Even in the throes of injury so, however serious or slight that injury might be; he remained one hell of a smarmy fucking dick.

"Oh FUCK OFF Bono, will you, you fucking KNOB!" Belinda spat out, before wandering off back to her drink.

She'd had enough of his bolloxology.

"She is raging" said Bono quietly to the St. John's dude, which given his performance to date, was unusually circumspect and pensive, even for him.

116

And then he burst into tears again, wailing uncontrollably; 'put out', apparently, by the sheer injustice of it all.

He has a tough life, old Bono.

Evans came rushing over to him then, and put an arm around him, before flashing a look of rage towards the rest of us that were there.

As if to say, 'Feck yiz anyway, yiz feckin' bastards, for upsetting me pal!'

"Bono's delicate, ye feckers!" he said, pointedly.

"He's very delicate".

He led him away then, with his arm around his shoulder still as the fucker continued to sob; and that thankfully - for then anyway - was the end of fucking them.

"Bye Bye fuckheads!" I shouted after them, to which everybody in our vicinity had a good old snigger.

"LET'S GET THIS FUCKING PARTY STARTED DUDES!" shrieked Axl Rose then, as he sauntered off stage and looked around at everybody that was there.

He had a bottle of JD in one hand and a smoke in the other, and the look of a dude also, almost certainly, who was looking to get fucked.

The crowd behind him were going absolutely bananas for more, but you could tell by his demeanour that he was definitely done for the day.

"What about another song dude?" asked one of the security dudes who was nearby.

A fat dude in a Pistols tee-shirt.

He looked a bit like Fat Paddy from the Off-Licence in Amiens Street now that I had a second glance, except a lot older looking and more spherical in shape.

It WAS Fat Paddy!

I hadn't seen him in donkeys' years - not since that Bowie Slane concert in '87 - but it was definitely him.

And the tee shirt that he was wearing was the very same one that he'd been wearing on that day also - gruesomely enough - and it was in tatters still!

Additionally - and I've definitely mentioned this before - from the infamous design on the pestilent garment in question, it was obvious that the letters emblazoned across its front should have *actually* read 'Never Mind the Bollocks, Here's the Sex Pistols'.

The multitude of clefts, cracks and gaps that joined abominably together to form Paddy's corpulent persona however, rendered the entire wording of the garment's front illegible.

So much so in fact that all we could make out was what appeared to be - well to us anyway, in our undoubtedly inebriated and therefore weakened mental state - the words, 'Vermin the Book She Extols'.

A volume about rats?

I was rambling, most assuredly.

Probably the acid.

I nodded across to Paddy anyway, and he nodded back to me, and that was the end of that.

Axl was having none of Paddy's 'next encore' bullshit though.

"Fuck them dude!" he answered.

"The axe is done for the day and ready to get fucked!"

"Say dude" he went on to Paddy as he messily took a slug of the JD, with a generous portion of it also landing on his shirt.

"Did you see how fuckin' pasty those kids were man? Like fuckin' pasty and, like, ginger and stuff too man? Like, there were some fucked up complexions out there, dude."

He looked around and about himself again and definitely noticed that we were there.

He didn't let on that he did though, the miserable bollocks.

"Hey, and guess what as well dude? I like, saw this chick that I boned in London a few weeks ago as well, like, I mean, how fucked up is that? She must be like, you know, followin' me around and shit? Say, one of the security dudes picked her outta crowd too, actually - I wonder where she is now? Oh yeah, and I like, showed her and the dudes that she was with my cock as well dude, like, that was a fuckin' blast man! This fucking skirt has many uses dude, like, you know, MANY uses. Say, is that a monkey up there? Far out dude!"

"I'M FUCKING HERE, ROSEBUD!" Belinda called over angrily, from the ten or so feet away from him that we were stationed.

"Nice to know that our liaison meant something to you as well, you fucking dick!"

She did not look best pleased.

"Oh, hey doll" he answered, not even missing a beat; fair play.

"Never even saw you there darlin'. So, like, you know - how goes it 'n shit?"

She just gave him an icy stare though and looked the other way.

Not that he cared too much about that either way, with the look on his face, unequivocally, the look of a dude that *very seriously* could not give a flying fuck about anything that anybody else there was doing or saying at the time.

He walked over to me instead, with Belinda fucking off to someplace else when she saw that he was on his way across.

"Hey dude" he said amiably, whilst simultaneously offering me a swig of his hooch.

"So, like, what's up man?" he went on.

"Did you enjoy the show?"

"Oh yeah, and like, sorry about the cock thing as well" he continued, sniggering, before punching me in the shoulder lightly to denote that all was ok.

I couldn't have disagreed with him more of course, but decided to let it go.

He seemed to be in good form so what was the point of rubbing him up the wrong way?

I nodded at him pleasantly, and encouraged him to go on.

"So, like, who the fuck are you dude?" he continued, directing his comments now toward Marcus, who was stationed by my side.

"I don't remember seein' you in London?"

"Marcus Quinn at your service, good sir!" responded Marcus amicably, before holding out his extended arm by way of an introduction.

"Otherwise known as the Quinnmeister! A pleasure to make your illustrious acquaintance my good man. I trust that the famous Irish hospitality that has been extended to you to date has been of a quality to defy your, already, no doubt, superior expectations? It is of critical importance, you understand, that the welcome that we extend to you is as exemplary as can be, and at a level indeed, that is unrivalled by any other nation".

Axl looked at him like he had two heads.

"Fuck you on about dude?" he answered, scratching his head.

He did offer Marcus a swig of his hooch though, so he can't have been *that* pissed off.

Although perhaps that was just a ruse to get him to shut the fuck up?

Many others in the past have employed similar stratagems.

"You'll have to excuse my pal" I piped up, by way of explanation.

"He'll use ten words always, when two, or less even, will do. It's just the way that he is."

Axl nodded to convey that he understood, but you could tell again by the expression on his face that he had already moved on.

"Say man" he continued.

"Was that like, that Bono fucking dweeb I saw earlier on? He is, like, one weird fucking dude, dudes!"

"Regrettably it was, young Axl" I answered.

"And you dodged a bullet there most assuredly. Marcus here gave him a couple of slaps - naturally enough - after which off he popped off with that Edge fucker, crying like a fucking baby with his tail between his legs."

"Really dude?" asked Axl of Marcus, to which the latter nodded with pride.

"Right on dude!" said Axl, clearly impressed.

"That fucker's been cruisin' for a bruisin' for frickin' years!"

I'd always thought of Axl as a stand-up dude, but he was going up very seriously in my estimation right now.

"Oh yeah dudes!" he went on, with a look of seriousness on his face.

"Like he was here earlier on and fuck me, he was, like, pissing EVERYBODY off. Although he did leave some beer and whiskey and shit, so I suppose that's ok. He's some dick though dudes. Like, an EPIC fucking phallus man!"

"So, like, what was he saying?" I asked, not *that* keen to know really, but anxious to be polite at the same time.

"Well that's, like, the fucking thing man!" Axl responded animatedly.

"He was like, saying, absolutely goddamn frickin' nuthin' dude! Except like, the odd fucking word here and there, and like, shit that was totally unrelated to the conversation we were having at the time! And do you know why man?"

I indicated to him that I didn't.

"I'll tell you why man! I'll tell you fucking why! That fuckin' dog shit guitarist of theirs told me just after in, like, you know, confidence 'n shit? But I don't care! I'll tell fucking anyone man! The world needs to know how big of a fucking dick this fucking dick actually, like, fucking is man, like, you, like - you fucking know?"

I toyed with the idea of breaking it to him gently that he was at present babbling spectacularly.

Considering the unstable nature of his ranting to date however, I decided to give it a miss.

Who knew what he might do when he was riled.

As it was anyway, he just gibbered on.

"Song lyrics dudes! His own fucking song lyrics! Like fucking WHAT?! Not that they're, like, any good in any case - I mean the dude is hardly fucking Bob Dylan, right?"

Much as I was in agreement with his pronouncement - I mean 'Bullet the Blue Sky' my arse - he appeared still to be talking in riddles.

"That's great dude" I said semi-positively, so as not to discourage him from reaching the end.

It would occur sometime, surely, this century.

He digressed further.

"So like, here's the deal dudes, or at least the deal like how their three chord trick axe man put it to me anyways. But seriously though like, that dude is like, straight outta fuckin' Spinal Tap man!"

I think he was waiting for an answer but Marcus and I just stood there waiting for him to continue.

There was a bit of a pause so, and tumbleweed flying across the floor, with a clock tower's solitary bell then also, peeling forebodingly some place off in the distance.

"So where was I?" he went on, when he realised eventually that neither of us had anything to say.

"Oh yeah, like, the, like, lyrics, 'n' shit!"

The world was still turning, indisputably, but if someone had told that me it wasn't, and that God - or whatever higher power there is that has his or her finger on the pulse – had decided to bring everything to a halt then, as a result of just the sheer ENNUI that had come about as a result of Axl's painful and seemingly interminable soliloquy – well you'd have got very little argument from me.

He meandered on then again - and eventually, believe it or not, got to the point.

"So the deal is this, dudes. Whenever anyone asks Bono a question, about like, you know, whatever, the bozo answers only with, like, lyrics from his frickin' songs. And if there's nuthin' that, like, you know, works for the conversation that's goin' on at the time, he'll like, you know, just say nuthin' at all! I mean how fucked up is that dudes? Some artistic shit that he's tryin' out the guitar dude said, but if you ask me, it's, like, a fucking crock man! I mean, like, you know, why can't the fucker talk like a fucking normal person talks dudes?"

Which coming from Axl just then, especially after his most recent excursion into drivel, seemed a tad on the ironic side to me.

It did explain to some degree however, why Bono was being such a total fucking dickwad earlier in the day.

Belinda had re-joined us now, and was listening to Axl with intent.

"Oh yeah" she said, remembering something from before.

"The short-arsed prick used a line from 'Gloria' on me as well earlier on, now that I come to think of it!"

"We cool now, sugar tits?" asked Axl of her, as he put his arm sleazily around her shoulder, to which she replied demurely that she was.

'Fucking women!' I was thinking, irritated now.

'As fickle as fuck every time!'

"I'd sometin' similar sweetie!" Axl continued, following on from what Belinda had said.

"I asked him if he, like, wanted to grab a beer with me and Slash later on in the, like, you know, city and stuff, but all the fucker kept saying over and over again was 'All I Want is You'! I mean, like, fuckin' bogus or what dudes?"

It was hard to disagree.

"So, like, then I said to him, like, NO FUCKIN' WAY MAN!" he went on.

"Do you think I'm, like, some sort of fuckin' faggot or fuckin' sometin'?!"

Belinda guffawed like a person that has never guffawed before.

Embarrassing really.

She must have nearly wet herself.

I mean if Marcus or I had thrown out anything as similarly sycophantic, she'd have just looked at us with contempt and turned the other way.

I mean it was hardly comedy gold.

"Fuck it anyway!" spat Marcus, who in his excitement at being around such a collection of eminent and well-known dudes and dudettes accidentally imbibed too liberal a mouthful of his stout.

An additional volume of excess beverage was discharged as a result of this so, messily, with the offending secretion splattering all down the front of his pristine white linen shirt.

"I always get chocolate stains on my pants!" Gary Moore shouted across.

He'd been hanging out with a couple of chicks on the other side of the stage.

This whole 'lyrics' thing so, replacing *actual* conversation, appeared to be endemic.

Axl shrugged at it anyway, as if to say, 'Hey, it's Gary Moore! He can do whatever the fuck he wants!'

And if you consider Gary's canon of work over his long and illustrious career up until that point, both as a solo artist and a member also of probably the greatest rock and roll band of all time, and compared that then, with our tearful midget's output, i.e., the diminutive bozo that had recently made his ignominious departure no more than a couple of minutes before, then there really was, when all was said and done, not that much of a contest there at all.

'Waiting for an Alibi' versus 'I Still Haven't Found What I'm Looking For'?

I rest my case.

"Say kids!" said Axl, moving on.

"Do you, like, wanna go to fucking Vegas tonight? There's like, plenny a room on the jet if you'd, like, you know, like to come with?!"

'Fuck yeah' I was thinking.

As in, you know, sign me fucking up!

Belinda and Marcus looked similarly enthusiastic; and why wouldn't they indeed?

Vegas!

The playground for the misguided and the psychotic!

'Bring it on' we were thinking.

Obviously.

I wondered what type of jet Axl had.

A lear jet?

A gulfstream?

Not that it mattered much.

I mean either way it was gravy.

And when we got there the whole shebang would almost certainly be compped too.

What was not to like?

I corresponded same so to our illustrious host.

"Fuck yeah duder!" I intimidated to him with fervour.

"We are in with fucking BELLS on man!" I elaborated further.

My companions expressed their enthusiasm similarly.

"Count me in lover!" said Belinda, before following this up with a girlish squeak and a coy little wiggle of her shoulders.

Marcus communicated likewise, albeit in a considerably more complicated manner.

"Your kindly invitation is gratefully received and accepted, my good man! I shall present myself to you at the required hour, after which the frolics and escapades that follow will go down in the annals of frolic and escapade history, as demonstrably legendary indeed!"

By the look on Axl's face then, following Marcus's words, I had the impression that he was beginning to second guess this extending of an invitation to my inarguably good-natured yet ridiculously over-verbose comrade in arms.

He shook his head though then, as if to say 'Well, like OK, whatever', after which we all breathed a sigh of relief and moved on expeditiously to the next item on the agenda.

Which bizarrely enough was a quiz.

Or a test really, in hindsight.

Perhaps the Vegas trip wasn't over the line *quite* yet.

Had Marcus fucked it up for us with his circumlocutory bolloxology?

It was a possibility.

"Favourite song dudes!?" Axl asked, pointing to me first and then Belinda, with Marcus I assumed required last.

Even though he had agreed so, in principle, that we could tag along with him and his crew later that night to the asylum in the desert, I got the impression nevertheless, that if I or one of the others were to throw out a favourite tune that didn't quite meet with the man of the moments' approval, that any one of our triumvirate could very easily be told to fuck off out of it in a nanosecond, if the number in question was not to his taste.

A Caesarean 'thumbs up' or Caesarean 'thumbs down' effectively, was the way that I saw things now.

A lot was at stake so; of that I was sure.

"Street Fighting Man!" I blurted out then, thinking, you know; why the fuck not?

I mean, who doesn't like the Stones?

It was a good choice.

"AND WHAT CAN A POOR BOY DO!" Axl screamed, practically delirious now it seemed.

"'CEPT TO SING FOR A ROCK 'N' ROLL BAND! COZ THIS SLEEPY LONDON TOWN IS JUST NO PLACE FOR A STREET FIGHTIN' MAAAAAAAAAANNNNNNNNNOOOOOOOO!!"

I was in!

There was no way in the world that a reaction like that would be leading to a rebuttal.

In my mind already, I was converting punts into dollars.

"Cloudbusting!" chirped Belinda.

And who could argue with that as well?

Axl nodded his head approvingly as if to say, 'Yeah. That's OK.

A bit of a curveball definitely, but how can anybody conceivably H8 K8?

"Night and Day!" blurted out Marcus.

'Fuck me' I was thinking.

'That's a risky move'.

He had to be on his way out now, opting for that doobie.

And don't get me wrong, I've nothing against Cole Porter or Fred Astaire; I mean they're both giants in their own right, of their, you know, respective genres.

That is, of course, being songsmithery and choreography.

But that's just it, you see.

Were such genres apropos?

Had Marcus read the situation wrong, spectacularly, and snatched thereby, unlikely defeat from the jaws of almost certain victory?

Bizarrely enough however, in this instance, not at all.

Quite the opposite in fact.

Grabbing Marcus's right hand with his own left, and placing his right hand on Marcus's left hip, Axl led him out in to the open expanse of the backstage floor and then, as if it was the most natural thing in the world for him to do, he started to waltz.

And then also - quite comically as it goes - to sing.

"NIGHT AND DAY!" he crooned, as the duo circled as per the dance.

"YOU ARE THE ONE,

ONLY YOU 'NEATH THE MOON OR UNDER THE SUN

WHETHER NEAR TO ME OR FAR

IT'S NO MATTER, DARLING, WHERE YOU ARE

I THINK OF YOU DAY AND NIGHT"

Given the overall euphoria of the day so, and the fact that most in attendance backstage were either already off their heads in a seriously major way, or well on their way to being just that - if they continued, that is, to ingest the mind-altering substances into their systems as per what they all appeared to be doing right now - it will come as no surprise to you, probably, when I describe to you what came to pass next.

Taking the lead from Axl, everybody that was there took a partner and followed suit.

I grabbed Belinda myself, of course, and before very long, the entirety of the backstage area was a sea of drunken fools such as ourselves, twirling and bumping into each other and having a great old laugh in general at the sheer absurdity of our present predicament.

Even Bono came back when he heard the commotion, and was dancing around now, similarly, with his monkey, which seconds earlier having seen him arrive, came scurrying back down from the lighting rig and curled itself around the pint-sized frontman's shoulders.

Which led me to surmise - as I'm sure it has for you too - that there really is, when all is said and done, no accounting for taste.

I noticed Slash and Duff then, from the band; over to the side and looking decidedly the worse for wear.

They were staggering about the place and sniggering away to themselves like giggly teenagers at a pop concert.

It was an absolute Glenn Hoddle so, I was thinking, that they'd been shooting up.

Having a little conflab to themselves then, they appeared to agree on some-thing - a lot of thumbs up and nodding of heads and what-not going on - before gathering together the rest of the band and moving 'en masse' towards the stage.

Taking up their instruments then they started into the song – although it was a somewhat darker and more off kilter version than the one that I was familiar with myself – with all of the waltzers, every one of us, twirling our way to the front in their wake.

Before long so, we were all there, and the band also, while the remainder of the audience - that is, those optimistic enough not to have left for home quite yet - the ones basically that had been hoping for another, at this juncture, very unlikely encore - being treated now to the ludicrousness that was to be perused on the stage.

And it was an odd scene indeed to behold.

Slowly but surely however they started to get into it, and edged closer to the front to see what was going on.

There were thirty, perhaps thirty-five thousand or so of them left still, so plenty to engage one's attention if at any time in the near to medium term future, a person was considering the option of taking hold of the microphone and adding words to the music that had been playing for the last few minutes, and was definitely - in my view anyway - in need of a lift.

I was thinking back to my time backstage in London some weeks earlier you see, and the fact that all of the Rock Star DemiGods there at the time – Axl included – had been impressed with what I could do.

Bearing this in mind so, and taking into account the fact that Axl was other-wise engaged with his waltzing, and showing no signs at all of moving towards the microphone himself and giving it a lash, I decided to take the bull by the horns and have a stab at it myself.

What did I have to lose?

Spotting that sleeveen fucker Bono though out of the corner my eye, making a beeline for the front himself, I grabbed his monkey's tail as he was going past.

This freaked the animal out so much that it started to jump up and down on Bono's shoulders then, and box him on the ears repeatedly with both of his fists.

Like one of those Japanese monkey toys with the cymbals, you know?

The upshot of this anyway, was that Bono started to have a good old whinge once again, with the only difference between that time earlier on when he'd been blubbering similarly, and now, being that on this occasion there were thirty something thousand more people looking on.

And they were not impressed.

As he left the stage so, melodramatically, with the monkey on his back showing no signs of letting up, the crowd in their infinite wisdom told him exactly what they thought.

"BOOOOOOOO!!!!!!!" they cried as one.

And then others towards the front contributed further.

"Fuck off Bono, ye short-arsed prick" said one.

"You're some cunt Hewson!" elucidated another.

He was not well liked.

Anyway, with that bollocks gone, the coast was clear for yours truly to weigh in.

Trying to remember so, all that I had learnt before - from David Bowie and Robert Plant among others - and relying instinctively also, on what I believed myself to be the right way to proceed, I made my way very slowly and deliberately towards the front of the stage.

CHAPTER 9

ONE HUNNRED AAAAAHHH!
TWO HUNNRED AAAAAHHH!
And I can see those fighter planes.
Yeah.
That's how many people have tried to have a conversation with me today.
At least.
Probably more than that actually, now that I come to think of it.
THREE HUNNRED AAAAAHHH!
And why wouldn't they indeed?
I'm feckin' Bono for feck sake.
If I was chocolate I'd feckin' eat meself.
Although the concert today is getting me down big style, which is mainly as a result of the feckin' MILLION hangers on, gathered here backstage.
And Axl's Axl-hogging friend.
He looks familiar as well, this cat; although from where I do not know.
A record company exec?
Nah.
Unlikely I would say.
Way too young for a start.
A confident fecker though.
Reminds of me.
When I was younger.
The swagger, you know?
Even though he's done feck all yet.
Knows that he will though.
I can tell.
Edgeward hates him.
Hates him like feck.
But I think he's ok.
Edgeward though?
If someone robs his gargle?
Gets his knickers into an AWFUL twist.

I definitely know the dude from before.

As I was saying.

For the life of me though, I can't remember from where.

I wouldn't mind but we gave that gargle to Axl and the lads as a like, you know, present?

So it's not even Edgeward's anymore to give out about!

What he needs is a monkey.

Seriously.

To like, you know, look after and shit?

It BIG TIME focuses the mind when you have another little life to look after.

My Pierre has been an absolute God send for me.

I don't know where I'd be without him actually, if I'm being totally honest.

A present from Francois Mitterrand, don't you know.

You know; the president of France?

It pays to have friends in high places.

One minute you're like, 'sans singe', and the next, you're like, so totally not?

I think that's why he gave Pierre to me actually.

You know, because the French word for monkey is 'singe' and I like, you know, sing?

Pretty clever really when you think about it; but then the French are kind of, really, aren't they?

When all is said and done?

Arrogant too.

Like, BIG TIME arrogant.

But arty too, which, of course, I love.

What with me being arty as well?

I gravitate towards them, you know?

As they do towards me.

But how could they not in fairness to them?

I mean, like, I'm feckin' Bono for feck sake!

As I was mentioning there before.

Wow, she's hot.

Punky too.

Lovin' the purple hair.

I'll chat her up with a line from one of my songs.

That'll impress her.

Which one though?

It's hard to know.

So many classics.

Gloria?

Yeah.

Gloria.

That'll work.

That's my thing right now.

You know, using lyrics from my songs with which to communicate?

Not only is it, like, really cool and mysterious and stuff, everybody loves it too, especially my fellow 'artistes'.

For example, those Guns 'n' Roses lads are going absolutely fucking wild for it.

Especially Axl.

He told me so himself.

"Let me be your lover tonight" I say to her, quite irresistibly to be fair.

From, you know - 'Even Better than the Real Thing'?

Not Gloria.

I changed my mind there.

Might use a 'Gloria' line later though.

I mean there's like, an absolutely perfect feckin' line in there that I could use to woo - so it would be a real shame not to, like, you know?

If it's in your arsenal of lyrical vocabulary you have to, like, you know; make use of it?

Shockingly though I have been knocked back!

What the actual feck?

Probably on the blob.

I'll try her again later.

Most people can't resist me for long.

Particularly the ladies.

Bullet the blue sky.

Not really a verb, is it?

As in you know, 'Bullet'?

More of a noun really, if anything.

But what else could we have used?

Cannon?

Possibly.

That's a verb, potentially, I suppose.

As in, you know; to 'cannon' into something?

Doesn't have the same ring to it though, does it?

'Cannon' the blue sky?

And 'Cannon INTO the Blue Sky' in actual fact, would be, from an overall 'syllables' perspective, two too many.

So that wouldn't work at all!

'Bullet it is lads!' I said to the others at the time.

"And feck anybody that has a problem with it!"

They all agreed with me of course.

How could they not indeed?

I'm feckin' Bono for feck sake.

As I was saying there before.

Relax Pierre.

I'll get you a pretzel in a minute.

Feckin' monkey is drivin' me nuts!

Although he is great in fairness to him.

Loves pretzels.

My little pal.

There's the castle.

Recorded 'Fire' in there.

Good times.

Opulent set up though.

A far cry from the Finglas streets on which we were dragged up.

And who the fuck does Christy fucking Dignam think he is as well, saying that we're not hard!

We're hard BIG STYLE!

Street.

And you would be too if you were brought up in the only enclave of suburban decency situated 'bang smack' in the middle of an otherwise downtrodden and loser-infested feckin' war zone!

We had it tough, me and the lads.

It wasn't easy being a blue nose on the north side.

As in, that is; random kicks in the bollocks for no reason at all.

A commonplace occurrence.

Compulsory you might even say.

But with n'er a Murphy or an O'Brien among us, I suppose it was to be expected.

Hewson?

Clayton?

Evans?

I rest my case.

And even though Mullen is Irish enough, as surnames go, Larry was always a bit of a blow in, whatever way you look at it.

Guggi and Gavin had blue nose names as well, and they weren't even in the feckin' band!

So we learned to be tough.

Oh yes.

But while we took our beating, we stuck to our principles too.

Fought the feckers with guile and, you know - our smarts.

Turning the other cheek basically, but throwing out the odd clever retort here and there as well.

That showed them.

An embracing of pacifism basically, regardless of the danger - and/or likelihood indeed - of impending digs.

Always.

And we never gave into it either; otherwise we'd have been, you know, as bad as them.

Worse even.

In short, we were like Gandhi.

Which, of course, he was.

'Short' that is, you know?

A midget really.

So I was a modern-day Gandhi!

Not a midget though.

Not at all.

I have it on very good authority in fact that I am of average height.

It was commonly considered anyway that I was - as I was mentioning there before - a modern-day Gandhi.

I still am really.

It's what most people love about me.

I doubt that there are many that know me in fact that would deny it.

I mean like, that is; that I am a benevolent soul?

A philanthropist extraordinaire and all-round decent skin.

Known for it.

ALWAYS doing stuff for people.

Not as short as Gandhi though.

I mean he was like, a feckin' midget!

And I am of average height.

A recent study.

Very well regarded.

"Ice" I say to the waiter, when he asks me if I want anything else.

The little bollocks has been annoyin' me for ages.

I nodded to him a minute ago, when he asked me if I wanted a drink, but the gobshite is still here!

Why is he still here?

I nodded, didn't I?

Thankfully enough I can use the lyrics from one of my songs with which to communicate further.

That's the deal.

Like I was saying there before.

My artistic challenge?

'Ice' being the first word, like the VERY first word of 'The Unforgettable Fire'

song, recorded just across the way there coincidentally, in the castle, as I was mentioning there before.

"Lemon" I intimate to him then, indicating that I would like said citric accompaniment for my drink as well.

With 'Lemon' of course being the name of a song from our new album.

I'm not just going to say 'Lemon' now, am I?

I mean, like, that would be cheating like, you know?

So we're, like, working on it now.

The new album that is?

How cool am I anyway?

Managing to communicate in this way?

Like Yoko Ono in that blackened 60's theatre.

Or Beckett even, with that light shining on the face thingamajig, whatever the feck that's called.

They really will be talking about me for years after I'm gone.

Cedarwood Road.

Our enclave, as I was mentioning there before.

Although not as pastelly at all as it sounds, when you say it out loud.

A bit of a shithouse really.

Did I mention that we were street?

We were like, so TOTALLY street.

Don't care what anybody says.

HAD to be.

Otherwise slaps big time from the local gougers.

'Lypton Village' we called ourselves; which probably sounds a bit on the homosexual side I know.

But we were, like, so TOTALLY not!

We were as hard as feck.

Gave ourselves nicknames 'n' all.

I'm Bono as you know.

Named after a hearing aid shop in the city centre, believe it or believe it not; which is mad really, when you stand back and actually think about it.

Like, ironic, you know?

As in, you know, deafness is not an affliction that you'd ever want to have when I'M singing!

I'm a great feckin' singer!

Probably the best around today, I'd say.

Everybody else says so too.

You're not dealing with muck here.

Edgeward - 'The Edge' that is, to you and you - well, we called him that because his guitar playing was like, so edgy?

And like seriously, who can honestly deny that he's not, like, a musical feckin' genius?

Like, the man is a total ledge!

I can't remember how Guggi got his nickname to be honest - something to do with eggs?

Not sure.

And Gavin.

Gavin was easy.

I mean his ACTUAL name was so fucking lame that he just HAD to be called something else.

Fionan!

I mean, like, Jaysus, for feck sake like, you know?

What were his folks thinking?

And it was on a Friday that we were all talking about it, so like, you know, why not?

'Friday' it was for the old surname.

Who is this feckin' bozo poking me in the chest?

He definitely needs a kick in the old New York Dolls.

But no.

I'll think peaceful thoughts.

Pacifism at all times.

Like Gandhi.

An Irish Gandhi.

A modern day Irish Gandhi.

You know, when I come to think of it actually, I'd say that Gandhi must have had a monkey.

Like, in fairness; a man in his position MUST have had a monkey!

Do they have monkeys in India?

I'd say that they have.

I mean like, there are elephants everywhere, and they let feckin' cows roam the streets as well for feck sake!

You'd never get a feckin' rib eye there!

Not that you'd call them streets!

Dirt tracks more like.

India is a hovel really.

But he definitely had a monkey.

I'd say that that's a certainty.

What is this fecker on?

He keeps poking me in the chest.

I'll find a handler to feck him out?

Feck it anyway.

No handlers about.
I'll stand him down, this young upstart.
It's hard to understand what he's saying though.
He appears to have swallowed a dictionary.
No wait!
I have the perfect line.
Not in a song yet, but I'll definitely use it sometime.
I'll make a point of it in fact.
That way I won't be cheating if anybody pulls me up on it in the future!
I must be credible at all times.
"Maybe you can educate my mind?" I say.
'Ha!' I'm thinking.
'How do you like THAT feckface? Where's your comeback now?'
Jesus feckin' Christ, the fecker has only just kneed me in the billix!
And it's really, really sore!
And where's Pierre as well?
He was here a minute ago.
Oh no!
This wordy accoster has only gone and like, frightened him off!
My little pal has done a runner up the scaffolding!
I'm starting to get upset now.
Welling up badly.
Need help.
I'm delicate, you know?
People don't realise it, but I'm very, very delicate.
"Don't let it get away!" I plead to anyone around that might listen.
I couldn't care less about song lyrics now.
I just want somebody, ANYBODY, to rescue Pierre.
Although that is an awesome line!
I'll have to use it somewhere, sometime.
Jesus, this dude is a feckin' lunatic!
He's only gone and smacked me in the feckin' nose!
What's that?
Blood?
Ahh here now, this isn't right!
A handler please?
Where's a bloody handler when you need one?
Don't they know who I am, these bastards?
I'm feckin' Bono for feck sake!
At last, somebody to help.
One of those St. Jude dudes or whatever it is the feck they call themselves.

134

He asks me how I am and I answer in the only way that I know how.
"Numb" I say.
Ha!
A line from ANOTHER song on our new album!
Back in the game!
Artistically, you know?
I impress him even further with my next line.
"Is it getting better?" I ask the St. Jude dude.
You know, from 'One'?
You can tell by the look on his face that he's like, REALLY impressed.
The punky bird comes over then again, for a chat.
Must be having second thoughts re; our proposed dalliance.
Which is no surprise really.
As in, you know; she's only human.
I'll continue along in the same vein.
That's sure to do the trick.
"Anything at all" I say to her softly.
"I'll give it to you!"
From, like, you know 'Gloria'?
On 'October'?
Told you that I'd get to use that line later on!
It's a cracker.
Quite ludicrously however, she blanks me again.
Must be on the rag I'd say, as I was saying there before.
No other explanation.
"She is raging" I say to Jude.
From like, you know, 'Running to Stand Still'?
On 'The Joshua Tree'?
This really is high art.
I actually don't know anybody that could think on their feet as impressively as
this.
Talking of art, Guggi is into beakers.
Yes indeedy.
All sorts.
Neolithic mainly though.
He's deep, Guggi.
Very deep.
Like, you know, spiritual and stuff?
OK so like, I'm getting quite emotional now.
Why is everybody being so mean to me?
Is it because I'm short?

OK so I'm short, I admit it!

I mean who wants to live in a world where shortism reigns supreme?

Not I, that's for sure.

Beckett again.

Which reminds me of a time that I said to some tall dude, I can't remember his name.

Anyway, I said to him, "You're shortist!" to which he replied.

"No. YOU are!"

As in, like, you know, you're 'the SHORTEST!?'

So, like fair play, you had to hand it to him.

Nice little wordplay there, it can't be denied.

OK, time for a blubber.

One, two, three, GO!

Waaaah!

Waaaah!

Waaaah!

Right on cue, here's Edgeward to take me away.

I do need time on my own.

This whole thing is like, too much, and I need my space.

Perhaps when I come back later on, people will be nicer to me.

And maybe Pierre will come back down too.

He's just scared, that's all.

A bit too much for him this whole brouhaha.

I know how he feels.

I'm frightened too.

I'll just sit here on this box type thingamajig and calm myself down.

I abhor violence.

As in, I am not confrontational at all.

Well not physically anyway.

I'm a bit of a jessy really, if the truth be known.

The battle of Clontarf.

That was the problem.

No, not that one!

The Viking thrashing?

Feckin' Belvo versus the Temple, I'm talking about here.

St. Anne's Park, '76 was it?

I think that was the year.

Fifty souls at least on either side, with n'er an inch of turf conceded, nor quarter given.

Us Knights Templar on one side of the divide, and those pesky Belvederians on the other.

And Per Vias Rectas my arse too!

Coming at us from all angles they were, the Jesuit pigs!

Rectas?

They nearly feckin' killed us!

I do believe anyway that that's where my pusillanimous persona was fostered.

But they had chains for feck sake!

And Nun chucks!

All we had was our fists.

What would YOU do?

What I did anyway, was hide behind a rockery.

The only option really.

There until 10pm I was as well.

Had to wait until it was dark before risking making a run for it.

It was summer, so you know, bright for feckin' ages.

I'd left my contact lenses at home too, so was like Mr. MafeckinGoo staggering about all over the place.

In the end I managed to make it to the Tonlegee Road anyway, before jumping on a 17A to Finglas.

I was certain that I was out of danger at that stage, but would you believe that I actually got hopped on when I got off the bus at the other end?

A right load of gurriers they were as well - little feckin' bollixes from the village!

"Givvus yorr bleedin' odds, ye fuckin' perrick!" they started, and with the ratio being a noticeably one-sided four to one against, I was very much resigned to the fact that my personal readies, what little I had on me at the time, would very soon be in the possession of these miserable little feckers.

Not content with just relieving me of the contents of my wallet however, they came to a decision collectively as well, that kicking the living feckin' daylights out of me was an activity with which they would be very much in favour of becoming involved in rather than not.

I just about made it back to Cedarwood Road anyway in the end, but the Dad and the brother couldn't have given two fecks about me at the time, even though I was in pretty drastic shape.

"Shoulda learnt to look after yourself better when you were a lad" they indicated to me to a man.

"Insteada hanging around with those Lipton tea merchants, or whoever the feck they are!"

In retrospect, they were probably right.

What's that?

Night and Day?

And our feckin' arrangement as well?

What gives?

It must be about time for me to greet my public.

Providence surely desires it.

And when they hear MY version of this, they'll be absolutely feckin' blown away!

I'll edge my way to the stage.

Sure nobody will notice that I had a bit of an old whinge before.

People have short memories.

I mean do you remember Live Aid?

I made a total feckin' arse of myself at that and still they bought my records afterwards in spades.

Joe Public is semi-thick really, when you take a step back and actually think about it.

Pierre!

My beautiful Pierre!

Here he comes again, down the gantry.

I knew that he'd make it back down eventually.

Oh my God, I am so delighted to see him!

He keeps me so grounded, my special little pal.

"Shall we dance my simian companion?" I ask of him, as he wraps himself around my shoulders.

Everyone else is dancing as we arrive to the stage, so I see no reason at all why we shouldn't dance ourselves.

It's all a trifle bizarre though to be honest, but the crowd is absolutely lapping it up so fair play.

It seems to be working, whose ever idea it was.

This is perfect timing for me as well, in fairness.

To like, you know, give the crowd what they want?

They must be absolutely GAGGING for a bit of Bono by now.

What's this?

My feckin' nemesis again!

He's only gone and pulled Pierre's tail!

Who, as a result, is going absolutely fucking bananas!

He's banging my ears now as well, violently, on each side of my head, which must surely look, to anyone looking on, like one of those little Japanese wind up 'monkey with the cymbals' toy type thingamajigs.

All of which, I really must say, is most upsetting.

There is no way that I can face my fans now.

I'll retreat with dignity so and return at a later stage.

Pierre probably needs a little bit of time to calm himself down as well.

I'm just too distraught right now also, to think about any kind of cohesive performance.

And cohesion is what I'm all about.
Although I AM a mountebank as well.
I do know this.
As in, I look around me, even today, and see talent at every turn.
What have I got in comparison?
A good singing voice?
Maybe?
A big mouth?
Most definitely.
But look at somebody like Peter Gabriel.
And for example 'San Jacinto'.
What I wouldn't give to have written that!
A feckin' masterpiece, for feck sake!
I mean our stuff is ok, don't get me wrong.
But nothing at that level.
Not even close.
But he was like, a feckin' prog rocker before that, so you know, there must be hope for me as well.
I have to be relevant.
And Bowie too.
As in, like, imagine having 'Low' in your canon?
Or 'Scary Monsters'?
I mean, like 'feck me' like, you know?
Hard to beat that.
Feck OFF Pierre!
He's annoying me now, the little bollix.
And my ears are feckin' killing me too!
I wonder what the terrain is like outside?
As in, surely that microphone hogging bollix has finished up by now?
Although in fairness to him, he does have a pretty decent voice.
Nope.
Still 'Night and Day'.
Although he's on to another chorus so will be done soon, surely.
I'm brilliant at that chorus actually, especially the harmonies.
Me and Edgeward are always doing it.
Actually, if I just sneak around the back here, on the opposite side of the stage, I can grab the spare microphone there that the bassist was using earlier on.
Everybody is sure to love it when I get going.
I mean, who doesn't like harmonies?
And of course, there's the obvious as well.
Do I even need to say it?

Again?

As in, like, I'm feckin' Bono for feck sake!?

What is going ON?

The crowd - quite insanely really, when you think about it - is not playing along.

Boos?

Harangues?

What actually gives?

Although it IS a metal crowd, so maybe that's it.

That HAS to be it.

I mean, like, they are ACTUALLY telling me to fuck off.

As the chant gets louder, my microphone hogging nemesis beckons me in.

"I think that's your cue to fuck off pal!" he shouts into my ear, most disrespectfully I believe.

Impudent pup.

I'll show him later!

Don't doubt that for a feckin' minute pal!

Off I pop again so anyway, with my tail between my legs.

Feck it anyway!

I'll just sit down here on this box type thingamajig again, until everything calms down.

Oh, but for a quieter time.

I'm sad for that now.

Think I'm losing it.

Getting weaker.

Yellow eagle flies down from the sun.

From the sun.

Gabriel again.

Better than our feckin' lyrics!

Pining.

Kicking a ball against a pillar.

ONE HUNNRED!

TWO HUNNRED!

And I can hear those fighter planes.

And I can hear those fighter planes.

I'll break my record.

All the time in world to do it in too.

Nowhere to be especially.

Just a feckless kid kicking a ball against a pillar on a 1970's summer's day.

And the Da coming home at 5pm.

Super Splits on a Thursday.

Yes!

Although Rolo from autumn onwards.

What sane person eats ice cream in October?

And the trees are still bare.

Of all they were.

What do I care?

Big Time bars occasionally though.

But like, seriously, the toffee in them would take your feckin' teeth out!

Hi there!

I'm on my way, I'm making it.

I've got to make it show.

YEAH!

Abnormal loved them though.

Abnormal being the brother.

Everybody else calls him Normal - he's Norman in real life - but like, I always go against the grain with most things.

That's just, like, you know; who I am.

So, shoot me, yeah!

I couldn't give a flyin' feck!

Abnormal it was so.

And everybody that I said it to thought that it was a great nickname as well, in fairness to me.

Although it never really caught on, more's the pity.

Wow, is that, like, 'Gimme Shelter'?

Now THERE'S a tune!

Surely I can make it back now?

As in, the crowd will be in such good form with a number like that, that they're bound to be ok with me joining in.

As I arrive to the stage, I realise that there's a rake of them there already at the front.

In my feckin'way basically.

Total Z listers as well by the way; Lesley Dowdall, Paul Brady and the like, you know?

Not one person that's even close to being as famous as me.

I muscle my way through anyway, and eventually make my way to the front.

It actually reminds me a bit of that time in Live Aid, when we were, like, singing that little Christmas song at the end?

You know, the one that Geldof and Midge Ure wrote about those starving kids in Biafra or wherever the feck it is?

There's this little trick that I have anyway, which works a charm most times.

In order to ensure that I'm remembered above everyone else on such occasions,

I just sing the line of the song a half a second after the rest of them, or even add a word or two extra in, at the end of the lyric.

'Oh Lord' or 'Lordy Lordy' or 'Hallelujah' or some crapola of that nature usually does it.

In the case of Live Aid anyway, I just added in 'It's coming' at the end of the line 'Do they Know its Christmas time at all', and I think that it's fair to say that my line was the most memorable of the night.

Everybody absolutely loved it and loads of people actually said it to me afterwards that that was, like, their favourite moment of the concert, as in, like, even better than Queen.

So I'll do the same feckin' thing here now!

This crowd are bound to love it.

Correct me if I'm wrong here but after a shaky start, I do believe that they're finally beginning to warm to me.

"It's just a shot away!" I sing, a half a second after everybody else.

Axl is bounding over to me now at a rate of knots.

Probably wants to congratulate me for being so cool.

In his eagerness to embrace me however, he appears to have lost his balance, with the general upshot of that being that he has accidentally pushed me into the crowd.

This IS a pretty pickle.

Thankfully enough though, the crowd is unsurprisingly receptive, and I immediately break into a pretty impressive crowd surf.

I spread my arms and legs apart, Da Vinci messiah like, and they whisk me along.

I knew that they'd come around eventually, the feckers!

The boos and harangues have been transformed into cheers, as they buffet me from Billy to Jack.

They're absolutely loving this now, in fairness to them, as am I.

Finally, I am at one with my public, after an admittedly inauspicious start.

I definitely blame my nemesis for that.

All now however, once again, is right with the world.

I appear to have drifted out farther from the stage though than what seems usual.

Which is not that strange at all really, when I think about it more clearly.

The crowd quite naturally, and instinctively, want more of their numbers to see me 'in the flesh' as they say; so are like, you know, passing me around.

Nothing wrong with that.

The cheers are getting louder now, as I am presented to all.

'Dia de Muertos' almost like, you know?

Iconoclastic.

Although I am very much alive.

A life FORCE you might say.

A person such as me in fact, comes along but once in a generation.

OK, so I'm quite far from the stage now.

Fifty metres at least, and no real sign of me being about-turned and deposited back from whence I came.

I must admit that I'm a tiny bit worried.

The crowd are actually quite boisterous now; and I believe also, strongly, that as general pastiness and overall gingerness goes, I've rarely experienced any more overwhelming.

They are positively Leitrimesque.

As in, you know?

Drumshanbo.

I am being carried all the way to the back, which although fine and dandy, and perfectly understandable when you consider the fact that they all want a piece of me - as I was mentioning there before - it still doesn't take away from the fact that it's gonna be one hell of a pain in the arse to get back to the stage.

It's time to let them know I think, that I've had enough.

"Guys?!" I say, as they continue to jostle me about.

"Ehh GUYS!?" I shout louder.

"Not bein' funny or nuthin', but do you think you could like, bring me back? The song is like, nearly over, and I'd like, you know, to be there when we close it out?!"

Rather than acquiesce to my wishes however, as I presume that they might, I am ignored.

Even worse actually, they're starting to take the piss.

What actually gives?

"Fuck you, you short-arsed blue nose prick!" says one.

The cheek!

I am of medium height, as everyone agrees.

Five foot six at least, but probably seven.

And my Cuban heels make me look WAAY taller as well.

I'm at the back now, like the VERY back, and the crowd is thinning out.

It's got to the point now in fact, where there are no more punters left for me to be passed over, so the last few stragglers just drop me to the ground, the feckers, and leave me for dead.

A few of them offer up some choice commentary also, by way of parting shots, and none of them - quite surprisingly to me being honest - are complimentary.

"Hey Bono!" says a potato-shaped looking character.

"Guess what pal? We absafuckinglutely CAN live with or withfuckingout you!"

"Hey shortarse?" says another.

"So like, in answer to your question, you know, the one about the fact that you still haven't found what you're looking for? Well let me help you out a little bit with that, by requesting that you turn yourself around there, and cast your eyes keenly on the edifice that is no more than fifty yards from where we are at present situated. It's called the EXIT dude. How's about doing us all a favour so and fucking using it!"

I am flabbergasted!

I go to open my mouth but some fecker actually grabs me by the lapels, and turns me around, before kicking me in the hole very smartly, with what has to be conceded are exceedingly pointy shoes.

Pissed off now, I skulk away moodily to the strains of 'Cheerio, Cheerio, Cheerio' ringing in my ears, but console myself once again with the fact that this is a metal crowd, so they were probably never going to like me anyway in the first place.

I'll make my way into Slane so, and convince one of the locals to give me a lift back into the city.

Once there, I'll head into Temple Bar and pop into the Kitchen to see if there's anybody buzzing around.

There are bound to be loads of people there I'd say, who, once I speak, will be hanging on my every word.

And why would they not of course?

I'm feckin' Bono for feck sake!

CHAPTER 10

'What the fuck was that'?' I contemplated, as I opened my eyes and returned from a slumber.

I shuddered in my seat then as someone long since dead danced a polka on my grave.

Another dip and my stomach arrived at my throat.

'Fucking turbulence' I realised then, before closing my tired eyes once again.

Still groggy from last night's shenanigans, I could definitely, I was thinking, be doing with more zeds.

I was awake now though, so falling asleep again especially with the turbulence, was probably unlikely.

Turning in my seat I gazed out into the night air.

'Where am I?' I wondered drowsily.

Oh yeah.

Axl's jet.

I remembered now.

All was quiet though, for a journey such as this.

As in, you know - hardly rock and roll?

There was a small degree of chatter behind me but it was hardly rip-roaring.

A 'glasses clinking at the bar/soft lounge music playing' kind of set-up.

Light laughter and conversation.

Not raucous at all.

Sedate if anything.

Although they were definitely getting louder as time went on.

I leaned my forehead against the window and gazed at the terrain below.

Dawn was breaking in the distance so I could see well enough where we were.

Sea.

Just sea.

Clouds in the distance though.

Rolling arcus spanning a majestic horizon.

In that direction we were headed.

'The Atlantic' I surmised, peering down again.

'Has to be the Atlantic'.

Which meant that there was still a good long way to go.

Fucking Vegas though man!

I couldn't WAIT!

Axl stirred in the seat across from me, which took me out of my reverie and back into the present with a bang.

There ain't no easing yourself into the day with Axl.

"FUCKING Bon Jovi man!" he spat out then, as he stretched his legs out before him and lifted his arse out of his seat sideways for a fart.

"Like, he's been buggin' me all frickin' day man!" he continued, settling back down again, before fumbling in his top left-hand breast shirt pocket for, I assumed, some smokes.

He found some there then, and a lighter also, so lit himself up, before flinging them both across to me also so that I could partake.

"Cheers dude" I said, grateful for the thought.

"Do you remember that shit your Bono dude was throwin' down in Slane man, like, you know, a few days ago?" he went on.

'That shit went down yesterday' I was thinking.

Which meant of course that Axl was still fucked.

"You know, like, that usin' the words of his own songs to, like, you know; answer shit and shit? Well FUCKIN' Bon Jovi man, he's, like, bin doin' the same goddamn thing all day man, only worse dude, like, MUCH fuckin' worse. Wanna know why man? I'll tell you fuckin' why. Because he's singing man! Fucking singing! Seriously! I dunno man, like, maybe they know each other and shit, and it's like, a thing that they do or sometin'?"

I have to tell you that at this point I was practically CERTAIN that he was bullshitting.

Lo and behold however, he proved me wrong within seconds.

"You don't believe me?" he spouted, annoyed I think that I appeared to be in disbelief.

"OK dude, well check this shit out!" he continued indignantly.

Standing up then, he waved across to Bon Jovi, who was just standing at the bar at the back of the jet - I could see him through a gap in my head rest - holding court with Belinda and some other long haired jerks with stupid fucking clothes on that looked just like him.

"Hey, JB! JB!" Axl shouted, after which the WAAY too heavily hair-lacquered dipstick turned to see who it was that was calling out his name.

"Wanna get a drink later dude?" shouted Axl further, to which Bon Jovi responded with the following.

But not before he had preened himself just that little bit more, and fixed his stupid girly hair, taking note also of everybody in his midst, so as to assure that his response, when it eventually came, was lost on absolutely fucking nobody.

Throwing his head back then, his 'sung' response was as follows.

"WE'LL GIVE IT A SHOT!!"

'Fuck me!' I was thinking.

So Axl wasn't bullshitting after all!

Maybe it *WAS* a thing that they did, and that he and Bono actually *DID* know each other.

Such a scenario wasn't inconceivable either I was thinking, especially when you took into account the fact that both of them were 'known' bell ends.

"Fucking 'Living on a Prayer' dude!" Axl went on, before wincing a semi-conciliatory smile at Bon Jovi and sitting back down; hoping desperately also, I assumed, that the fucker would just stay where he was and not come over for a chat.

"Goddamn SHIT toon man!" Axl went on.

"And the fucker was singing it last night as well dude, when we were, like, you know, playin' Texas 'n shit?"

"How so dude?" I asked; interested to know, I suppose, how *that* shit went down.

I was sorry I asked.

"Oh yeah man!" he continued.

"We were like, back in the penthouse 'n shit, scoring chicks 'n charlie and you know, like, just gettin' wasted man. Some bozo suggested a game of 'hold 'em' then so, you know, why the fuck not we were thinkin', sometin' different, you know?"

As I mentioned before.

I was sorry I asked.

I just waited for him to get on with it.

"So like, I'm sittin' opposite JB and there's like, two other dudes playin' too. Not Sambora though. That chicken shit dick was just standing behind JB, givin' him advice. Not that I fuckin' cared about that man, coz like, I had the hand to beat all fuckin' hands man, no fuckin' way I'm losin' tonight! A straight flush dude, all the frickin' way, nines to kings, diamonds on my frickin' windshield man!"

'I guess you had to be there' I was thinking.

He carried on.

"Although technically he *could* beat me man, with, like, you know, a Royal 'n shit? But like, you know, how fuckin' likely was that? But anyways, we never got to play out the hand, because I, like, ha ha, I fuckin' turned the table over man!"

"You did what dude?" slightly more interested now, now that the story had taken an unlikely twist.

"Oh yeah man, like totally! And like, fuck man, I found out as well after that that he was waitin' on just one card for a Royal - although he was probably gonna stick anyway, the chicken shit dick! He wasn't happy anyway man, when I did what I did. But like, fuck it man, I didn't care! The shithead deserved it man! I just grabbed some chick then anyways, who was sitting nearby, and like, you know, took her out to the balcony to get laid!"

'All very interesting Axl' I was thinking.

'But how's about getting to the end of the fucking story?'

I decided to let my views on the matter be known.

"All very interesting dude" I said.

"But how's about getting to the end of the fucking story!"

"Alright, alright!" he answered, somewhat piqued for sure at my impatience.

"Keep your fuckin' hair on dude! So like, yeah, JB and Sambora are having a major fuckin' conflab over sometin' man, with like, lots a whisperin' n shit goin' down, and you know, tryin' to figure some shit out, I dunno, like, to stick or twist maybe or, like, you know, fuckin' fold maybe dude? Anyways, Sambora whispers sometin' into JB's ear and then like, JB only goes and sings the fuckin' words man! That's right, you fuckin' heard me right! Only like, SINGS his fuckin' answer dude?"

Axl sang it then, under his breath, so that I could understand where he was coming from, but not let on to Bon Jovi also, that he was singing Bon Jovi songs.

"WE'VE GOT TO HOLD ON TO WHAT WE GOT. IT DOESN'T MAKE A DIFFERENCE IF WE MAKE IT OR NOT!"

"Like, come on man! What the fuck was I supposed to do?" he elaborated further.

And in fairness to him I could see where he was coming from.

In circumstances such as the ones he had just described, turning over a table would be the least that could be expected.

I'd be thinking slaps myself.

Slaps, big time!

And if you consider the 'musical' output of the duo in question too, and then align that logically with the odious personalities of which they must almost certainly be in possession, it was hardly surprising in fairness, that they were the way that they were.

Although Sambora was a musician, so at least that was something.

By way of a, you know, redemptive trait?

Bon Jovi was just a dick.

I considered my recent foray into rock superstardom then, as I peered through the window once again.

Faux pink snowfields below me, colours changing with the dawn, belied what lay beneath.

Much like, I imagined, the superficial nature of fame and the trappings that it brings too.

Or so I've heard.

Like this private jet, for example.

Were we not as liable to crash in this as anybody else tonight, utilising a similar mode of transport?

Perhaps not so luxuriously, admittedly, but a similar mode of transport nevertheless?

Is there not an absence of hierarchy also after said demise, when everybody is gone and we've all been returned to dust?

My maudlin reverie was disturbed then momentarily by an escalation of debauchery at the back.

"Come on Freakers!" Belinda shouted across.

"You're missin' the craic here, ye boring prick!"

I decided to ignore her though, and stay where I was.

I don't know what it was but after my performance earlier in Slane and the subsequent adulation from the crowd; being around and having to listen to Belinda now, was for some reason or other considerably more vexing than it had been before.

On that note in fact - and regarding the reaction to my performance general- ly - it had been far better, immeasurably, than I could ever have expected.

Although that might have been also - as I'd considered many times over since the momentous foray in question - as a result of the fact that I'd sent that dufus Bono packing with a flea in his ear, with the crowd's subsequent positive reaction to my singing and overall display being perhaps for that reason alone.

Night and Day.

You recall that that was the song?

And ironically enough also, the version of it that I sang, or the version of it that the band played, and on which I had accompanied them – very competent- ly, it has to be said - was the same version that U2 themselves had recorded a year or two earlier, on some compilation album or other, in which they had been involved.

Bono so, must have been absolutely fucking seething backstage when he heard it coming on.

But anyway, as I mentioned before, the crowd that were left - some thirty thousand of them or so, roughly - had made their way tentatively back to the stage.

They had no idea who I was of course, so the entire scheme could have gone very seriously pear-shaped if I'd been hesitant in any way or failed to nail it from the very instant that I began.

I had just one chance to win them over and if I didn't take it, they'd be letting me know about it in no uncertain terms.

Slowly approaching the microphone so, I perused the swaying throng below.

Axl was right.

They *were* pasty.

And ginger.

BIG TIME fucking ginger.

Despite this fact though, it was a daunting experience even so.

The inebriated waltzers to my rear also, were taking no notice of me at all, but the band, to their credit, were very much aware of my impending performance.

They were right on the money, delivery wise, and as tight as you like as well.

They might have been off their heads in all ways imaginable, but that didn't take away from their ability to be consummate professionals if an occasion such as today demanded them to be such.

Effecting my thousand-yard stare then, and pointing to nobody in particular in the front row - although it might have been *any* of them, as Bowie had informed me before - I started to sing.

"NIGHT AND DAY. YOU ARE THE ONE!" I crooned in a Newleyesque type falsetto.

'Why not?' I was thinking.

I could mimic most singers now I had come to recently learn, so Newley was as good a choice as any, and certainly befitting for the number in question also, genre wise.

The faintest of ripples was to be observed across the heads in the crowd, and a slightest of murmurs as well.

Mercury rising.

"ONLY YOU 'NEATH THE MOON; OR UNDER THE SUN!".

I grabbed hold of the microphone confidently and strode with purpose towards the front of the stage.

Heightened cheers abounded as I moved closer to the edge.

They'd no idea who I was but it didn't matter.

Only two things mattered as things stood then.

Perception and delivery.

And fortunately for me on this most momentous of days, both were in heavenly synchrony as they had never been before.

The longer the song went on in fact, the more entranced they became.

Some became emotional even – although I wasn't putting that down necessarily to the excellence of my performance.

It was good – don't get me wrong – but I believe myself that their elation was probably more so related to the fact that they were all pretty exhausted following the exertions of the day, and were emotional anyway, as a result of the euphoria that they'd experienced already, earlier on.

The arrangement of the song also - which, in fairness to them, U2 had made a not insignificant contribution towards - was of a nature, I believe, that encouraged reflection.

Not melancholy necessarily, but almost definitely a vibe that might urge a person to look inwards.

"COME ON, YOU BEAUTIFUL PEOPLE!" I lied, shouting the words assuredly to the clod hoppers below.

"RAISE YOUR HANDS FOR ME NOW" I went on.

"AND JOIN ME IN THE CHORUS!"

Dusk was upon us, so the words, as luck would have it, were fortuitously germane.

"NIGHT AND DAY!" we sang in unison.

"YOU ARE THE ONE!"

We WERE the one.

A salient point lost on nobody.

I was theirs and they were mine and nothing could change that, not now, not ever.

Except fucking Bono of course, who believe it or believe it not, actually came back for more.

Unbeknownst to us all he'd snuck around the back of the stage and sneakily grabbed a spare microphone while nobody was looking, the conniving little git.

He attempted to harmonise with me then having rushed over to where I was standing, but it just didn't work.

In an instant so he had ruined the mood and the crowd was not hp.

A volley of boos and harangues commenced with none of the tirade, thankfully, being directed towards me.

"FUCK OFF BONO, YOU PRICK!" they started, with the words very soon becoming a chant.

"FUCK OFF BONO, YOU PRICK! FUCK OFF BONO, YOU PRICK!"

And that was the moment; the EXACT moment that I knew I had arrived.

"I think that's your cue to fuck off pal!" I intimated to the bollocks, leaning over to shout the words into his ear.

True to form anyway, he broke down once again, before leaving the stage in a teary huff.

The crowd then, naturally enough, sang the only song that was appropriate for the moment; so it would have been remiss of me I believed, as things stood at the time, not to have done the right thing and helped them along.

I duly weighed in so with our communal articulation rousing in the extreme.

"CHEERIO, CHEERIO, CHEERIO!" we chanted gaily.

"CHEERIO, CHEERIO, CHEERIO, OH!" we continued.

Our euphoria had returned.

I smiled at the fans and gave them a peace sign, before twirling nonchalantly and transforming my two fingers into a backwards facing midget-berating, one digit rebuke.

A 'flipping of the bird' basically, to send our abominable little elf on his way.

I was smiling of course; but not *too* much.

Aloofness was critical.

I mean, there has to be a layer.

You can't give everything away.

I continued with the song for a few moments more, after which Axl untangled himself from Marcus and came over to join me at the front.

The crowd became even more euphoric then, when they noticed who it was that was coming in for a duet.

"WE FUCKIN' ROCKIN' TONIGHT DUBLIN!" he screeched into a microphone then, which I have to confess made me wince just that little bit.

They always make the same mistake these fuckers.

As in confusing the absolute fucking BACKWATER that is BOG WARRIOR Meath, with the thriving metropolis that is delectable Dublin.

I'd never make that mistake.

I decided to keep schtum on it though for now.

As in Axl was, at present, my best friend in the world, so it was of crucial importance to keep him onside.

As things were he was pretty much 'championing' me, so this really was a once in a lifetime opportunity and not to be fucked around with in any way.

The drummer cut in then with a quite rapid change in tempo, banging the snare in quick time succession as the bass drum thudded away simultaneously on a similar beat.

Recognising the number immediately Slash and Duff joined in, with the crowd going absolutely ape shit as a result of the change in direction.

"YEAH!" screamed Axl, as he prowled the front of the stage, stomping back and forth as he nodded his head up and down aggressively.

'You KNOW it!' his moves insinuated.

"YAAYASS!" he screamed again, as the crowd became ever more animated.

"Y'ALL READY FOR SOME FREAK SHOW?!" he went on, pointing towards yours truly.

Fuck me!

He *DID* know my name.

Wowzer!

Belinda must have told him.

"I SAID!" he went on, waving one arm around demonstratively, and pointing very directly towards me then again, so as to ensure I assume that there was no confusion at all regarding who or what exactly this 'FREAK SHOW' was.

"ARE Y'ALL READY FOR SOME FREAK SHOW!?" he shrieked again.

The answer from the crowd was unanimous.

"YEAH!!" they said.

They said 'YEAH'!

Which considering my anonymity mere minutes before, was quite unbelievable.

It was my cue also, to continue.

I could not fuck this up.

Striding to the front confidently so again; as the bass and lead guitars introduced the main motif of the song; I waited for the right moment before starting to sing.

"AT A POINT BELOW ZERO" I began.

"WHEN THERE'S NO PLACE LEFT TO GO".

'MASSACRE'!

Majestic 'MASSACRE'!

The audience knew it alright and sang along to every word.

And why wouldn't they indeed?

What self-respecting Irish person worth their salt doesn't know and want to sing along with fucking 'Massacre'?!

And it WAS a massacre too, even if I say so myself!

Axl took the second verse, with things then going from great to even better.

Although he could have left the old 'Aye, Aye, Ayes' out of it in fairness, if there were any negatives at all that I could have brought to his attention.

The third verse I fucking OWNED - and it was fairly apocalyptic, even if I do say so myself.

'THERE GOES THE BANDOLERO

THROUGH THE HOLE IN THE WALL

HE'S A COWARD BUT HE DOESN'T CARE THOUGH

IN FACT, HE DON'T CARE AT ALL!'

We closed the song out then, to clamorous applause.

But if they thought that that was the end of it they had another thing coming.

Segueing dramatically some seconds later into the opening bars of the 'unrecognisable only to those living on Mars' guitar riff from 'Gimme Shelter', the band and everybody on stage, of which at this point there must have been thirty individuals at least, collaborated wondrously in the eponymous vocalisation that represented the incontestably monumental introduction to the song.

"Ooooooo – Ooooooo – Ooooooh!" we sang together.

"Ooooooo – Ooooooo – Ooooooh!" we continued, as the by now ecstatic crowd joined in.

The band took the song then to where it belonged, as the mood gradually, as cadence heightened, became rapturous.

"WAR, CHILDREN. IT'S JUST A SHOT AWAY!" we sang together; incongruously joyful when you consider the words.

"RAPE, MURDER. IT'S JUST A SHOT AWAY!" we wailed, even more ecstatically, and more contradictorily also, when you consider those words as well.

But they were just words really, with their meaning today insignificant.

Our exhilaration was interrupted then unbelievably once again, by our perennially aggrieved but staggeringly more persistent than you can imagine Sméagol Hewson himself.

The numbers on stage were gathered at the front now, and were serenading the crowd heartily as per the lyrics above.

Gollum Bono however, spotting his chance once again to grab a piece of the limelight, wormed and squeezed his way covertly through the singing throng to the front, before grabbing a microphone off someone and joining in, the complete and utter bollocks.

And as per his performance at Live Aid also indeed, almost seven years before, he inserted a sly vocal subterfuge, exactly as he had perpetrated a similarly calculated 'all about me' ruse all those years before.

As in, do you remember the line at the end of that number, where it goes 'Let them know its Christmas time'?

Well Bono at the time, the treacherous prick, waited until the line was finished by everybody else on stage – including absolute fucking legends like McCartney, Bowie, Geldof AND Townshend - before adding the words 'it's coming' at the end, a half of a bar or so later, just so that the crowd could hear his own voice last and that their abiding memory above all others, would be his own despicable and miniscule self and the words that he was singing.

I mean what a total and utter fucking dick!

'Just a shot away' thrown out there now today, sneakily by the bollocks, a second or two after everyone else there had sung the same words.

I made a conscious decision so, there and then, that he would not be prevailing any further today.

Whatever way I went about it – and I hadn't figured it out *quite* yet - there was just no way in the world that he could be allowed to continue.

Thankfully enough however, I wasn't the only person there that was of a similar mind.

Axl, noticing Bono hogging the limelight also, made a conscious decision of his own to bring said situation to an expedient and undeniably non-negotiable end.

Striding over to the Lilliputian imposter in question, he grabbed the microphone from him decisively, and pushed him away.

Bono though, in his attempts to get closer to the crowd, had been teetering already precariously close to the edge.

That, and the fact that he was wearing the most ridiculously high-heeled -

although quite well-disguised in fairness - Cuban heels, led to the ignominious events that were to come to pass next.

Losing his balance as a result of the situation already outlined, he fell backwards into the waiting crowd below.

OK so as I'm sure you are aware, the whole notion of 'crowd surfing' - as it is clear to me anyway - is that the rock star be plunged into an expectant audience and passed along then for a few minutes by adoring hands below - with the odd pinch of an arse here and feel of a John Thomas there – after which those same adoring hands return said rock star back to the stage and safely deposit him back from whence he came; free to continue with the show basically, secure in the knowledge that he has given them what they wanted and that although he will never actually be 'one of them', that he was, at least for a few moments anyway, *almost* 'one of them'.

On this occasion however, *that* situation was not *in any way* how things eventually went down.

The crowd, sick of the fucker by now and dearly wanting to see the back of him more than anything else in the world, did what any large gathering would do, logically, under similar circumstances.

Holding him up as per the 'crowd surfing' scenario referred to in the narrative before, they carried him along as described.

Rather than directing him back towards the stage however, they did the very opposite, to the extent that within no more than ten or so seconds, he was already thirty metres away from us, and being pushed along in the opposite direction.

Spotting what was going on then, the rest of the crowd joined in exuberantly, with their enthusiasm and desire to get the job done driving Bono along even more swiftly than they had been driving him before.

Within no more than a minute or two so, he had been harried and bustled to the back of the crowd, where as soon as he became arrived at a point where the crowd had thinned out and there were no more hands to carry him along, he was just dropped there on his arse and left to fend for himself.

I might have imagined this also - and it was a good old distance away so my eyes may have been playing tricks on me – but I'm almost sure that someone in the crowd, as Bono was being deposited where he was being deposited, gave him a right old kick in the arse before indicating to him aggressively, in no uncertain terms, that he was to be on his way.

Although, as I said; I might have just imagined it.

Either way though, that was the end of fucking him!

Back on stage, things were coming to a close.

"GOOD NIGHT DUBLIN!" Axl shouted, with his mistaken geographical reference rankling with me once again.

"YOU'VE BIN FRICKIN' AWESOME DUDES!"

"AN' GIVE IT UP FOR ONE OF YOUR OWN AS WELL, JOHNNY FREAK SHOW RIGHT HERE FOLKS! LIKE, WHAT A FRICKIN' VOICE DUDES! ALRIGHT JOHNNAAY!!!"

The crowd went wild again, which although totally fucked up and not at all like anything I could ever have imagined would eventuate when I raised my head from off the pillow that morning, was a thrilling feeling nevertheless.

This shit was new to me of course, but I was certain also, right at that very moment, that I wanted more.

The thought of it indeed and how I might be able to sustain that wondrous feeling of power and exaltedness that I'd experienced as I'd been standing there on the stage singing, with the crowd in the palm of my hand as I'd been delivering the songs, consumed me in an instant.

"You fuckin' love it man!" snickered Axl from his seat across the way.

"I can tell. I can ALWAYS tell dude! You been bitten by the fuckin' bug man!" he continued, stretching in his seat and nodding to the trolley dolly to come over to take an order.

I smiled and shook my head as if to say no, but he could read me like a book. Sure hadn't he been there himself, all those years ago?

"I'm tellin' ya dude!" he went on, straightening himself up as the waitress arrived by his side.

"Seen it a million fuckin' times before man! S'written all over your face Bubba!" he continued, before putting his order in to the girl.

The very cute girl by the way, who looked to be - certainly on the basis of how she was dressed - considerably more than just a trolley dolly.

"Two JB's on the rocks" said Axl.

"Doubles darlin', for Freakers and me, and then after that, like, you and me, we'll go back to my room for some fun – you fancy that, little darlin'?"

She giggled suggestively before turning on her heels to fetch us the drinks, but not before Axl had slapped her on the arse playfully to send her on her way.

"Rock 'n' roll dude" he said, shrugging, as if to say that you can get away with pretty much anything when you're a Rock Star Demigod.

Belinda was at the bar still and by the sounds of her cackles - which were louder now and ever more persistent - she was definitely well on her way to being plastered.

Fuck it anyway, I was thinking.

Another five or six hours of this and a refuel somewhere probably - Chicago maybe - before getting back in the air and continuing on to Vegas.

It had to be at least another three or four hours on to there as well, so the thoughts of having to put up with Belinda's bolloxology, and Jon Bon Jovi and his crew as well, was a proposition that was not appealing to me in any way.

"Fuck me dude!" I said to Axl with a pain in my heart.

"Have we gotta put up with these gobshites for like, the next ten fucking hours?! I'm seriously thinking of throwing myself out into the goddamn Atlantic so, if that turns out to be the case!"

"Fuck you talkin' about man!" he answered, and by the look on his face he was not entirely in tune with what I was saying.

The reason for which, following his next words, became clear.

"That's Lake Michigan dude! We only three or four hours outta Vegas man, if that!"

"Really dude?" I answered, both shocked and elated at the same time.

"Like when did we refuel?" I went on.

"Surely we didn't fly all the way from Dublin to here on one tank?"

"Course not dude" Axl answered, looking at me again like I had two heads.

"We filled up in the Big A while you were out for the count!"

"Thanks doll!" he continued, as the waitress returned with our drinks.

Settling down then some moments later, as I sipped on my double JB on the rocks, at thirty thousand feet high in the sky, two thoughts came to my mind.

The first was that three or four hours in comparison to ten hours, when known fuckers and imbeciles around you are talking what appears to be incessant and practically interminable shite, is a considerably more agreeable predicament to find yourself in than not.

The second, as I looked through my window, to my left and to my right, seeing nothing but water below; stretching out before me and as far away even as the newly illuminated horizon that must surely have been many hundreds of miles off into the distance; was that Lake Michigan, as lakes go, was one hell of an outrageously sized fucking lake!

157

CHAPTER 11

Come hither, come thither, and hear what I say!

As town criers of yesteryear bolstered your illiterate selves, so I will bolster your catachrestic inadequacies today!

I would have made a good town crier.

Indubitably.

But I was born too late.

And that dream that I had?

About giant blue turtles devouring my hedgerows?

Please!

Nuclear submarines people.

Metallic blue and primed for conflict!

The general lower orders will believe anything though really, most of the time, with the most basic of subterfuge and clandestine of activity all that's required usually, to hoodwink.

Take this simpleton before me now for example.

Accepting my benevolence?

He seems nice enough but it's just pathetic!

I mean I barely have to try!

And six million attenuated Jews killed by marauding, psychotic Nazis?

What on God's earth has that got to do with me?

It's gone now and consigned to the past.

A more righteous path for humanity will prevail.

And I'm the man to guide us there.

Mephistopheles is MY name!

Cologne, 1993.

That's where we're at.

Although I'm not entirely sure why I am here, being honest.

Ho hum.

It matters little.

I'll show this chap that I've been saddled with the Stolperstein while I have the time.

That should maintain his awe and convey the impression to him also, of course, that my overall altruism is beyond reproach.

The world at large has bought that bullshit to date, so why not this bozo?

He does seem like a nice guy though, as I mentioned before.

Albeit a little green.

The Stolperstein so, just so as you know, are these commemorative brass cobblestones that a German artist instigated last year, as a, you know, gesture or 'memorial' to the victims that fell at the hands of the Nazis in World War 2.

And a noble gesture it is indeed.

But ahem, HORSE, BOLTED!?

As I was mentioning there just before.

Well that's what I think.

Markedly more drastic measures are required.

We must terminate mankind's perpetual cycle of barbaric hostility.

It's not like, you know, there isn't a precedent there already, for drastic short-comings on the part of the human race?

These brass cobblestones anyway, or 'stolperstein', are embedded into footpaths outside the last known residences of the victims in question, to remind humanity that it happened and that it was easy for it to happen and that it must never happen again.

Like, seriously?

A brass cobblestone outside a house in Germany is going to discourage a future crazed despot from seizing power, and then wielding that power indiscriminately over a suitably brainwashed and apathetic proletariat?

I don't bloody think so.

I had a dream alright.

And it was nothing like MLK's, let me tell you!

My dream showed me the light.

A calling.

Greg Stillson.

You know, from that 'Dead Zone' flick?

And with power like that at one's fingertips one owes it to one's self, in my view anyway, to start again.

And in case there are any that disagree, to make the decision for everybody on everybody's behalf.

To NOT annihilate the world basically, by - in the short term - annihilating it.

Humanity is its own worst enemy - as you know - so with humanity no longer in the picture, surely nature and all material things that are pristine and beautiful and innocent will flourish once again?

So this calling of mine.

I've never had more clarity about anything either before or since.

And with my elevated public persona I can get there, most assuredly.

It will take guile and cunning of course, but most of all patience.

A changing of the guard will not happen overnight.

An extinction level event folks!

That's what we're talking about here.

To gain access to a vast arsenal of nuclear weapons, one way or another, to bring the Earth, in its totality, to an end.

I will gather together a cabal of like-minded luminaries.

And when I say 'like-minded' I do of course mean, ostensibly so, merely.

I am referring to individuals – you know who they are - that want to do GOOD in the world, not bloody end it!

This 'entente' will be my means to an end; but it will take some amount of time to arrive there.

If hob-nobbing with the likes of Geldof and Bono so, is a prerequisite to positioning myself 'politically' as it were, on the global stage - then hob-nobbing with Geldof and Bono it will have to be!

But they will know nothing ever, of my grander design.

THAT I will keep to myself.

Something tells me though - call it intuition - that neither of those two bloody do-gooders will be THAT positive about a potential annihilation of the entire human race!

Most will scoff also at my political ambition - of course they will.

But I prefer it that way.

Lull them into a false sense of security, you know?

You think it inconceivable?

Well what about Reagan?

Did he not have his finger on the button?

And he was B list celebrity status at best, certainly back in the day.

And look what he was able to achieve?

Damn near brought the world to its knees.

He was way ahead of his time old Ronnie.

Knew how to play the game.

And he might have got there in the end too but for the failing of his health scuppering his plan.

And that was his plan alright!

I could see it in his eyes.

Ronnie was a proper mentalist.

And whereas my own plan might appear to be insane also, to anyone that might find out about it - if they ever actually do - which of course they won't – I'm convinced myself, as I've alluded to before, that it's the right thing to do.

I mean, what is the point in continuing?

Now is the time.

They'll thank me in the end.

If any survive, that is.

Of course they will!

Morlocks and Eloi - but more Eloi than Morlocks, one would hope.

Otherwise the cycle begins again, and it's all been for nought.

Ha!

Wells had it right.

But with no time machine at my disposal, I must eventuate now.

Or as soon as is practicable.

Once near inaudible murmurs of discontent from middle-eastern caliphates are gathering bluster.

Proud and noble nations, fatigued now of their third world inferiority.

Giants of yesteryear.

Do we honestly believe that they're all going to, you know, just go away?

I don't bloody think so.

Unrest is afoot, of that there is no doubt.

Dastardliness is imminent.

So it's the right thing to do, unquestionably.

In for a penny, in for a pound, as I've always said.

It's been leading to this moment for centuries.

I mean, who can honestly deny that?

Consider all of the countless conflicts since the dawn of civilisation, and tell me then that it shouldn't be so.

Have we learnt nothing?

Our race has regressed.

We had our chance and we blew it.

Homo sapiens do not deserve anymore, to be the dominant species on earth.

And global warming?

That ever-widening hole in the ozone layer?

Don't get me started.

It calls to mind actually that Kubrick movie.

You know - that 'dawn of man' scene in '2001 A Space Odyssey'?

With the obelisk thing or whatever the hell it was?

How long ago was that meant to be?

I mean if you think about it seriously in the grand scheme of things?

A hundred thousand years?

Two hundred thousand years?

The latter probably.

So if the Earth was formed 4.5 billion years ago - as it is commonly thought that it was - it has been around, give or take, for approximately 22,500 times longer than the human race.

I would say so that we are just lodgers.

Wouldn't you?

As in, how did the Earth manage without us on its' own, for the preceding 4,49,98,00,000 years?

It will survive again so, one would think, when we are gone.

Take organised civilisation also.

When did that initiate exactly?

5,000 years ago?

10,000?

Neolithic times?

Ancient Egypt?

If you consider the fact so, that man started to be truly civilised no more than let's say between 7,000 and 12,000 years ago and then take into account the God-awful mess that we are in right now, here in the latter half of the 20th century AD, surely then you would have to concede, that as a species we have ballsed it all up in a not inconsiderable way.

And it could have been so much better.

"All this world is heavy with the promise of greater things, and a day will come, one day in the unending succession of days, when beings, who are now latent in our thoughts and hidden in our loins, shall stand upon this earth, as one stands on a footstool, and shall laugh and reach out their hands amidst the stars."

Wells again.

Sometime in the early part of the 20th century.

But a tad optimistic really reading it now, despite mankind's impressive enough forays into space since he penned the words.

If only that were it alone, instead of our noble and farther-reaching pursuits being perpetually tempered by a hell bent and relentless drive for mindless self-destruction.

The fecundity of human achievement to date has not, regrettably, softened our similarly indomitable propensity to fuck things up.

"Would you like to get some bratwurst?" I say to the chap, who's just a kid really.

It's nice to be nice, even to chaps that I barely know.

"Yes" he answers warmly.

"I'd like that a lot".

I know a great little stall between Rathausplatz and Alter Markt so I'll take him there.

It's only a couple of minutes' walk anyway and I'm hungry myself.

That's another thing.

Famine.

I mean how can famine exist in a world where others, including myself, throw away perfectly good food?

Have we no shame?
This kid is Irish so he knows about famine surely?
Will I ask him?
Perhaps not.
I'm not that interested anyway in what he has to say.
We'll just enjoy our bratwurst here and I'll keep my thoughts to myself.
The less that everybody knows - including this chap - the better.
I am a scarlet pimpernel, is what I am!
What were they thinking though, those paddies?
Back in the day?
As in, are there no fish in rivers and seas?
Apples on trees?
Does it all really have to be about the potato?
Although us English had a fairly sizeable hand in events too.
Make no mistake about that.
As Disraeli put it in fact, Ireland's woes were, to paraphrase, as a result of an 'absentee aristocracy' (being the landowners for whom the peasants worked the land), an 'alien established Protestant church' and the 'weakest executive in the world'.
He wasn't wrong.
The world also, to a one, looked the other way.
It IS human nature though really, isn't it?
Survival of the fittest?
I mean we don't give THAT much of a fuck really.
There are oodles of precedents of insouciance as I was mentioning there before.
Hence my plan.
It's no more than we deserve.
"What's that kid?"
The kid is trying to speak.
"I was just wondering" *he asks.*
"If you ever come up…"
Spit it out kid!
He definitely needs to be more confident this youngster vis-à-vis public speaking and such?
Project himself better, you know?
I think I'll order some apple wine.
"Ein Apfelwein, bitte" *I say to a plump waitress who is wandering close by.*
I should probably get one for the kid too.
"Entschuldigen" *I say, calling her back.*
"Zwei, bitte".
The kid seems pleased.

Ok so there has been some fantastic human endeavour also - don't get me wrong.

Great strides made across countless disciplines.

Science, The Arts, and Medicine to name but a few.

But is it enough?

The answer to that question, my friends, is an emphatic NO.

The apple wine has arrived and very appetising it looks too.

An earthenware jug with floral designs around it being the main receptacle, along with two small goblet type wine glasses for accompaniment.

Quite deceptive is apple wine.

It looks like apple juice to all intents and purposes but nothing could be further from the truth.

The clue is in the name people!

It's a Frankfurtian speciality really, but you can get it in other parts of the country as well, if you know where to look.

Like here!

If you drink this shit like apple juice though, you're gonna know all about it in the morning.

Your arse?

A Japanese flag!

Talking of which, what about Pearl Harbour and the subsequent entry into the war as a result of said travesty, of the old septic tanks?

And septic they were too; make no bones about that!

Clinical.

And THIS is human 'endeavour'?

Please!

How much proof does one need so, of mankind's inherent capacity for wanton and bloodthirsty slaughter?

Child sacrifices in Carthage?

How's about that?

Do you want more?

Wartime abominations, that is?

Ok then, I'll give them to you, seeing as you've asked.

Jebel Sahaba.

The first, really, I suppose you might say.

In recorded history anyway.

That is, the oldest known recorded evidence of systematic warfare carried out by the human race.

So 'homo sapiens' arrive 200,000 years or so ago, give or take, and it takes 188,000 years, roughly, before modern day warfare can be said to be born.

That is, to be clearer, 'proven' to be born.

164

For that is what Jebel Sahaba is.

If you consider so, the fact that we had lived peacefully enough as a species for approximately 85 per cent of the time that we had been here, is it not odd to think of how little time it took for us to, you know, catch up?

And yes indeedy, we soon stepped things up with great gusto, especially in Neolithic times.

Sedentism, you know?

What's mine is mine etc.,?

This is my patch pal and I'd rather stick a spear in your gullet than share it with you.

Oh, and your family and your friends?

Well, I'll stick a spear in their gullets as well, just in case they come after me for revenge at some other point down the line.

And then the bronze age, with weaponry to match.

A whole other ball game people.

We're hotting up now.

Hamoukar, then Kadesh.

The Mycenaeans in Greece?

All pre-cursers to further dread.

As Russell says, 'War does not determine who is right, only who is left'.

Shall we do it by numbers?

Rather than chronologically?

Yes, I think so.

I think that that would be best.

The top 10.

Yellow Pearl.

Russian Civil War 1917 – 1923. Nine million dead.

Dungan revolt in China in the 1860's. Sixteen million dead.

Tamerlane in Mongolia – 1370 – 1405. Twenty million dead.

Sino Japanese War 1937 – 1945. Twenty million dead.

Qing conquest of the Ming dynasty 1616 – 1662. Twenty-five million dead.

An Shi rebellion against the Tang dynasty 755 – 763. Thirty-six million dead.

World War 1. 1914 – 1918. Thirty-nine million dead.

Taiping Rebellion in China 1850 – 1864. Forty million dead.

Mongol Invasions – 13th century. Sixty million dead.

World War 2 – 1939 – 1945. Eighty million dead.

So, what of an apocalypse?

Are we not hurtling in that direction anyway?

Do the frankly UNBELIEVABLE numbers that have been lost to war to date, not dictate such?

I foresee it now in my imagination and it is beautiful.

A future that is, one hundred or two hundred years from now.

Two thousand even!

Nature unfettered by the tumult of humanity.

Architectural edifices from the past, tall and looming but empty now, save for creatures that exist at this time without malice, bar a malice that comes from an instinct for survival rather than avarice.

A feral form of mankind exists, but he is wizened and weak and lives in a state of persistent dread.

No longer the 'dominant' species, any number of other less obvious contenders vie now for that historically unenviable top spot.

I'm thinking birds.

Or some form of flesh eating bug?

Probably those actually, as it's far more likely to have survived the atomic blasts before metastasising over subsequent centuries, into a more sinister and foreboding entity.

They live in the hollowed-out halls and floors of long since vacated buildings, tall and large, in cities created by man but no longer inhabited by him.

The feral man lives on hills and mountains now, far away, too afraid to travel to the cities for fear of being eaten alive by these barbaric and blood thirsty flesh-eating hexapods.

The insects have evolved now and are the size of dogs.

They are rampant and carnivorous, but nature despite this remains unimpeded.

Skies are bright and the air every day is clear.

Starry nights are comparatively crystalline, and with no air pollution their luminosity is blinding.

The Trolhogs – for that is what they are called – are nocturnal, so all is well for most other life forms during the day.

As sunset looms however, impending chaos is inevitable.

Other creatures retreat to their abodes in preparation for the night time battles that will commence forthwith.

One such creature, a favourite of the Trolhog, and a rodent of a hamster or guinea pig type ilk - Priggles they are called - are easy and obvious fodder.

They DO know this though, instinctively, and although hardly 'an intelligent life form' as we perceive 'intelligent life form' to be at this time, they have devised a plan nevertheless, that enables for their survival.

Aware intuitively that as prey they are the most vulnerable by far, they have developed a system of sacrifice that allows for them to endure, so long as they adhere to their routine.

Nightly, and without fail, the Priggles will push the least able of their lot to defend themselves to the top of the earth (they retreat into burrows at dusk, and remain there insofar as they can, until the sun rises on the following morning) so that when the Trolhogs arrive, which of course they inexorably do, their appetites will be satiated by these 'lesser' Priggle 'runts' that have been forced through the earth to the top, to meet with their gruesome and unenviable fate.

Other dangers loom though, in the clear light of day.

Whilst Trolhogs sleep, other similarly savage beasts are hunting their prey.

Giant flying bird-like creatures, similar in appearance to storks, save for their size - which is gargantuan - with bills, the razor-sharp teeth of tigers embedded into them, top and bottom, and monstrous eagle-like talons attached to their legs, survey the terrain for their quarry.

Grizzywarks they are called and they are fully the size of a horse.

They are lithe also, which enables them to swoop easily and expertly from on high to low, whilst darting in and out amongst and between the branches and leaves of trees, searching for Nennos.

Nennos are small frog-like creatures that although clever and chameleon-like in their ability to blend into their environment seamlessly, are no match even so for the Grizzywark.

The slightest twitch of nervousness whilst hiding from their nemeses, and they're gone.

With a flit, flit, flit, the Grizzywark has arrived, devoured and departed again, all within no more than a second.

Thankfully for the Nennos the appetite of the Grizzywark is slight, so after three or four forays per day into the forests, they usually retreat to the hills where they make their home.

And as all of this goes on, the world still turns, and the sun still shines.

Oceans and flora flourish in turquoise and green and a rapturous regeneration of our beautiful planet prevails.

Carnivorousness is rampant admittedly - as I have alluded to before and described - but mere Trolhogs killing Priggles or Grizzywarks devouring Nennos has no lasting effect on the thriving nature of 'nature', as the earth replenishes itself and sheds the brutal several millennia-long effects of mankind's abuse.

How to formulate my plan though, without anybody finding out?

That is the conundrum.

Feigning interest in a battle against conglomerates that pollute the world is one thing; I mean that's easy.

If a halfwit like Geldof can get away with it, then it certainly shouldn't pose any difficulties for an intellectually superior being such as myself.

Getting my greasy mitts on as many nuclear warheads as possible however and then devising a plan where I can place these bombs in situ at the desired locations and then detonating them at the required times, simultaneously for maximum effect, is a whole other story.

That takes planning my friends, and probable collusion on the part of other individuals that are of like mind.

The key I believe is this Bono chap.

He's always hob-nobbing with that Mitterrand bloke.

You know, the French president?

That's the individual who, I think, above all of them, will be my easiest route.

I mean, think about it - am I really going to be able to infiltrate the United States Security Services or Russia's or China's even for that matter?

Those are major league long shots by any stretch of the imagination.

The French however?

The French are an entirely different kettle of fish.

So much so I would say, that if I was to offer to whomever the chap it was that was in charge of the codes, FOR the codes, a ten thousand-dollar bottle of Château Mouton-Rothschild, I doubt that there would be very much, if any, deliberation on his part, before he parted with same in exchange for said plonk.

Most of the Frenchie's arsenal is attached to submarines also, so are far easier to access, you would think, than nuclear warheads that are stored in like, you know, actual 'facilities'?

At least that's my take on it.

The kid is trying to speak again.

"Just as an FYI" he says.

"But I do actually know Bono, kind of?"

I'm not sure why he's bringing up such a thing now but I suppose that most Irish people think that they know Bono in some form or another, give or take.

I mean the bastard is fucking everywhere right?

Co-incidental though, all the same, considering the fact that I was musing on him just then, only a couple of moments ago.

Ok, so I've done my research and know that there are roughly fifteen thousand nuclear warheads held globally - by the nations worldwide that is, that are holding them.

And France has around three hundred, would you believe?

That's way enough so, in my view, to get my Armageddon under way.

The deal anyway so is to get as close as possible to this Mitterrand individual, and well, I don't know, get him drunk or something, before cajoling him into giving me the codes.

Once I have them - which should be easy enough to acquire - you remember what I was saying there before about the wine - it'll just be a matter of getting myself on to one of those submarines, to, you know, get the ball rolling.

I won't have to launch them all though, of course.

That simultaneous shit that I was talking about earlier on won't work.

Just one will do and then, you know, watch them all go nuts.

The Yanks are great at that anyway, so the initial target will definitely have to be there.

I'm thinking the eastern seaboard?

If all of those landmarks are obliterated, well that will just drive them crazy!

The Statue of Liberty?

The Chrysler building?

How many people live in New York anyway?

Seven million?

In the city probably.

Way more in the state though of course.

And if I think of it in numbers, it definitely doesn't seem that bad.

I mean, I'm not a violent man per se.

And if it's quick - as it will be of course - then nobody will really know that much about it anyway, will they?

As in, you know - instantaneous evaporation?

Probably the best way to go I'd say.

Just think about it people.

Just think!

A Grizzywark can wake up of a day and not worry about imminent extinction.

He can just fly off to wherever he wants to and catch Nennos.

A Trolhog, similarly, can munch on as many Priggles as he wants, without even the merest thought for some idiot in a gasoline guzzling super truck, mowing him down indiscriminately as he attempts to cross the road in search of his next snack.

And I know you're probably thinking, well what's so bloody special about Trolhogs and Grizzywarks.

And well you might.

But it's not about them.

The Trolhogs and the Grizzywarks are immaterial.

It's about the controls being taken away.

Enough is enough.

I feel a tugging on my sleeve.

It's the kid again.

He seems nice this kid but he's no good at maintaining his own council.

That's three times in the last ten minutes that he's interrupted me.

"I'm sorry" he says.

"But are you like, ok?"

In truth I'm not.

But it's nice of him to ask.

I like this kid.

I wonder if he'd like some schnitzel.

I would.

"Would you like some schnitzel?" I ask of him.

"No" he says.

"I'm ok for schnitzel right now" he verifies.

It doesn't take much to set me off.

Which drives me to tears usually.

And then I get my fanciful ideas.

Nuclear warheads indeed!

Even if I was allowed to get close to one, which is probably unlikely, I absolutely abhor submarines.

And being underwater freaks me out as well.

So how is that supposed to work if I can't even set foot on the vessel on which the weapon is armed?

I never think things through.

Everybody is always saying it.

"What's your name kid?" I ask.

It's nice to be nice, even to minions and such, such as this young chap.

I'm great that way.

"Johnny Fortune" he answers.

"'Freak Show' to me pals".

"So, what has you here in Cologne, my young Irish counterpart?" I ask.

Intimating to him once again that he is on an equal footing.

Which, of course, he is not!

I mean how could that be the case?

I'm fucking STING for fuck sake!

Which is in fact my ACTUAL name.

Some people in interviews and what not try to call me Gordon, but no way, I'm not having fucking that!

Even the missus calls me Sting, so I think that that pretty much seals the deal for me.

And I can have like, so much fun with it too, as in, you know - having a laugh and stuff?

For example, I was talking to a journalist the other day, and he was doing a piece on me, so I asked him to, you know, give me a general synopsis of what the article was going to be about.

So he basically said that it was just a general interest piece on where I came from, a bit about The Police, what I'm doing now etc., so I said to him then, as cool as you like don't you know, without even thinking, 'Well there'll definitely be a sting in that tale!'.

Talk about laugh!

We were beside ourselves for ages, well bloody minutes anyway, especially him.

The article was shit though.

A real let down to be honest and not nearly laudatory enough, which it should have been of course, especially when you think of all the great things that I've achieved in the past.

"You may recall" answers the kid.

"That Axl from Guns 'n' Roses introduced us earlier on at the hotel and that you asked me at the time, no more than an hour ago really, if I would be interested in accompanying you on a short tour of the city. So, like, ahem, here we are like."

I detect a slight twinge of cynicism in the kid's delivery although I'm not sure why.

Ok so I forgot that I'd suggested our walk, but I do have a lot of things on my mind.

The annihilation of humanity for one!

Yes indeedy, its back on!

A slight wobble there earlier, but I'm back on point once again.

"Say kid" I say, remembering what he mentioned there before about being acquainted with that midget, Bono.

"What would you say, knowing Bono as you say that do, are his overall views regarding the continuance of humanity as a, you know, species and such? As in, you know - for or against?"

The kid muses for a while before coming back to me with an answer.

And an odd response it is too.

As in, much as what he is asking me is prominent in my own thoughts, I have no idea as to how he comes to know what he does.

Is he some form of a medium or a mind reader of some ilk?

Upon hearing what he says anyway, I stand up and gather my things together before rushing off at great haste in the general direction of the hotel.

What is it so, you may ask, that he says to me that disconcerts me so much?

And well you might.

"Much as I do know Bono, Sting, vaguely" he has elucidated.

"And would be more than happy to give you my thoughts on whether his views regarding the planet are apocalyptic or otherwise, I have a much more pressing question for you myself, which I'd very much like for you to answer, if you don't mind, that is. My question is thus".

And at this point he pauses for effect.

"What the fuck" he says, continuing.

"Can you tell me please, is a fucking Grizzywark?!"

I mean, seriously?

What a total and utter fucking weirdo!

CHAPTER 12

So that Vegas trip never actually happened.

Which should come as no surprise to you really, when you consider the 'minute by minute' and quite honestly farcical 'about turns' that were being perpetrated outlandishly by the gobshites that were in situ on the plane.

It turned out anyway that Bon Jovi at some point during the course of our flight and unbeknownst to myself or Axl or anybody else for that matter - and for reasons best known to himself - had decided that it would be a *far* better idea today for us to be travelling to Germany rather than the US, so took it upon himself whilst nobody was looking to direct the pilot to do exactly that.

The fact that he had asked for nobody's permission to do such a thing should of course come as no surprise.

Don't forget that he's a Grade A bollocks to beat all others.

So while I'd been peering out the window of the jet and surmising, quite logically I believed at the time, that we must be somewhere over the Atlantic - especially when I considered the vastness of the body of water below - it transpired in the end that I was in actual fact, correct.

The only difference now being, of course, that we were flying in the opposite direction.

It was definitely NOT Lake Michigan so, as Axl had intimated to me before.

And what with him being as unstable as he was generally, I'm a little surprised at myself for believing him in the first place.

As in, I'm not usually that gullible.

The acid and the coke and the gargle so, were quite clearly having an unduly adverse effect.

I *had* been out for the count though, as all of this had been going on, so whatever about whether I should or shouldn't have been believing or disbelieving of Axl vis-à-vis his spurious views regarding our location, I definitely had a better excuse myself - i.e., unconsciousness – for accepting this 'now known to be completely false' information regarding our geographical co-ordinates at the time.

It was pretty amazing though I considered, whatever about my own slumbering self, that not one of the other passengers there noticed the aircraft - at whatever point that it did - doing a 360° fucking turn!

I definitely think that I would have noticed such a dramatic change in direction myself had I been awake.

None of them did though, which illustrated to me quite evidently, how irreversibly fucked up they all were at that time.

Here we were so anyway; in Cologne of all places.

Which is not exactly the glitz and glamour of Vegas, I'm sure you agree.

And what a bizarre place it was too, especially when I observed how few old edifices or buildings were there.

A modernist nightmare really; so much so in fact that when we *did* see an old building, we'd stop in front of it for longer than one might usually, just to pay homage to the fact that it had actually survived the war.

"Fuck me!" said Axl, with a look of distaste on his face.

"This place is fucking grim dude!"

He was not wrong.

We arrived at the hotel anyway, eventually, in a state of great brouhaha.

And not just with the staff, who were hysterical enough, but with our own party as well.

Isn't it amazing how excitable people can get once there's even the slightest change to a plan?

Axl was stressed out enough, but that Bon Jovi bollocks was in veritable conniptions.

'WE WANNA GODDAMN SUITE MAN!' he bellowed to the dude at the desk.

Followed by 'AND WE'RE TAKIN' THE WHOLE GODDAMN FLOOR TOO MAN!'

Gobshite.

And what the fuck is wrong with blue M & M's as well?

Yes indeedy; if ever there was a dude that needed a kick in the hole as a matter of priority at a particular place in time; it was John Bon Fucking BELL END Jovi right then.

'Halfway There'?

I don't think so pal.

You are fully ALL THE WAY there.

All the way there, that is, to being a fucking DOUCHE!

The mayhem in the foyer was exacerbated further by the fact that there was another star also, residing in the hotel at the same time as ourselves.

The venerable Sting no less.

Imagine that!

An establishment having to deal with an unscheduled event?

Something unexpected happening that required them to think outside the box?

It was chaos.

And I thought that the Germans were supposed to be organised!

They got us booked in anyway, eventually, before some bright spark suggested, I can't remember who, that we should all congregate in Axl's suite, to like, you know, 'party'?

Although I don't believe that the word 'party' is an actual verb?

Not where I come from in any case.

There we all were anyway, a few minutes later, with Belinda flinging herself at anybody that might give her a second glance.

Marcus was sniffing around her too, so I let him know in no uncertain terms that he'd be far better off just knocking one off.

Less heartache unquestionably, and a considerably more expedient fulfilment of his immediate needs.

Once he got *that* out of the way, he could enjoy the rest of his night with the lads.

"Forget it pal" I told him.

"She's only interested in Rock Star DemiGods, and although I regret to be the bearer of the bad news, you are definitely not one of those!"

He nodded resignedly before heading off purposefully in the general direction of the jacks.

The sensible decision without doubt.

I was hovering around myself anyway on the outskirts of things, just minding my own business and sipping on a double G & T.

I heard a rap on the door then, so being the closest person to it I headed across to see who was there.

Little did I realise that this simple and apparently innocuous move on my part, would signify the beginning of a short chapter in my life that would represent one of the most bizarre that I would ever experience.

Opening the door then anyway, I was delighted to see that it was Sting.

This 'initial positive feeling' however, was an 'initial positive feeling' that would dissipate very soon.

Unlike his more usual confident and overbearingly hubristic persona, the ex-law enforcer himself at the time, cut a considerably less upbeat personage.

He entered the room a 'broken individual' as far as I could make out, painfully conscious of all that he surveyed, and our group's immediate and intimate examination of his self.

This was not the self-satisfied mouthpiece that we've all come to know and tolerate, reluctantly, over the years.

Even Belinda I believe, despite her perpetual propensity to pursue poon tang with Rock Star DemiGods, regardless of the circumstances that are prevailing at the time, appeared to have looked the other way.

174

She became otherwise engaged anyway, soon enough, as I found out from somebody else not long after Sting's arrival.

'Fucked off with some rocker dude' I was told, so I came to the fairly obvious conclusion that she was probably boning Richie Sambora someplace else, when I noticed a few minutes later, perusing the suite, that neither of the duo were accounted for and/or available for selection at the time.

My assumption - quite rightly as it goes - was that the pair of them had wandered off to some other more private location for the ride.

Desiring a leak anyway, as I was, and knocking on the bathroom door to encourage whomever was in there to get a fucking move on, I was left in no uncertain terms some moments later, as to the unified views of the parties that were at present ensconced.

"Fuck off Freakers!" wheezed Belinda - knowing and recognising me obviously, from my voice - in between what I can only assume was fairly full on fornicating, given the slap, bang and clattery type noises that were emanating from within.

"Richie Samfuckingbora is boning me here, ye dozy prick!" she shouted out again, semi-breathlessly.

What a tart!

I was BIG TIME wise to her now.

She'd get up on anything!

"Yeah" shouted Sambora also.

"Why don't you, like, fuck off kid?!"

'Jaysus' I was thinking.

'Another fucking bonehead!'

I went back to Sting so, anyway, to check how he was getting on.

I was concerned, genuinely, for both his physical and mental well-being.

By now he had shuffled over to a protruding window sill on the far side of the room, perhaps two feet in breadth, and hoisted himself up.

He pulled his feet up from off the ground then and rested them on the sill, meaning that his thighs and knees were pulled now towards his stomach and his chest.

He had the look of an adult foetus; perched there precariously, rocking back and forth.

Looking to all intents and purposes to anyone looking on, like a PROPER fucking nut job!

His appearance was unkempt and sloppy also, and not at all what you would expect from such a figure.

He wore grey tracksuit pants that were ill-fitting and stained in parts, particularly around the crotch, whilst an oversized black t-shirt with a protruding Jagger tongue on the front, was his choice of chemise.

A red Yankees baseball cap pulled down over his eyes - with more curvature on the peak than usual – 'squeezed in at the sides' kind of thing - completed the look - which was, to be fair, not great.

His personal hygiene was pretty drastic also, to the extent indeed that Marcus, who would usually keep his thoughts on such matters to himself, asserted to me the following, not long after Sting had arrived.

"I can say this to you, pal" he pronounced, with a tone of genuine regret in his voice.

"Hand on heart, without fear of contradiction; that every breath he takes is fucking rank!"

Sting's on-going mental state also, left a lot to be desired, which led me to the conclusion that it would be a good idea, probably, to get him out of there ASAP, rather than leave him to be torn apart by the particular set of individuals that were present at the time.

He was in no fit state to fight back basically, and when I heard the comments that were being thrown out there then by Axl, upon noticing the state that the poor bollocks was in, I was in no doubt as to the fact that we needed to be departing from the place sooner rather than later.

"Hey Sting!" he shouted out from across the room.

"I'm just saying dude, but I'd like, be thinking about maybe givin' rehab another fuckin' shot man!"

"WE'LL GIVE IT A SHOT!" sang Bon Jovi loudly again, as he had on the plane earlier on; and it was just as fucking annoying on this occasion as it had then - more so indeed.

What a gimp.

The situation for Sting anyway remained harsh; to the extent that I felt morally obliged at this point to remove the poor bastard from the scene.

He was totally helpless as things stood, and a translucent globule of dribble had started to drool from out of the side of his mouth as well.

It was not a good look.

I asked Marcus if he wanted to come with, but he informed me then - pretty icily it has to be said - that he'd rather stick his head into a bucket of warm poo than assist me with, as he called it, my 'stupid feckin' altruistic endeavours''.

"The dude is a space cadet" he suggested, which in fairness to him, and as an evaluation of how Sting had been coming across to date, could hardly have been argued as an incorrect synopsis of the scene.

He wanted to stay put also he said, to get stuck into more of the free gargle that was on offer, and although that's an undeniably noble enough aspiration in itself, I *do* believe that he might have come along even so, to give his old pal a hand.

With the state that poor old Sting was in, it definitely looked to me as if it was a two man job.

As it turned out in the end anyway, it was just 'yours truly' and the lunatic of the hour that departed the hotel, five or so minutes later on.

And that was *his* idea rather than mine; despite my previously stated desire to assist him by taking him away.

He was out of his box most assuredly; but that didn't stop him from being instinctively aware, I believe, that if he stayed there for very much longer, things might get ugly.

"Take me away please" he whispered into my ear; recognising me - 'instinctively' again I would say - as the only person in the vicinity, probably, that might be happy to assist.

It was early in the evening as I remember it thinking back - perhaps 7pm?

Sting had been mumbling away to himself since I had made his acquaintance earlier on, but his words as we pushed along now were increasing in volume - perhaps he was becoming more accustomed to my presence?

He was becoming a good deal more animated also, with his previously semi-inaudible words and expressions at this point, markedly more exuberant.

Which I have to inform you was not that good a thing.

He relayed to me then - well not me, specifically - the world really - or anybody within earshot that might be in a position to listen - a dastardly plan.

It was patently obvious though, lamentably - that he was totally unaware of the fact that he was speaking out loud.

The words were one thing - I mean they were bad enough - I'll explain to you further as I go on - but his overall demeanour or 'carriage' even as you might call it, was of far greater concern.

I mentioned to you before about his rocking back and forth?

Well this was replaced now whilst he was walking, with a Mohammad Ali shuffle.

More recent Ali though that is; not the glorious '1-2 BANG' majestic in-ring sporting foxtrot of yesteryear.

He commenced a wringing of his hands also as if concocting a plan, Mr. Burns-like, I'll bide my time, with his prior to this unnoticed by me, bony and fisherman-like gnarled fingers weaving in and out as he made fantastical statement after fantastical statement, one after the other; apparently - as I was saying there before - to himself.

He spoke of blue turtles munching on vegetation in his garden and metallic blue submarines.

He referred to me also, quite early on in his monologue - and quite insultingly also - as a simpleton.

I thought about interrupting him at that point, but given his initial intensity and the fact that even though he had said it, it appeared still that he believed himself to be talking inwardly, I concluded that it was probably more trouble than it was worth to pull him up on the matter.

He did call me 'nice enough' though, in practically the same breath, so that was another reason why, probably, I was inclined to give the bollocks a break.

His ramblings from there on however, had to be heard to be believed.

We stopped in front of Cologne Cathedral to have a look at a brass cobble-stone on a path.

Which might have seemed innocuous enough if we had just come across it, but the aspiration by which it came to be there, as Sting 'explained', was inarguably august.

A commemorative tribute to the Jews lost in the war.

These cobblestones anyway, or 'stolperstein' as Sting just about managed to inform me, were inserted into footpaths outside the last known dwellings of the subjects of tribute; or indeed the actual spot where they were dragged, kicking and screaming into the street, usually in front of their less denominationally ill-fated neighbours, leaving all of their worldly possessions behind them as they were marched to the living hell that would very soon come to represent their existence from that moment forward.

He spoke then of his plan to destroy the world.

Yes, you heard me right.

Although not the 'world' exactly, per se.

The human race, more accurately.

The world *after* Armageddon however, would replenish itself he said, with nature flourishing and an earthly 'cleansing', generally speaking, taking place.

This would take hundreds or even thousands of years he went on to state, but could be executed only, if he could manage somehow to get his hands on some nuclear weaponry, with a view to firing a warhead at the United States and then standing back to let all hell break loose.

He would enlist also, the help of rock star luminaries that were known to rub shoulders with individuals at the highest political level – and he mentioned Bono and Geldof in particular at this juncture – with a view to cajoling whichever of them he could to give him access to politicians – French mainly – who would in turn - in exchange for expensive red wine - give *him* access to the nuclear codes that would facilitate ultimately, the perpetration of his contemptible act.

He spoke of HG Wells then, and of time machines and Eloi and Morlocks.

He referred to middle-eastern nations, formerly superpowers, rising from the ashes to reclaim their rightful place at the forefront of the world.

He mentioned human conflict since the dawn of man, Stanley Kubrick, and global warming, before pointing out the need for humanity to no longer be a dominant species on earth, as we had had our chance and had fucked it up in a not inconsiderable way.

And then he asked me if I would like some bratwurst.

Yes indeedy.

This was a dude that was not stable in any way.

I *was* hungry though, all the same, so not averse to a partaking of the meat based German delicacy if it was going.

I was of a mind also that if Sting had some form of menial task to be carrying out; that is, in this instance, the acquisition of in number, two, the sausage based snack referred to above; that there was a reasonable chance that it might actually shut the fucker up for a minute or two, perhaps; which would be good.

"Yes" I answered so, with a pained expression on my face.

"I'd like that a lot".

He grabbed me by the wrist then and we headed off in the general direction of a stall that he knew he said, near some market or other that was situated close by.

Him shuffling as before, and I shortening my stride so as to not trip up as a result of the change in my usual pace.

And regarding my desire that this new assignment on his part might focus his mind and encourage him to shut the fuck up?

I regret to tell you that this was not the case.

If anything the fucker became worse!

He spoke of apples and fish and Protestants and famine.

He insulted the memories of millions of my ancestors then, as if he was flicking a crumb from off his lapel.

He quoted Disraeli, referenced Darwin and once again spoke of the annihilation of the human race; and all the while as he was stuffing his saliva stained face with admittedly very delicious bratwurst.

I was getting a right pain in my bollocks now though with his blathering, to the extent that I made a decision to ask him if he ever came up for fucking air.

"I was just wondering" I asked.

"If you ever come up…"

But the prick only went and interrupted me AGAIN!

And although his initial delivery pertained to the fact that I needed to speak up for myself, and that my communication skills generally, were of a notably inferior essence, he went on to suggest, more positively it has to be said, that he might at this stage in the proceedings, like to partake of some wine.

'Apple' wine he suggested actually, which apparently was some form of local regale.

Given the tedious nature of my present circumstances so, I found it hard to conceive of a suggestion that was more agreeable; despite the fact that the advocator of said intoxicant was the very individual from whose lunacy I was desirous of clemency.

He ordered just one for himself though initially; but thankfully did the right thing then and revised his original order to two.

This was a singularly capital idea all told, especially when I was considering, just a few moments later, the virulent content of the next instalment of his verbal diarrhoea-laden rant.

He moved on to the horrific and grotesque nature of all of the wars and conflicts that have come to pass, from the dawn of civilisation to date.

Starting with Pearl Harbour, and the entry into World War as a result of that debacle, the yanks, he went on to list all of the worst conflicts, one by one, in order of how many lives had been lost in each of them.

A kind of 'top ten' as he referred to it himself at the time.

It was painful.

And do you know that part in 'Top of the Pops', where they count down the top ten songs in the land to the strains of Philip Lynott's 'Yellow Pearl' playing in the background?

Well he was only humming the tune also, with the drum machine fills included also, believe it or believe it not, as he listed off all of the major wars that had taken place many centuries and millennia ago.

It was at the next point in the proceedings however (as if they weren't already, I state with bitter cynicism) that things became *really* weird.

His rocking back and forth increased in ferocity and was accompanied now by a manic nodding and shaking of his head, up and down and from side to side, as his delivery increased simultaneously in both velocity and volume.

'Ahh here, come on now Jaysus, will ye, for fuck sake Sting!' I was thinking to myself at the time.

'As one absent-minded gravedigger said to another absent-minded gravedigger, you've definitely lost the fucking plot now!'

On he rambled though, deliriously.

His hands were shaking erratically now too, as he raised his tumbler to his lips to partake of the admittedly very impressive apple-based imbibe.

The lion's share of it made it on to the table before him only though, and his lap, rather than down his throat; and I do have to admit also to a mild degree of concern for his teeth as a result of the tumbler chattering off them quite aggressively every time that he did eventually manage to raise the receptacle to a point that was close enough to his mouth where a portion of the liquid might be consumed.

He spoke then again, bizarrely, of an imagined world in the future where mankind was no longer the preeminent species.

We existed still, yes, but had regressed as a race to the extent that we had gone full circle as a genus, and were living now in the hills and mountains, afraid to leave there for fear of the giant flesh eating bugs - 'Trolhogs' he called them -

that had come now to rule the cities where mankind had flourished before.

Other similarly strange flying birds, the size of horses - Grizzywarks I believe he referred to them as - feasted on smaller, amphibious, tree-dwelling creatures; and although this was harrowing enough as you might imagine, mainly as a result of the fact that a lesser or weakened human race was living now in a state of perpetual fear high in the hills, Sting put forth a celebratory image of an earth that was rejuvenating itself. The air was cleaner, with man-made pollution a thing of the past and malicious 'acts' prescient now only, also, as a result of a desire for survival rather than anything of a more avaricious or self-serving nature.

New age psycho-babble mumbo fucking jumbo, I was thinking.

And if he wanted to 'sell' this story to anyone else also I surmised at the time, and be 'believed' or taken seriously, at any point in the near to medium term future, I was certain myself, of one thing and one thing alone.

That if his desire was for an audience to take his points on board in a logical and fair-minded manner, that constant drooling as a part of his delivery would not at all get him to where he needed to be.

He babbled on about nuclear weapons then again, and how he might be able to get his hands on one.

He mentioned Bono and the French president Mitterrand, and the fact that he might perhaps be able to get close to Mitterrand, and thereby a bomb, if he befriended Bono further, and enlisted his assistance in said ruse.

I mentioned the fact that I knew Bono, kind of; but quite honestly, I might as well have been talking to the fucking wall.

I had intended to elaborate further and assist him by letting him know that Bono, being Bono, would almost certainly not be able to help, as a result of the fact that most world leaders tolerated him merely, and that behind closed doors they *actually* regarded him as being a bit of a dick.

He just ignored me though again, completely, and continued rabbiting on about bombing the US, getting Mitterrand drunk - so as to access the warhead he would need - and those fucking Trolhogs and Grizzywarks again!

He began to get quite emotional then after which, to be honest, I actually started to feel a bit sorry for him.

"I'm sorry" I said, tugging at one of his sleeves as the tears rolled down his face. "But are you like, OK?"

True to form - that is, ignoring my actual question - he answered by asking me if I would like some schnitzel.

Which in fairness, I did.

I was fucking famished, even though I had only just finished that bratwurst not thirty minutes before.

Listening to this gobshite was hungry fucking work.

But having to stay there for longer than completely necessary was an issue also, so I gracefully declined his offer.

I could always get something later, back in the hotel, in the company of, I was thinking, decidedly more equitable minds.

"No" I answered.

"I'm ok for schnitzel right now".

He appeared to be having second thoughts then, and looked to all intents and purposes, to be amending his abominable artifice for an atomic Armageddon.

And then, in keeping with his propensity for circuitous incoherence, he asked me for my name.

I told him it to him so, after which he asked me what I was doing in Cologne.

And if somebody had walked up to me then, at that precise moment in time, and presented me with a box of semi-agitated and oxygen-deprived budgerigars, I quite honestly believe that a considerably greater degree of intelligible discourse would almost certainly have been contained within.

The gibberish remained at a consistently ridiculous level.

He spoke then of a piece that a journalist had written about him and an amusing little vignette that he'd thrown out there, during the course of their tête-à-tête.

"There'll be a sting in that tale!" he had intimated to the journalist at the time he said, to which they both, apparently, nearly wet themselves with their respective jollity and mirth.

I felt an urge to inform him, right at that moment, that if it was a career in comedy he was looking for, that based on his sartorial presentation today alone, he had already very much achieved his goal.

Given his constant jabbering however, I was unable - as indeed had been the case from the outset - to get my point across.

Besides all of that anyway, the 'conversation' – or lack thereof of any that was lucid - was not improving in any radical or perceivable way.

To the extent indeed that I felt compelled to pull the bollocks up on one or two of the issues that he'd brought to the fore, earlier in his rant.

Those carnivorous creatures from the future, for one.

I mean, what the fuck was all *that* horseshit about?

Before I got to that though, he came out of his babble-laden reverie for just a moment, to enquire of me as to what my own personal views were regarding Bono and *his* feelings as I myself surmised them to be, either positive or negative, as to the overall continuance of the human race.

To which, bearing in mind what I have just mentioned about those beasts from the future, I replied to the fucker as follows.

"Much as I do know Bono, Sting, vaguely" I stated, with no small degree of derision.

"And would be more than happy to give you my thoughts on whether his views regarding the planet are apocalyptic or otherwise, I have a decidedly more pressing question for you myself, which I'd very much like for you to answer - if you don't mind, that is. My question is thus."

At this point I paused for effect.

"What the fuck" I said, continuing.

"Can you tell me please, is a fucking Grizzywark?!"

And on this occasion, I *definitely* meant for it to, ahem, STING!

Rather than answer me however, he stood up instead with great haste, and made what appeared to be pretty implicit designs to depart.

Bizarrely also - as if his behaviour to date had not been bizarre enough - he gathered into his arms the earthenware jug and tumblers, both of them, which led to a spillage of liberal quantities of the apple wine contents of the aforementioned receptacles on to his general person.

He shuffled out of there then, like some sort of a deranged bag man, without so much as a 'Cheerio Johnny', or 'Thanks for looking fucking after me Johnny, in my hour of MENTALIST need!'

Nope.

Not a fucking dickey bird, the prick!

I had a *right* pain in my bollocks now.

There I was, alone in a strange northern European city, where surrounding me on all fronts were fuckers who to communicate, were required, it seemed to me, to release fuck knows how many pints of phlegm from their throats in order to just speak.

Dulcet tones they were not.

Guttural if anything.

I got to thinking then of my general predicament as it was at that moment.

Yes, I had been on a rollercoaster of a 'free for all' junket for the last 24 hours; that much was undeniable.

But did I actually *like* the people with whom I was associating?

Axl was ok, fair enough, but Bon Jovi was an undisputed gobshite and Sambora wasn't any better.

And as for Sting?

Well let's just say that I won't be rushing to be in his company again anytime soon.

It was Belinda however, who had pissed me off the most.

Notwithstanding her predisposition to want to fuck whomever or whatever lay in her path, I was annoyed with her more so, really, as a result of the fact that I was no longer at the top of her agenda.

If a person was famous in any way, or had rubbed off anybody even, that was famous, they were of far greater interest to her than I could ever have been, no matter what.

This innate shallowness of hers basically, was what I found to be so offensive.

I resolved so, at that very moment, to just leave them the fuck to it.

Paying the bill then - Sting had left me with *that* doozie as well - I left the stall/cafe type affair and headed back to the hotel.

The plan in my head was to check in with Marcus to see if he wanted to accompany me back to Dublin and then, whether he did or he didn't, to find a way to the airport in Cologne anyway, and see what standby Aer Fungus flights might be available to Dublin.

I'd have to ring the old man up beforehand though, to get him to put me on the list.

Arriving back to the hotel, I made my way across the foyer, and then up in the lift to the suite.

Rapping sharply on the door, I was relieved a some moments later to see my old pal Marcus standing there before me.

"It's all kicking off in here pal!" he said to me breathlessly.

I noticed then that he was dressed in nought but a bathroom towel.

"You can join in with us if you like?" he continued.

"Although I fancy that it will almost certainly modify our relationship somewhat for the worst going forward".

I followed him so, into a large bedroom at the far end of the suite, before doing an immediate about-turn and making my way back out.

I had seen enough you see, during my short few seconds within, to verify that this was not a scenario with which I would ever have any desire to become embroiled.

There, on actual display, were three phalluses, in a state of erect prominence, with the subsequent addition of Marcus's appendage rendering it a quartet.

Belinda was present also, in a state of complete undress, and finding somehow a way to make use of, one way or another, all of the members that were on display.

Suffice it to say that there was no personal 'orifice' on her part, that was not in some form of utilisation, gratuitous or otherwise.

Marcus was right.

It would tar our relationship irreversibly if I hung around.

He's a great pal of mine undeniably, but I draw the line at familiarising myself in any way, shape or form with his JT.

And besides, who wants to be in an environment where there are four other pricks on display, especially when at least two of them are connected in some way or other, to the ghastliness that is 'Bon Jovi'?

Not I.

And of course I'd be afraid that I'd like it too much as well.

The altogether hedonistic nature of the set-up also, was jarring with me.

As in, was there anything that these Rock Star DemiGod fuckers wouldn't do?

I'd been annoyed with their self-satisfying antics anyway before I had arrived back, but this really was the last straw.

I walked over so to a little incidental table that was nearby, upon which a phone was situated, and picked said handset up.

Calling 0 for reception, I asked the girl who answered for an overseas line.

A few seconds later, I was talking to the oul fella.

"Dad" I said.

"Ahh son, what's the story?" responded the familiar and friendly voice of the old dominant progenitor.

"The 'story' Father dearest" I answered drily.

"Is that I need you to call Aer Fungus as a matter of the most extreme urgency, to get me on a standby list for a flight from Cologne back to Dublin. Can you sort that shit out?"

"Game ball son" he answered calmly.

"I'll sort that 'shit' out. Leave it with me and I'll get on the case ASAP. Oh and by the way, did you hear about the concert?"

I had no idea what he was talking about, but would have to wait until some other time to hear about it, as he had already hung up.

"I'll call you back!" he had said in a panic, as only old people can panic about what is usually nothing at all.

"There's someone at the door!" he said, before presenting me with a dial tone.

As I said.

A panic about nothing all.

He didn't call me back also, which was even *more* annoying.

WHAT about the concert?

What concert?

It would have to wait.

I tried to call him back a couple of times after that but to no avail.

There was a constant engaged tone on every occasion, which meant, almost certainly, that he had found a way to incorrectly replace the receiver.

Call me unfair anyay, but old people are shite at fucking everything!

I mean once you get over 40, what is the point of even carrying on?

Anyway, I wasn't prepared to wait around for the old man to get his head out of his arse.

Assuming that he'd do the right thing and speak to whomever he needed to speak to at some point, eventually, I made my to the airport, having found out, just about, where it was from the barely competent and emphatically disinterested girl in reception.

Taking a bus there, with that mode of conveyance being the only mode of conveyance that I could now afford, I arrived there approximately one hour after I had set out.

Making my way to the appropriate Aer Fungus desk then, I enquired as to whether a certain disoriented and somewhat semi-senile individual that answered to the name of Thomas Fortune, had been in contact with anybody there, at any time in the near to recent past.

I held out little hope.

Surprisingly enough however, and very much against the run of the habits of an entire lifetime, the old bollocks HAD in fact been in contact, with everything now being, quite amazingly, all in order.

All that was required of me now, was to just hang around until a seat became available on the next plane back to the old sod - of which there were three departing that day so the odds were definitely in my favour - and then take up the offer of said seat if there were no other familial airline grifters ahead of me in the queue who were looking for a similar outcome.

It turned out that there were none anyway, fortuitously enough, so I was winging my way back to Baile Átha Cliath within less than the hour.

Nothing though, could have prepared me for what greeted me at the other end, after I made my way through the baggage reclaim area and onwards, through the double doors then that led directly into the arrivals hall.

Let's just say at this juncture - to give you a little clue - and indeed before I get into it in more detail later on - that the broadcaster Gay Byrne, on the whole, was not long after this point, looked upon very differently by the general proletariat and/or anybody else indeed that was familiar with him, or knew of him in any way.

From the moment after I jousted with him on national TV no more than 48 hours after I had arrived back into the country - if I can even refer to our one-sided exchange as such - his career, and everything that goes with it, went into an uncontrollable state of downward spiral and melee.

Which - as I am sure you agree - is no more than the condescending bollocks deserves.

Before all of that however, there was that *other* surprise that awaited me when I sauntered through.

But sure I'll tell you about that again in a minute.

CHAPTER 13

Dis kid is gas.

Fuckin' GAS!

He's owndly a'ter rippin' de bleedin' hoewel owra Burddin.

De poor fucker duzzen know wayer te be bleedin' lookin'!

Ha ha, dass bleedin' excellent!

Abou' bleedin' tiyam 'n all!

He's been a bollix for bleedin' ages Burddin, annee's owndly like, a bleedin' spanner!

Why duz everywan tink darrees so bleedin' grea'?

Colleh's alrigh' doe.

Ye know, darrould dear 'studio assistant' wan?

De wan dah 'Rowills i' der Colleh' as de Burddin prick is always sayin'.

She waz always nice te me in anyway, de odd tiyam darreye waz on de show.

I come back de odd tiyam as well, just te like, ye know, checkirrou'.

For de gas like, ye know?

Ders always somewan good on, an' de odd bleedin' gobshite as well.

Like dah Ustinov perrick.

Now der's a bollix dah loves de sowend of 'is owen voice.

Iss gas bein' dead in anyway.

Annis norras bad as ye migh' tink needor.

Ye can fly off te wherever ye want te fly off te whenever ye want, an' no-one knowez de fuck dah yiv even been dayer as well.

I do miss ridin' doe defo.

An' garglin'!

Ders no worries doe.

Dass de mayen ting.

All dah shite dah made ye run arowend like a blue-arsed feckin' fly wen ye worr aliaave?

Dass all gone.

Yorr juss happy all de tiyam an' ye get te see all de people dah ye wanna see darrar still aliaave, juss by imaginin' dem an' den yorr, like, ye know - juss dayar!

Irris hard doe wen der ravvin' a rough tiyam of i'.

Ders nu'in'dah ye can do abourrih, ye know?

Irrid defo be nice te be able te juss purran arm arowendem like, an' tell dem darris ok.

Ye can't doe, so ye juss have te gerronwirreh.

An' droppin in in mid-wank is no fun needor!

Seein' Scotty Gorham knocking' one off innis hotel rooyem is nawra prirry sigh' lads.

Nawra prirry sigh' arrall!

I'm juss tellin' yiz like.

Yiv nevvor seeyen me moowiv fuckin' faaster.

Bu' Burddin in anyway, de prick!

Embarrassin' me Ma dah tiyam on de show.

Dah waz annoyin'.

She's shy enough in anyway a' de best a tiyams wirrou' dah bleedin' spanner givin' 'er stick.

I nearly gevvim a straightnorr righ' der an' den meself, te like, sort de bollocks bleedin' ou'!

An' de gammy fuckin' head on 'im as well, wha'?

Hard te beleeyav darrees so confident 'n' all, wha' wirra gammy fuckin' head like darronim!

He star'ed wi' me den, in anyway, goin' on abou' me sui'.

Cream i' waz, which de prick said waz a nice contrast.

So irrowndly took 'im tirty bleedin' seconds te gerrin a dig abou' me bein' black!

I taw darrih lookt deadly meself in anyway - bu' shore dats needer heeyor nor dayor, wha'?

An' dennee he owndly starts shitin' on abou' de fact darreye bawwra gaff in bleedin' Howt'?

Like dat's any a his bleedin' business?!

An' anyway izzen dah wayer he bleedin' lives as well, de feckin' sap?

He's some fuckin' stockin' dah Burddin.

I told 'im in anyway dah dass wayer all de big knobs hang ou', ye know, which gorra good oul laugh owra de audience!

An' I meant bleedin' KNOBS as well - not darree bleedin' got dah doe, de dopey bollix!

An' dennee starts talkin' abou' de missus an' marriage, and why did I ge' married 'n all, wha' wi' me bein' a rock 'n roller 'n all dah, so I towelt 'im darrih waz te serrill dowen an' look a'ter me geddles an' be faithful te wan woman 'n all dah, bu' de bollocks only trea'ed me wi' like, bleedin' darrizhinn!

'Really?' he sez, wirris head off te de siyad like - de sanctimonious PERRICK!

And den one mower 'Really' for like, effect.

An' den a bleedin' nudder!

If I haddena been on de box in anyway, or de oul one haddena been dayer in de audience, I'd a bleedin' deckt de prick!

Burreye kinda juss lerrih go, ye know?

I waz brawrup dah way in anyway by de grandparents.

Dey worr bleedin deadly dey wayer, 'n' lookt a'ter me brilliant.

De Ma cudden doowih ye see, wha' wi' her bein' in work 'n' all, so she brough' me back from England te her folks, for dem ta look a'ter me while she waz away 'n' dah.

Annih waz bleedin' grea'!

I bleedin' lovt Crumlin back in de day, an' even dow I stood ou' like a sower bleedin' tumb, dah waz cool as well.

De geddles worr always mower interestet in me as well, tinkin' darraye had a bigger dick dan alla de resta de lads!

Which a course I bleedin' did!

I'll fly over heeryor in anyway, te de udder side a de studio, te gerra berrer look a' de kid.

Burddin looks MAJOR uncomfortabiddle now, de bleedin' sap!

An' looka de stayrovvis bleedin' jackeh!

Sack yorr bleedin' wardrobe organiser chief - der makin' ye look fuckin' stew-peh.

So dennee gawrawnta fame an' dah, so I juss toweld 'im darrawl dose bollixes dah give owra bowrih are talkin' troo der bleedin' hoewels.

Alldoe I didden say 'bleedin' hoewels' a course.

De Ma waz dayer, so I had te show a lirrel birra respect 'n' dah, ye know?

I toweld 'im so, darrye I juss bleedin' went forrih in anyway - hook, liyen an' bleedin' sinkor!

An' why de fuck would I norras well?

A young gobshite from Dubbillin wi' people givin' me free gargle an' women trowin' der selves at me 'n' all sorts?

Bring i' bleedin' on lads I waz sayin'!

Rock 'n' Rowell, ye know?

So anyways, I juss hover arowend now, an' look a' tings.

Dass de deal wi' dis bein' dead shite.

Ye juss do worrever de fuck ye like, an' buzz off te wherever de fuck ye want te as well.

Ye rallready know dah tings are gonna happen too, so ye can be like, dayer befower dey do like, ye know?

Dass how I knew dah dis Johnny kid waz gonna be a star even befower 'ee noowih 'imself.

When yorr dead ye can see de hoewel lot, ye know?

Everytin' da went befower an' everytin' dass gonna happen a'ter too, like.

Iss bleedin' weird too knowin' dah de wordeld is gonna rend in 2051– bu' sure der ye bleedin' go, wha'?

Dah mad bastard Sting is gonna start Armageddon on his 100th birthday!

Don't ask how, he juss bleedin' duzz.

De feckin' French president gives him de bleedin' cowwds!

Ye sorrah ge' useta knowin' shite like dah in anyway.

I tell ye wha' doe, snuffin' it young wazza major bleedin' surpriyez.

I BIG TIME taw darreye waz invincible.

Darreye'd go wan for rever, ye know?

Bu' de 'Great Gig in de Sky' ain't tree bad lads.

As de Floyed say.

'I am NOT frightened of dyin'.

'Any time will do.'

Achally I waz fuckin' brickin' i'!

Diddin wanna leeyev de geddles, ye know?

But ye reap watch ye sow wha'?

Nobody te blame forrih bu' me bleedin' sellef.

Feckin' gobshite!

I waz tinkin' back den te when I waz youngar, ye know, a teenager 'n dah, dossin' on a beach dowen in Tramower.

Me an' a few a de lads from Crumlin mitchin' i' for de day, 'n' jumpin' a train dowen der for de laugh.

Ye know worreye meeyen?

One a de lads in anyway - I can't remember which wan - achally brough' jam sambos an' a big borril a TK Oddenge, so fair fucks te him like, whoever de fuck i' waz.

Myra beeyen Larry Duffy now darreye come te tink abowreh.

He waz a daycent skin, Larry.

Not a hundreh per cent shooer darrih waz him doe.

It myra been some udder bollix.

An' den some creamers dayor gave us a lend an ol' nag, so we went racin' up an' down de beach on de poor owel ting, usin' a frayed blue fishin' rope for like, reyans.

De poor ol' bollocks, he musta nearly diyed dayer an' den from exhaustion ableedinlowen!

I'd say 'ee waz turdint in te glue in anyway, defo, not long a'ter dah.

An' den de creamers triyed te charge us twenty notes for usin' de horse, so we told 'em te fuck off owrovih a course.

We went toe te toe wi' dem den, kickin' de shite owrov each udder for twenty minutes a' leeyest.

No weppins doe.

We fough' fayer back in dowez dayez.

Digs 'n' boots waz all - no kniyevs 'r ant'in'.

We won in anyway, so headed off te Wawrerford for gargle, wi' some odds an' a few dollars dah we took offa de nackers as well.

Some boozer callt 'Philly Grimes' i' waz - nayemed a'ter some famous bog hockey bloke' from a few yeeyors befower.

We gargled dayer all day in anyway, and playet poowil, bafower gerrin' de last train owra dayer arrabou' 10 a clock, an' sleepin' all de way back den te Hueston.

I waz only tinkina darrinanyway, as I'll nevvor ge' te spend any mower days on de beach, 'specially not wi' de geddles.

Bu' fuck irrinanyway wha'?

Ders fuck all darreye can do abourrih now.

Irriz weird dyin' doe.

Ye expect i' te happen in a bed like, wen yorr in yorr bleedin' ayries, ye know?

Me Granda brang me to a hospital once in anyway, wen I waz a nipper, to see some relation o' his - an uncle I tink - an' de poor oul bollox waz like, a sack o' bleedin' bowens in de bed, ye know?

He cudden even say nu'hin' annee waz so feckin' weak dah me Granda had te feed 'im 'is dinner wirra spoon 'n' 'is warrer too troo a bleedin' straw.

I remembor 'is arms reachin' out dayer in anyway, tryin' ta sirrup 'n dah, an' I'm not bleedin' jokin' yiz, i' put de heart bleedin' crossways on me.

His pleadin' skinny arms, barely held owrabove 'im 'n out tawards me - 'Take me away from this son pleeyez' I waz imaginin' 'im sayin'.

'I'm bleedin' beggin' ye son. I'm in a livin' fuckin' hell heeyor!'

Not de best way te go alrigh' burreye still taw dah darrid be me all de sayem.

Dyin' old in some bed somewayer, ye know?

Imagine me surpriyez den wen I woke up a' tirty six yeeyors of ayege, an' realiyezed darrye waz bleedin' dead?

As dah Peerer Hamill bloke owra 'Van der Graaf Generator' useta say, wha'?

No warnin' or bleedin' nuthin' needor.

Juss fuckin' owra heeyor.

Alldoe probably berrer dan dah poor oul bollox in de bed, wha'?

I always remembert his feeryor too.

He waz fuckin' brickin' i' - ye could see irrinis eyeyez.

Me Granda' waz feckin' gas too a'ter, like, on de way ou'.

"If I ever get to be like that, young Philip" he said te me as we marched owra der with his giant hand on me shoulder, as we pusht troo de doors o' de hospital an' back owrinta civilization.

"Just find a gun from fucking somewhere son, and shoot me in the back of the fucking head!"

Me ol' Granda waz bleedin' deadly he waz!

Anudder gas ting abou' bein' dead as well, is dah ye can get te see insiyad people's miyends.

Not der brayens or de blood an' guts parrovvih or ant'in like dah – no bu' ye rachally get te tink worrudder people are tinkin' wen der tinkinnih der selves.

Like now for eggzample wi' Burddin heeyor.

He's absaloo'ly bleedin' bullin' i wi' de kid now, who's still takin' im apart like a bleedin' good ting - burree can't do fuck all abourrih ye see, azzee has te remayen all professional-like an' above boward.

In reality doe, inniz head - an' I know coz I can bleedin' see i' - he'd much rahder give' de kid a kick in de bollix dan be nice to 'im!

"Let's talk to de mammy so" he said te me, back den befower.

De bleedin' spanner.

As iffee like, ye know, had knowen 'er all 'is bleedin' liyeff.

"I've never met the mammy" he even sayez.

As if she walks in de circles dah you bleedin' walk in pal?

I don't bleedin' tink so Burrdin!

An' I'm scarleh forrur as well, me poor oul Ma.

She duzzen know wayer te bleedin' look!

And dennee goes on abou' me rock 'n' rowell wayez 'n' all de ridin' 'n' dah, as if dat's a proper conversation te be havin' wi' somewan's oul' one.

Who duzzee tink 'ee bleedin' is?

De Ma wants de grouwend te open up beforerurr in anyway, she's darrembarrest.

Bu' de bollix juss carries on in anyway.

Fair play to 'er doe, she hoewelds her owen grand so she does.

One worerd answers, ye know?

Monasyllabic like.

She knowwiz darrees a bleedin' gobshite alrigh'.

She waz well useda dem by den I suppowez, havin' had te live dah long in bleedin' England 'n' all.

"Where's the house, it's on the main road, is it?" he's owndly a'ter askin' 'er.

'None o' yorr bleedin' business pal' I'm tinkin' bu' de Ma is noddin' arrim as if te say yeah.

'For fuck sake!' I'm tinkin'.

'Every bleedin' scrote in Dublin'll be out der now temorrah, te check out de pad'.

"What is your reaction to the sort of carry on that he gets up to?" de bollocks gowez on even mower.

I mean wha' sorra question is bleedin' dah?

She's embarrest enough already, annees only a'ter makin' er even mower flustorred askin' 'er dah.

In fairness te de oul wan doe, she playez dumb an' asks him, like, ye know, wha' 'carry on' duzzee meeyen.

De fucker backtracks den, an' pretenz darree waz owndly takin' abou' me songs.

He's some bleedin' PERRICK dah Burddin.

"I've always enjoyed his music" sez de Ma.

Fair fucks to 'er, dass purrim inniz bleedin' playess!

"And you're very close together, the two of you" he rabbits on.

Ahh no Burddin, we bleedin' hay reach udder!

Dat's why werron de bleedin' show tagedder.

Ye big fuckin' stockin' o' shite!

"Oh we're, two great friends", answers de Ma, all jovial like ye might tink, if ye didden knower darris.

Burrye can tell dah she'd much rahdder be givin' 'im a kick in de old liathroidi if she'd half de chance like, an' der waz like, ye know, no-wan lookin' on.

"Are ye really keen on de mammy?" de prick goes on den, te me.

Ahh no Burrdin, I bleedin' hayror like I waz sayin' der befower.

Dass why I ast her te come on te de show wi' me, ye bleedin' plank!

"Ahh yeah. I love her very much" I say te de fucker, juss te shurrim de fuck up!

I' duzzen work doe.

"And do you see quite a lot of each other, you're running up and down to each other?" he shites on.

No' really Burddin - we live a few hundred meerurs away from each udder, bu' we don't keep in contact arall.

"Ahh yeah, she duzz all de babysittin'" I say te de bollocks, juss te shurrem up again.

Dah duzzen work eeddor!

He talks abou' America den and de Ma comin' wi' me an' all, burreye kinda switch off den he's annoyin' me dah much.

I mean if evvor a prick needet a slap for bein' such a bleedin' gobshite, den its dis bleedin' prick, bleedin' now!

De Ma is keepin' i' tagedder doe still, fair play to 'er.

An dennee gets on te me powetry as if de prick has ever even seeyen a dactyl or a bleedin' caesura in his life.

(Der powetry terms by de way, in case yiz wor wondrin')

Burriss de condescendin' way darree goes on abourrih as well, as if, ye know, if i' waz me dah rowrih i' muss be bleedin' shite!

An' what's he evvor bleedin' done as well, bar bein' a PERRICK every tiyam darree opens 'is bleedin' mout'!

It's harder dan i' looks doe, wri'in' daycent powetry.

An' I'm norras hard as I look needor.

Me Ma calls me a big pussy ca'!

I useta love me powetry doe.

Sittin' der in a dark rooyem tinkin' abou' tings.

I' waz bleedin' deadly achally - an' denneye useta star' tinkin' abow RALL sortsa stuff.

'600 unknown heroes, killed like sleepin' buffalo'.

Dah juss cem te me a'ter I waz eatin' pizza in dis WELL bleedin' dodge Italian kip der in Milan, righ' rafter a gig we did dayer, a few yeeyors back.

De Mozzarella, ye know?

Dass worrinspieord me.

Deep, wha'?

A bleedin' deadly liyen darriz.

Burriwaz a few weeks ago in anyway, wen I saw de kid first.

I glided on dowen te Slane te see 'Guns 'n' Roses' who worr playin' dayer - ye probably remembor?

Dass anudder ting abou' bein dead - ye can still keep up de date wirrall de new bands darrar comin' ou'.

An' dey worr bleedin' deadly as well, aspecially de guitar playor - some bloke in a black ha' callt Slash.

De ginger singer doe, waz weardin' a skirt, so dah waz well suss.

Ledder striyads are yorr owndly man pal!

Dey finisht up in anyway, so I waz juss floatin' arowand backstage heeyor an' dayer seein' wha' waz goin' on.

A few ol' heads were dayer darreye knew from befower, so i' waz gas te see wha' dey worr doin' an' how dey worr gerrin' on.

Gazza waz dayer a course, an' dah bleedin' tick Bono, alldoe I don't know warree waz doin' dayer – i' waz a merril crowad, ye know?

He'd go te de openin' of a bleedin' envelope doe, dah bollix.

An' himself an' Burddin gerron like a house on bleedin' fiyor as well, sowee MUST be a bleedin' prick!

I never knew 'im dah much doe meself wen I waz aliaave, bu' Geldof towelt me once dah de spanner waz te be avoidet like de bleedin' playegg.

So whenever I sawrim arrantin arrall, I juss walkt away in de opposite direction.

Dey playt 'Massacre' in anyway.

Guns 'n' Roses darriz, annih waz bleedin' massive!

Not wantin' te blow me own trumpeh or an'tin bu' de lyrics on dah are de bleedin' biz!

Shore how could dey no' be in anyway?

I'm Phil bleedin' Lynott for Jaysus sake!

An' de kid took over halfa de vocals as well, annee waz bleedin' deadly!

'Massacre' is de wan wi' de buffalos – ye know, darrye waz talkin' abou' dayer rearlior on, darreye I wrote dayor in Milan.

Probably aar best numbar tibbee honest, alldoe most people say 'Still in Love with You' or 'Don't Believe a Word' which are both grea', don't ge' me wrong; bu' 'Massacre' is me owen fayvrih meself.

We recordet darrin England in 1976 I remembor, in some studio callt Rampart in London; owwind by De Who I tink i' waz.

'Johnny the Fox' waz de name a de album in anyway, anniwaz bleedin' deadly!

Robbo waz annoyin' me at de tiyam doe, as I had a woejious dose on me wen we weyar like, layin' dowen de tracks.

Which achally turnt ou' te be jaysus Hepatyris, would ye believe dah lads?

Too much gargle said de doctor – which waz fayer enough, as I waz bleedin' lashin' irrin te me a' de tiyam.

Me ol' pal Phil Collins - ye know, de Genesis drummor? - well he waz dayer for a few dayez as well, just te like say hello 'n dah, but dah pissed Brian off big tiyam as well, as he's de drummer, so' like, 'dass bleedin' dah' waz de way he sawrih.

He owndly wantet wan drummer in de studio ye see, so I tink he felt threatent or sometin' maybe, I doe know.

Phil playet percussion on wan or two a de songs in anyway, which defo pissed Brian off even mower.

All in all so i' waz a bleedin' shite atmosfearyor in de studio.

Iss gas so den darriz waz such a grea' bleedin' recordt!

Bu' back te Slane in anyway.

D'ye know wen ye see somewan on de stayedge an'ye juss know dah der like, destint te be a star?

Like dey bleedin owen de place, ye know?

Well dassworriwaz like wi' dis young Johnny Freak Show youngfella in anyway, wennee waz singin'.

He waz bleedin' brillant an'like, had de audience eerin owra de palm ovvis hand.

I' waz gas doe as well, coz dah Bono bollocks kep' comin' back to gerrinvolved, bu' de crowet - a bleedin' merril crowet as I waz sayin' dayer bafower - worr givin' de short-arsed bollocks unmerciful stick!

De band worr doin' 'Gimme Shelter' den in anyway - de Stowens song, ye know - wi' de kid an' de Guns 'n' Roses singer doin' a grea' job, I have te admirreh.

Bono owndly decideh den doe te do abirra crowet surfin' de bleedin' spanner, alldoe I tink dah de ginger singer myra pusht 'im in!

De crowet den in anyway, fair play te dem, carreed 'im all de way ou' ti de back a de feeyeld, an' gave 'im a kick in de arse den ou' de bleedin' dower wen der waz no mower people dayer te carry 'im along.

Iwwaz a bleedin' deadly buzz watchin' all dah, anneye could juss flowrallong above dem all as well, as iwwaz all goin' on!

He shoulda knowen berrer in anyway, turnin' up arra merril concert an' expectin' tegerrany joy ourrov a crowet like dah.

Anyways, I bleedin' love Dublin me.

I waz owndly sayin' dah te Burddin on de show as well.

I useta ge' fierce homesick, 'specially if I waz away for like, ages 'n' dah.

Any mower dan a mont or two an' I'd be goin' up de bleedin' walls!

Aspecially if I waz in England, wer dey normally trea' de Irish like bleedin' shite.

I waz gerrin' a taxi achally, from de East End o' London once, a yeeyor or two back owndly, on me way in te de cirree for a programme on de Beeb.

It waz owndly gas den worrye saw ourra de bleedin' winda!

Even Sykesy fowendih funny, an' back in doze dayez Sykesy fowend fuck all funny.

"Fuck me man!" sezzee a' de tiyam.

"You're a dog right? Like, I've seen you with the ladies man, so like, I fucking KNOW that you're a fucking dog!"

He wazzint wrong needor.

I defo always gave i' large wenever I waz ou' wi' de burds.

I'd no idea warree waz bangin' on abou' doe, untillee pointet owra siyen dah waz hangin' in a winda o' some guest house as we worr drivin' past.

Somewayer on de Bermondsey Rowed I tink i'waz.

I remembar de siyen well enough in anyway, as i' knockt me for six big tiyam wen I sawrih dayer.

'No Dogs, No Blacks, No Irish' righ' dayer in big black lerrers, scrawlt wirra a marker on browen cardbowward by some English prick wirran evil heart.

I copped wha' Sykesy waz goin' on abou' den.

"Shit man" he went on.

"Like, you're unwelcome in every way fucking possible! As in, like, you're ticking every box dude!"

He waz fuckin' right too.

Even de dogs were gerrin higher billin' dan me heeyor!

But shore so fuckin' wha', I waz tinkin'?

I waz fuckin' rollin' innih a' de tiyam, so wha' de fuck did I cayor?

I'm wan stewpeh fucker doe a' de sayem tiyam.

I meeyan dyin' is grand an' all, an' norreeven as bad as ye might tink.

Bu' livin'?

Fuck me lads, nuthin' bates fuckin' livin'!

I waz owndly talkin' te Bruce Springsteen der befower in anyway at some party somewayer, right a'ter he got faymis heeyor in Yoorip.

He waz faymis in de states for way longer dan dah doe, like a good bi' befower darralbum 'Born in the USA'.

He waz tellin' me in anyway abou' wennee waz livin' in a tree wirra loada pals on de west coast, befower he waz even dah well knowen.

Dis waz wen dey had no dollars arrall between anyadem an' were like, lookin' for gigs juss like annee udder band ou' dayer doin' de sayem ting.

Dey worr stayin' way ourrov LA in anyway he said, somewayer on de foothills ovva big mountain - 'Big Sur' I tink he calltih?

Dis pal darree waz stayin' wi' in anyway, juss built a gaff arowand de trunk ovva mad lookin' owelt giant tree, an' dah waz fuckin' dah!

Dats wayer de bollocks decideh te live, juss like dah, off de cuff like, as if iwwaz de most normal ting in de wordeld for him te do!

He soundet like a righ' bleedin' mad bastard te me!

Springsteen waz stayin' wirrim in anyway for a wyell, and on de first mornin' a'ter himself an' de udder lads arriyaved, he gorrup before anyone else, te like, ye know, go for a walk an' gerra birra fresh ayor.

He walkt ourra de front door in anyway he towelt me, an' saw dis big massive udder tree, righ' in front a him like - like de wan dah dey worr livin' in owndly bigger - wirrall deese mad colourt flowers all overrih everywayer, all over de branches and de trunk 'n' all.

He walkt towards irrin anyway, te have a closer look, burrih turnt ou' dah dey werrent flowerz arrall burachally tousands a burrerflies instead dah worr juss havin' a birrov a rest like, on de tree.

Wen dey saw Brucie comin' over tewards dem in anyway, dey just flew off de tree an' fecked off in te de sky, de hoewel lorrovem, somewayer bleedin' else.

Now dat's fuckin' livin' lads.

Imagine seein' dah?

I taw iwwaz class in anyway.

Murmurations are grea' as well, are int dey - ye know wen a loada starlings ge' tegeddar an' do dah mad bleedin' dance in de ayor, dah looks like waves or a kaleidoscope kinda ting up in de sky?

Mad how dey dowent fly inte each udder as well issineh?

Somewan towelt me dah dass wayer sowels end up eventually, so I'm hopin' dah der righ'.

I'd love te gerrinvolved in some'in' like dah, an' I'm gerrin plenty o' practice in as well, wha' wirrall me floatin' arowend heeyor an' dayor over de last lirrel wyell.

I mean when ye see a ting like a murmuration, ye have te take a step back an' say te yorrself dah der has te be a God like, ye know?

Burrin case yizzer wondrin' - der bleedin' izzint righ'!?

I meeyan I'm dead an' I've never even merrim!

Iss all a big con in anyway lads, juss te get yorr bleedin' dollars!

Anyways so I waz some dozy bollix givin' all DARRUP, wha'?

An' me geddles as well?

Burreye can do fuck all abourrih now, so ders no point in complainin'.

I'll meet dem again defo somewayer else dowen de liyan.

Back te de present in anyway, wi' Burddin an' de kid.

Burddin is lookin' big time uncomfortabiddle now, even mower dan befower.

Squirmin' arowand innis seat kinda ting, an' tryin' te loosen up de oweld collar.

De kid has callt 'im ou' on lowidza tings.

All o' de tings darrees said owver de yeeyors mainly, includin' howee waz talkin' ti me oul Ma like I waz tellin' yiz der befower.

'Fair play te ye pal' I'm tinkin'.

Ye defo have Burddin's fuckin' number!

Dis kid is bang on.

De owndly surpriyez achally, now darrye come te tink abourrih, is dah no fucker has said dis shite te Burrdin befower.

Ye know, forrawla de stupi' bleedin' tings darrees said in de past?

It's some stick darrees gerrin' from de kid in anyway, annee can't handle irrarall.

"De ye know wha' actually Byrne?" sez de kid now befower standin' up.

I tink he's had enough.

"You're some cunt!" sezzee.

Ders a sharp intake a breath from de audience den a'ter darrowl chestnu'!

'Cunt' is norra word dats yewezzed much on nashnal telly in Ireland.

"And if there was a shortage of cunts as well" de kid goes on.

"For whatever reason......you'd be TWO fucking cunts!"

Class.

Fuckin' class.

Burddin duzzen know wayer te bleedin' look.

So de Johnny kid heads over te him den an' owndly fucks a glass o' warrer all over de poor gobshite's head.

"THAT'S FOR ALL THE POOR FUCKERS 'TO WHOM' YOU'VE BEEN A BOLLOCKS OVER THE YEARS BYRNE!" he shouts den righ' in te Burddin's face.

"AND IT'S LUCKY FOR YOU THAT YOU'RE SITTING DOWN AS WELL, YE PRICK" he goes on.

"OTHERWISE YOU'D BE GETTIN' A SWIFT KICK INTO THE TOWN HALLS AS WELL!"

An' dennee juss fucks de glass on de flowar and turns te face ou' te de audience, raisin' 'is arms up den as if te say, 'Well what de fuck else were yiz expectin' me to do?!'

He's defo not surpriyezed by de positive reaction as well bu'.

Anneez like, ye know, defiant a' de sayem tiyam - de ye know worrye meeyen?

As in, fayer enough, yiz are happy darrye gave Burddin a soakin' burrye wudden givin a bollix eedor way wedder yiz liked irror no'.

I like dis young fella.

He has balls, ye know?

I'm leavin' now in anyway now dah de fun 'n' games is ohvor.

I want te check in on de oul one befower I head back in te town for some barrel o' de banz tingamajig darrye check ou' every mont' in McGonagles der on South Anne Street.

I'll be keepin' an eye for dis Johnny kid doe in de fewchar.

He's defo destint for grea' bleedin' tings!

CHAPTER 14

Do you remember that feeling of coming through the double doors in 'Arrivals' at Dublin Airport and watching out for a family member or friend that might be stationed there, perhaps, to welcome you home?

Even though in your heart of hearts you were sure, almost certainly, that there was be nobody there to greet you on the other side?

I do.

That prospect anyway, after recent events, was no longer on the cards for my good self.

And all as a result of my cameo appearance at Slane with Axl Rose just a couple of weeks before.

It turned out anyway that I had gone down rather well with the travelling proletariat on the fateful day in question, to the extent that when I came through the aforementioned double doors, after my ill-fated and supremely irritating sojourn to Cologne, the reception that awaited me was unexpected in the extreme.

The masses had amassed.

No sooner had I wandered aimlessly through the exit in question, with my earphones in and a vaguely unoptimistic eye out for the individual in question that as I mentioned before, would almost certainly not be there, a veritable throng of people that I'd never met before in my life, burst forth in great haste in my general direction.

And although they all seemed positive enough, and had nothing but my general well-being and best interests I am sure at heart, it didn't take away from the fact even so, that it was one hell of a shock to the system when said shit went down when it did.

Descending upon me like biblical locusts, with additionally no end to the mindless chatter and general gibberish that was accompanying their unwanted advances, I was, at that moment, fearful for my life.

"Johnny, we love you dude, you magnificent freak!" shrieked a pasty looking girl who was positioned directly before me.

And I don't mean to be *too* harsh here, but she definitely bore an uncanny resemblance to a potato.

Others there just drooled and pawed at me as I made efforts to push way through.

"You're the new Bono dude!" said some gormless fucker behind me as well; to which when I heard said utterances, I turned to from where I believed they had emanated, to administer to the utterer of same, a straightener of an unequivocally disciplined variety.

Sadly however, my haymaker did not land.

Before retribution could be meted out for such an unforgivably 'off the mark' correlation, a strong arm from where I did not know at the time, grabbed me by the wrist and pulled me forcibly away in the opposite direction.

Swatting all-comers away nonchalantly with the ease and panache of a POTUS minder, the masses within nanoseconds were swept aside.

They never stood a chance really, given the dudes no nonsense efficiency, to the extent that no more than sixty seconds later, if that even, having ducked through various passages here and pushed through any number of surreptitious and otherwise inconspicuous doors there, I was deposited gingerly into the back of a sleek and frankly *waay* too large 7 series BMW, with the disappointed and badly dissipated throng very soon a mere series of dots in the rear view mirror of our shiny charabanc.

The handler sped away, whilst I familiarised myself concurrently with my luxurious new surroundings in the back.

A figure to my left then - hitherto unnoticed what with all of the recent kerfuffle and commotion – enigmatically, from under a white fedora, and through his glistening teeth and excessively long Cuban cigar, made his presence to me known.

"Sup kid?" he whispered softly, smiling at me genially as he transferred the cigar to between his digits, before holding out his other hand to be shaken.

I took it so and shook it, before waiting for him to go on.

I recognised him from somewhere, definitely; but was fucked if I knew from where.

It wasn't as if he looked like a rock star or anything.

He had a distinctly ordinary demeanour about him if anything, despite the hat and cigar; like an accountant or an undertaker perhaps; decidedly nonde-script clothes and an unassuming disposition to match.

Nothing though - when I eventually cottoned on to who he was a few minutes later - could have been further from the truth.

Although when I consider now his involvement in what must surely be regarded as an annihilation of music on THE most persistently consistent basis that has actually ever come to pass (you'll get it when I tell you who he is), perhaps the second profession that I mentioned there before, vis-à-vis the ultimate expiration of the corporeal form and subsequent 'dressing up' of same then to render said form ostensibly and superficially 'presentable', wasn't *that* far off the mark.

"You get used to it" he went on.

"One way or another. The 'intrusiveness', you know? If I can call it that? It becomes manageable. Although from time to time kid, I'm not going to lie to you, it *is* a struggle. Make no mistake about that".

Where did I know him from?

His face looked so familiar.

"Like for example" he continued.

"When they want to know your shit. Seriously kid. No shit. As in, you know - your *actual* shit? The colour of it, its consistency, its various constituents etc., whatever they might be, how regularly indeed, also, that you actually *emit* your shit. I kid you not, kid. That, in this day and age, is what counts for a scoop. If they could get away with installing cameras up your arse in fact, they'd do it in a fucking heartbeat!"

He was quite animated now, the dude; with the idea of people investigating the general composition of his excretions vexing him in a not inconsiderable way.

I came to the conclusion so, after listening to him rabbiting on about the curious (considering the fact that we had just met) subject of his bowel moments and subsequent potential journalistic investigation of same, that there was a very strong likelihood that he might continue in this vein for actual ever.

I needed to take the bull by the horns so, and stop him in his tracks post-haste, as a matter of the most extreme exigency.

"Nice to hear that dude. NOT!" I indicated to him with fervour.

He looked a tad taken aback; as in, by the look on his face, he was not used to people reacting to his musings as I had myself just then.

But fuck that!

I wasn't going to putting up with any fucker's shit (literally) just because he believed that that was how he should be treated as a result of his apparent eminence?

If there's one thing in my book in fact, that's more detestable than any other trait that a person can display, its sycophancy.

Get to know a person first I say, and then, if you like them, fine - be their pal if you want to be their pal.

Not before that though.

What if they end up being a dick?

You'll look like a right fucking bell end then yourself, when everybody realises that your famous mate is a twat!

So I gave it to him from the hip.

"The nuances of your digestive system dude" I opened.

"Are not essential material for our exchange. Regardless of the fact that you seem to be of the view that information of this nature is ok for public consumption. I can tell you right here and now however, as a reasonable judge I believe of what is right and what is wrong, that it is not. I will be happy to inform you in the future however of the next time that I am in your company and a desire comes over me to know and understand further the general make up of your poo. In the words of my old English teacher in fact, O'Rahilly; a lady who was never afraid to call a spade a spade, particularly when her heart was filled with trepidation amid choppy academic waters that were required to be negotiated with no small degree of guile or skill...

'*Who's the wanker in the corner with the stupid fucking hat on, spouting what can only be described as mindless drivel. Discuss.*'"

And I meant it to sting.

And then it came to me who he was, and it all made sense.

As in, that is - why the dude was such an insufferable fucking arse!

Paul McfrickingGuinness!

You know - U2's manager?

It was no wonder so - as I was saying there before - that he was such a fucking dick.

I mean how could anybody hang around with those bozos for any significant length of time and not have such damnable exposure affect them in anything but a profoundly negative way?

Surely their dickheadedness had to rub off in some capacity or other, right?

I wondered what he wanted from me.

"Look kid, let's cut to the chase" he put forth, ignoring my riposte and sitting forward in his seat; all business-like now, and ready to move on to the next phase of our engagement.

"You're the flavour of the month now, ok, whether you like it or not. Your life from this moment on will never be the same".

Once again, I wondered what he wanted from me, but was starting to guess what it might be.

I had a fairly strong inclination, having heard and considered his opening gambit, that he had a burning desire to be my manager.

My appearance at Slane had obviously gone down very well and grown legs.

So THAT'S what the oul fella had meant about the 'concert' when I'd phoned him that time from the airport in Cologne.

My rising star must have made it to the 6 o'clock news.

"You're gonna need help kid" McGuinness continued.

"A lotta help; and I'm the man to have in your corner at a time like this. I have a proven track record, as I'm sure you know, and can get things done. For a small and relatively nominal fee, I propose to become your manager. What say you to that so, young man?"

I had guessed right.

He *did* want to become my manager.

And although that was fine and dandy, and a good idea perhaps, I harboured, instinctively, a strong degree of initial reluctance to accept; which was mainly as a result of the company that he kept.

That is, the one *other* heinous act that I knew to be in his stable.

I was certain also that if you were to take the two words 'small' and 'nominal'; as in the two adjectives that he had utilised to describe the fee for his services; and replaced them with two of the most diametrically opposed antonyms that you can glean from any reputable thesaurus, that these two *new* words would almost certainly represent a demonstrably more honest appraisal of what his *actual* fee would represent, when all of the ledgers were reconciled and we were perusing what was in the coffers at the end of a given financial year.

Regardless of his fees though, exorbitant or otherwise, he *did* have a point.

As in, if the debacle at the airport was anything to go by, I'd be requiring assistance from somewhere, sharpish; and ideally from professionals in the game that were specialists in their field.

I had initial misgivings of course, given - as I have alluded to already - his proven track record of associating, publicly, with known bollixes.

Despite this undeniable truism however, it was important for me to consider, when I reviewed the whole shebang more seriously, that he might very possibly have been carrying on with said association as an outcome of a previously agreed and therefore unavoidable professional arrangement that was already in place, and that his subsequent affinity with said bollixes was as a result merely of contractual obligation.

Not to put too fine a point on it so, I was considering the option of giving him the benefit of the doubt.

He elaborated further then, so I decided to allow him to proceed without interruption.

"This debacle so, young Johnny, at the airport".

He knew my name.

That surprised me a little, I have to be honest.

It must have been from off the news.

"That now, is your life" he continued.

"It is however, manageable. Two handlers are a minimum requirement first of all, to sweep any areas around establishments and venues and such before you arrive. The same thing also, of course, must be repeated before you depart. It will be beholden upon said handlers additionally to shield you from the great unwashed at all times, and to ensure, basically, that there's never a situation that comes to pass where their greasy mitts are pawing all over you in any, way shape or form. Additionally - and David Bowie will verify this for you if you ask him -

creating a furore around 'a star' who isn't in fact 'a star' *quite* yet, is what ultimately gets you to the place you want to be. Cordoning off areas in hotels so - in addition to any public events that you might be attending - and employing handlers to hold people back as an apparent 'star' - in this case you - comes floating through a busy hotel foyer or what not, is an essential part of the strategy in this early stage of your metamorphosis from standard bozo to bona fide Rock Star DemiGod. Flamboyant dress also on your part and a bizarrely put together entourage as well, will help you immeasurably. Tony DeFries, Bowie's manager in the 1970's, was a master of this approach, and you can see, quite obviously, that the results were spectacular. When Bowie came to the US in 1972 he was a virtual unknown, but by the time he left in 1973, no more than six months after his initial arrival, he was the hottest topic on everybody's lips. It was the best marketing coup that anyone had seen in popular music since the Beatles had done the exact same thing, just ten years before, in the exact same place. Nobody, and I mean NOBODY, has been able to repeat anything even remotely close to it since. Not even U2, with their rooftop stint for that opener off 'The Joshua Tree'. Anyway, this is where I come in, young Johnny. So waddya say? Are you prepared to dance with the devil?"

I liked what I was hearing.

As in, if I could keep individuals like that pasty potato-headed girl at the airport away from me, and that this was the course of action that I needed to take to ensure that that would be the case, then surely it would be money well-spent.

Talking of money, he moved on next to the vulgar subject in question.

"Let's talk about money" he said, with a hungry look in his eye.

"I will manage all of your affairs" he went on salaciously - clearly delighted to have moved on to a theme for which he held great esteem.

"Aside from the recording aspect of your contract - which will, of course, be a separate arrangement between you and the record company, whichever one we end up going with - the fee for my services will be 20% of all of your earnings plus expenses. This is a fair percentage, market-wise, for the work that I do, but do please feel free to check that out with your own legal representatives if you so desire. I can assure you however, that it is fair"

It didn't seem overly onerous I was thinking at the time, so once again I allowed him to carry on.

"First things first though son" he proceeded, in a considerably more animated fashion than before, as he swivelled himself around in his seat to face me.

He undid his seatbelt then also, and slid across the sleek cream leather back seat of the saloon, until at some point not long after that his pockmarked and wizened looking visage was no more than an inch or two away from my own.

I could smell his rancid breath as he spoke, all whiskyish and garlicky and

'Shanahan's on the Green', in addition to being accompanied by a faintest spray of snow white spittle as he spoke and his excitement intensified, with the gathered moisture on his lips becoming loosened and airborne as a direct consequence of his more heightened frenzy.

Which led me to surmise then, I have to admit, that he couldn't have been *that* much of a manager if this was how excited he became whilst embroiled in the early stages of what was no more than at this juncture, an exploratory and therefore embryonic at the very least, negotiating phase.

"You need to be exposed" he said then whispering it into my ear, and leaning in even closer than he had been before.

Which I must confess, worried me a great deal at the time.

So much so in fact that prior to him speaking his next words, I had been in the process of trying to think of a way of explaining to him that flattering though his advances were, that he needed to be understanding at the same time, that I was definitely not that type of girl.

"I've got a slot for you with Gaybo on the Late Late Show this weekend!" he animated then, leaping back, as a result of which my heart both soared and plummeted in equal measure.

Soared as a result of the fact that his apparent amorous advances and references to 'exposure' had been no more than a simple misunderstanding on my part, and confusion also, around a word that has more than one definition.

And 'plummeted' as a result of the fact that when he said the words, 'I've got you a slot for you with Gaybo on 'The Late Late Show' this weekend!' he could not have deflated my spirit any less than if he'd hit me over the noggin with a baseball bat and left me there to die, alone and friendless, bleeding to death in the middle of the fucking street.

For those of you that don't know, let me explain to you as best as I can why this reference to 'Gaybo on the Late Late Show' sent such shivers down my spine.

McGuinness was referring to a weekly chat show on terrestrial Irish TV that is hosted every weekend, on Saturdays I believe, by an individual that goes by the name of Gabriel, or 'Gay' (so not the great Irish actor) Byrne.

Adored and revered by a bizarrely fawning multitude, this *actual* idiot hijacks Irish screens for nigh on three hours on the nights in question, and has been doing so on a continuous basis from the early 1960's right up until the present day.

It's all that I can do in fact, whenever I see the fucker coming on, not to put my foot through the screen.

To convey this correctly, let me just say this.

If you're looking for a definition of the word 'sanctimonious', forget any of the trusted lexicons that you might refer to usually for such a purpose.

Just look this bozo up.

He quite honestly has got to be seen to be believed.

'Okey doke, alright now folks' he will say, followed by 'Thank you now, thank you now!' - but in such a way that is not thankful at all, and more so in a fashion that indicates that he is the boss, and that you'd better shut the fuck up or else.

Not unlike a Christian Brother schoolmaster basically, urging some boisterous teenage pupils to settle down.

Venom there, bubbling just beneath the surface, ready to be unleashed at any moment, as soon the old celibacy induced rage that's inherent within can be contained no more.

Not that Byrne is *that* bad though.

I can't remember him ever attempting to beat up any of the audience members.

And I'm sure that the missus also, probably, engages with him in some form of 'ben jessy' from time to time.

He is a supercilious bollocks though nevertheless.

The type of dude that when you are speaking yourself he is not listening to you at all, but rather instead, formulating sentences in his own mind for the next time that he'll be talking himself.

It was the fact that he was so revered though by everybody, that stuck in my craw.

And also that he has never been brought to task at any time, for the quite interminable shite over which he has presided for so many years.

That interview with your one that rode the bishop from Galway for example.

Or the middle-aged socialite that Charlie Haughey was boning?

All bollocks really, and Byrne should have called it at the time for the salacious claptrap that it was.

But no.

He just lapped it all up like the rest of the bloodsucking populace that constituted the main elements of Irish society at the time.

And as for the way that he spoke to Phil Lynott's oul one as well, regarding her apparently promiscuous son's comings and goings?

A shocker really; but fair play to Mrs. Lynott for remaining dignified and pleasant throughout.

If it had been me, I'd have been levelling the fucker!

The worst though was with Gerry Adams, the shinner, and that playwright bollocks Hugh Leonard.

Whatever your political persuasions Byrne, your job is to facilitate, not to fucking opinionate!

So when Adams during the interview says, referring to his public persona versus his private persona, 'I think I'm a nice guy', surely the answer from Byrne should have been either a 'yes' or an 'ok', or some such other similarly bland riposte; not a 'YOU think you're a nice guy??'

207

It was clear anyway that reconciliation was far from his mind during the exchange, a stance that was corroborated by the witless Leonard, who actually refused to shake Adams' hand at the beginning of the debate.

As impartial interviewing techniques go so, this was a shambles from beginning to end; and some people have the gall to call the fucker a broadcasting genius?

But anyway, as McGuinness had alluded to just now, I would be meeting with the spanner at the weekend.

In some other respects though, the more I thought about as were driving along, perhaps it might afford me an opportunity to take the fucker down.

It was hard to deny that he didn't have it coming, and I'd be doing the nation a great favour at the same time as well.

"And after the Late Late is over……" McGuinness continued.

"…And whatever you do by the way, don't fuck it up - we're doing an album and a tour. I'm looking into getting a studio booked for you for next week in London. We need to strike while the iron is hot, young man!"

You had to hand it to him; McGuinness was one hell of a piece of work.

I mean if he could make those 'popular beyond human comprehension' idiots U2 successful, then who knew what he could do with a potential superstar such as myself?

I mean, I was able to actually sing, you know?

And the last time I checked also, my fact wasn't *that* slappable.

Worried about the album that he had mentioned though - and in particular about the fact that I had no original material to speak of that could actually be recorded - certainly not in the short term anyway - I opened my mouth to voice said concerns.

Sensing my anxiety however, like the consummate professional that he is - and with some sort of a sixth sense thrown in there as well I'll wager - McGuinness nonchalantly headed me off at the pass with a swish of his hand.

"It's an album of covers son, don't worry about it" he said.

"And I've a rake of special guests lined up to appear on it already, hopefully. You've won't actually believe who I've got to be honest, if I can confirm even half of them!"

I couldn't begin to imagine who he had, but having met so many of these so called 'Rock Star DemiGods' over the previous number of weeks, I had to admit to myself that I was a good deal less excited at the prospect of meeting more of them than I would have been before all of the shit that I'd had to contend with in recent times had gone down.

As in - and I've said this before - not one of the fuckers were any great shakes really, when you scratched between the surface and got to know them as they were in actual 'real' life.

We had taken an unusual route from the airport, detouring through Coolock, and then on down the Tonlegee Road and the Kilbarrack Road towards the sea.

I had no idea why, so put it down to the fact that McGuinness must have just wanted a more scenic route.

The Beemer zoomed up the coast road anyway, past The Sheds pub in Clontarf, and onwards in the general direction of Fairview, the Five Lamps, and the city centre.

I could see the Pigeon House and the Ringsend gas towers to my left as our beast of an automobile powered along.

"Where we going dude?" I asked McGuinness, desirous at this stage to know where.

"The Shelbourne" he answered.

"Where else?"

Where else indeed?

That was where those U2 fuckers hung out.

Them, and all other shapes and sizes of brain dead fuckwits desperate to be seen in this apparently trendy public domain where G & T's cost a tenner and pin striped suits and paisley cravats are NOT considered, unlike anywhere else in the world of which I was aware, to be ridiculous couture.

The *only* place in Ireland like that I'll warrant.

Sure didn't the lads and I meet Bono and 'The Edge' there as well, as I was saying there before, when we were in our teens?

When we gave them a really rough time of it as a result, mainly, of the fact that that 'Edge' prick was wearing what is more commonly known as a 'teacloth' on his head.

He referred to the headwear himself at the time as a 'bandana', but there were no two ways about it as far as we were concerned.

It was a fucking teacloth!

That anyway I supposed - looking back on it now - was the beginning of my general distaste for the bilge that the fuckers dispense, and have dispensed, over such an unfeasibly protracted passage of time.

Although their music is probably not *that* bad in fairness to them.

It's just their stupid gombeen heads that annoy me more than anything else.

"Ok so is there any viable reason, Mr. McGuinness?" I enquired, unhappy with the choice of venue, and anxious to make it clear to him that my preference was for a more agreeable alternative.

"Why we are going to *that* fucking hellhole, and not another more convivial hostelry, where infinitely more civilised and less feeble-minded individuals might be congregated?"

He looked at me and smiled.

"You just don't get it yet, do you kid?" he went on, shaking his head from side to side and smiling at me patronisingly, as if I was some sort of a fucking idiot.

"I'll say it to you again. This is your new life now. That previous chapter of your existence where you rubbed shoulders with 'Joe Public' and the great unwashed? That's over now, for good".

I was beginning to wonder if I had made a very grave mistake.

Were the things that I had desired all this time all that they seemed?

Was this new world that I had entered - populated by no more than buffoons and halfwits and 'desperate to get to know you' liggers and hangers on - a world in which I held a desire to reside?

Ahh well.

I was in through the door now.

I supposed that I'd better just get on with things and see how I fared from here on in.

"We're not going to that Horseshoe Bar kip though, are we?" I enquired, remembering it better now, the more I reminisced.

There were two bars in the Hotel, but this Horseshoe Bar shithole was the worst of the two by far.

A dark cloud formed over me then, as I recalled the ghastliness of the place in greater detail.

The 'bar' itself was ok; don't get me wrong.

I mean they sold gargle right?

What was not to like?

That wasn't the problem.

The problem, as I was saying there before, was the collection of boneheads and morons that frequented said venue on a consistent and very much on-going basis.

An ominous and sudden feeling of foreboding came over me, which was copper-fastened further by the grave and harrowing words that were emitted next from out of my insouciant companion's despicable larynx.

This dread that I refer to - as if you haven't guessed already - was related very specifically to whom we might encounter when we arrived at said bar.

"Oh yes we are!" McGuinness responded jovially, which considering the gravity of the situation that was looming, was a disposition that I regarded to be bordering on deranged.

"It's a great spot, the Horseshoe, so it is?" he went on, deliriously.

"What the fuck is your problem with it anyway?"

I toyed with the idea of having it out with him there and then, but thought better of it when I considered the debacle that was likely to follow over the coming minutes and hours.

I would have enough to contend with, without having him as an enemy as well.

My apprehension and suspicion was substantiated further, when I listened to what he elucidated next.

"Oh and by the way, one of the guests for your new album will be there also" he added breezily; as cool as you like, don't you know, as if words of such a nature laden with such foreshadowing, could be just thrown out there casually, all willy-nilly like, without a care in the world or consideration for one's own fellow man.

Had the fucker no soul?

How could he be so cavalier with respect to such an imminently perilous fiasco?

I was hoping against hope anyway, that the guest to whom he was referring was not who I thought that it was.

Surely providence would not be that cruel.

To put me in the same room as that spanner again?

So soon after seeing the bollocks in Slane?

Although if my life was to be transformed as radically as McGuinness said it would be in the future, I would probably be in contact with the fucker on a regular enough basis.

We pulled up outside the Shelbourne so, ten minutes later on, after which instead of alighting as any normal person might do under similar circumstances, McGuinness waited, and encouraged me to wait also, for one of those doorman dudes with the funny top hats to wander over 'as is their job' he indicated tersely, and open the door.

"NEVER open the door son!" he said in earnest.

"From this moment onwards you must NEVER open the door!" he continued.

I was beginning to get the feeling that to be a star, you must also concurrently - certainly if McGuinness's behaviour was anything to go by – be a total and utter fucking dick!

I waited for the door to be opened anyway - reluctantly on my part - before following the surprisingly nippy rock star manager through the revolving doors at the front, and then the foyer, before turning right at the end and entering the incongruously titled hellhole bar as referred to earlier on.

'Horseshoe Bar' my arse, I was thinking.

There ain't nothin' lucky about this fucking joint!

CHAPTER 15

I'll 'ave te kill 'im naow, me ol' mace.

An' dass a real shame dah te be fair.

Irish John, I call 'im.

Ee's a good lad is 'Irish' – 'Irish' I call 'im for shortce - burree likhe, knows too much!

Ye know worreye mean?

He'd firrinn very well in Liverpool achthly would 'Irish'.

Very witty likhe.

As John useta say about Liverpool, 'Dis is where de Irish came when all de potatoes ran outce'.

I rang Jurgge befurr anywees, annee knew wha' te do straight soff.

Jurgge ALLWEES knows wha' te do.

Didden think darreed suggest dah doe!

As in, likhe, ye know, bumpin' de lad off.

Anneye've no idear owwee waz able te gerra peece dah quick as well, likhe.

Not shore wen I'll be gerrin araound te doowin de deed doe.

Too bizzy 'ere likhe.

Loadza people araound 'n' dah.

Good te be' backh doe.

In Abbey Road likhe.

S'bin ages rearly.

Not since I last saw 'Irish' acthly, naow darreye come te think abaarrih.

When I waz 'avin a birrovva 'mowmence' outsaaide, likhe.

An 'emotional trauma' I think iss called?

I get lihke dah sometaimes.

Wen irrall gets too much, likhe.

Ye know?

We stole all de songks ye see!

Me an' de boys, likhe.

Betcha didden see dah one comin'!

Me an' John achtly te be toesilly correct - backh in de day.

Off my 'ol piana teacheh, Mostyn.

He's dead naow is Mostyn, de poor ol' bassted.

Dead as fried chicken, likhe.

I'd mosey on up der anywees evree Sattdee aftnoon for me piana lesson; juss behaaind Mathew Streece iwwaz, ryrabove a pub.

I can't rearly remembeh which one doe te be honest.

In Temple Court doe, for shore.

I do remembeh dah.

De streece, likhe.

One time I waz der anywees - de last time acthly - an' John waz, likhe, der too.

He juss cem alongk on de day likhe, forra laugh.

He gorrin to a serious diggin' match with ol' Mostyn doe, which I gorra be honest didden end well.

He waz a big ol' lad Mostyn so wennee fell oveh – darris, wennee slipped on de rug, likhe – which waz, likhe, a toesill accident - iwwaz neveh gonna be a soft landin' der la'.

It turned outce anywees darree acthly DAAIED from de fall, burriwaz all put daown to i' bein' likhe, a tragickh accident, likhe - azzye waz sayin' der juss befour - an' waz forgorren abaarrin no taaime arrall.

De thing waz doe dah wennee took de fall darracthly dunnimmin, he knockt oveh dis chesta droars type thingamajig an' out fell all dis sheet musickh, likhe, 'undreds an' 'undreds o' deese amazin' peessis, all toesilly compleece, an' some wi' lyrics written on dem as well likhe!

John legged i' wirrim anywees, while I hung araound afteh, te go through everythin' wi' de bizzies.

I waz te act 'all innocent likhe' John said, ye know, as if busseh wudden melt 'n me mouce.

He said darreye looked a lot more 'docile' dan 'im – good werd dah, docile - which is probably rice te be fair, wha' wi' me cute lirral babyface 'n dah - so darriv der waz any suspicion likhe, darrih probably wudden last for longk.

We gorraway wirrih anywees, an' hooked up backh a' mine laycer dah day te go through de songks and, likhe, formulace err plan.

We decaaided te go to 'amberg den, de five uvvus - me, John, Juurge, Stu and Peece - te hone de songks as best we could, likhe, and, ye know, pu' lyrics on 'em as well - darris de ones darrole Mostyn hadden already compleeced.

By de taaime we came backh te Liverpool so, we wur ready te rock n' roll.

Likhe, ye know - lissrallee!

We only 'ad enough decent songks doe for abarr eight years - maybe a hundred and fifty or so - an' den after dah we'd be likhe, done.

Some o' de udders were allrice but not so good dah we could gerrall ovvus to agree te dem bein' releest.

We did use some o' de crappy ones doe for err solo werk.

I got 'Jet' an' Juurge got 'My Sweet Lord'.

Ringo got 'Photograph' I think, an' I'm almost certain dar 'Instant Karma' waz a Mostyn reject too; which as ye know John releest rightce afteh we brokhe up likhe.

We tried te wrice some of err own material too from taaime to taaime, burrih alwees ended up soundin' all stupid likhe, an' oh I doe know - chaaildish?

'Octopuses Garden' for example.

And 'Yellow Submarine'.

I mean how can doze two songks compare to an absolute classickh likhe 'Tomorrow Never Knows'?

He waz some fuckin' songwricer darrole Mostyn.

So everyone waz sayin' likhe - wen we broke up 'n dah - darris waz all because o' Yoko an' me an' John fallin' ouce - bu' dass likhe, toesill bollocks darris!

Dah waz nuthin' 'te do wirrih.

We juss ran arra songks!

I met dis Johnny kid so anywees – 'Irish' likhe - a few years ago in London in a waaine bar type place darree waz workin' in a' de taaime - an' I likhe, told 'im de whole stoury den.

I waz toesilly bladdehed anywees, an' I usually lerroff a birra steam wen I'm likhe dah.

An' denneye merrim again, outsaaide de studios 'ere in Abbey Road likhe, only a few weeks afteh dah ferst taaime, an' told 'im de exact same thing again!

An' naoweez threatnin' te go publickh likhe, an' blab irrall te de werld an' its' muddeh!

I GORRA take 'im outce so.

I likhe 'im doe is de only problem.

He kinda remaainds me a birra John likhe ye know - wennee waz youngeh?

Iss a birrova conundrum so rearly.

I got dis call off Bono's manager anywees - ye know, dar Irish singer - de midgety chap?

Well dis manager – Paul's 'is name as well – wellee calls me up anywees lookin' for a fayveh for a pal ovvis dah needs a bass player for ees new recourd.

So I told 'im darreye'd help out likhe, ye know - just te be nice.

Ye gorra stay daaown wi' de kids, ye know?

Imagine my surpraaise so wenneye saw my ol' mace 'Irish' walkin' in te de studio der, likhe, earlier today!

An' iss funny too cozzih looks likhe Bono an' 'im likhe, absolutely fuckin' hayce each uddeh!

Alldoe dass no' surprise rearly when ye consider 'ow much ovva fuckin' knob'ead dah fuckin' Bono lad is.

He told me befour anywees - Bono darris - dar 'Irish' waz recourdin' 'is 'Magnum

Opus' ee said - bu' by de way ee pronounct i' it saaounded likhe 'ee waz sayin' 'Magnum o' Piss'.

'Bono mace' I said to 'im so at de taaime.

'It rearly saaounds likhe yorr sayin' 'Magnum o' Piss' la'. You know likhe, a big borrill a champagne likhe, burrinstead 'o champagne bein' innih, achtual YORRINE bein' innih instead mace!'

I waz only takin' de piss doe likhe - ha ha, are yerravvin' dah folks?

Only takin' de piss?

Dass comedy gold darris!

Burree wazzen findin' me funny arrall and toesilly ignored me den afteh, de short-arsed midget fuckin' get!

Darrannoyed me a lo' te be honest, burrye lehrih go, bein' all magnanimous likhe, as I usually am.

'I think ye need to learn how to talk proper Macca' de tosser went on doe burreven I know dah dass meant te be 'properly', which I told 'im so as well juss te likhe, ye know, get de last werd in likhe.

He buggered off den anywees te talk te some utheh bell end across de way, so I decaaided den te juss gerron de ale, likhe, big style, as I usually do.

Backh wen Bono's manager called me befour anywees, I told 'im darree could tell ees mate darree could use Abbey Road to recourd de album iffee likhed.

I'd square i' wi' de Studio Manageh so der'd be no problem der arrall.

As in, how could de Studio Manageh refuse me?

I'm Paul McfuckingCartney for fuck sakhe, likhe!

'ere we are naow so anywees, an' worra bad idea iss all turned out te be.

As in I'm stuck in Abbey Roadce 'ere naaow, wirra load of uddeh Rock Star DemiGod types hangin' araaound, and not one ovvem dass even fit te likhe, ye know - lace my bootce!

We're all juss hangin' araaound anywees as I said, waissin' for 'Irish' te make a decision abou' wha' songs we'll be doin' an' in worrordeh!

Fuck dat so mace.

If I'm kept waissin' for any longeh I'm juss gonna push off likhe, an' ge' blad-dehed somewhere else.

Maybe dah waaine bar on de Strand where I ferst met 'Irish'?

Alldoe maybe noss.

Think darrye might be barred owra der naow darrye come te think abbaarih.

But why wouldee wanna say somethin' likhe darranywees?

'Irish' darris.

Ye know - abou' leakin' me an' de lads seecriss?

I mean ees known abarrih for years naaow, annees neveh blabbed befour.

Unless ees lookin' for likhe, 'notoriesee' 'n' dah!

Very impoursint te rav dah doe in fairness, so I can defo see whereeze cummin from der.

Like playin' a concert on a random rooftop in London in de middle o' de day.

Or sayin' dah yorr likhe, more popular dan Jesus Christ!

Dah waz all brilliant PR rearly, worrever way ye look arrih.

An' all publicity is good publicity rice?

Good OR bad.

Ders Gary Moore oveh der smokin' a joint.

Some axe man ee is.

Shockin' face doe.

Norreven a muddeh could love dah face.

Loadsa faces araaound Liverpool are likhe dah doe deese days.

'ave you met my friend Stanley?'

No' like i' waz in de '50's.

Fists 'n' boots waz all 'n' dah waz dah mace.

Der bloody killin' each uddeh naow deese kids!

Talkin' o' killin' acthly, I rearly 'ave te ge' me plan straice.

Juurge said darreed get de peece so no problems der, burree said too darrye should purrah a tail on de kid as well te likhe, ye know, gerran idear ovvis movements an' dah - worree gets up to likhe - every day afteh ee leaves de studio te go 'ome.

I'll sort darrou' naow acthly.

"'ey, Bill!" I shouce oveh to me trusty mindeh whose just across de way.

He's standin' next to a coffee machine der, talkin' to one o' de engineers.

"Come over rear Billy mace - I wanna ravva lirrel chat with ye".

Bill drops everything o' course an' comes oveh te where I am.

"Alright scouse?" I say to 'im wennee arraaives across.

Billy is from de Wirral.

"Yeah, good boss, good boss" he says, all poncy-likhe and smarmy, likhe ees tryin' to impress.

"I'm boss, boss" he goes on, which leads me te thinkin' darree probably needs te broaden up ees vocabulary likhe, just a lirrel bi'.

Less 'bosses' likhe, ye know?

Naaow's not de taaime doe, te be bringin' darrup.

Naaow I juss need te be callin' on ees expertise in de area of securissee an' likhe, ye know, 'clandestine' type activiteeze.

Dass a big werd darrissinih?

Clandestine!

Jurrge taugh' me dah.

Jurrge knows all sortsa stuff.

"De ye see de kid oveh der Bill?" I say te Bill anywees, draggin' im in a bi' closeh den likhe, so dah no-one else cannear.

216

"De one darreveryone's 'ere for likhe?"

Bill nods backh at me to indicate darree understands.

"Well Bill mace" I go on, beckonin' him to lean in even closeh.

"I want ye te stick a tail on 'im laycer today, an' den every day afteh dah for de next week or so at least".

Bill looks at me den likhe I've go' two 'eads.

An' den I realise darree thinks darreye want 'im te give de bloke a good knobbin', likhe.

"For fuck sakhe Bill!" I say.

"I don't want ye te bloody shag 'im, soff lad! I juss want ye te, likhe, ye know, follee 'im araaound 'n' dah!"

Billy finally gets de message so and nods backh at me te indicate darrees on board, likhe.

So as I waz sayin' der befour, iss important te know Irish's routine so dah when I do bump 'im off, ders nothin' suspicious der likhe, darranybody can nab me for if dey do eveh follee up on a lead?

Ee'll be recordin' ere for de next month or so anywees at least, sowwees shore te gerrimself into a birrova routine.

If I can juss find outce where de fuckeh's stayin' I'll 'ave a great chance a gerrin away wirrih wirrou' anybody bein' any de wyseh.

Billy from de Wirral can defnitly 'elp me wi' dah.

Ee's in for a rude awaknin' so, is 'Irish'.

Not de dyin' part doe - alldoe darrill be bad enough forrim as well te be fair.

No I mean likhe, wi' de fame 'n' dah, an' de adulation.

Iss allrice a' de startce, don't ge' me wrong - bu' den i' gets te be a right pain in de arse afteh taaime.

Burririll only be for a month or two forrim so likhe, ye know – worreveh!?

Talkin' 'o which achtly, err ferst eveh TV interview waz done by an Irish chap.

A bloke called 'Gay' - Gay Byrne I think 'is name waz - backh in de days when 'gay' meant bein' 'appy.

We were on wi' Ken Dodd as well, who's one werrd characteh.

An' a scouser too.

'Ken Odd' err John called 'im.

Annee took de toesill piss owrovvim on de same day as well!

"Hey Ken Odd!" he said in a friendly type way - burree waz defo juss takin' de piss.

"I waz juss thinkin der la' dah likhe, ye know, te be a comedian an' dah, don't yerrav te say stuff dass funny likhe, evree naow an' again? Likhe, ONCE migh' be a startce mace, rice?! What de ye think abou' dah, Ken Odd?"

Norrimpressed arrall waz wha' Ken Odd waz thinkin' abou' dah, annee acthly gave John a clip araaound de ear for 'is trubble, rice afteh 'ee said worree said.

217

He could gerraway wi' dah backh den, Ken Odd.

We were only nobodies at de taaime ye see, so nobody rearly cared.

Not long afteh dar interview doe, wennar star had likhe, risen, we'd 'ave juss lifted an eyebrow te some 'andler somewhere, an' Ken Odd woulda been taken outsaaide an' given a rite bloody good 'iding for bein' such a git.

'Irish'll be 'ere for at least a month or so anywees, likhe I waz sayin' der befour, sowwih should be easy enough te learn ees rooseen.

I'll need te think abarra disguise doe.

As in, if I'm gonna take 'im outce arrees 'otel, I can't run de risk o' Joe Public recognisin' me likhe, wen I end up doin' de dirty deed.

Which o' course dey will.

I mean I'm likhe, Paul McfuckingCartney for fuck sake!

Likhe I waz menschnin'der befour.

I do remembeh a taaime doe, wennih wazzin likhe dah.

Wennih wazzin likhe darrarall.

'appier taaimes rearly, wen every numpty in de werld didden wanna a peece o' yorr arse.

Good taaimes.

Loadsa greatce memories from wen we waz likhe, anonymous.

Likhe jumpin' on a train te Southport for de day wi' de rest o' me scallies!

Long hot summehs wi' nothin' on err 'anns bu' taaime.

Chewsdees wer de best.

Bunkin' on te Birkdale over a fence likhe, te take de piss owra de golfehs.

Some knob'eds dey are, golfehs.

Take demselves way too serious, likhe.

Dah Bowie fuckeh izza golfeh!

I ress me case!

John useta piss in de holes on de greens anywees, juss so as de golfehs'd get piss all oveh der 'ands wen dey were takin' der balls backh owragain, after der pars or der pigeons or worrever irris de fuck dey call 'em.

An' den we'd 'ed down te de beach te drink de cheap sherry dah Peece nicked off 'ees old man, which waz likhe, de only ale darreeze old man wudden notice waz gone likhe, norrin a million fuckin' years la'!

I mean likhe, who drinks sherry anywees, 'cept de Queen Muddeh maybe, an' most folk's grea' granny once a yerr a' Christmas, an' der so far gone anywees dah dey could be drinkin' cow's piss an' still be thinkin' darrih tastes allrice.

Oh an' scally scouse teenagehs!

We drink i' too, on beaches wen derz nowt else available an' we wanna gerras bladdehed as we can, on de cheap likhe!

We shared a bond doe me an' John.

Muddehless in err teens.

No-one can prepare ye for dah, I don't care worranybody says.

At least I 'ad a Dad doe, an' a bruddeh - so dah waz somethink I suppose.

Poor ol' John waz surraaounded by ol' grannies an' aunts an' dah, so iwwaz alwees gonna be 'arder for 'im.

Iss no wundeh rearly, darree waz such a narky buggeh for mosta de taaime.

'Muddehless an' ruddehless' my ol' Dad useta say abarrim.

"Dass why ees alwees lashin' out see lad" he'd say from behind 'is paper on err armchair in de backh room.

"Ee's a lost soul ee is dah lad" ee'd go on.

"I do 'ope darree finds somethin' to engage 'im in life doe, err Paul. Uddehwise ee'll juss go off de rails for shore. Nothin' more certain dan dat lad"

Lirrel diddee know.

My ol' man waz nice doe.

Encouragin' likhe.

I remembeh one taaime wen we were workin' on lyrics for one of ol' Mostyn's songs in err front room an' we cem in te play it for me Dad who waz in ees usual spot on de armchair in de corneh.

De song waz a winner for shore musickh waaise, bu' we juss wanted someone else's opinion on de lyrics likhe, te see if dey werked.

Burree wazzin impressed one bi'.

Wazzin impressed arrall.

"Come 'ed lads!" ee said to us a' de taaime.

"Yorr from Liverpool soff lads, rice? Not de blummin' Bronx. De ye rafta use all doze American slang werds likhe? Irrid be much betteh if ye juss used plain old King's English an' forgorrahbarr' all dah nonsense from across de pond!"

John an' me decaidded te stick wiv err original plan doe, which waz just as well rearly.

Uddehwaaise de whole o' de English speaking werld for de last thirty years or more, woulda been singing alongk te de chorus laaine of one of aar most famous songks likhe dis.

'She Loves You, YES, YES, YES'!

Can't see dah catchin' on.

Sometaaimes parents talk through der arses doe, ders no denyin' i'.

As dah baldy poet bloke Philip Larkin says,

"They fuck you up, your Mum and Dad".

S'true dah.

True big taaime.

We wur bluddy ace in 'amberg doe.

Knocked 'em dead every nightce, 'specially dah last taaime.

No' like doze early yerrs in Woolton wen John waz playin' skiffle wi' de Quarries.

'ee waz just a kid doe, bidin' ees taaime rearly until somethink besseh came alongk.

Nice lad doe Pete Shotton.

Boss rearly.

Funny likhe.

Dey wurr all good lads acthly.

Sad taaimes doe in 'amberg.

Stu dyin' likhe.

Amazin' rearly darra lirrel kickin' from some local louts could lead to 'ees passin' away.

Dah coulda bin me!

Or John.

Mad dah.

Burree waz a real pussy cat err John rearly, despite likhe, ye know, bein' a toesill fuckin' mouthpeece.

Would run a' de first sign o' trouble ee would, which is exachly worree did on dah night too!

An' on de day wi' Mostyn wennee ran off with all de sheet musickh, likhe.

Stu didn't maaind us goin' doe, azzee waz kinda driftin' away from us anywees.

More interested in paintin' pictures likhe, an' dah lass darree waz hangin' araaound with, dar Astrid.

Astrid waz alrigh' doe te be fair, even if she waz a birrova leech, 'er an' er mates likhe, in darrold Kaiserkeller joint.

She waz neveh away from der rearly, wi' Bill an' Ben 'er flowerpot men - doze two German boyfriends ov 'ers dah neveh left 'er saaide.

All over us she waz anywees, 'specially Stu.

Dass wen me an' de uddeh two lads - John 'n' Jurgge darris - decaaided dah Stu could neveh know abou' de songks bein' suss.

Doze German hanger-on's looked way too square te be able te keep a seecriss like dah, an' we cudden take a chance on Stu not tellin' Astrid too - anybody coulda known abbarrih afteh dah if we'd let darrappen.

And we cudden tell Peece eetheh.

Burree waz likhe, juss de drummer, so waz neveh rearly involved in anythink important likhe.

Felt propeh bad doe, shaftin' 'im in dee end.

'ee neveh did owt to any ovvus so lerrin' im go waz 'arsh, I'm not gonna lie.

An' none ovvus 'ad de balls te tell 'im to ees face neetheh.

Bu' we wer only young I suppose an' everybody makes mistakes wen der young.

Well dodgy name dah doe, rice?

Astrid.

Likhe one o' doze cars for de middle classes likhe.

De Vauxhall Astrid!

For all yorr middle class needs, likhe travellin' te Woolworths for yorr weekly shop an' ferryin' yorr mediocre kids te mediocre comprehensives in shit'oles likhe Amersham and Sidcup!

I tell ye what doe, iwwaz unbelievable 'ow quick irrall went daaown.

I mean likhe, goin' from playin' te fifty people in de Indra teravvin' two number 1 singles within a month ov each uddeh, and den goin' te de states likhe, and cleanin' up oveh der too!

People don't realaaise 'ow fast irrall 'appened!

Likhe, we 'ad a big enough hit with 'Love Me Do' an' den an ACTUAL number one hit with 'Please Please Me', bu' we were still playin' support te Helen Shapiro in de clubs in Engand while all o' dah waz goin' daaown!

We'd likhe, commissit te de shows doe so, ye know; we juss 'ad te gerronwirrih.

Brian wazzen gonna lerrus lerranybody daaown even den.

'elen waz nice abarrih doe.

She knew dah de kids were der te see us, bu' she went ahead an' did 'er own show anywees after errs, te less dan 'alf de crowd.

'The Great Shapiro' John called 'er, alldoewee waz defnitly takin' de piss.

As in likhe, comparin' 'er te doze magicians dah play to abou' four kids on Blackpool pier, pullin' rabbits owrov 'ats likhe, an' pretendin' te be currin' der sequinned assistants in 'alf.

He waz some dick'ead err John wennee wannet te be.

Which I 'ave te be honest waz mosta de taaime.

Alwees tryin' te be cleveh likhe, but not dah clever arrall rearly.

He shoulda juss left poor 'elen alone.

She waz greatce err 'elen.

Alldoe she waz just a kid too if I remember it right; way younger than uz, an' we waz only kids as well likhe.

Jinnow wha' - I think she waz likhe, only fifteen or somethink at de taaime.

So she actually WAZ 'The Great Shapiro'!

A magical singeh an' a magical gurl.

John waz wrong abararr 'elen.

Burree waz wrongk abbarrah lorra things.

Derree is anywees – 'Irish' - talkin' te dah do-gooder Geldof get, an' de two of 'em are juss havin' a good ol' laugh a' my expense, likhe.

"What do you think Macca?" he shouts across to me.

'Irish' darris.

"Isn't it about time that the world at large was aware of it? As in, should it not be, at this stage, in the public domain?"

He waz oveh wi' me der befour rearlier on, an' promised me darreed keep mum.

An' naowees sayin' darree migh' not!

Likhe, wha' de 'ell is wrongk wi' de lad?

Can't ee see darreye'm rearly stressed abarrih?

I can't stay 'ere any longeh.

I'll hook up with Bill laycer and find outce wha' de kids movements are den for de next few days.

Alldoe I myrafta move on dis fasteh dan I originally thortce.

De only thing naow as well of course, is darrye migh' rafta kill dah Geldof fuckeh too!

I buggeh off anywees, slammin' de door on me way outce.

Dey'll be well pissed off naow, naow darreye've gone.

All dee uddehs likhe, ye know?

'Shyce' I'm thinkin' doe, as I'm standin' on de steps outsaaide.

I need Billy from de Wirral te drive me 'ome'!

I'll 'ave te go backh up naow an' call 'im backh outce.

Bloody 'ellfire!

Dass annoyed me dah naow.

I'll 'ave te trudge back in der wi' me tail between me legs, likhe.

I open de door te de studio again anywee,s an' wave te Billy te come across.

Ignorin' everybody else der o' course.

He comes oveh den, rushin' likhe, likhe de lackhey darree is.

"I need a lift, soff lad!" I say to 'im, annee he can tell righ' away darreye'm, likhe, rearly annoyed.

"Oh yeah, soddy boss, will be righ' der boss" as he rushes back oveh te gerris coat from de uddeh saaide o' de room.

More bloody 'bosses'.

'ee needs te sort dah shyce ouce.

We're outsaaide soon anywees, an' in de car befour longk.

"Did ye rear dah lirrel shyce in der Bill" I ask de lad, wundrin' iffee 'eard wor 'Irish' waz sayin' der befour abou' de songks.

"Talkin' abou' likhe, err kid John an' de songks likhe, from, likhe, ye know, way backh in de day wen we waz fab?"

"No boss" ee answers, so I decaaide te tell 'im all abbarrih so darree understands why I've gorra do worreye've gorra do.

He's shore te think dah bumping de kid off is a birrextreme, so if I tell 'im de backhground likhe, he should 'ave no problem doin' de dirty deed when I explain to'im laycer woss gorra be done.

Anneye've decaaided as well te gerrim te doowih ratheh dan me.

Why not likhe?

'ee's sure te be ok wirrih if de price is rice!

I go through i' wirrim anywees, annee listens to me all attentive likhe, as I explain de whole stoury from startce te finish.

"Dass some story boss" he says wenneye'm done.

"Burriss a bi' hard to take in, likhe - not bein' funny likhe. As in likhe, ye know, you've all 'ad prissy successful solo careers since den as well likhe, ye know?"

Issa fair pointce in fairness te de lad.

I can tell dah Bill is no blert even iffee is likhe, a birrova woollie.

I decide den te givvem a medley - seein' azzees after referrin' te de songks likhe, darreye've releest since afteh de Beatles brokhe up.

Der all allrice as it goes, even if Denny an' Jimmy wroce most ovvem.

I startce wi' 'Pipes of Peace' and Frog's Chorus (Billy duzzen join in der doe, which is a bit disappointing for shore), den 'Live and Let Die' befour followin' darrup up with 'Band on the Run' and 'Say, Say, Say'.

I can tell darrees rearly enjoyin' i' likhe - 'is own personal solo concert - so I, likhe, ye know, caddy on.

'Say, Say, Say' is folleed by 'Ebony and Ivory', 'Jet' and 'With a Little Luck', befour I finish irrall off with 'The Girl is Mine' and de 'piece de la resistance' 'Silly Love Songs'.

Iss rearly obvious dah Billy is impressed wirrih all, azzee likhe, nearly crashes de limo on more dan one occasion on err way backh te de flatce.

We ge' te my place in Mayfair anywees, abarran 'alf an hour laycer, wi' Billy pulling de limo up next te de main entrance when we arraaive.

De doorman Winston comes oveh den te bring me in, burreye roll de window down ferst befour 'ee gets all de way across.

"Givvus five minutes der Winston Lad" I say, stoppin' im innis tracks.

"I just wanna rav a quick werd 'ere with Bill befour I go in".

He heads backh to de door den, and I roll de window backh up.

"Alright der, Billy lad" I say to 'im, all earnest likhe and serious naow dar- reye've important business wirrim darreye wanna discuss.

"So do ye know de way dah dah kid, Johnny Madhouse, or worrever de fuck ee calls 'imself – I know 'im as 'Irish' - izz gonna give de game away on me an' de lads? Ye know, abou' de songks 'n dah? Well I cantce allow dah te happen, rice? So I need you te kill 'im for me, Bill, OK?"

Why not let Billy do it, as I waz sayin' der befour?

I mean why should I be takin' a chance likhe dah meself?

He could do wi' de readies as well I'm thinkin', an' I can definitely make it worth eez while.

"You wha' mace?" he replies, all shocked likhe an' busseh wudden meltce, burreye can tell darree'll be happy te doowih if de money is rice annee thinks darree can gerra way wirrih, likhe.

"No way boss!" he continues.

"I'm no merderer!"

Ten seconds laycer doe, wen I tell 'im 'ow much I'm prepared te pay, 'ee chang- es 'ees tune prissy quickh!

Propeh made up ee is naaow.

"Oh well when ye purrih like dah boss, yeah, I can do dah, no problem, likhe".

A million big ones?

I knew darreed come araaound wennee 'eard dah!

"De only thing doe Bill" I go on.

"Is darris gorra be tenice"

I waz 'avin a think abarrih earlier on in de car on de way backh, and realised den wen I thortce abbarrih some more, darreye can't rearly delay wha' needs te be done.

I mean worrif de kid's plannin' te go te de press ferst thing tomorra mornin', likhe?

Der can be no delay.

Winston's at de windeh again so I roll i' daaown te see worree wance.

"A package arrived for you earlier tonight sir" he says as 'ee passes a small box through.

"Oh, rice" I say to 'im.

"Thanks mace" I go on befour rollin' de windeh backh up.

I wonder worrih could be as I undo de string on de box an' open irrup.

Would ye believe i' bu' Jurrge 'as only got de peece for me already!

Der irris befour me, all shiny an' mad looking, wirra box o' bullets in der as well.

"Bloody 'ellfire Bill!" I say to Bill, who's leanin' in oveh into de backh an' starin' arrih as well.

"Jurrge 'as only gone an' come up wi' de peece"!

"No excuses naow mace" I continue.

"Let's strike while de iron's hot. Backh to de studio la', pronto! We'll follee de kid backh te whereveh ee's stayin' an werk irrall outce from der!"

"Rice-oh boss" Billy responds, befour turnin' de ignition backh on an' speedin' away.

And wi' dah, Johnny Madhouse's days are numbehed!

Or 'Irish' as I call 'im meself.

An' Geldof too.

An' any uddeh fuckeh dah tries te gerrin my way!

CHAPTER 16

As I sat there listening to the fucker, it was difficult to conceive of anybody more annoying that had actually ever lived.

I'm talking about Gay Byrne here folks.

You know - that bollocks that presents 'The Late Late Show'?

OK, so Hitler and Stalin were psychotic, murdering bastards, fair enough; but had anybody ever, besides them, in the history of time, been as irritating as this gobshite?

I considered it to be unlikely.

Unless you took into account Marty Whelan of course, who was, and is, in all ways imaginable, a similarly reprehensible buffoon.

And that's without considering even or taking into account the fact that at no time ever, over the vast and virtually incalculable tracts of time that have elapsed since the dawn of the universe and before, the name 'Marty' has and will NEVER be, a moniker that is befitting for a man.

A three year old toddler perhaps.

But not a man.

And 'Gay' of course similarly.

"Okey doke folks, settle down, settle down" the fucker had started anyway, a few minutes earlier, as I'd been waiting in the wings, urging the audience with his words to come under his command.

They would come under his command 'OR ELSE' was the way I saw it, looking at him there in all of his finery and his pomp.

He was unequivocally - in his own mind at least - the master at the head of the class.

McGuinness was standing beside me also at the time; with the pained wince on his visage indicating to me plainly enough that he was similarly piqued.

He raised his eyes to heaven then, before nodding to me slowly and encouragingly; as if to say, 'Come on lad, you can do it! Sometimes you just have to take one up the arse for the team!'

I gritted my teeth so, and braced myself for the ordeal to come.

"Alright so, okey doke, that's it, thank you everybody, THANK YOU!" Byrne continued, with really quite overwhelming superciliousness.

And yet the people here today appeared to be happy to endure the disdain. 'Go figure' as the yanks oft times say.

"Our next guest so folks" the bollocks went on.

"Is a young man from Dublin, who, over the last number of weeks, has taken the world QUITE by storm, don't you know. Hitherto unknown to us, his image now is on every magazine cover that you care to review, and you can't turn in the street as a matter of fact, for seeing his face on some billboard or placard or other, wherever you may go".

I could taste the bastard's bitterness.

He had obviously been making a vain and pathetic attempt to be humorous, but in that regard - if the audience's muted reaction was anything to go by - he had MONUMENTALLY fallen flat on his face.

Seething resentment, as I'm sure you are aware, is a difficult emotion to conceal.

A reasonably discerning crowd so, they had sensed and disliked, evidently, his unnecessary antagonism.

"Anyway folks" he continued, unabashed.

"Despite the expedient nature of our young star's meteoric rise, he appears nonetheless, to have a modicum of - or so I am told – talent. With that being the case so, I encourage you folks, to please give a very warm welcome to our first guest of evening, Mr. JOHN FORTUNE folks. JOHN FORTUNE, everybody! Okey doke."

And with that the crowd erupted and out I popped.

Our host though, as you've heard, had got off to a bad enough start, so I was not in the best of form.

As in, that is - how about getting my fucking name right at least?

It's JOHNNY, for one, not John.

And 'FREAK SHOW' really, if I'm being pedantic.

I considered then, internally, at that precise moment in time, that the whole scheme as things stood, was almost certainly destined to end in some form of travesty or other.

The audience calmed down then eventually anyway, after which I took my seat.

My nemesis then, for the next little while, warbled on some more.

"Well, young John" he began, as snivellingly as you like.

"You are VERY-WELCOME-TO-DA-SHOW! We are all APSALOORY DELYRAH to have you here!"

"Thank you Gay" I answered, as evenly as I could under the circumstances.

"It's good to be here" I continued, lying.

I had an incredibly strong urge to punch the fucker in the face.

"Let us begin so, young John, shall we?" he threw out then, settling back in his chair, all 'lord of the manor' like, and would yiz all look at me and the size o' my bollocks in comparison to the size o' your bollocks, ye young upstart!

I was in a negative state of mind alright, I can't deny it.

"Ok so let me see" he continued patronisingly.

"You're at this 'Guns and Roses' rock and roll concert, is that right? Just a few short weeks ago? At the country seat NO LESS of our good and most venerable friend of the show, young MASTER HENRY, Lord Henry Mountcharles himself - and you happen to find yourself on DA STAYAGE towards the end of the concert I believe, as a result of what you must surely agree, was no more than sheer blind luck and chance. And then, lo and behold, HA HA HA, the patrons on the day decide to take a shine to you, well I say folks, WADDYA ALL TINK 'A DAH? And here we are so, today! Is it all a bit of a shock to you so, young John, this new found fame and fortune? THANK YOU FOLKS, THANK YOU, SETTLE DOWN NOW PLEASE, OKEY DOKE!"

Some mad bird at the back had started to shriek.

By the way that Byrne had asked his long-winded question though, and the smug way even, in which he was sitting back in his throne now, all self-satisfied like, and holier than thou - as if he himself, in his own life that is, had ever done anything more important than just fucking chat to people for a living - I could see immediately that he was fucking BOILING with animosity.

Absolutely fuckin' bullin' he was, the sap!

"I just sang my tunes on the day, dude" I responded to him so, cockily.

"And gave the fans what they wanted".

I was disgusted with myself for sounding so arrogant, but his despicable attitude was pushing me in that direction.

It was almost certainly a defence mechanism on my part as well; as in, there was no way in the world, ever, that I'd be letting this fucking bozo get the better of me – you know, like he did with Phil Lynott and his lovely, dignified mother, a few years before on the very same show?

And Kate Bush as well, now that I came to think of it.

For no reason at all he had given the wonderful Kate a hard time of it as well, before she was famous, and was like, you know, just starting out.

I elaborated further so; just so as he could be 100% clear as to where I was at.

"I was meaning to ask you actually Byrne" I said.

"Are you always this much of a fucking bollocks?"

A sharp and collective intake of breath was audible distinctly among the masses, with the odd stifled giggle evident here and there as well.

Unanimously positive rumblings they were though - of that I was certain.

Zero dissent anywhere.

Which encouraged me, naturally enough, to proceed in a similar vein.

As in…

And I definitely paused here for dramatic effect.

227

"And if I might enquire also Byrne - does it take much practice on your part, to like, you know, be such a fucking PERRICK!"

I was on a roll.

Byrne was on the ropes big style now, and didn't know WHERE to be fuckin' lookin'.

Although in fairness to him, he *did* make a valiant enough attempt to turn things around.

"HOW DARE YOU SPEAK TO ME LIKE THAT, YOU INSUFFERABLE LITTLE GUTTERSNIPE!" he snapped.

"TO WHOM DO YOU THINK YOU ARE ADDRESSING?"

Grammatically correct as well, so fair play.

I was warming to the guy actually, if the truth be told.

But I was already well on my way vis-à-vis my controversial public attack on the king of the Saturday night tube, so there was definitely no way that I could ease up on the old offensive now.

'In for a penny, in for a pound' kind of thing, you know?

"I do Byrne. I do know 'to whom' I address!" I answered breezily, taking great care at the time to establish for him by my brazen attitude, that before him was an individual that quite honestly couldn't give a flying fuck about anything.

I continued on then with what I believed at the time was fairly admirable gusto.

"And I doubt that anybody here in the audience today Byrne!" I intimated, "Or looking in at home this evening even, would disagree with me when I declare to the world at al, that you are the greatest sack of shit that has ever drawn breath. I know *exactly* who and what you are, you sanctimonious scumbag. Do you seriously believe that the public at large can forget your treatment of the great Philip Lynott and his mother, just a few short years back, on this very show? Do you honestly believe that it's better to be a toady to the likes of weasels like that talent void, Hugh Leonard, than treat the aforementioned Philo and his wonderful old dear with the respect that they deserved? AND you practically fawned over that sad, fat-arsed old gobshite, Peter Ustinov as well – who, by the way, has never put forth anything funny or regaling in his entire life - in addition to chastising the legend that is Oliver Reed, just because he availed of the opportunity to partake of a litre or two of whiskey next door in the Montrose Hotel, prior to appearing on your quite staggeringly mediocre revue. And all of this as a result of you and your producer's decision-making foolhardiness in positioning the great man as the last guest on your show on a Saturday night? Were you not aware that there are public houses open in this city at such a time, and that as a result of this fact, there would be no other place, ever, that Oliver Reed was more likely to be? That is, you fucking nitwit, if he was scheduled to come on to your show at 10.30pm in the evening, rather than at the more sensible entry time of say, 8.30pm?! What else was he going to be doing with his time Byrne, while he was hanging afuckinground? Sitting patiently in the wings, sans bois, whilst you lorded it over the rest of the Z list celebrities that were on before? I don't fucking think so dude!"

I was definitely not holding back.

Byrne tried to move things forward then to a more convivial footing, but with zero success of course.

I was too far down the road now to even contemplate turning back, so any compromise or adjustment to my manner at this point, was a U-turn that I was not prepared to consider.

And besides, there was something quite refreshing - liberating even – about the prospect of being a national pariah.

"Ok so, well moving on and besides all that" he countered so, in vain.

"How are things otherwise, young John? The family are ok etc., etc., yes, yes?"

I could tell that he was back-tracking now, so I went in for the kill.

"Game ball Gaybo!" I said, in a not unhostile manner, before leaning back confidently in my chair for a bit of an oul stretch.

I threw a few shapes out there then also, here and there, for like, you know, show.

"Game ball! And your good self?" I continued, with no small degree of nonchalant abandon.

Byrne was at a loss for words though, which was definitely a first.

He was aware, unquestionably, that a further onslaught was imminent.

"And what about that PERRICK Bono!" I carried on.

"You fucking love him, don't ye? Oh yeah! The miserable little short-arsed CUNT!"

The 'c' word on national TV!

That had to be a first!

Certainly for Ireland anyway.

And what with yours truly being the 'perpetrator premiere' of said 'mot'; I can't deny at the time that this was a singularly proud moment for me in my short life thus far.

Talking of cunts actually, I was thinking at the time, I might as well just go for the jugular.

I persevered on.

"De ye know wha' actually Byrne?" I continued.

"YOU'RE some cunt!"

The audience were loving this now.

"And if there was a shortage of cunts as well" I went on.

"For whatever reason......you'd be TWO fucking cunts!"

I was definitely on my last legs though vis-à-vis the continuance of my tenure on the show.

The audience were grand; don't get me wrong.

They were fucking loving it as I was saying!

It was the plethora of producers, executive producers and studio types that had gathered in the wings that were the problem.

All stressed out and nervous looking, this collection of miserable and pasty looking grey-suited bastards, were just itching to pull the plug on me.

It was of critical importance so, I was thinking at the time, that any impending removal of yours truly from the stage, would be on yours trulys' terms alone.

There was just no way in the world that I'd be permitting any fucker to be manhandling me off the set.

Given how quickly the bastards had mobilised though, to my left and to my right, I would have to be moving fast.

Standing up so, I strode briskly across to the charlatan of chat.

Stationed before him then, I purposefully lifted the near full glass of water that was on the table before him, and deposited the contents of same, slowly and deliberately, over his barely believing and undoubtedly startled countenance.

He just sat there open-mouthed as the audience whooped and hollered with delight.

"THAT'S FOR ALL THE POOR FUCKERS 'TO WHOM' YOU'VE BEEN A BOLLOCKS OVER THE YEARS BYRNE!" I shouted loudly.

"AND IT'S LUCKY FOR YOU THAT YOU'RE SITTING DOWN AS WELL, YE PRICK" I went on.

"OTHERWISE YOU'D BE GETTIN' A SWIFT KICK INTO THE TOWN HALLS AS WELL!"

And with that I fucked the glass on to the floor and turned to face the audience, raising my outstretched arms up and out and towards them confidently, whilst nodding my head up and down simultaneously, as if to indicate the following.

'Well I can't fucking believe that no-one has ever done THAT before!'

They were going absolutely fucking bananas now.

"G'WAN FREAKERS, YE FUCKING LAD YE!" shouted one fucker.

"POWER TO THE PEOPLE!" shouted another; which just goes to show you on one level how misunderstood a person can sometimes be – i.e., me – and on another, how in all of the crowds that have gathered, ever, over the grand expanse of time, that there's always one fucking billix that takes advantage of that fact that because it's a large gathering, that he or she can take advantage of the fact to further his or her own personal agenda.

As in, that is, if this 'power to the people' fucker believed that at any stage before, ever, in my short life to date, I desired any affiliation with those 'An Phoblacht' reading, 'haven't washed for actual fucking weeks', crusty left-wing, 'never did a day's work in their fucking lives' bastards, then he very clearly didn't know me for who I was.

Capitalism all the way for me, folks.

Survival of the fittest etc.

The weak and the meek and all those other fuckers on the social, can go and fuck themselves.

I made it to the wings anyway, just about, assiduously avoiding producers and security dudes as I went on my way, with no small degree of finesse.

Eventually arriving at McGuinness's side then, I punched him playfully in the shoulder, before tousling the decidedly thinning remains of the thatch on his head that once upon a time, quite a few years before I supposed, had been growing there abundantly of its own accord.

Not so anymore though, regrettably for him.

"All publicity, right, my son?" I intimated to him then with a smile, shamelessly quoting the great satirist himself.

"What do you think of that so then, son of the black stuff?" I continued, realising very soon though, that the fucker had no idea at all as to what I was inferring.

McGuinness?

Son of the black stuff?

I mean, Jesus Christ, it was hardly fucking rocket science.

I considered then the fact that the poor fucker had probably been required no doubt, for most of his waking hours, to spend the majority of his time fraternising with those U2 bozos, so when I contemplated that, and then consequently, his inability to work out what was no more than a simple word-play around what was really, let's not forget this, his own *actual fucking name*, I came to the conclusion that it was not that surprising at all that he was such a fucking dunce.

I just put it down to experience so, and moved on.

"What the fuck was that?!" he responded tersely, but I could tell by looking at him just that little bit more keenly, that he was actually, secretly - to anyone that was bothering to pay any attention - very pleased indeed.

You could tell by his face in fact that it couldn't have gone any better – regarding, that is, the creation of my Rock Star DemiGod persona - so even though outwardly he was required to give the impression to the 'public', that he was incensed to a point of near horror by the erratic and boorish behaviour of his new and reckless charge, he was in *actual* fact delighted by how the entire event had eventually come to pass.

He verified this to me further mere minutes later, as our limousine pulled out of Montrose and took a right turn towards Donnybrook and the city centre.

"Nice work kid!" he said, with a smirk of self-satisfaction smeared all over his smug looking face.

"Really, REALLY, nice work! We couldn't have choreographed the whole thing any better actually, if we had tried!"

You'd swear that he'd had something to do with it himself so conceited was his delivery.

I toyed momentarily so, with the idea of pulling him up on that, but decided in the end that it would be better, probably, if I said nothing at all.

This was the dude who held the purse strings I was thinking, so the less that I said or did to piss him off at this juncture the better.

And when I say 'held the purse strings', that was the whole point.

Not only was he buying the scoops in the Horseshoe bar, which was where we were headed to again right now, he was footing the bill also - and it had to be a fairly sizeable one at that - for the studio sessions that would be taking place in London at some point in the very near future.

I definitely needed to be keeping the bollocks onside so, especially given the fact that his continuing patronage would be having a direct and immediate influence on my general prosperity and success going forward.

I only had the four or five so anyway in the Horseshoe, before making my excuses and doin' a Dexy's.

The usual pricks were in situ - barristers and recruiters and the like - so hanging around there for any more than the sociable few was more than I was prepared to endure.

It was of critical importance also, that there was no repeat performance of what had taken place there earlier in the week.

Do you remember that I was on my way there with McGuinness, right after he had picked me up from the airport after that flight back from Cologne?

Well it turned out anyway that the place was completely fucking mobbed on the night in question, but that he'd managed to blag us a corner booth near the bar even so.

The only downside to this otherwise positive 'state of affairs' however, was having to spend time with that bell end Bono, and his admittedly half daycent skin of a drummer band member, Larry Mullen.

Larry's alright as it goes, and on the evening in question was taking the piss out of Bono almost as much as myself.

He drew the line however at fucking a full pint of gargle over his pint-sized partner in crime, which, as an approach to his dealings with the prick was significantly more reserved than my own.

As in, that is, I DID fuck a full pint of gargle over the bollocks.

But sure the fucker was annoyin' me, right?

And I'd had a long day.

He just kept shitin' on about the war on poverty and the fucking peace process, but the last time I checked – and I definitely said this to him at the time - he wasn't exactly throwing his gazillions at some poor bollocks who was living in a cardboard box under a bridge in the Dominican fucking Republic!

He had annoyed me at the 'Guns 'n' Roses' concert in Slane a few days before as well, so it was kind of a combination of things that led to me doing what I did.

McGuinness ushered me away at the time anyway, amid the commotion, and calmed me down over at the other side of the bar.

It was agreed that it would be better for everyone if I left, he said, but that I was to drop into meet with him first thing the following Monday morning, in his accountant Ossie Kilkenny's offices in Lower Mount Street, to talk through plans for the future in further detail.

He'd organised a recording session in London already, he said – things move fast in McGuinness's world - that would take place, all things going well, sometime the following week.

I did fuck all so for the weekend bar scratch me arse and pull me plum in the oul one's house in Donaghmede, before heading back into town on Monday morning for the meet.

I couldn't have left the gaff though anyway over the weekend, even if I'd wanted to, as around two hundred or so of my new fans had camped themselves outside for the duration, waiting for me to make an appearance.

And not a fucking looker among 'em either!

I checked, of course.

Otherwise I might have shown them a bit more interest.

Belinda showed up though, unsurprisingly, so I let her in, naturally enough.

Guaranteed blowie there.

It was mad as well I was thinking, as she was sucking my knob bone fucking dry, how when I was a nobody she didn't want to know me, but now that I was a bone fide Rock Star Demigod, she couldn't wait to get her chops around the old John Thomas.

BIG TIME fucked up in the head was our Belinda!

Gave great blowies though - you had to hand it to her.

Deadly.

She fucked off anyway eventually, but not before blagging an invite to the recording session in London the following week.

A moment of weakness on my part there, being honest; and almost certainly agreed to mid-fellatio.

There she'd be anyway, I could see her now, sitting in the corner, all demure and Yoko Ono like - as in, that is, no discernible talent to speak of at all, but an unshakeable belief, despite that obvious shortcoming, that she as much as anybody else there, belonged in such a rarefied environment nevertheless.

As I said.

Fucked up in the head.

I arrived at the accountants' office anyway in Mount Street on the Monday.

McGuinness had sent another limo to the house, so besides having to wade through the fuckers that were stationed outside still - even though it was 7.30am in the fucking morning - it was definitely a far easier journey than I'd been anticipating before the jammer had arrived.

And no Dart journey with the great unwashed as well!

I'd no idea how he had got my address also but that's McGuinness for you.

Organised to a tee and a bit of a miracle worker really.

How do you think U2 have been so successful for all these years?

As you are no doubt aware, it is not for their musical exemplariness.

I was shown into the office anyway by some secretary or other – a good looking ginger bird with a nice arse - to be greeted by the man himself and another spanner with glasses; which turned out to be the accountant, Kilkenny, as referred to before.

He shook my hand anyway, the accountant – limp and sweaty - before making his excuses and leaving the room.

McGuinness bade me sit down then before a large, old-fashioned looking leather-topped desk, which I did, before stationing himself similarly on the opposite side.

He opened up a large black A4 diary then, and started to speak.

"It is a TOUR-DE-FORCE young Johnny! A TOUR-DE-FUCKING FORCE" he announced excitedly.

"Unadulterated and inarguably fucking BRILLIANT is what it fucking is!" he announced again, chuckling away to himself, before looking down at the pages before him, and me again, with a soft little twinkle in his eye.

He shook his head then a little bit more, in apparent disbelief, before turning to the pages again, with another little chuckle thrown out there for good measure, and a bit more shaking of his head.

'Get to the point dude' I was thinking.

As in, you know; less of the feckin' histrionics?

Spit it out man.

We *do*, after all, only get the old three score and ten and whatever about me, you yourself are WELL on your way already to that heady number!

He eventually, anyway, came to the point.

"Okay so, young man, brace yourself for it" he gushed excitedly.

"The following list is a 'Who's Who' of contemporary icons, who as a result of the sterling work that has been carried out on your behalf by yours truly behind the scenes over the last number of days, have agreed to guest on your new album. Your new album which, BY THE WAY, is to be recorded over the next few weeks, in the eponymous and legendary 'Abbey Road' studios in dear old London town.

In no particular order so, young Jonathan, we have, as follows;

Geldof, Rogers, Nelson, Collins, Gabriel, Waits, Bush, Bono, McCartney, Rose, Moore, Waters, Bowie.

Well? So what do you think of fucking that pal?! Are you not impressed beyond your wildest fucking dreams?"

His enthusiasm was heart-warming, I had to admit it.

And it was hard to deny that it was a pretty impressive list as well, despite the odd name here and there that was dubious.

Some were worrisome also, for entirely other reasons, and would require further investigation/clarification before agreement might be reached.

Regarding the dubious ones though; I do actually like Kenny Rogers – 'Islands in the Stream' aside of course - but there was no way in this fucking world that I would ever in a million years, be sharing a studio with Willie fucking Nelson!

The Bono issue was contentious too, and I was fairly concerned as well as to what Geldof, musically, would be bringing the table.

Legend he was, and is, of course; don't get me wrong.

But had he had a hit single at all over the course of the previous fifteen or so years?

I was struggling to think of one.

Other than that however, I had little reason for complaint.

I indicated such, but made my reservations known also, as alluded to above.

"Don't be such a fucking pillock Freakers!" McGuinness responded, gesticulating wildly with his arms as a reaction to what I had just said.

"PRINCE, you fucking idiot! PRINCE ROGERS FUCKING NELSON! Not Kenny Rogers and EMPHATICALLY NOT Willie fucking Nelson? Have you gone mad? There will be no slack-jawed redneck yokels on this recording! Let me make that perfectly plain to you right now. The collection - and I trust that you are in agreement with me on this son - will be a work of the 'avant-garde'".

Eats, shoots, and leaves wha'?

Jaysus.

My bad.

I liked what I was hearing though.

'Avant-garde' was working for me big style.

I was thinking that Rogers and Nelson were a bit off the mark alright, genre wise.

It all made sense to me now.

The Bono issue however remained disquieting.

I voiced my concerns so, again, re; said issue.

"Look Johnny" McGuinness answered, quite serious now, before placing his hands on the table and leaning into me closer.

"Will you give me a fucking break on this pal? Paul, for some reason, I don't know why, has taken a bit of a shine to you, even though by all accounts you've treated him like a piece of dogshit during most if not all of your encounters to date. The pint over the head in the Horseshoe bar last weekend being a case in point. For some obscure reason however, I don't know why, he wants to be involved in this project. He specifically asked me to be in fact, which is not like him. I dunno, maybe he's gay for you or something. Fuck knows. Anyway, whatever. The point is, is that he holds a lot of truck in this town kid, and you don't hold dick, at least not yet anyways. The bottom line so, is this. I am advising you Johnny, as your manager, and his manager also, to cut the fucker some slack. There are honestly no disadvantages at all to him being involved. Quite the opposite in fact. It's a racing certainty actually, that we will sell double the records as a result of his involvement. The public love him – I've never known why, but they fucking do! I need you to agree to this right now Johnny, before we proceed. Its cards on the table time son. What's it gonna be? I need an answer from you one way or another. Bono's involvement? We're good to go. No involvement? We're shelving the entire enterprise!"

Fuck me!

Talk about a dilemma.

A cock and a hard place.

I mean Bono is such a fucking bollocks that it was difficult to conceive of him being on my first ever recording?

But it wouldn't be happening otherwise if I didn't concede.

The question really, was this – and as McGuinness had mentioned to me also, some time before - was I prepared to go dancing with the devil?

It was a conundrum indeed; no question about it.

But FUCKING SUREDIN I was prepared to go dancing with the devil!

Of course I was!

I'm not that fucking proud!

There had to be something in return though.

I couldn't give in *that* easily.

Or at least I couldn't *be seen* to be giving in that easily.

"Look can we just move on please?" said McGuinness wearily then, with his head now resting in his hands.

"We need to think about the songs; that is, you know, the 'covers' that we'll be doing? You remember that I mentioned to you last week, that it is a 'covers' album that we'll be recording?"

I nodded to indicate to him that I did.

"Yes indeed" he went on.

"We don't have enough time to come up with new compositions, obviously, but with a 'covers' album, we can put a pretty decent compilation together in no time at all".

"But hang on there just one fucking minute pal!" I interjected, cutting across him decisively before he elaborated any further.

Referencing the Bono 'situation' once again, it was critical that I let him know that I wasn't going to be a complete pushover when it came to potential involvement from the faux philanthropic midget bollocks that we all love to hate.

"I'm not having that Bono pox anywhere up in the mix, de ye hear me? Backing fucking vocals only pal, alright?"

He sighed and nodded, which was a noble enough concession in fairness to him, especially when I considered the fact that U2 were his largest client, clearly, and the single biggest reason why he was in the position that he was in today.

It was time so probably, I was thinking, to be giving the bollocks a break.

We went through all of the songs then in detail, but I'll tell you about them again, when I talk about my visit to Abbey Road.

Which, would you believe, was even *more* fucked up than anything that I had experienced thus far!

CHAPTER 17

Dying is focked; don't you agree?
Like, really, really focked.
Young Michael.
Just four.
Leukaemia.
Focked.
That's when everything started to turn sour.
And then there was that recurring dream.
My father dying in a hospital bed.
Fock knows where.
In the dream, I am he, comatose and unresponsive.
The setting is ethereal; clinical and misty.
Sterile with a thin blue hue.
I am surrounded by avaricious offspring, curiously enough, my very own self, tall and imposing and peering downwards; accusatory and stern, with my stone-faced siblings alongside me on either side, similarly austere.
They (we) do not fare well in my father's (my) imaginary state.
Inwardly belligerent is my imaginary entity.
A twisted Havisham whose apparent inability to communicate is vexing his audience to a point of near apoplexy.
It would appear also that they (we) want his (my) money.
A sea is visible in the distance through a window at eye level.
A deeper sleep within the dream peculiarly, arrives.
The sea is adjacent to a long and deserted beach.
Gentle waves ebb and flow and approach and recede; their minor flurries as they arrive harbingers of choppier waters on the horizon.
I see these, clearly, looming ominously; yet invitingly also.
I drift further out as the tide recedes; one final time, never to return.
Imagine that!
A moon that halts, orbiting no more.
Celestial worthlessness.
Suspended and immobile.

It might as well just fall from the sky now that its purpose, bar incandescence, is defunct.

There they are above me – the rapacious troop!

Sarah Pocket's, one and all.

And the gangly, scraggly-haired lout that I call my son.

My very own self.

'How much dosh does the old man have?' they contemplate.

'SURELY he is loaded. A widower for most of his life with sizeable state pension contributions accruing for the last twenty plus years as well? He MUST be loaded'

Little do they know however; these ingrates; of my mental state.

Although how could they?

Externally I am vegetative and hebetudinous – yet I see and hear all.

They will receive nothing.

I saw to that, many moons ago.

That'll learn 'em!

Their bothersome visits will bear no fruit.

The doctors are no better.

Similarly gormless, with their white coats and nametags the only differentiator between them and my scavengers.

I am compos mentis; although not to anybody looking on.

Simultaneously I am a passenger jet, doomed and plummeting to earth on a path that is already set.

A macabre silence is extant in the cabin, as the 'sudden loss of air pressure' that nobody believes will ever come to pass has - quite decisively, it must be conceded - come to pass.

Unused oxygen masks are swinging from side to side as the ill-fated craft maintains its eerie descent.

Too late for the passengers on THIS manifest!

The damage has already been done.

In unconsciousness I slip in and out of consciousness, to a point where I am uncertain of which is which.

Not long for this tired old bag of bones.

Lights grow dim on the shore, as the welcome embrace of an infinite number of aeons gathers me fulsomely to its bosom.

A diffusion of lifetime events merge as the dull mist that has been present but unseen since the beginning clears before my eyes.

Pain as I once knew pain to be, dissipates.

A state of heavenly suspension metastasizes above, around and beneath me, as hitherto material elements disperse.

I drift away then, on the wind out to the sea; a wisp with no name that was never really here.

As dreams go so, it's certainly up there, right?

I'm sure that there's a message there too, somewhere, that's like, you know, supposed to mean some focking thing!

I'm pretty wealthy though - as you probably know - so I definitely don't need the cash.

Nothing to do with that so.

I do have a question on my mind though, that has been vexing me for a while.

From where do I get my curmudgeonly nature?

Societal most likely; as my family in general were - and are – considerably more even-tempered than I.

Or from my grandfather?

He was a miserable old bollocks by all accounts.

Something my Dad used to say.

'A right old focking git he was' he intimated to me once.

'And a total bollocks on his deathbed as well!' he inferred further.

My grandfather's apparent suggestion for the inscription on his gravestone was (albeit in my view hilarious) extreme in the extreme.

"Here lies Zenon Geldof" was the alleged advocacy.

"Who, although he didn't know them specifically, despises everyone that decomposes here with him today in this Godforsaken boneyard. He will be aggrieved eternally by the fact that his non-corporeal remains must decay in an area that's adjacent to such similarly succumbed cadavers, who in real life he would have avoided as assiduously as an Andalucian Grand Inquisitor of old might have pursued despicable heretics for an imminent but regrettably undersub-scribed auto-da-fé".

Yes indeedy.

Old Grandpa Geldof was not sociable.

A misanthrope really.

Not unlike myself.

Thankfully anyway, following his expiration - and only after some last minute and hard fought intervention from other more socially decorous members of the extended Geldof family - his headstone was inscribed with a notably more moderate epitaph.

Names and dates etc., 'May He Rest in Peace', blah, blah, blah.

But what else does one need?

When you're gone, you're gone, and that's focking that!

Look at us anyway, gathered here today.

In venerable Abbey Road no less!

A collection of 'super beings' really if I'm being totally honest.

Are we not rarefied?

I know that I am.

Is not Joe Public beneath us?

The fact is indubitable.

If Geldof's arse for example, releases - as the great Billy Connolly often says - a wee jobby - as is its wont and an oft time metabolic necessity - with said wee jobby remaining unflushed in some hotel toilet convenience or other as a result of the buoyant nature of its overall consistency, is not said wee jobby now an object of material value?

'BEHOLD GELDOF'S TURD, GOOD SIRS!' I hear them cry, many years hence, in some Sotheby's type establishment of the future.

"WHAT AM I BID TODAY FOR THIS PRECIOUS ITEM?"

I recall indeed - whilst I am on the subject - young master Bowie regaling me once on the very theme, recounting a similar occurrence in his own experience when a pair of shysters that were loitering outside his own hotel room door, engaged themselves in a comparable conversation regarding the general purloining of one, or indeed two, of his apparently valuable - and only as a result of the fact that they were his - short and curlies.

The world is focked up people!

There ain't no denying it.

I know them all here anyway, pretty much, including the kid.

You know - that young Johnny Freak Show chap?

He's everywhere now anyway, by all accounts, and quite famous too, as far as I have been made aware.

Strange as well - he was a 'nobody' the last time that I saw him, at that shite 'Queen' tribute thingamajig in Wembley just last month.

He wasn't famous a few years ago as well when he was shitting his pants in Bad Bobs!

That was the time that I lent him a pair of jeans so that he could get himself home.

Sure didn't I tell everyone the story in Elton John's dressing room backstage the last time that we met?

What a focking twat!

Imagine shitting yourself because you can't tell the difference between a fort and a Barry White?

I'm good like that though, me.

Philanthropic, you know?

Always saving people and what not.

I'm famous for it indeed, as you probably already know.

Africans mainly.

Loads of those fockers would have died if it hadn't have been for me.

AND THE LESSON TODAY IS HOW TO DIE!

That was the moment folks.

241

MY moment.

The very first day of the rest of my life.

Do you remember it?

At Live Aid?

I'm sure that you do.

I focking do!

And what was to occur afterwards would define my existence from that very moment onwards.

As in, that is, much as staring out over a sea of eighty or so thousand sun-drenched, drunken kids in Wembley stadium can freak a person out - especially when you're acutely aware of the fact that in addition to the numbers that are in attendance here today, that there are one or so other billion individuals watching you on TV from any number of countries that are tuning in from across the globe - nothing can prepare you for the emotions that you experience when you find yourself perusing a vaguely similar, but considerably larger gathering, in another less fortuitous corner of the world; particularly when you take into account the fact that there's a very good chance that if the people that are gathered here before you right now, don't find sustenance of some description from somewhere, ANYWHERE, within the next one to two days, that there's a reasonably fair chance that they and their family, and most of their close acquaintances also, will perish from ACTUAL starvation for the want of what you and I deposit nonchalantly and without consideration, on a daily focking basis into our household bins.

It was a scene from hell.

You can't imagine it really, unless you've seen it up close.

Inconceivable.

And if you think that Michael Buerk - very ably, admittedly - purporting to you the biblical nature of the catastrophe - whilst you sit in the comfort of your front room, eating and then being put off eating what you are eating as a result of the scenes that you've just been coerced into witnessing, when all you ever wanted to do was to go to work or school or wherever, and relax then in the comfort of your own home afterwards, at the end of a long and taxing day out there in the 'normal' world, doing whatever the fock it is that you do - is a problem, then fock focking you!

The stench.

The desperation.

The hopelessness.

The eventual realisation that as a parent you CANNOT actually feed your focking child?

If you do nothing afterwards so, having witnessed this and seen truly, what REAL suffering is; well you're a soulless bastard who is beyond redemption.

May you die screaming in fact, as one of my old aunties used to say about the clergy.

What else could I do?

Let them perish?

No way.

Anybody else would have done the same thing.

And the look on poor old Mark Ellen's face when I dropped the 'f' bomb on national TV?

Focking priceless!

I didn't give a fock though.

It was of critical importance to stir the shit in whatever way that I could.

Controversy was essential to encourage the consistently languid and miserly British public to get off their fat lazy arses and pick up the focking phone.

And that video from 'The Cars'?

Fair play to Bowie as well for, you know; giving up his song.

Probably the noblest thing that he's ever done to be fair.

To convey the horror, you know?

It was a wake-up call for me as well.

The compass of my moral obligation after that was well and truly set.

Practically overnight, I became a figure of stewardship and enlightenment, socio and political, rather than a washed-up Rock Star DemiGod who was long since passed his sell-by date with the kids of today.

As a matter of fact, and if the truth be told, there was no way in a million focking years that 'The Rats' would have picked up the Live Aid gig if I hadn't been organising the thing myself.

Harvey Goldsmith would have told me to fock right off actually, if the circumstances had been different and the decision regarding our participation was based on popularity alone.

In the end anyway it worked out fine, with our songs standing up well enough when compared to most of the other acts that were performing on the day.

Back to today anyway.

There's the kid again, over there across the way; chatting to that gimp, Paul McCartney.

I'll call him over for a bit of an oul chinwag.

"Hey kid!" I shout across.

"Come over here te me, ye little poxbottle!"

Over he comes so; somewhat reluctantly though, I notice.

It definitely looks as if there was some unfinished business between himself and Macca before he wandered across; certainly by the way in which they appeared to part in any case.

"Howya Bob, what's the story?" says the kid gloomily.

"Not too bad kid, game ball" I respond, chummily enough.

"So what where yourself and Macca arguing about there?" I go on.

"Ahh nothing much at all, Sir Bobsalot" he answers.

"He was just being his usual narky fucking self."

Fair play to the kid; he's clearly a discerning judge of character.

His personality synopsis of Macca is of no surprise to me at all.

I've had lots of experience of dealing with the bollocks myself, and it's fair to say that he's one hell of a narky prick when he puts his mind to it.

He puts even me in the ha'penny place I'd go so far as to say.

The focker is always banging on about some shite or other.

I have a brainwave then, to beat all brainwaves!

The kid should tell him the greatest joke of all time!

You know; that one about Noddy, and why he has a bell on the top of his hat?

I defy anyone to not laugh at that gag.

It'd put a smile on any bastard's face, including Macca.

"Tell him the joke kid!" I encourage him excitedly.

"You know; the one about Noddy? He'll focking love that, guaranteed! How much is the bets?"

The kid appears reluctant to do so however, which is unusual enough.

He couldn't wait to throw it out there that night in Dublin a few years back, after he shit his pants.

And it went down a storm backstage in Wembley a few weeks ago as well, when I told it meself.

Something is not kosher.

Something is not kosher here at all.

McCartney looks weird also; almost as if he's seen a ghost.

But fock that!

The punters here today need to be hearing the joke is the way that I see it.

"Hey everybody, gather 'round!" I shout out.

"The kid has something to impart to you!"

Most of the people there start to wander over then, which is no surprise really, when you consider who I am.

As in like, you know; I'm Bob focking Geldof for fock sake!

Everybody listens to the Bobmeister these days.

I carry on.

"No, listen, seriously. This is an absolute focking REVELATION! I kid you not! You've never heard anything like it before in your life! It's that good!"

Ok so I'm bigging the gag up a bit, I can't deny it - but what's the problem with a bit of good old fashioned PR?

"What do you think Macca?" the kid shouts across then to McCartney.

"Isn't it about time that the world at large was aware of it? As in, should it not be, at this stage, in the public domain?"

Macca looks even unhappier with the situation now than he was before, to the extent in fact that he's like, just stood up and grabbed his jacket from off the back of his chair and focked off!

Well mental, that!

Off the scales looniness to be fair.

"What the fock is wrong with focking him?" I ask of the gathered luminaries.

They shrug to each other as one, as if to indicate that it's not that unusual really, when you consider the subject under present scrutiny more forensically.

Or to put it another way; that Macca is as mad as a box of frogs dude, so what the fock were you actually focking expecting?

"Anyway folks" I say, moving swiftly on.

"Wait until you hear the kid's gag! It's an absolute focking corker!"

"Come on kid" I continue.

"Let's be having it!"

The kid seems more into it now – thankfully - now that he has a captive audience that appears to be keen.

"Ok folks, here goes" he says.

"The greatest joke of all time, period!"

He takes a deep breath then and readies himself for the off.

And then he lets loose.

"Why does Noddy have a bell on the top of his hat?"

The crowd waits, with their mouths open slightly in anticipation of what I know already to be a glorious punch line.

The excitement is palpable.

Our intrepid young jokester then, moves in for the kill.

"Because he's a cunt!" he says.

Silence.

Not a dickey bird.

Like, what the actual fock?

And then, EUPHORIA!

But from just one individual alone.

Kate Bush, who as everybody knows is about as balanced as a two legged chair, shrieks with delight.

Regarding the rest of them though, they're just standing there, feckless idiots one and all, wondering what the fock is going on.

I'm inclined to think so, looking at them all, with their imbecility on show for the whole of the world to see, that in addition to Enid Blyton's plucky young (albeit dubiously hatted) hero, that most of the dudes and dudettes that are on display here today, have personality traits that are of a similarly questionable persuasion.

"Well its ok, I suppose" says the charlatan, Bowie, who's heard it before also of course, I'm remembering, that time I told it backstage in Wembley just a couple of weeks ago.

He liked it then though, so what's his problem with it focking now?

"But let's be honest Geldof" he goes on.

"It's hardly rib-ticklingly uproarious, now, is it? And the course language also I believe, is quite objectionable - I'm sure that most here would agree? I myself much prefer the one about the two nuns in the bath".

Trust that Bowie bollocks to position himself on morally higher ground.

"OK so, well what's that one about then dude?!" I retort narkily, more to humour the focker than anything else.

"Oh yeah!" he responds gushingly.

"It's class. Like totally fucking class man!" the bollocks goes on, not worried about course language now of course, now that he has the floor.

"Well, tell the bleedin' thing, will ye then, for fock sake, if you're focking gonna!" I say tetchily, starting to lose my patience now, the more the prick goes on.

He aligns himself centrally then where everybody can see him, before shaking his arms around a bit and limbering up, kind of, as if getting himself ready for some sort of a prize focking fight or something.

"Two nuns in a bath" he says then, all confident like, and full of himself.

"One says to the other - 'Where's the soap? The other nun replies, 'Yeah, it does, doesn't it?!'"

The whole room erupts.

Like what the actual fock again!

Ok so it's daycent enough, but not exactly at the 'Noddy being a cunt because of his stupid focking hat' level.

'Where' being replaced by 'wear', you know?

With the inference being that if you rub the soap against your nunnish fanny for long enough, its general fullness will, depending on your own personal meticulousness, deplete in size accordingly.

You'd think anyway, by the way that the fockers are guffawing and rolling about the place with glee, that the Bowie spanner is some sort of a comical focking genius or something.

When all he is really when you think about it, is some focker with a half daycent voice and floppy hair.

And no arse!

That's right!

No focking arse.

I'm surprised that more people don't bring it focking up.

At least I have a focking arse!

"I think that it's good actually" says the kid magnanimously.

"I'll definitely be using that one again".

"But anyway" he goes on.

"Seeing as you're all here now - gathered together in one actual corner of the studio - do you think that we can take this opportunity to go through the running order of the songs, and decide then on who's going to be doing what?"

Fair play to the kid; he's confident, I'll give him that.

"I'm thinking 'Intruder' for the first number. Are you cool with that?"

He is addressing his comments to that feckin' weirdo, Peter Gabriel, who quietly, and 'just about' to be honest, murmurs a response.

He was singing some shite earlier on, but had to shut up as a result of it being so focking tragic.

Kate Bush had to convince him to stop, which he did, thankfully.

"Sure kid" he whispers in response.

"Whatever you say".

I think that he's still pissed off about being asked to pipe down.

This is going to be one hell of a strange focking album anyway I'm thinking, if 'Intruder' by Peter Gabriel is the opening track.

A great number though, don't get me wrong; but hardly Top 40 fodder.

"Kate? Phil?" the kid continues, turning around to address some others.

"Are you two ok to add backing vocals and drums as per the original number on the LP?"

Kate Bush, one of the duo to whom he is supplicating, giggles girlishly as if to denote acquiescence, but says something then about it being some other song that she had sang on before.

They sort that shit out anyway, whatever it is, and then Phil Collins, who I've only just noticed is there, indicates that he's up for it as well.

"No FACKING problem, moy san!" he says, all cheeky chappy and London wide boy-esque.

"Pukka!" he remarks further, like some sort of a bleedin' dope.

I have to say also, that he is wearing THE absolute worst focking jumper that I have ever seen in my entire focking life.

It's bleedin' woejious!

A Freddy Kruger type number in white and red.

A shocker really to be fair.

"No takin' the piss owra the jumper vis time though kid, owite?" he puts to Johnny, as if reading my mind.

Once again, they must know each other from before.

This Freak Show kid sure gets around.

"Oh yeah, sorry about that Phil" answers the kid, looking genuinely remorseful, I think, probably for the first time ever.

Or certainly since I've known him myself.

"I was having a pretty bad time of it back then dude" he explains further.

"Prince over there gave me some seriously dodgy pills just before, hence my shitty attitude on the day in question. Apologies again duder".

Ok, so he is like, WAAY overdoing the apology now.

He must be looking for something, defo.

Absolutely focking guaranteed!

"No worries kid" says Collins, with everything now forgotten about apparently, and like, all water under the bridge and shit.

I'm inclined to think myself though that it's decidedly optimistic of Collins to believe that anybody in their right mind who is reviewing the putrid specimen/ jumper of choice today, will in any way be able to restrict themselves from taking the absolute and utter focking piss out of it; unless of course they can call on some very seriously impressive attributes of self-control and restraint.

It is ALL OVER the focking shop!

"Cheers" says Phil to the kid, before moving on to the next thing.

Whatever happened to Phil Collins though?

Now there's a dude who bought a one-way ticket to Palukaville.

'Sign me up' said he.

I'll make that deal with the devil.

And there it was.

Shite numbers for ever more.

'And he ain't never comin' home' as Tom Waits across the way there says in one of his songs.

'You want my dignity?

Go right ahead and take it pal.

Toss around my bizarrely popular golden eggs as you see fit, and keep on sending me the cheque'.

The Rats would never stand for that.

No focking way man!

Do I look like Lionel focking Richie?

Collins on the other hand is happy to lap it all up – don't forget that he went from 'Blood on the Rooftops' to 'I Missed Again' in less than four years.

Like, how focked up is that?

From the sublime to the ridiculous.

Axl Rose is here too, with an interesting selection of nubile totty in tow.

He's an omnipresent scourge though, that focker.

As in, is there anywhere that he isn't?

MTV?

Slane?

Random tribute concerts?

Here?

It would appear not.

He's totally locked also of course, which is no surprise.

The majority of his party as well, females mainly, are in various stages of undress, which is sadly not as a result of any orgy that's imminent or anything of a similarly decadent nature, but more so related to the fact that this is the way that they actually turn themselves out.

"Hey, you can carry a toon doll, right?" Axl intimates to one of them, a buxom blonde girl in denim shorts and a flimsy item of clothing on her top half which I believe is referred to as a 'boob tube'?

"How about a Derry air?" he goes on, which seems like an odd request to be putting forward, until I hear then, subsequently, the way that she speaks.

A feckin' Northerner!

"Aye, but not niyee lover" she answers.

"I'm tayee dronk?"

I toy with the idea of explaining to her that neither 'now' nor 'two' are words that carry two syllables, but consider then, wisely probably, that most in attendance would regard such an intervention, almost certainly, as a churlish intervention indeed.

And besides I'm keen to remain on her good side for obvious enough reasons.

Whatever about Axl's desire to hear her bang out for the masses a dulcet tune that originates from the north-north-west coast of the Emerald Isle, I'm inclined to assert to her myself instead, whenever such an opportunity might arise, that I'd be considerably more keen to familiarise myself with another 'derriere' of which she is in possession; one that is, one might say; of an altogether more tangible constitution.

She is very well upholstered indeed!

I decide so; wisely I believe; to maintain my council for now.

There's Macca again, popping his stupid focking head around the door.

Looking for his minder most probably, who's still here.

'Fock off Macca' I'm thinking, irritated to be seeing the focker again.

Definitely the worst focking Beatle - of that there is zero focking argument.

And there's that feckin' gobshite Roger Waters.

We're good pals usually, but he's being one hell of a narky focker today!

I'm trying to get him to let me sing on at least one of the longer Floyd songs of the three that we're going to be doing for the album, but the bollocks is having absolutely focking none of it.

"So let me get this straight" I say to him, eager to convey to him that I am not best pleased.

"You want to do ALL of the vocals on 'Empty Spaces', ALL of the vocals on 'Young Lust', and have DEIGNED to allow me to sing one focking line on 'Is There Anybody out There'? Being namely, the line 'Is there anybody focking out there'? Additionally, you large-veined bollocks, you are telling me - having me bothering my arse to turn up to this focking thing in the first place, to assist this no-mark kid with the untrustworthy excretory organs - that I can't even play acoustic guitar on said number? You can fock right off Waters, is what you can do, ye lefty,

communist cock-sucking prick!"

"Oh fuck off Geldof" he responds, clearly not best pleased with things himself.

"You're shit man, and everybody knows it!" he goes, before breaking into, for who knows why, 'You'll Never Walk Alone', that anthem type thingamajig that the Liverpool football fans are always singing.

He's focked off as well, across to the other side of the room to talk to Axl.

Good riddance I say.

Let the feckin' spanners get on with it!

I'll definitely shout a few insults across to them though, later on.

Imagine not letting me play guitar on that other instrumental number as well?

I'm a focking great guitarist - well acoustic anyways - and besides, it's picking, merely, around just A Minor and C.

A child could focking play it!

"'Banana Republic' my arse!" Waters shouts across then, the cheeky bastard.

"Why don't you fuck off and write a proper political polemic that is venerated the world over – like, you know, I fucking did!?"

What a feckin' pillock!

'The Wall' is a load of old shite!

I can't believe that I did that movie now; I mean what the fock was I focking thinking?

"Ask me bollocks Waters, ye prick" I respond anyway.

I'm not prepared to take THAT shite lying down.

"And tell your Aorta also while you're at it" I go on.

"That it is an INTERNAL focking artery and not usually within the context of conventional physiological systems, meant to be located anywhere that is remotely adjacent to an individual's epidermis!"

You'd want to see the state of the veins on his arms.

Focking shocking!

He's come over to me again anyway, which is definitely a pain in the arse.

But one of the geddles has followed him over as well, so that's a positive development somewhat, I suppose.

There's no focking way in the world when she sees ME here that she'll be choosing that big veined bollocks over the Bobmeister!

She's Irish too, which is good, and a southsider as well, from what I can make out from her accent.

I wouldn't be going near any focking Northsiders!

It definitely looks like I'll be in like Flynn here so anyway, soon enough!

The skirt that she's wearing also – if I can call it that – is all the way up to her arse!

I can see her keks an' all, but it looks as if she doesn't give a fock about that either way, one way or another.

She might be locked though is the only thing.

She's DEFINITELY locked.

Locked and focked.

Probably best to leave it so.

I don't want to be accused of anything suss anywhere down the line.

She seems more into Waters though; which is definitely a bit mad.

Although I'm probably giving off negative vibes.

"Are all these your guitars?" I hear her ask of him then, which I believe is a line from of his songs.

And then "Wanna take a bath" which I recognise also, from one of their tunes.

Might be the same one.

She focks off with Waters then anyway in the general direction of the jacks, so I've definitely missed out on my chance there to score.

If I'd made any sort of an effort though, he would definitely have been left trailing in my wake.

I mean how could he not, the elephantiasis of the capillaries suffering prick?!

I'm Bob Bobmeister focking Geldof for fock focking sake!

CHAPTER 18

"Can you tell me where my country lies? Said the unifaun to his true love's eyes".
Unifaun?

Bloody hell Peter Gabriel!

Whatever the fuck you're on dude, cut the bleedin' dose!

I would say this to you also pal - and I mean it with the greatest sincerity - think of a number between P44 and P46.

He was sitting on a high stool anyway, singing his song.

The words of said song also - as you have just heard - were in no way what one might ever be in a position to describe as satisfactory.

The atmosphere so, as a result of this malarkey, was malevolent.

I scanned the room before me, taking stock of the eminent luminaries within.

And sad as it might seem, as I reviewed these blankest of faces - given what I believed to be on a personal level, a grand and auspicious occasion; that is the recording of my debut album of covers - I saw nought but negativity throughout.

Total misery really, being honest - but with the sounds that were abroad, such a scene was not unsurprising.

"It lies with me, said the Queen of Maybe" Gabriel continued.

"For her merchandise, he traded in his prize".

The mood was not improving.

'The Queen of Maybe?' mouthed Prince to Gary Moore, with a pained display of incredulity evident across his general demeanour.

"Unifaun? Like, 'What the Actual Fuck' dude?" mouthed Axl Rose to Tom Waits, who shrugged his shoulders in response, as an individual similarly nonplussed.

He was a man of few words, Peter Gabriel.

When he sang however; as was the situation right now; the ensuing barrage was contrarily interminable.

He would stop soon anyway; eventually and thankfully; aware finally I would say that these 'unifaun' and 'queen of maybe' type motifs - as per what he'd been wittering on about for the last little while - were failing to scale the heights.

In that regard he was not incorrect.

The prevailing verdict, as I have mentioned already, was a unanimous and collective inversion of the thumb.

252

The 'a capella' delivery was the main source of distaste I believe; but Phil Collins informed me reliably (and he would know, as he had played drums on the *actual* original recording), that this was how it had been delivered on an early Genesis album, many years before.

Even he so, also, in the clear light of day, was cognisant of the song's short-comings - although he did tell me that despite the ridiculous nature of the content lyrically, that it held up rather well actually, even now, from a musical point of view.

I was unconvinced myself though, but not knowing the number in question I had no choice at the time but to just take his word for it.

I couldn't deny something of which I had zero knowledge.

And besides I *did* know their 'Foxtrot' album from the early 1970's, so his description of how they put their songs together at the time definitely rang true.

They'd one track in fact, if I remembered it correctly, that took up the entire-ty of one side of a vinyl LP!

I do recall that it was decent enough though musically, despite - as Collins had attested to just now - the librettos to said melodies being a good deal more pretentious as to be palatable.

So here I was anyway, in Abbey fucking Road.

Would you actually fucking believe it?

McGuinness, true to his word, had gathered everybody together that he had said he would, so here we all were now.

And it was a Motley Crew indeed!

If the collected individuals in situ however could deliver on all that I was looking for them to deliver - well everything would definitely be OK.

It was pretty obvious though to anyone that might be looking on, that most of the individuals that were gathered here today were incontrovertibly unstable.

Regarding their musical capabilities however, and what they might be in a position to bring to the table, I was feeling very positive indeed.

Despite their obvious shortcomings vis-à-vis general sanity and what not, it was hard to deny that from a musical point of view we were dealing with actual 'rock royalty' here.

It would be a challenge to contain them, admittedly; but I reckoned that I could just about keep them on track.

If I could only get Peter Gabriel to shut the fuck up though, I was thinking.

Maybe then, finally, I'd be in a position to get the ball rolling on my new foray.

Thankfully anyway, and on that very note, Kate Bush, spotting that he was struggling, swooped in majestically to lend him a hand.

Gliding imperiously across the room to where he was situated, she arrived at his side soon enough, before whispering something inaudible softly into his ear.

Gabriel stopped immediately then and stepped down from off his stool, before being led away slowly by Kate to the other side of the room.

At last!

His farcical songsmithery was at an end!

I'm not sure what Kate said to him to be honest, but it was abundantly clear to all that were there, that he was infatuated by her beyond a level that could ever be considered to be healthy.

He was like putty in her hands.

It was time to get busy now though, regarding getting my new tracks laid down.

Time was money and all that, and the fuckers here today would not be providing their services for free.

I had a quick scan around the room then again to see who else was there.

Prince and Gary Moore as you've just heard, so axe wise we were definitely sorted.

Axl Rose and Tom Waits were present also, as I was mentioning there before too, so overall fruitiness and a general likelihood to aggress was box ticked as well.

Macca was in attendance additionally, which was a bit of a surprise.

That bollocks doesn't get out of bed for less than fifty grand a day I'd say, and from what little I knew of McGuinness, I was certain even so that he wasn't going to be forking out wedge like that for anybody, whether they be an eminent musical patrician of legendary status or not.

Kate Bush was there also as I said; looking as beautiful as ever; with Peter Gabriel as I alluded to there before, following her every move.

Phil Collins was in situ too; but his jumper was so grim that he was being ignored by and large by everybody that was there.

Bowie was hovering around the place additionally, trying to look cool.

And Geldof as well!

That fucker is everywhere!

I was hoping that he wouldn't mention my soiling 'episode' from Bad Bobs from a few years before.

I could do without that shit – literally - rearing its ugly head today.

ESPECIALLY today!

He'd brought it up at that Freddie gig a few weeks earlier as you may recall, and it had done little for my street cred at the time.

Thankfully anyway, he appeared on *this* day to be happy to shite on about matters of a different nature.

You may recall my meeting so, going back to it, with McGuinness at his accountants' office in Mount Street?

That was when we came to our agreement regarding the songs.

It had started well anyway - as I'm sure you'll be no doubt delighted to hear - and had got better and better as our meeting had gone on.

I couldn't believe the artists that he had lined up for me being honest, and on top to that also, the songs that they had agreed to let us cover.

I'd had to concede to Bono being involved though, which was the only downside really, to the whole thing.

And here he was now, sitting in the corner in Abbey fucking Road - the short-arsed oily prick - trying to look all suave and mysterious as if the fucker had invented what it was like to look urbane.

I was at a loss as to why he wanted to be there though.

I'd fucked a pint over him in the Horseshoe bar only a few weeks before, and had treated him like absolute horseshit also, just a few days before that at the Guns 'n' Roses gig in Slane.

Perhaps he WAS gay for me, as McGuinness had mentioned to me before.

"Ok well let's go with 'Tomorrow' for the U2 number" I had suggested anyway to McGuinness at the time, which was the only U2 number that I could think of that was tolerable.

"Definitely their best three minutes" I continued, piling on the saccharine, just to keep the fucker onside.

This was a great opportunity for me, so I didn't want to fuck it up.

If suffering Bono for a few days in Abbey Road was the price that I had to pay for success, then pay that price I would pay.

"Excellent!" McGuinness responded at the time, perking up; considerably happier now I believe that I had decided to play ball.

I had definitely been a narky bollocks up until that point; I don't mind admitting to it.

"Let's have a think about the other songs so, as well!" he continued at the time, leaning forward now with renewed excitement.

"I've some solid ideas myself of course, but would welcome input from your good self too. And again, just as a reminder, young Johnny, it is imperative that the tunes be avant-garde".

Fortunately enough looking at the list again, it was clear that most of the artists in question had a fairly obvious leaning anyway in that general direction.

Finding *unusual* songs so from their already weird and wonderful repertoire, would not be as challenging as it might otherwise have been, had the artistes in question been less fucked up in the head.

I moved in closer so to have a more meticulous look at the names.

Next on the list was Gabriel, erstwhile frontman for Genesis as I was mentioning before, (when they were, believe it or not, as I kind of mentioned before, semi -daycent) and eventual world music icon/thinking man's 'alternative rock' hero DemiGod extraordinaire.

"Peter fucking Gabriel!" said McGuinness warmly.

"You have just GOT to love Peter Gabriel. He's a bit like Bono really, isn't he? Except not so much of a pain in the arse. And taller too. CONSIDERABLY taller; which wouldn't be difficult in fairness."

It WOULDN'T be difficult.

I'd been about to suggest that also as it goes, but had decided to keep it to myself.

There was no point in annoying the bollocks again I was thinking, now that he was in better form.

He might have said the words himself of course, but that didn't mean that I could just jump on the band wagon myself.

I suppose it's a bit like when black dudes use the 'N' word amongst themselves, you know?

As in, you know that it's ok for them to do it, but if any other fucker, particularly a white fucker, starts acting the bollocks and doing the same, then they'll be taken to task for it soon enough.

"Agreed" I answered so; leaving the diminutive aspect of Bono's stature to the side for now.

"The best thing that Gabriel EVER did actually dude" I went on.

"Was to leave Genesis in 1975, and go out on his own. I mean look at the car crash that they've become since then? Fuck me man!

'Land of Confusion'? Land of fucking BOLLOCKS more like!"

McGuinness nodded sagely to denote his acquiescence.

"You're right young Freakers" he said, nodding in agreement.

"I was thinking something off PG4 anyway?" he continued, as he stared at the ceiling and nibbled at the end of his pen.

"But then I thought to myself, like, you know, come on Paulie, what the fuck is actually wrong with you dude? As in, basically – and I'm sure that you will agree with me here Freakers - for pure and unadulterated fucking weirdness, you're not gonna find any number that is more fitting than 'Intruder', the opening song on PG3. Would you agree with THAT, young Freakerino?"

I DID agree with that and told him so with a considerable degree of éclat.

"FUCK YEAH, BUBBA!" I blurted, leaping to my feet with excitement.

"'Intruder' is the fucking DOGS man!!"

"INTRUDER'S HAPPY IN THE DAAAA-AARK!" I sang then further with great fervour.

'Intruder' is a fucking ANIMAL I was thinking, and the perfect number also with which to kick off the new disc.

As in, you know - I am 'INTRUDING'?

Entering into the public domain, and about as subtle as a brick wall across a motorway.

THAT'S what I'm talking about!

"Oh and another thing" he said, in a fairly off the cuff manner I was thinking at the time, especially when I considered afterwards the perilousness of the statement that he was putting forth.

"We'll be having Phil Collins drumming on that one as well".

'He's definitely trying to squeeze that doozie in there while I'm in good fucking form' I considered then, as he avoided my gaze and pretended to look at some papers and shit to his right.

I mean, like, you know - it wasn't even his bleedin' desk!

Did he think that I was a *total* fucking sap?

As it happened anyway, I didn't care about that *too* much.

Collins is on the original cut anyway and does a decent enough job.

He uses no cymbals on the track also, which is unusual, and proper belts it out as well.

"That's cool" I responded in a calm and collected manner, to which McGuinness did a bit of a double take.

He had definitely been expecting me to be a bit less agreeable there.

"I've met Collins before as it goes Paulie" I admitted to him further.

"And whereas he is a poxbottle undoubtedly, to beat all other poxbottles, and wears additionally, THE worst fucking jumpers that you have ever seen, he remains, nevertheless, despite 'Against All Odds' etc., a seriously great fucking drummer".

"I have to admit to you though Paulie" I went on.

"That my last encounter with him did not end well. I gave him a thick lip in some underground club in London for slagging off Prince, and got fucked out of said venue, would you believe, for the very same action? Most clear-minded people, I considered after the event, would have given me a fucking medal! Anyway - just in case there's any needle in the studio like, when he cottons on to who I am".

"Not a problem Johnny" said McGuinness.

"Not a problem at all. I wouldn't be overly mad about him myself."

"And another thing!" I piped up, thinking of something else.

"There is no way in this fucking WORLD that I'm doing any of *his* numbers!"

"Jesus Johnny!" responded an animated McGuinness in apparent disbelief.

"I would have assumed that that was a fucking given! I mean Collins' music is BEYOND tragic, everybody knows that! No son, don't worry; we'll be doing just the Gabriel number with Collins, and then a Beatles number as well, with Collins drumming on that one as well. 'Tomorrow Never Knows', do you know it? Collins actually does a half acceptable version of it himself in fact, on one of his own albums - surprisingly enough - so I think we'll be ok."

257

I was dubious enough about that I have to admit, but decided to let it go.

So long as the bollocks wasn't singing 'A Groovy Kind of Love' or some such other similar bolloxology, I should probably, I was thinking, be thankful for small mercies.

"Prince next so duder" said McGuinness.

"And you are not going to BELIEVE what he is permitting us to use!"

'Excellent!' I was thinking.

Prince's music is weird enough at the best of times, so whatever it was, it was bound to be hitting the nail vis-à-vis general screwballishness.

"Go on dude!" I asked excitedly, hoping for something that was off the wall.

I would not be disappointed.

"What is it?" I enquired further.

"Only fucking 'Crystal fucking Ball' dude!" answered McGuinness.

"Would you Adam and Eve fucking that!" he went on.

'Wow' I was thinking.

'Crystal fucking Ball'!

Fuck me, what a tune!

Underground and rare and never officially released.

I'd heard it once before on a bootleg that Marcus had picked up in Amsterdam, but hadn't been fortunate enough to hear it again since.

From what I could remember of it though it was a real knockout, and also, as was our requirement for this collection, seriously fucked up in every way that you could imagine.

Right up our street so.

"Next up" said McGuinness, "Is the great Macca himself! Guest starring on the album as a result of a favour being called in by our very own diminutive frontman himself, Master Hewson. Paul has put himself out for you here, young Johnny, I do hope that you realise that!"

I think that he was expecting me to be impressed, but having met McCartney before I was inclined to think that I could take him or leave him, one way or another.

Given that I was supposed to be remaining on my new manager's good side however, I contemplated that it was probably best at this juncture to give the impression that McCartney, rather than being a knob end to beat all other knob ends known to man, was in actual fact, conversely, the greatest thing since sliced bread.

The fact that Bono was doing me a favour also was neither here nor there.

I quite honestly could not have given a flying fuck whether he was putting himself out for me or not.

That said though, it was important nevertheless to maintain my bonhomie.

"Fantastic!" I said so, with faux enthusiasm.

258

"That's fucking brilliant Paulie!" I continued.

"I've always liked Macca" I went on, taking great care to come across as sincere.

"I've actually met *him* before also, would you believe? And I don't give a bollocks what anybody else says about him Paulie; you know, about being a stupid, miserable fucking talentless cunt and all that? Defo my favourite Beatle Paulie, one hundred per cent!"

McGuinness gave me a funny look then, as if to indicate that he thought that I might be taking the piss.

I assured him however, that I was not.

"Seriously dude, no kidding. Macca is the fucking bollocks!" I went on, trying my best again to appear genuine.

'The' bollocks, rather than 'A' bollocks I clarified for him again, when he asked me to repeat what I had just said.

He remained sceptical however, and then I considered that he had probably met with him himself before at some point, and was aware therefore of the famous scouser's shortcomings.

That had to be it.

He shook his head anyway and moved on.

"OK well he'll be on it and has agreed to let us use 'Tommorow Never Knows' as I mentioned before, from the incomparable 'Revolver album – in my opinion their best – fuck Sergeant Peppers – but only on the condition that he shares the vocal with you 50/50 all the way through"

I was dubious enough about this at the time also; but having the chance to record such a fantastic track as the aforementioned masterpiece, was too good an opportunity to forego.

I would maintain my council on it for now so I was thinking, and put up with this mild affront in the interests of getting it over the line today.

I could always push back on Macca on the day.

"Sounds great dude" I answered so.

"I'm happy with that for sure" I continued, lying.

"Okey doke, Johnny" McGuinness replied, who at this stage was looking as pleased as punch with himself.

"Next we have Geldof, who as you know is fucking EVERYWHERE. That said, he does pack a lot of punch and is the only reason why we have Waters on board as well. They know each other quite well apparently, from that time Geldof that played the lead in that woeful movie that they made based on the great Floyd LP, 'The Wall'".

It was true in fairness to him.

The movie of 'The Wall' was a shocker indeed.

Which was mad really, when you considered the fact that the album was such an absolute fucking classic.

Say what you want about the Floyd, but you can never slag off 'The Wall'. Even punk rockers like it and that's saying something.

I was genuinely pleased to hear that Roger Waters would be involved.

He is a bit of a communist undeniably, but anybody that can pen something as off the wall as 'Dogs' is alright with me.

Definitely their finest moment.

"What's the Floyd number Paulie?" I asked of him, eager to know.

"Well I'm keen to limit Geldof's input to a minimum" he answered, on a positive note.

"Given how absolutely fucking shite he is in every way, so we're going to do a short semi-instrumental one from 'The Wall' called 'Is There Anybody out There'. Are you familiar with it? He wants to do the acoustic guitar bit on that as well by the way, which he insists that he can manage on his own. I'm not convinced about that myself though, but sure I suppose we'll just have to wait and see on the day. We'll have plenty of other guitar players there either way anyway, so we're not gonna end up stuck if it turns out that he reeks".

"Excellent boss" I responded.

"I do know and like that number; it's definitely one of their best, although short, which in this case as you say, is not the negative that it might otherwise be. Will Waters not be put out though, if that's the only Floyd number that we're doing? I mean it hardly requires a huge amount of input from him, you know?"

"Well spotted Young Freakers, well spotted!" McGuinness responded with a laugh.

"There is no way in hell that a raving fucking megalomaniac like Roger Waters will be turning up to something like this just to make up the numbers. We have 'Empty Spaces' and 'Young Lust' lined up for him as well, with Gary Moore on axe on both of those too. Or Prince - it doesn't matter. Maybe one do one and one do the either? Either way, both of those numbers will be fucking rock dude! Waters will do vocals on the first and you can take over on the second if that's alright? As I'm sure you know already, both of those tunes run into each other."

"All good Paulie" I said.

"All good. Loving your work here dude. Who's left?" I went on.

"Can't be more than the one or two, right?"

"Correctimundo young Johnny!" McGuinness answered, rubbing his hands in anticipation I believe, for what he was about to impart to me next.

"Next up" he went on.

"Is the legend known as Thomas Alan Waits! A little number known as 'Tango 'til They're Sore' from his 1985 tour de force 'Rain Dogs'. He'll be tinkling the ivories pal, while you take over on the vocals. I can't believe that he has agreed to let us do it to be honest, as it's a pretty difficult number to take on. I assume that you're up for that?"

"Fuck yeah!" I exclaimed loudly, in an effort to impress upon him my confidence in my ability to take on said task.

I was not convinced particularly though, as attempting to emulate the great man himself, tonally at least, would be an assignment that would not prove to be easy in any way.

"No better fucking buachaill!" I intimated further, for additional effect.

"Excellent" McGuinness went on.

"And last but not least - and admittedly, not hugely avant garde - we'll be going with 'All the Young Dudes' by Mott the Hoople. Bowie will share vocals with both yourself and Axl Rose, while the chorus will be taken up by anyone else there that can sing. What do you think? I think that it's a magnificent fucking closer myself personally dude".

I couldn't deny that the anthem in question was a definite crowd pleaser, and although not hugely avant-garde as he had said, it was a great closing number indeed for what seemed to me to be, in every fucking respect, a great track listing generally from start to finish.

I couldn't have been happier if I'm being honest, so made that sentiment clear to him then, with a more than exuberant degree of aplomb.

"You're a fucking legend Macker!" I stated to him demonstratively, before standing up and walking over to the other side of the desk, and planting a big wet smacker right on him, full on the lips.

"If you were a Doris, I'd be bangin' ye!" I went on, to which he quite rightly nearly fetched up his shredded wheat.

The meeting ended then, not long after, after which I found myself, no more than a couple of weeks later, in Abbey Road, as I mentioned at the start, along with the collection of rock and roll misfits as have been alluded to to date.

And I was getting a right pain in my arse dealing with them as well, as things stood.

Whatever about their exemplary ability to create seminal music that many years hence will compare more than favourably to anything else that has gone before, handling them on a personal level, and trying indeed, to get them to do anything at all in what most other people would consider to be a reasonably decent timeframe, was more challenging than anything that I had experienced to date.

It was like herding fucking cats!

Axl Rose and Tom Waits were in one corner, smoking weed and talking in close, whilst Gary Moore and Prince were comparing shoes at the other end of the studio.

Cuban heels for Moore I believe, while Prince's choice – and it was an iffy enough one at that – was a pair of gold stilettos.

Which would lead to the question - at least in my mind anyway – was there any *specific* reason pal, as to why you got dressed this morning in the dark?

Macca was there as well across the way, talking to his minder, all secretive like, just the two of them.

I'd been over with the legendary scouser earlier, just to say hello.

He'd been on about his songs again and the fact that neither he nor the other Beatles had actually written them at all, and had actually instead, purloined them from his old piano teacher in the late 1950's, right after he and John had accidentally murdered the dude but got away with it, and then headed off to Hamburg directly afterwards, to develop the new tunes and render them superior.

Macca had told me this yarn several years before while I'd been working in a wine bar on the Strand, and encountered him there while he was drunk and slobbering pathetically at the bar.

I hadn't believed his bullshit story then and didn't believe it any more when he'd been telling it to me again, earlier today.

I had met him then again some weeks after the first occasion, on the steps of the very studio that we were in now in fact, and he'd laid the very same claptrap on me once again.

I found it hard to believe that he was still hawking this bullshit around town to be honest, when everybody already knew about it, and nobody even so was taking him seriously in any way.

At this stage so, I believed that sarcasm of a stinging and wounding nature would be the general order of the day.

"Ahhh yeah, the stolen songs; I forgot about them Macca!" I responded, taking great care to appear earnest and true.

"Haven't they fucked you in jail for that yet?"

"SSSSSHHHHH!!" he hissed at me then, pulling me in closer, and telling his minder to fuck off somewhere else while we spoke.

"Nobody else 'ere knows abarrih la'" he went on.

"Except you, me, and one or two select udders dah shall remain nameless for now, ok?"

I was beginning to get a right pain in the hoop with the prick.

I mean, how long was he planning to keep this bolloxology up?

It was time to teach the fucker a lesson.

"Look Macca" I answered, once again feigning seriousness and intent.

"I honestly believe that the world has a right to know. Do you seriously believe that this charade can be allowed to continue? It has gone on for long enough. Tomorrow morning so, first thing, I will go to the press and tell them all that I know. They'll believe me for sure, especially now that I'm famous and have a voice that will be heard".

I had no intention of course of doing anything of the sort, but just wanted to teach the fucker a lesson for being such a douche.

I was certain that he would understand that I was just taking the mick.

Geldof called me over then anyway, for some crapola or other, so I made my excuses and left Macca to himself.

In retrospect though, and thinking about it now, he was pretty upset, but I was too busy and stressed out to be aware of it at the time.

Regrettably later that day, this lack of awareness on my part would come back, very seriously, to bite me in the arse.

I arrived over to Bob anyway, who true to form, was as plastered as fuck.

He asked me then what Macca and I had been arguing about, so I just made something up about the bollocks being his usual narky self.

Rather than heading him off at the pass though from this unusually inquisitive line of questioning, my indicating to him that Macca was in bad form had the opposite effect.

"Tell him the joke kid!" he encouraged me excitedly.

"You know; the one about Noddy? He'll focking love that, guaranteed! How much is the bets?"

'Fuck me!' I was thinking.

'Will any conversation that I engage in with Geldof ever' I mused further.

'Not have either this fucking Noddy joke or the fact that I soiled my pants in a nightclub about a million fucking years ago, as the main elements of said exchange?'

He kept egging me on though, and gathered everyone around as well, to the extent that it became easier to tell the joke than not, if only to shut the fucker up.

I decided though – stupidly, as that decision would turn out later on to be – to have a little bit more fun with Macca whilst the opportunity to do so was there.

Determining that as a result of the fact that he was too far away from us to hear what Macca and my recent exchange had been about, I decided to give him the impression that I was about to impart his little secret to all and sundry that were there.

"What do you think Macca?" I shouted across.

"Isn't it about time that the world at large was aware of it? As in, should it not be, at this stage, in the public domain?"

Talk about an overreaction.

The bollocks just stood up and grabbed his jacket, and fucked off out of the studio, without so much as a goodbye to anybody.

The ignorant scouse prick!

Not that anybody there was *that* bothered.

I just carried on so and got on with the joke.

"Why does Noddy have a bell on the top of his hat?" I asked.

"Because he's a cunt!" I answered.

Silence.

Not a fucking dickey bird.

And then a raucous cackle from Kate Bush, fair play to her.

At least she had a sense of humour unlike the other pricks that were gathered around.

Although on a separate note she's about as stable as the sun in 'Ice Cream for Crow'.

Bowie told another joke then, the bollocks; as ever trying to steal somebody else's limelight.

Something about two nuns in a bath?

To be fair to him though it was pretty good, and I told him so too.

There's nothing wrong with being magnanimous from time to time.

"I think that it's good actually" I said.

"I'll definitely be using that one again".

Time anyway was moving on, so I needed to get my arse in gear regarding the running order of the tracks.

Do you think though, that I could get any of them to fall into line?

Suffice it to say that over thirty minutes later, I was no further on than when I had made my initial attempts to corral them as one.

And then I had to deal with another bollocks later on - who shall remain nameless for now - who was actually trying to take me fucking out?

As in, you know, attempting to relieve me, unbidden, of my youthful and barely utilised thus far, mortal coil?

It was going to be a long fucking night, I was thinking.

There were no two ways afuckingbout it.

CHAPTER 19

The cooing of a bird outside disturbs my reverie.

A wood pigeon I'll warrant.

Right from the belly like a note from a sax.

Into the mystic.

Ronnie Ross.

I had drifted off, despite the cacophony.

Everyone is here, with most vying to be louder than the other.

Prince is present also, but as ever he is keeping himself to himself.

Prince is a pal.

No more than that of course; although he would dearly love for it to be the contrary.

As I have told him before however - jokingly of course;

'Whilst not being frigid, I will nay fraternise with a midget'.

The joke is on me though, as I'm only a wee titch myself.

This Johnny Freak Show fellow however is another matter.

Now there is a chap with whom one could be amorous.

And of moderate height as well.

5'10"at least.

A person that another person might 'look up to' as it were.

McCartney is here also; prized buffoon that he is.

Definitely my least favourite Beatle.

Geoff regarded him as an oaf too.

Brought nothing to the songs, he always said.

None of them did in fact.

Arrived with them complete apparently, and just played them as they were.

If anything, Geoff affirmed, George Martin was the key driver in rendering them exceptional.

Last week anyway was when Johnny became known to me.

I was in Ireland visiting relatives, as I quite often do.

My low profile permits me to do so, which is sadly not the case for many of the others with whom I am ensconced here today.

Although I do believe that they prefer it that way.

Court it even?

The fame and the adulation, that is.

This Johnny Freak Show fellow though?

He appears to be the opposite.

That is, I mean, that he could probably take it or leave it.

Like me.

His eyes though.

His beautiful eyes.

The eyes of a thousand year old man.

We will walk for miles he and I, tracing my ancestral footsteps on beaches in Clonea and Inch, before stopping for steamed mussels and stout in small country pubs, hiding in corners, stooped over fare, fireside and whispering, my crown and his, concealing each other's.

We will fashion for ourselves then - hermit-like and somewhere remote - an existence that is bucolic.

He stands for decency and decorum I suspect also; albeit in a singularly - from what I can deduce from his display to date - uncompromising fashion.

Not one for nightclubs or external hostelries generally - particularly when the masses are amassed in their droves - I tend to stay in when I am home.

Visiting with friends so last week, I see Johnny for the very first time, speaking with the idiot Gay Byrne on Irish TV.

Not a person to be taken seriously, I recall in minute detail a similar encounter of mine own with said Byrne arse, on the very same show, many years before.

'Condescending' I would say, is a gross understatement of the debacle.

He walks towards me slowly, following my mimed performance of 'Wuthering Heights', with ignorance and arrogance accompanying his every step.

He has the brazenness then to enquire of my mother within no more than the first ten seconds of our engagement.

He has no idea clearly as to what I am about.

I fend him off anyway, grinning and bearing it as best as I can.

Some years later then, I recall, I am sitting with Del in a hotel in Waterford, and there he is again, laying into the great Philip Lynott and his poor old mother as well.

A rookie mistake that on Phil's part, bringing his mother along.

Notwithstanding said blunder though, there is no excuse still, for the host's quite outrageous display of pomposity.

And then last week as I mentioned already, co-incidentally, I am on home soil once again – 'The Late Late Show' does not air in the UK – and before me is Johnny in conversation with our perennially inane compère.

Rather than accept his contemptuousness though, and just roll with the punches – as indeed did both the bashful Phil and I – Johnny's reaction to Byrne is quite emphatically the opposite.

Seething clearly after Byrne's scathingly churlish and scornful introduction (with the inference being that because Johnny is new to the scene and as a result of this, untested, that he must clearly be a charlatan of dastardly ilk, with zero talent to account for at all), he gives it no more than twenty seconds, before laying into the moron with no small degree of malicious intent.

"I was meaning to ask you actually Byrne" he puts to him forcefully.

"Are you always this much of a fucking bollocks?"

I think – probably - that this was the precise moment when my heart became his.

I made a solemn pledge to myself then that from that moment onwards, I would do everything in my power to ensure that we would be as one.

Imagine my surprise so when no more than a couple of days later, Paul McGuinness called me up to ask me if I wanted to guest on this new artist, Johnny Freak Show's new album of covers, to be recorded in Abbey Road over the following number of weeks.

Paul must have been surprised so, I would say, that I accepted his offer so expeditiously.

I generally say no to such advances straight off the bat, or wait for months or years even, to respond; after which they usually lose interest and don't bother to ask me to do anything at all, ever again.

Which, being truthful, is exactly the way that I like it.

Oh dear.

Peter is at it again.

That is, being a mad bloody bastard!

Another whose unwanted advances I have spurned.

No matter what I convey to him however, his infatuation remains immutable.

He is singing 'a capella' at present to a markedly unimpressed crowd.

Prince and Gary Moore are glancing at each other askance, whilst Axl Rose and Tom Waits look similarly bewildered.

"Can you tell me where my country lies?" Peter starts, gazing directly and lovingly at me.

"Said the unifaun to his true love's eyes".

"It lies with me, said the Queen of Maybe" he goes on.

"For her merchandise, he traded in his prize".

A notable quietude is conspicuous throughout.

Metaphorical tumbleweeds tumbling across a silent studio floor, whilst a whistling winter breeze pervades the bleak terrain.

I actually know this song as it happens and it's excellent usually.

Musical accompaniment however, I really must attest, is critical to the success of its delivery and a subsequent positive reception.

'A capella' does not work.

I have told Peter this before also, but he doesn't listen.

That's his problem really.

Peter NEVER listens.

It is the first song in any event, on the 1973 Genesis album known as 'Selling England by the Pound', and it is truly a humdinger.

'Dancing with the Moonlit Knight' it is named.

Today however it is not going down well.

Not for the first time so, I will be required to put Peter - and everybody else here present - out of our collective misery.

I glide across the room so - as I do - and arrive at his side before long.

"Stop being such a fucking plank Peter!" I whisper softly into his ear before taking his hand and leading him slowly away to the other side of the room.

A resultant sigh then, of an unmistakably mutual essence, is ubiquitous.

We stand at the window Peter and me, hand in hand, gazing wistfully outside in silence.

It is a clear day with intermittent clouds flitting at speed across an otherwise azure sky.

Which gets me to thinking – is there anything more flocculent than a cloud?

Going nowhere but with such purpose.

Today fluffy and fleeting, a gossamer wisp.

Tomorrow, looming and ominous; a giant snowdrift lurching towards a dark and nebulous horizon.

A train to Dover it was; boarding at Bexleyheath.

Giggling schoolgirls, of which I count myself, one.

Giggling though?

Not I.

Friendless today, as I would have it.

Urged to join in, I resist.

Upon arrival and disembarking, I detach myself from the others by the by, before wandering off, far from the madding crowd.

Of hardy stuff I am made; I climb to the edge via a scrubby path that conceals well what lies ahead.

A castle in the distance lends the place majesty.

Although blustery I am fearless nevertheless.

Opening up then, vast fields before me lead to the sea.

Various trails lead on from there, as the wind becomes more turbulent and my gait, as a consequence, unsteady.

A peregrine falcon hovers expertly on a draft directly overhead, as yachts off the coast negotiate the choppiness of the waters as expertly as they can.

'If they find me racing white horses, they'll not take me for a buoy.'

Considering then, the beauty that is all around, the desire of the others to frequent 'amusement' parks on the pier stupefies me to a point of disbelief.

Looking further out into the strait, I spot an outline of Normandy on the misty horizon.

How bizarre that such a peaceful scene, can belie such carnage as has come to pass before?

"But he never even made it to his twenties. What a waste".

Un baiser d'enfant.

He is much younger than I.

That much is indisputable.

Perhaps ten years?

But what of it?

He is of age.

What feelings are these, stirring within?

How odd that I cannot bring myself to go across?

His lack of desire to impress is as uplifting as it is unaffected.

He was engaged in a conversation with Geldof earlier, when they appeared to be having a joke at McCartney's expense.

That's good.

McCartney needs taking down a peg or two.

Especially after what Geoff said.

"No, listen, seriously," said Geldof at the time, to everybody there.

I moved in a little closer to hear better what he had to say.

"This is an absolute focking REVELATION!" he continued.

"I kid you not! You've never heard anything like it before in your life! It's that good!"

Encouraged then to take up the reins by Geldof, Johnny shouted across to McCartney the following words.

"What do you think Macca?" he exclaimed.

"Isn't it about time that the world at large was aware of it? As in, should it not be, at this stage, in the public domain?"

I wasn't sure exactly what was going down, but McCartney looked decidedly uncomfortable at the time.

Picking up his jacket then tetchily, he just stood up and left.

'Good riddance' I was thinking to myself.

A turd in human form.

There are no two ways about it.

Johnny went on with what he was saying anyway, which on a positive note, turned out to be a joke.

I had been feeling pretty down earlier in the day, so a good old rib tickler was most probably what I needed at the time.

And so it turned out to be.

"Ok folks, here goes" he continued.

"The greatest joke of all time, period!"

I sincerely hoped that he wasn't setting himself up for a fall.

He took a deep breath then and readied himself for the off.

And then he let loose.

"Why does Noddy have a bell on the top of his hat?" he said.

We waited in anticipation, the excitement palpable.

"Because he's a cunt!" he said.

What a gag?!

I just fell about the place!

Everybody was staring at me then as if I was some sort of a bloody lunatic.

But why would I care about that?

I'm Kate bloody Bush for fuck sake!

Unusually enough however, nobody else there - bar Geldof, Johnny and I - found the joke to be funny; which copper-fastened my view even further that Johnny and I were meant to be.

Not Geldof though.

That gangly arsewipe has no class at all.

David Bowie told another gag then – yes, that twit was there as well – something about two nuns in a bath; which, bizarrely enough, everybody else there regarded as a superior yarn.

It was if we were living in a parallel universe so laughable was the contradiction.

As it goes anyway, Johnny was magnanimous enough, telling Bowie at the time that he thought that his joke was funny also.

Geldof though, being Geldof, was unconvinced.

But he's a narky enough bugger at the best of times, so no surprise there.

Anyway, back to the present.

Johnny has had enough of the tomfoolery and has gathered us all together in one corner of the studio to converse.

He seems keen to talk through the songs that we'll be doing, particularly the running order, but also to get a handle on who exactly will be doing what.

But 'what the deuce', I'm thinking, wandering off in my mind once again.

(That's something that I do).

What are we, really, I muse?

You know, when all is said and done?

I consider this further before Johnny gets started as I look around at this gathering of 'stars'; all of us jostling vaingloriously for attention.

Such pathetic naivety!

To believe that there is permanency in anything?

This notion of 'lasting' – as in our understanding of what 'lasting' actually is - is as preposterous as it is untrue.

All that we experience is temporary.

And yet we strive for constancy even so – at home, at work, with family, with friends – when we know truly, deep inside, that we are destined, all of us are destined, to succumb.

Does not the grim reaper visit with us all?

'Nirvana' however, I like.

As a 'notion', you know?

With of course an added 'twist' of my own.

One must always be original, right?

Sorry Buddha!

We die so, is the deal with this Buddhism, and are reborn.

This is how I understand it; as they do also, I believe.

From there onwards however, I see things in a different way.

Rather than be reborn immediately, we must first of all prove our worth.

How one performs during this 'test' will determine what 'entity' one will return as.

Additionally, if one has acted badly during one's prior sojourn on earth, one will return as a 'lesser' entity as a form of retribution, incapable of attaining corporeal embodiment again for several hundreds or even thousands of years.

Although human form, believe it or believe it not, is not the 'ultimate' temporal actuality.

That accolade goes to the most mysterious and enchanting creature of them all - the starling!

But more of that anon.

Additionally, there is creativity.

That is, if a person has been creative during one's lifetime on earth, they will return as a slightly more appreciable entity – that is, NOT as insignificant an entity as a non-creative person.

This entire cycle anyway is so that we can achieve a state of true enlightenment through continual death and rebirth, until such time in a distant future when our 'Nirvana' has been achieved.

'Non-creative' people also will exist in a kind of 'purgatory' until their soul has conceived of something original and new.

This can be anything from as complex an idea as a new form of flora – a variation of a daisy perhaps – or the germination of an idea in the future, that will be of benefit to the human race, as and when said idea appears.

An idea that is supplanted into the embryo perhaps of an 'as yet unborn' child, who in adulthood will bring said concept to the fore and assist mankind thereby in his on-going quest for amelioration.

Sounds mad, you think?

Perhaps.

271

I think myself though, that it is perfectly reasonable.

As 'reasonable' certainly as a chap in a dress being murdered, and then rising from the dead three days further along.

Now THAT is unreasonable.

Moving on anyway, humans that are evil or who do NOT create - or indeed who create things that are by their very nature abhorrent – Oppenheimer say, for example – whether by design or default, will NEVER return as humans.

They WILL return eternally however, as more repugnant entities – rats and snakes and the like - doomed to remain like that as eternal punishment for their previous malignant deeds whilst on earth.

Creativity so is the key - crucial now and in the future - to the natural evolution of the human race as a genus.

Those that oppose it - 'creativity' that is - as they maintain their bunkered in positions of lethargy and apathy, will be punished accordingly also, as another form of repercussion.

Or conversely, my theories as outlined above might be just poppycock!

Who knows really?

Either way, I am not for this world; whatever about my wanderings.

That is this more 'earthly' world of imagined 'celebrity' and 'luminosity' in which I at present reside.

I will slip away so soon unnoticed.

A barely recognisable shape concealed beneath a blanket, in the back of a nondescript boxcar that's trundling out of town.

Cacophony and bluster will clatter to my left and to my right, whilst peace, tranquillity, inner peace and harmony will lay before me on the road ahead.

I detect similar reflections in the eyes of my prospective paramour.

He has known this madness for five minutes merely, but already within him I see hesitancy and doubt.

We will elope so, the two of us, and be of the land.

And then, one day - with his consent (or possibly not) – I am confident that he will thank me afterwards either way – we will jump into a river holding hands.

I am strong so will drag him in after me if he resists.

And then our centuries long - millennia long even - adventures will begin.

Twin souls separated by mortal cessation alone, before being reborn and reborn and reborn again over aeons, until we are united eventually in our mutual states of Nirvana.

The entire affair here now however in the studio, has descended into Bedlam.

Axl Rose is babbling at Tom Waits in what can only be described as a sickening display of sycophancy, whilst Bob Geldof and Roger Waters are embroiled in a bitter war of words also, regarding who will be doing what over the course of the coming days.

And if you think that Geldof is bad, try getting Roger Waters to ruminate on anything that isn't related in some way to Roger Waters and what Roger Waters' likes.

As everybody is aware we are talking about a chap here who is the very embodiment of megalomania.

He wanders off anyway to somewhere more private, with some disgusting little groupie type slut with a skirt up to her arse.

No prizes for guessing what she's after.

To cap it all off then, Peter has returned – I had managed to shake him off before by returning to the main group on the other side of the studio – and is at present before me; and regrettably also, on bended knee.

'Bloody hell' I'm thinking.

'Will he ever, at any juncture, get the blasted message?'

"And I, I, I, I, I, I, I - I love it when you give me things" he snivels.

"And you, oo, oo, oo, oo, oo, oo - you ought to give me wedding rings" he whines further.

Lines from a song I suspect, considering the fact that he is singing the words.

But Jesus fucking H, does he ever give up?

A proposal of marriage yet again, clearly; this time in genuflection as inferred before; and sang forlornly also, with his doe-eyed cocker spaniel peepers pleading up at me, waiting for some form of beyond unlikely affirmation.

Johnny is well pissed off now also, with his mood not lightened at all by the decidedly lukewarm reaction to his most recent proclamation.

Bowie and Prince have wandered away to a less populous area of the studio, where they appear to be simulating what I believe is a golf swing, whilst Gary Moore has just picked up a guitar and cranked it up the max; rendering any further conversation until he stops, an actual impossibility.

It's a decent riff though, undeniably.

The beginnings of 'Tush' by the great ZZ Top.

And much as said tune is excellent and as 'rock and roll' as you can get, it does not appear to be doing the job vis-à-vis improving Johnny's mood.

If anything his demeanour has darkened further as a result of the new interruption; which adds fuel to the fire also I believe, following the tepid response to his previous pronouncement regarding his general desire for everybody there to get their shit together.

Bono joining in then also, vocally, renders the entire interlude semi-unbearable, with a cheerily percussive Phil Collins adding then merely to Johnny's general chagrin.

And then without warning he just leaves.

That's right.

Just stands up and tells them all to fuck off, before grabbing his jacket and high-tailing it out the door.

I have a decision to make so.

Do I remain here in this music studio/faux lunatic asylum and attempt to make polite conversation with what is at best, as has been alluded to before, a collection of decidedly less than stable Rock Star DemiGods – whilst at the same time fending off the amorous advances of an 'a capella' singing-voice-wielding Peter Gabriel, who just won't get the message – or do I depart myself also and just follow my heart?

I decide on the latter of course, and make waves to abscond.

Peter is not happy naturally that his advances have been spurned yet again; but what are you gonna do?

It's not my fault that the chap won't listen.

Peter never listens.

Saying goodbye to nobody so, I wander across to the door and then exit the building some moments later, before following Johnny down the street.

I arrive at the famed Zebra crossing - à la the Fab Four in 1969 - and Johnny's side, no more than a couple of minutes after that, before slipping my hand warmly into his.

Together then as one, we cross to the other side.

"There is a clearly defined hierarchy within a murmuration" I say to him as we walk along; and judging by the way that he reacts I can tell that he understands.

He nods back at me with a sage and steady gaze, not losing eye contact with me for a second.

It's obvious that he is anxious for me to expound; so I duly oblige, of course.

"Given your lack of creative output to date however" I continue.

"You may be required to go through several passages of transformation before you arrive at the stage that is 'starling'. I myself however, following our imminent demise at some point later today; and as a result of my own creative input thus far also in life; will be, I regret to tell you, considerably ahead of you in that respect. But that's ok my darling. For you, I am prepared to wait."

I veer him down Hall Road in the direction that I want us to go.

"Are you sure that this is the right way Kate?" he asks, eager it would seem, to know if I know where I am going.

"I'm staying at The Dorchester, which I believe is straight ahead" he carries on, pointing straight ahead.

"Yes, yes, don't worry" I answer hurriedly, not wishing to give the impression to him that there is anything wrong.

"This is a nice little short cut through Little Venice. Please trust me on this." I continue.

"Way more picturesque".

I gave away way too much earlier on, talking about our 'imminent demise'.

I need to be more careful about that.

My love must know nothing of my intent until it is too late for him to do anything about it.

We turn right into Lanark Road then, and a couple of minutes later, Clifton Road, which is no more than a few hundred metres away from our eventual destination.

I have been here before so know the locale quite well.

Linking his arm then I pull him even closer; ostensibly to keep me warm in the close early summer evening air, but actually, also, so that I can have him near to me when I put my final plan into effect.

Before that however - and in an effort to ensure that he has at least some understanding of why I am doing what I am doing, when I do eventually do it, an explanation of sorts, albeit tenuous, is undoubtedly required.

"Buddhism is the thing you see" I commence, in an effort to keep things simple; at least initially.

"In that" I continue, as we stroll along.

"We all die, of course - humans, that is - but come back again to earth many times over as lesser creatures or entities, until such time as we have learned all that we have needed to learn and achieved a state of Nirvana, or ultimate peace."

His grip on my arm tightens, and I can tell that I am getting through.

Oh my love, wouldst that thou understand?

I was not certain that you would, but now that you do, my love for you is even greater than before.

More confident now, now that I am certain that he is on my wavelength, I elaborate further – with more information perhaps, than I had originally intended to impart.

"The stage whereby our souls arrive at 'homo sapien' also, is, believe it or not my love, no more than halfway through the cycle.

Several other life 'forms' will be experienced further along - including Lion, Eagle, and of course Le Papillion - which on earth also, as you know, experience various stages of transformation as preparation for a final journey, which, at that point, is very near. Papillion is an advanced level."

We turn down Warwick Avenue and head on in the general direction of the blue bridge over the Canal, which is directly ahead.

"Our penultimate journey however, is very different" I continue.

"And requires us to go through many different phases that are in fact 'educational'.

This will prepare us however, ultimately, for our eventual goal."

We reach the bridge, at which juncture I bid him stop.

"Yes my love, it will take longer than expected for us to be together, but I am ready for that and prepared to wait, as I mentioned to you before. I might have to flunk a few tests, and remain as a Netherfeather for longer than I had anticipated,

275

but that's OK. In the grand scheme of things, let's not forget that we are talking about actual eternity here!"

He unlinks himself then and I can tell that he is afraid.

"Do not be fearful my love" I say to him, pulling him back towards me.

"We WILL be together forever – hold on to that thought my darling, and all will be well."

He has no knowledge of the hierarchy of the murmuration – although I did mention it to him briefly before – which is why he is probably looking at me now a little askance.

I don't have time to educate him on it now however, now that we are arrived on the bridge.

No matter I suppose.

He'll find out soon enough, when he is dead.

A Netherfeather though; just for your information and as I mentioned there before; is pretty much 'entry level' for a murmuration, and as low, I suppose, as you can go.

This will be - several transformations from now of course - Johnny's eventual murmuration entry point; as it will be mine - albeit as a result of my creative endeavours to date, a lot sooner than he.

You don't think that starlings arrive at a murmuration trained up already, do you?

It talks many years of learning and countless ignominious plummets and deathly splats before any serious level of competency can be attained.

Over time however, one climbs through the ranks.

A Liftwaffer for instance, who reports into a Soar Sergeant, is a pretty decent next step up for a Netherfeather.

Liftwaffing is a difficult skill to acquire though, and attained only after many years of application and practice. It requires a delicate and barely perceptible flapping of the wings that permits one to maintain a steady and even motion as one waits for a next squall or heavy gust of wind to arrive.

A bit like treading water in swimming, but in this case with air.

Treading air.

Another good level, and above a Liftwaffer in terms of rank, is the Glide Officer, who reports directly into, usually, a Flutter Chief.

The Glide Officer is more adept than a Liftwaffer, where timing and communication are critical to the success of the discipline. A thorough understanding of the key nuances of geometry is of vital importance here also, in addition to having an encyclopaedic knowledge of sophisticated air flows and ultra-specialist level atmospheric weather systems and aerodynamics.

The Hover Head is a rank above Glide Officer - at the same level, give or take, as the Flutter Chief - and can train up to one hundred Netherfeathers at any given time.

Outside of actual murmuration 'action' in fact, the Hover Head, usually, will take these young cadets under his wing – excuse the pun – and chaperone them on short training runs; to give them the basics initially, before providing them then, later on in the lesson, with further more in-depth instruction around the key aspects of advanced scapular and covert oscillation.

If ever you see a small gathering of starlings in fact, and think to yourself, 'well that's a pretty shit murmuration in comparison to the other more populous gatherings that I've seen before', it's a distinct possibility that what you are ACTUALLY witnessing, is a training session that's being facilitated by a Hover Head, along with any number of Netherfeathers that are in the very early stages of their schooling.

There are various other disciplines at management and mid-management level also - Vapour Major and Gust Geometer to name but a couple – but the ultimate level to attain – or levels, as there are two main ones really – are Air Commodore; who is the key organiser and administrative head for a murmuration - think of him as a HR Director I suppose, for a large global multinational company; and the Wing Commander, who is the actual technical head for the entire flock squadron, and as high as you can go in terms of seniority within a murmuration configuration.

And when you consider that the starling is the greatest living thing, the Wing Commander, is the greatest level of existence that a soul can aspire to whilst on earth.

Bloody hell, what was that!

A bullet has just whizzed over my head!

What the actual deuce?

"Get down, ye doxy fucking bint" shouts Johnny, whilst at the same time trying to shield me from what appears to be a veritable barrage of steaming hot miniature pellets of lead that are being propelled at high speed in our general direction.

"Some fucker is shooting at us!" he continues.

"And whereas for the last little while - whilst you have been banging on about whatever the fuck it is you've been banging on about; and I, as a consequence of said banging on, have been losing the will to fucking live - when ACTUAL potential demise is presented to you like this, in such stark and realistic terms, I'm inclined to think that I'd prefer to hang on to my mortal coil for just that little bit longer, if it's all the same to you - you really quite off the scales and incoherent fucking mentalist!"

I've no idea what he is saying but realise now, more than anything, that now is the time for us to be succumbing to the depths.

Standing up then and grabbing his arm fiercely at the same time – I'm stronger than I look – I drag him across to a gap in the railings where we can both just about squeeze through, before I hope for us to be plummeting soon, the ten metres or so to our near certain demise, and the next stage of our transformative journey towards inner peace.

Regrettably though, I am hit by a bullet in the chest before we can reach said destination, and crumple to the ground in a heap.

Checking to see that I am OK, I inform my lover that I am.

"It's OK darling" I say to him breathlessly, whilst at the same time withdrawing a ball of mustard from inside my cleavage.

Fortuitously for me the bullet has become lodged in the condiment.

"A ball of mustard" I say to him.

"I keep it on me at all times.

You know?

For emergencies".

"For fuck sake Kate!" he answers tetchily; and for the first time since we have known each other, I am seeing his darker side.

"Would ye ever ask me bleedin' bollocks!"

And with that he rushes off into early evening air.

He'll definitely be back though.

I mean how could he not?

Return that is?

It is merely a matter of time.

I mean, I'm Kate bloody Bush, for fuck sake!

CHAPTER 20

"But anyway" I continued, addressing my comments to everyone that was there.

"Seeing as you're all here now - gathered together in one *actual* corner of the studio - do you think that we can take this opportunity to go through the running order of the songs, and decide then on who's going to be doing what?"

I had managed eventually to corral my disparate troop together, with no small degree of pitiable pleading and cajoling on my part to effect said result.

But I couldn't shut them up, especially Axl, who had a real hard on for Tom Waits and was practically sucking the fucker's dick now he was that enamoured with him.

In deference to Tom however he appeared bemused; well initially, at least.

Time was getting away from us though – especially after that humorous 'Noddy joke' interlude as per what had been instigated by Bob Geldof a couple of minutes before – so I needed to be putting some structure into the day as a matter of urgency before the whole shebang went south.

It was fairly excruciating however to regard that Axl's sycophancy - as per almost exactly as he had been laying on Robert Plant just a couple of weeks before, that time when we were backstage at Wembley for the Freddie Mercury tribute thingamajig - was even more extreme on this occasion than it had been then.

Such a degree of brown-nosing in fact, as per what he was pushing out there now, was more loathsome than any that I had experienced to date.

Even Tom; who, by his very nature I understand, is a reasonably even-tempered character; looked just about ready to punch the fucker in the face.

"Fuck man, it's like, a GODDAMN pleasure to be in your company man!" warbled Axl.

"Like FUCK man, Tom FUCKING Waits man! We are not FUCKING worthy, dude! Say dude, like, how did you come up with the idea for 'Trouble's Braids'? Like, what a fucking toon man! Pure fucking genius man! And '9th & Hennepin'? Jeez man - like, with that spoken word shit and shit? Fucking AWESOME man! Say, what's that toon about anyways? Could never figure it out dude. Not that it matters anyways Bubba, coz it's like, fucking GODDAMN GENIUS man! Say, do you wanna beer dude? Or a broad? Lots o' broads here dude, lots o' broads; just say the fucking word man - FUCK man, it's like, great to fucking SEE you man! Say, you see that Lindsay chick there; like, over there man, the one in the leather skirt and shit? I tell you what man, like, she sucks fucking cock like her goddamn life depends upon it man; I kid you fucking not!"

Tom held up his wedding ring finger then and pointed to the band of gold, waving it then directly beneath Axl's servile visage as if to emphasise that such a proposition for the reasons outlined, was not at present on his radar.

He might as well have been presenting his bare arse to him though for all the good that it did.

The dude just wittered on as before.

"Oh yeah and there's like, this Northern Irish chick here too dude; fuck knows what she's saying man, but like, FUCK dude! What a rack man! Like, what a fucking rack?!"

"Say friend" drawled Tom from under his hat, his face all but concealed by the cloud of blue joint smoke in which he was enveloped.

"Have you, like, you know - had a lot of coffee today?"

Axl ignored him however and just bleated on.

"I think she said 'NOW' earlier on as well dude - when I asked her some shit about somethin'. I dunno - when she wanted to leave, maybe? But fuck man, I swear she pronounced 'NOW' with, like, two fucking syllables! And 'TOO' with two too!"

"An owl performing a ballet?" suggested Tom, cryptically enough.

Axl stopped momentarily with a quizzical look on his face, before moving on swiftly, when he realised that his brain would not be catching up with this particular line of dialogue anytime soon.

"Say, I got somethin' to ask you dude" he went on.

"I was only sayin' it to Slash last week, or last month, or some time anyways - like, whatever dude! Anyhoo, like, we saw 'Ironweed' and that Robin Williams flick, I can't remember its' name dude – somethin' to do with Fish? And we were sayin' like, FUCK man, how come Tom Waits is so good at fucking acting man, you know, and, like, on top of that shit, on FUCKING TOP of that shit, he's, like, such a totally fucking awesome rock star and shit as well dude, like, you know? So, like, what gives dude? Joo get training or fucking some shit like that man?"

Everyone was listening in at this point and it's fair to say that there wasn't a closed mouth to be observed.

This was babbling on an epic scale.

"Well friend" answered a pained looking Tom, exactly as before.

"I would regard myself as a plumber that does some electrical work from time to time".

And as much as that was a great answer and, believe it or believe it not, actually stopped Axl from rabbiting on as per how he had been rabbiting on thus far, the subject of work brought me right back into the moment.

Sadly, such an aspiration - as in the notion of getting any of these fuckers to remain focused for any more than ten seconds at a time - was very much, on my part, wishful thinking.

"So let me get this straight" said Geldof to Waters.

"You want to do ALL of the vocals on 'Empty Spaces', ALL of the vocals on 'Young Lust' and have DEIGNED to allow me to sing one focking line on 'Is There Anybody out There'? Being namely, the line 'Is there anybody focking out there'? Additionally, you large-veined bollocks, you are telling me - having me bothering my arse to turn up to this focking thing in the first place to assist this no-mark kid with the untrustworthy excretory organs - that I can't even play acoustic guitar on said number? You can fock right off Waters, is what you can do, ye lefty, communist cock-sucking prick!"

"Oh fuck off Geldof" Waters responded.

"You're shit man, and everybody knows it!" he continued before breaking into, for fuck knows what reason, a version of 'You'll Never Walk Alone' from the musical 'Carousel', and standard bearer crowd anthem of course also, for the great Liverpool FC.

Which is fine usually of course; but seriously?

Taxi for Waters.

Regrettably however, this was not to be.

Waters anyway, pissed off with Bob for being such a cantankerous git, prised himself away and wandered across to Axl to say hello.

I'd be having words with McGuinness about these fuckers later on, I was thinking.

He had given the impression to me before at our last meeting, that they'd been the best of pals.

It looked now however as if they couldn't stand the sight of each other!

Axl was back with the girls now as well – he had arrived with three; Belinda and two others; Northerners I think – as per what was decipherable, barely, from his meandering rant just before – so it was not unsurprising to see Waters ending up over there.

It's worth noting at this stage also, that none of the girls could ever have been described by anyone that was looking on, as being, as the expression goes, 'fully clothed'

I decided so anyway to stick with whom I had for the moment; which was Peter Gabriel and Kate Bush.

"Peter" I said to Gabriel.

"I'm thinking 'Intruder' for the first number. Are you cool with that?"

"Sure kid" he responded softly.

"Whatever you say?"

Gabriel is cool.

He's a daycent enough skin in fairness to him, if perhaps a tad on the needy side.

He was BIG TIME infatuated with Kate Bush though, as I was mentioning there before.

And fuck me, it was overpowering!

You could tell as well that she absolutely fucking hated it.

'You need to relax pal' I was thinking.

'Treat 'em mean, you know?'

He was way beyond that though.

I asked Kate then, and Phil Collins also, who was nearby, if they were OK to do backing vocals and drums as per their original similar turns on PG3, and they both appeared happy enough with that.

Kate reminded me then though that it was actually 'No Self Control' that she had sang on on the album – my bad there - but that she was happy to help me out on 'Intruder' either way, if I thought that it could work.

I asked Peter what he thought about this so, and he said that it could be done, almost certainly; although I *do* think that he just wanted to contrive of a situation where both he and Kate could be together in a booth.

They had sung together before also of course, on 'Don't Give Up', his big hit from the 1980's.

Kate seemed to have his best interests at heart anyway, at least on a platonic level; sure wasn't she responsible earlier on for ensuring that his a capella 'bombing' for his and everybody's else's sake, was brought to a close?

"No FACKING problem, moy san!" responded Collins also.

"Pukka!"

And as much as I wanted to slap him in the face for being such a cheeky chappy cockney feckin' wide boy – with, it has to be noted, *the* worst jumper on him that has actually ever been - I did have three individuals on board now, so at least we could start.

He actually mentioned his jumper to me then also; bizarrely enough asking me NOT to wind him up about it for the rest of the day.

Talk about an impossible request!

Given how much I had taken the piss out of him before though, that time that we had met in the basement club in Kensington a few years earlier, I decided that it was probably best to do the right thing on this occasion and give him a break for the day.

And besides, he was the only drummer that I had there as well, so why would I want to be shooting myself in the foot?

I apologised to him so, just to be nice, blaming my bad attitude on the day on some dodgy pills that Prince had given to me just before we had met.

Which was a true story also, believe it or believe it not.

I was fucked for absolute fucking days after it!

I needed a pianist for 'Intruder' also, and with Macca already departed, I had a scan around the room to see who could deputise.

Tom Waits had just come off the receiving end of that Axl Rose gibberish, so timing wise with him, vis-à-vis asking him to step in, was probably a bit off.

Wisely so, I think, I made a conscious decision to give him a wide berth for now.

Waters and Geldof were arguing still also, throwing insults at each other from across the room; with the situation there if anything, deteriorated even more.

"'Banana Republic' my arse!" shouted Waters across.

"Why don't you fuck off and write a proper political polemic that's venerated the world over – like, you know, I fucking did!?"

"Ask me bollocks Waters, ye prick" retorted Geldof.

"And tell your Aorta also while you're at it, that it is an INTERNAL focking artery, and not usually, within the context of conventional physiological systems, meant to be located anywhere that is remotely adjacent to an individual's epidermis!"

As put-downs go, in fairness to them, they were both daycent enough.

Axl was back with the girls also as I mentioned, and was attempting once again to make conversation with the northerner; she of the two syllables, that is, where one will suffice.

Belinda was there too, mooching around, trying to look all 'femme fatale' and alluring to anyone that might give her a second glance.

Which on this occasion was Phil Collins, who made a beeline straight for her when he realised that she was on her tobler.

Knowing Belinda though, I had to concede that I wasn't feeling overly confident about the poor bastard's chances.

His departure also however meant, somewhat annoyingly, that I was back to just two in my troop, while all of the others, once again, were dispersed elsewhere throughout the room.

I was beginning to get a right pain in my arse.

Macca came back then and motioned sheepishly for his minder to come across.

I think he was looking for a lift back to where he lived; which, if I remembered correctly from the last time, was Mayfair.

Not too far from The Dorchester so, where I was staying myself.

I'd need to be watching out for him so.

How unpleasant would that be to accidentally meet up with *that* fucker in the street?

It doesn't bear thinking about in fairnesss.

He'd probably start singing songs at me again, like he had done a few years earlier.

Bowie was a few yards away from me also, standing next to a drum kit and advising Prince - using a drumstick as a hastily fashioned teaching aid - on the nuances of the perfect back swing in the game of golf.

"Start it slowly" he said, with a bizarrely engrossed Prince hanging on his every word.

"And whatever you do mate, don't break your elbow. Your left arm must remain straight at all times. On your downswing also, the first thing to move must be your hips back towards the ball. Don't worry pal; everything else will follow."

"Thank you SOO much dude!" said Prince, genuinely delighted it seemed to me, that his problem had been solved.

"I had three shanks last week that came out of absolutely fucking nowhere!"

It was as if we were living in a parallel universe.

Three shags I could handle.

Wanks, even, more feasibly.

But shanks?

Three shanks?

Prince?

He did not look like a golfer in any way that you cared to envisage.

Standing there, in his glittering gold stilettos, attempting to simulate the perfect back swing under the tutelage of David Bowie?

You couldn't *make* this shit up!

Bowie left Prince then - who remained stationed where he was, trying out his new swing – and wandered over to Waters and Geldof who were still arguing of course, but sitting next to each other once again.

They had been joined now also, by Belinda – or Lindsay, as Axl Rose prefers to refer to her as.

Waters stopped arguing with Geldof then, thankfully, now that Belinda was there and he had a potential muse to impress.

"Are all these your guitars?" I overheard Belinda asking of him.

Referencing of course, the great 'One of My Turns' from 'The Wall' – Waters' venerated political polemic!

And then following that up with,

"Wanna take a bath?!?!"

She knew her Floyd alright Belinda, fair fucks to her.

He looked impressed also, Waters, and conveyed his desire to get to know her better by taking her by the hand and leading her off to the jacks.

There was no fucking around with *that* bollocks, despite the mad fucking veins that were protruding out of his arms.

He was not an attractive dude.

Off Belinda popped with him anyway, regardless of the quite unsightly disfigurement of his forearms; but not before blowing a coquettish kiss in my direction as she skipped away in her black leather mini skirt and similarly-hued stiletto heels.

She was some brazzer Belinda.

It was fairly undeniable.

As the Aussies say - and they're not wrong about much – 'That Sheila, mate? She bangs like a dunny facking door!'

The opening strains of 'Tush' by ZZ Top began then as Gary Moore, clearly bored by the Northern Irish chick with whom he had been attempting to communicate - even though he's a Northerner himself – and in fairness to him, she rendered indecipherable speech a near art form – decided that enough was enough and that it was time to liven things up.

The only problem with that being though – and much as I love ZZ Top and 'Tush' in fact, even more – that said number was not on the playlist, so not a number that we needed to be rehearsing in any way.

Not that Moore gave a fuck about that.

All that *that* dude ever wanted to do was to play his guitar.

Which would have been fine and dandy of course, if it hadn't have been for that Bono poxbottle, once again, heading over to a microphone nearby and muscling in on the act.

I mean – and I'm sure you agree with me on this – there is just NO WAY that *that* fucker has a voice for the blues!

Do you remember 'When Love Comes to Town' with the legendary BB King? Tragic!

Fucking tragic!

To compound the situation also, Phil Collins and his jumper joined in on the drums.

The jumper was bad enough of course, don't get me wrong, and enough to make you want to ram your fist through the wall; but Collins' fancy fills at this particular moment in time, were totally wrong for the tune.

It's a fucking blues riff dude!

As in, there is no need at all for the use of the Tom Tom!

The jumper anyway, I think, was the last straw.

Looking around me then again, it was as plain as day to me that we were getting nowhere fucking fast.

Peter Gabriel, whom we had lost along the way, but who was back now to where Kate and I were at present stationed, began to serenade her once again; this time on bended knee, as if, it seemed to me, that he was singing to her a proposal of marriage.

"And I, I, I, I, I, I - I love it when you give me things" he whimpered pathetically, with his pleading and doleful eyes gazing up at her in desperation.

"And you, oo, oo, oo, oo, oo, oo - you ought to give me wedding rings" he blubbered further, at which point I came to the conclusion that enough was efuckingnough.

"Well fuck yiz anyway!" I shouted out suddenly, meaning to shock them all I supposed into some sort of reluctant submission.

Not a dickey bird though, except for Kate, who for some unknown reason was regarding me with a strange yearning kind of look in her eye.

'There's something not quite right about her' I was thinking.

I would find out later that day, to my detriment, how precise that pronouncement was.

"If yiz aren't going to take things seriously" I went on anyway, attempting one more time to bring the bozos to attention.

"Then yiz can fuck right fucking off!"

Once again however n'er a peep.

Moore, Collins and that short-arsed poxbottle Bono continued on with 'Tush', whilst Prince carried on with his swing practice in the corner.

Axl Rose and Bowie were chatting up the Northern Irish bird with the incomprehensible accent, while Geldof and Waits just sat there, talking to nobody; waiting for the world to end I imagined, or some such other dastardly disaster to descend upon us all.

Waters and Belinda were nowhere to be seen as well, so it was a pretty good bet that she was still sucking off his cock in the jacks; his ginormous cock, that is, with the oversized, throbbing and protruding veins; if, anatomically, that is to say, it looked anything at all like his deformed and weird looking arms.

No-one there so, bar Kate; who was still gazing at me with an odd look in her eye; was taking the blindest bit of notice as to what I had to say.

Off I popped so.

I mean, what was the fucking point?

I just grabbed my jacket and exited the building right there and then.

I'd ring McGuinness later on to tell him that we could give it another go tomorrow.

Or not at all.

I was so pissed off at that point that I actually didn't care.

I reached the famous zebra crossing then on Abbey Road, before stopping there momentarily to check if there was any traffic coming from either side.

It was then that I noticed Kate Bush standing beside me who silently then - and in the absence of any logical reason for doing so that I could think of at the time - slipped her hand into mine and semi-guided me across the road.

'What in jaysus does this mad fucking bint want?' I was thinking to myself.

286

'She's as nuts as the rest of them, if not *more* fucking so!'

I decided at the time though, weighing everything up, to let her tag along.

As in, it was hard to know how she might react if I did anything untoward that might antagonise her.

I'm sure that we all know one, but she DEFINITELY had the look of an individual who believes that it's perfectly alright to rub ones' personal faeces all over one's living room wall.

"There is a clearly defined hierarchy within a murmuration" she said to me then; and if I thought that she was for the birds before said uttering, this latest offering did little to dissuade me from what was now on my part, quite clearly, an exceedingly precise summation of the facts.

She was as off the scales as a Geiger counter in Chernobyl.

I gave her a look so to convey to her the notion that I believed that she was a bit of a fruitcake; in the hope that she might, you know, get the message and fuck off back to the asylum.

Regrettably however she remained by my side.

"Given your lack of creative output to date however" she continued.

"You may be required to go through several passages of transformation before you arrive at the stage that is 'starling'. I myself however, following our imminent demise at some point later today; and as a result of my own creative input thus far in life also; will be, I regret to tell you, considerably ahead of you in that respect. But that's ok my darling. For you, I am prepared to wait."

'What the fuck is she babbling on about?' I was thinking.

She had without question, long since before this juncture, gone past a point of no return.

She appeared also to be leading me off in some other direction; that is, away from The Dorchester; so this of itself was another even more worrying development.

"I'm staying at The Dorchester" I mentioned to her so.

"Which I believe is straight ahead."

She indicated to me then that she knew of a short cut through Little Venice, wherever the fuck *that* was, so given the fact that she was very insistent that we remain on this course, and the fact that the further we travelled, the more frantic she became, I made a decision to just go along with things for now.

When the time came however, and I spotted some alley way or other that I could leg it through, I'd dislodge myself from her at that point, and make a run for it like a fucking good thing.

She looked also to be concealing something in her bosom; so until I knew what *that* was, it was of critical importance for me to keep her onside.

It was hard to make it out, but it was bulging significantly.

Based upon its' positioning also - that is, centrally - it was almost certainly not of a mammary-like configuration.

What so, could it be?

A revolver?

As in like, you know, one of those small, silver 'ladies type' gizmos that you sometimes see on 'Dynasty' or 'Murder, She Wrote'?

Or a miniature rapier of some variety?

As in a covertly concealed dagger to be withdrawn at some unforeseen time in the future, with a view to causing grievous bodily harm to yours truly for no logical reason at all, bar an assuaging of her, by now, quite undeniably psychotic tendencies.

Given her display to date anyway, it could quite honestly have been anything, so I wasn't going to be taking any chances.

I would bide my time, and just wait for my best opportunity to abscond.

She started to bang on about Buddhism then, which was the point where I realised that I was in grave, grave danger.

I made an attempt to prise myself away at this moment, but this served merely to encourage her to grab my arm even tighter and pull me closer to her still.

I understand a basic notion of Buddhism of course; that is, that we die and are reborn several times over until we achieve, allegedly, an ultimate state of 'Nirvana' or shall we say, 'inner peace'.

By the way that she was babbling on about it now however, it seemed to me that she had taken her simplistic 'teenager-like' notion of what it was all supposed to mean, and then carried it off somewhere else in her mind; that is to a place where notions such as lucidity and sanity are conspicuously absent.

According to her anyway, we're all coming back as lions and tigers and butterflies and what not, but that the *ultimate* aspiration for our souls is to achieve the highest status of ALL living creatures; that is, oddly enough, the starling.

And that people that have been bolloxes on earth are coming back as rats and snakes and beetles and what not.

Like, what the actual fuck!

She kept referring to me as her 'love' also, and additionally, even more worryingly, that there'd be an 'imminent demise' for us at some point later that day.

And what the fuck is a Netherfeather as well, when it's at home?!

I tried to pull away from her then again, but her hold on me was as tight as a limpet.

She was stronger than she looked.

"Do not be fearful my love" she said to me then, as she pulled me in closer to her again.

"We WILL be together forever – hold on to that thought my darling, and all will be well."

'What a fucking nutjob' I was thinking, and vowed to myself at that very moment that if by some minor miracle I managed to get out of this scrape alive, that I'd be giving the old fairer sex a considerably wider berth in the future than I'd been giving them to date.

As in, you know - surely they're more trouble than they're worth?

And then, suddenly - as if things couldn't get any worse - some other lunatic from somewhere else started taking pot shots at us!

That's right!

Actual bullets being shot at us from an *actual* gun, with a view to said projectiles, I assumed, causing grave corporeal discomfiture or worse to either myself, Kate 'mad as a brush' Bush or us both.

For why I did not know, but our immediate safety now, was my primary concern,

"Get down, ye doxy fucking bint" I shouted at her, whilst at the same time trying to shield her from the assault.

"Some fucker is shooting at us!" I went on.

"And whereas for the last little while - whilst you have been banging on about whatever the fuck it is you've been banging on about; and I, as a consequence of said banging on, have been losing the will to fucking live - when ACTUAL potential demise is presented to you like this, in such stark and realistic terms, I'm inclined to think that I'd prefer to hang on to my mortal coil for just that little bit longer, if it's all the same to you - you really quite off the scales and incoherent fucking mentalist!"

I'd hoped that she might; following on from my pointed little monologue there; get the point - but I am sorry to say that she did not.

Quite the opposite in fact.

Instead of just lying low and attempting between us to conjure up some kind of scheme to get us out of this sticky situation, she stood up instead and dragged me over to a gap in the railings on the bridge where we were now situated, endeavouring then, following on from this, to squeeze both myself and herself through this small opening.

It was a drop of at least thirty feet though, so there was no way that I was allowing that to happen.

Was she trying to get us both killed?

As all of this was going on anyway, the bullets continued to spray around us like fuck, with some of them whizzing past us and ricocheting off the metal railings of the bridge fuck knows where, and others missing their target altogether, with the 'pfft' sound as they made contact with the water below conveying to me how amateurish the antagonists' marksmanship really was.

The dude – if I can assume it was a dude – was no sniper!

One shot was lucky enough though, hitting Kate square in the chest and felling her to the ground.

And much as I was keen to get away from her and regarded her at the time as a pustule on the arse of mankind to beat all other pustules on the arse of mankind that have ever been, it was important also, to ensure that she was alright.

One must be gallant always, don't you know; even when known blights such as the specimen before me are in distress.

As it happened anyway, it turned out that the object that she had been concealing in her bosom had come to her rescue, right at her very hour of need.

"It's OK darling" she said to me, whilst struggling at the same to catch her breath.

After which she withdrew a small brown tennis ball shaped object from within her cleavage.

"A ball of mustard" she indicated to me then.

"I keep it on me at all times. You know? For emergencies."

This was the last straw.

Whatever about dodging bullets from a person or persons that wanted either myself or this lunatic before me expired, I draw the line at associating with individuals that see it as a necessity to carry condiments of a savoury nature about their person, and to regard said condiments as objects that they might be needing at any time in the future for 'emergencies'.

Although bizarrely on this occasion it appeared to have done the trick.

"For fuck sake Kate!" I said to her anyway, sick at this stage of her shite.

"Would ye ever ask me bleedin' bollocks?!"

After which point I fucked off; keen to get away from her of course, but anxious also, to avoid the bullets that were raining down upon us still from whatever location nearby that they were raining down.

Who though, had been their intended target?

Was it I?

Or, more feasibly, the mad fucker with the private stash of seasoning, whom I had just recently left in my wake?

It stood to reason that given her *own* personality traits, she most probably associated with others that were of a similarly psychotic regard.

It was highly probable so that at some point along the way, she had pissed one or several of them off?

Surely this was the case?

And that she was the intended target?

I would find out, anyway, soon enough.

CHAPTER 21

As it turned out it *was* yours truly that they were after and not, surprisingly enough, the fucktard with the mustard.

And what was the story with that as well?

Prince had fucked the very same object at me also - that is, a ball of mustard - in Heathrow airport just a few years before.

Do all of these Rock Star Demigod types carry condiments about their person as a matter of course?

I had a fuzzy recollection of it being relevant to something although I couldn't figure out at the time what it might be.

Perhaps it was a dream?

It was hard to be sure.

But such matters as things stood right now, were of secondary concern.

Seasonings aside there persisted on my tail, assassins, in numero duo, with my immediate termination their predominant desire.

Darting in and out of alleyways and side streets so, after I had left the bridge and was dashing frantically on my way, it became apparent to me very soon that the shooters were very much still in pursuit.

A fusillade of bullets endured, but the marksmanship of the assailant or assailants; I was unsure still if there were just one or two guns; thankfully remained below par.

I ran further on so, taking great care to stoop lower than usual so that the parked cars and intermittent trees on the road I was on right now might afford me some form of shelter, however negligible, as I continued on my way.

Twilight had arrived now also, as the early summer evening drew to a close.

The area was becoming more populous as well, as we re-entered civilisation from Little Venice; this was a definite plus.

The gradual fading of the light that was brought on by the closing of the day you see, determined also that my pursuers were taking far fewer pot-shots at me now than they had been before.

Spotting a zigzag of train lines then to my left; ten of them at least, criss-crossing back and forth; I made an assumption that I must be close to a railway station; and a major one at that probably, given the number of tracks that I could see that were intertwined.

This was good news of course.

Railway stations have bridges and culverts under bridges - which as you no doubt know, make excellent environments for concealment.

Noticing one such culvert then to my right, which was perhaps ten metres high and five metres in breadth, I darted towards it hastily with the zeal of a rapacious racoon.

'I can hide here temporarily' I was thinking, 'and afford myself at least some degree of respite from these maniacs for a while'.

I needed to figure out urgently what to do next.

Another added advantage to being obscured in such a darkened tunnel was that I could identify very easily what was outside.

My pursuers however, conversely, would find it considerably more challenging to ascertain what if anything, was lurking within.

I was eager to ascertain as well who was trying to take me out, and in doing so piece together the rationale behind why such a pursuit of me, and what appeared to be my attempted assassination, was taking place.

A few moments later so I ventured out to the adit of the tunnel, to have a bit of an old gander and see if I could spot where my pursuers might be.

It was difficult to see anything in the paling evening light, but I identified them then at last, hiding behind a canal bank wall, no more than twenty metres or so away from my present position.

Hunched down there on their hunkers, there they were: barely visible but detectable from time to time as a result of them lifting their heads occasionally in an attempt to establish where I was.

Hasidic Jews they were, weirdly enough; two of them, with the standard traditional garb donned as you might expect.

Dark clothing, naturally - black trousers and black silk jackets - with the obligatory wide-brimmed fedoras on their heads, and solitary curled side locks worn on either side of the face.

Something was not quite right about *these* dudes though.

Their furtive actions and general demeanour overall, seemed very un-Hasidic to me.

I came to the conclusion so, that they were probably in disguise.

Who the fuck *were* they though, if not Hasidic Jews?

I covered my mouth then - when the visual eupnoea came to my attention - but charged and breathy clouds of exhalation into the clear night air had very regrettably I could now see, given my location away.

Aware so, as a result of the insufflatory faux pas on my part, that my pursuers would be upon me before long, I left my erstwhile hiding place in the tunnel and was on the move once again in a flash.

With great haste I made my way back up to the road, sprinting as quickly as I could so as to avoid any more hot-leaded projectiles that might be blasting in my general direction.

I spotted a road sign then which indicated to me that I was on London Street. Not very original I know but how and ever.

More crucially, there was another sign just next to this, which said that Hyde Park was in *that* direction - that is, away from the train station – Paddington, as it goes - and even more critically, away from the unhinged Hebrew hit men.

Reaching Hyde Park would be advantageous on two fronts.

One - on its perimeter there is an abundance of foliage and trees, so hiding from my foes would be considerably less challenging than it had been to date.

And two - it was quite close to The Dorchester so if I could at the very least make it back to the old temporary domicile in one piece, I could raise the alarm then from there when I arrived, and bring these Hasidic - or otherwise - fuckers to task.

I managed to make it to the outskirts of the park anyway, and ducked under a bush as soon as I arrived.

And not before time either, as a bullet whizzed directly over my head mere nanoseconds after I had taken cover.

Peering out then from behind said bush, I spotted the two miscreants directly across the road, pointing frantically here and there – surmising, I suppose, where I was likely to be going next – whilst one of the two, from what I could gauge anyway, was reloading a pistol agitatedly with a view to launching another attack on me imminently, as soon as the task of replenishing said firearm was complete.

This was quite obviously so, my best opportunity to escape.

I probably had ten seconds max to get the run on them, so it was imperative that I utilised this short window of opportunity to my best advantage.

I was aware also that if I continued along the perimeter of the park along the Bayswater Road, I would arrive eventually in the general vicinity of Marble Arch.

It was no more than a three minute dash then from there to The Dorchester – I had walked it just the other day so knew the route well enough - if I hung a right at that junction and ran as fast as I could down Park Lane.

Emerging then so from the bushes and turning on my heels, I sprinted as fast as I could in that general direction.

They were not pleased - the two bozos with the twizzlers for earrings - judging from the shouts of consternation that I heard when my sudden flight and bid for freedom came to their attention; with their diligent pursuit of me recommencing once again, not long after and in even greater earnest.

Their voices also – well, one of them at least – seemed oddly familiar.

293

I could worry about *that* however, at some other time.

Right now I had other more pressing matters to be dealing with.

I arrived at the hotel anyway before long, but they had been gaining on me over the preceding minutes, and were no more than twenty metres behind me now as things stood.

Spotting the hotel awning then just a few strides away, I was fortunate to discover that a party of tourists were in the process of disembarking from a coach and were readying themselves for check in - organising luggage and what not - which meant that Bill and Ben behind me would no longer be in a position to be as free and easy with their snipering as they had been thus far.

Entering the foyer so, I immediately scanned the area for a porter or a concierge that might come to my assistance.

Spotting one then to my right, adjacent to the elevators and a weird oversized potted-plant type thingamajig, I darted across to him with no small degree of celerity.

"Pal!" I splurted breathlessly as I arrived by his side.

"You have just GOT to help me!" I went on, whilst at the same time watching the doorway to check if the desperate duo had followed me in.

"Hasidic Jews……" I continued, gasping for air.

"Men you…" I struggled further.

"Don't wanna meet…" I just about got out.

I was going to finish my sentence by saying 'on a dark night' but the by now very indignant porter stopped me in my tracks with no small degree of umbrage and pique.

"I can assure you sir" he said, with a level of haughtiness that is reserved solely I would say for dudes of such an ilk, that work for establishments of such an ilk, where you are unlikely to find a room at any time ever, for less than five hundred sovs a night.

"That the menu at this heralded hostelry is of the highest order in the land!"

'What the fuck is this fucker banging on about' was the first thing that came to mind.

With 'lay off the wacky backy duder' being the second.

"Our JUS is of the finest quality" he went on.

"And compliments ALL of our meat dishes with masterly aplomb! I would thank you to remember this, good sir!"

It turned out anyway that rather than being a porter he was in *actual* fact a waiter on his way back to the restaurant from the jacks, who took great offence at the fact that I was insinuating that their 'jus' was 'acidic' and that as a result of this fact, I would not be choosing any 'meat' dishes from their 'menu' in the hotel restaurant later that night.

Talk about an inopportune moment for a 'lost in translation' event.

All of this bolloxology became irrelevant anyway, soon enough, when I spotted my two nemeses sprinting across the foyer, with my immediate liquidation at that moment in time their principal goal.

The one with the pistol was to the fore I noticed, with his sidekick not far behind.

I looked around me then for some item or other with which I might defend myself, but saw nothing in the vicinity that would suffice.

Not being craven in disposition also, I made a decision of course NOT to cower behind the waiter.

'Take your medicine like a man, my son' as my oul fella always used to say.

Too many fuckers in this world are limp-wristed cunts.

Aware of the fact anyway, that there was probably nothing that I could to at this stage to avoid it; I prepared myself for the end.

Imagine my surprise so when from behind the giant plant-pot type thinga-majig to my right, a diminutive figure in Cuban heels emerged at speed.

Rushing the assailant closest to me - that is, the dude who was armed - the figure rugby-tackled him expertly from the side, as a result of which the weapon flew out of my enemy's hand and clattered across the marble floor, ending up eventually next to a reception desk that was several metres away.

The would-be assassin made an attempt to rise then with a view to retrieving said pistol, but the pocket-sized knight in shining armour latched on to him like a leech.

The sniper was going fucking nowhere.

The second assailant looked at me then as if to say 'Look dude, I'm probably not up for this Mexican stand off – do you mind if we call it quits?', but before he had time to say or do anything two security guards had arrived by his side and taken him out as well.

Well what was a turnip for the books as the greengrocer suggested to the librarian!

I didn't see *that* coming.

All so now you would imagine, was fine and dandy and as rosy in the garden as it could be.

You'd think so, wouldn't you?

Nothing however could have been further from the truth.

Fucking Bono, that's what!

THAT prick was my grand defender!

My Guardian fucking Angel!

Can you imagine how beholden to him I was going to be now?

As I regarded him there, sitting on the assassin, with a smug look of 'Aren't I great to be such a fucking hero, while the rest of yiz here are nothing but a bunch of fucking saps!', I considered the fact that if I had a choice between this *new* situation – that is, Bono being my saviour - and the gunman *actually* taking me out as had very nearly come to pass, I'd very probably, given how things appeared now to have panned out, have opted for the latter.

What the fuck was he doing here anyway?

I didn't remember inviting him along?

Yet here he fucking was, astride of Macca, like the cat that's caught the proverbial cream.

And yes.

You heard me right.

Fucking Macca!

THAT'S who had been trying to take me out since I'd arrived at that foot-bridge in Little Venice with Kate Bush.

And his minder too.

What was all THAT about?

It was time to find out what had been going on.

"Lemme go la'!!" squealed the famous Liverpudlian from beneath his dwarf-ish adversary.

He wriggled back and forth then a bit in a bid to break free, but in fairness to Bono he held his ground admirably enough.

"I've done nuthink wrongk!" Macca continued, clearly not privy to some of the better known and fairly standard in my view civic mores - that is that attempting to kill random citizens in the street for no apparent reason at all, is a practice that is widely frowned upon, usually, in most free-thinking democratic societies of today.

I strode over to them so, and made myself known.

"Evening Macca" I declared, as nonchalantly as you like.

"Billy from the Wirral" I said also, nodding to his partner in crime.

Macca had told me his handle earlier on.

"You can get off him now Paul and thanks for your help" I said to Bono.

"Macca and Billy from the Wirral pose us no further danger. The weapon, as you will see if you turn to your right, is in the hands of a security dude".

Sure enough it was; a big burly chap with the widest shoulders and squarest head I think that I have ever seen.

There'd be no fucking around with him.

"Are you sure Johnny?" Bono responded; worried I think that once released the infamous scouser would be making efforts to abscond.

"No, its OK Paul" I answered.

"I think that between the two of us and this unfeasibly large security dude – you're an Islander, right dude – that we have the situation under control."

"Yes sir" responded the security dude.

"Tonga".

'I could have probably guessed that' I was thinking.

The fucker was a tank.

Bono stood up then and dusted himself off, after which Macca did the same.

"Scoops?" I ventured then; which under the circumstances I felt was the only logical course of action with which to proceed.

They all nodded in agreement – some convincingly; some less so – after which off we all popped into the lounge for said refreshments.

The security dude followed us in also, and took me the side before we reached the bar.

"Don't you want me to call the police, sir?" he asked.

"The gentleman did after all, come at you with a gun."

"Not at all, not at all!" I answered.

As things were I was absolutely fucking parching for a pint, so viewed any potential obstruction to that inclination, as an obstruction that I could very much at this stage do without.

"Sure isn't it all water under the bridge now, wha'?"

He fucked off then anyway, which meant that we could AT LAST get stuck into the beer.

"So what's the fucking story Macca?" I asked of the man, right after of course I had got the first round in.

Never wait for some other fucker to look after the gargles.

If you're there and you've got cash on the hip, just get them fucking in.

Sure you'll be getting them back anyway as soon as the round moves along.

That's the norm anyway with most clear-minded and decent thinking people.

"Why the fuck were you trying to take me out?" I went on.

"I wazzin mace, I swurr!" he answered, as indignant as you like, before taking a nervous little sip from the glass of red wine that I'd purchased for him just a few moments before.

"Look Macca" I responded, leaning in closer to him so that he could hear better what I had to say.

I was sitting on a high stool at the bar – the only way of course to be ensconced in a pub – whilst Macca was sitting directly before me similarly at the bar.

Bono and Billy from the Wirral were sitting next to us, although not at the bar.

Bono was stationed adjacent to me, while Billy was adjacent to Macca.

"You've been taking pot shots at me since that bridge in Little Venice! Poor Kate Bush copped one in the chest as well by the way, but you're lucky there, as she had some mustard ball type thingamajig in her cleavage which cushioned the shot".

"Ehh yeah, dah waz me achally boss, soddy abou' dah boss" said Billy from the Wirral.

"I've neveh shorra gun befour mace, so I don't rearly know worrye'm doin' likhe."

It turned out anyway that Billy from the Wirral had been responsible for the initial volley of bullets whilst Kate and I had been stationed at the bridge, but that he had been so bad and his aim so off, that Macca had lost his patience with him and taken over marksman duties pretty much immediately after I had left the culvert next to the station.

And in fairness to the dude the shots that had followed after that were markedly more on target than any that had gone before.

"Well to be honest with you Billy, that's all very well" I answered.

"And very nice to know; but it still doesn't go any way at all towards answering my question. Which is, just to reiterate; why the fuck were youse bollixes trying to take me out?"

"YOU KNOW WHY MACE!!" Macca responded then loudly, as he placed his wine glass unsteadily back on to the bar.

Surely the fucker wasn't going to start blubbering again?

He was, you know.

Uncontrollably.

He'd done the very same thing before you may remember me saying, all those years ago in that wine bar on the Strand.

The dude had issues clearly.

We all looked at other then, uncomfortably, for the next twenty or so seconds until he eventually, and thankfully, brought his emotions under control.

"You were gonna go te de paypehs abarrar songks!" he pronounced then, sobbing still and just about managing to gulp down another half-mouthful of his wine.

"Ye toult me so in de steeyoudio la'!!

'Duzzen de werld deserve te know all abarrih', you said!"

He was right.

I *had* said that.

But I'd only been joking about it at the time and had in actual fact as you may recall, been talking about the Noddy joke rather than the songs.

"Hang on a second" said Bono, butting in.

"Are you guys talking about that Beatles songs rumour that's been doing the rounds for the last, God knows for how feckin' long? You *do* know that that's, like, total bullshit, right?"

This was interesting.

What did Bono know about this situation that I didn't?

Macca tried to answer him back then but I stopped him in his tracks.

"Hang on a sec there Macca" I said, raising my hand abruptly to encourage him to desist.

"Let's hear what the short-arsed fucker has to say".

Bono winced a bit then at the last little reference to his height; so I was thinking at the time that I should probably do the right thing and apologise to him for being so derogatory about his diminutive stature.

But then I got to thinking.

HEY!

FUCK HIM!

He decided not to press the point anyway - the limp-wristed fuck - and went on with his story without taking me to task.

Fucking wimp!

"Oh yeah" he continued on.

"I was talking to Johnny Rogan about it only last month – you know; that rock star biographer type bloke? I think he wants to do a book on us actually, which is hardly surprising in fairness. I mean if you look at our impressive canon of work to date like, you know; how could he not?"

He stopped then momentarily as if he had lost his train of thought.

"Sorry, where was I?"

Where were you *indeed*?

I'll tell you where you were, fuckwit!

You were in the middle of the most interminably boring sentence of all time.

That's where you were!

Sadly for us anyway, he prattled on.

"Oh yeah, that Beatles rumour. So Rogan has done his research anyway, particularly around that Mostyn piano teacher character – that's the name, right Macca? – and it turns out that there was no such dude with that name that existed in and around Matthew Street at the time, and certainly no piano teacher in the area either, that had rooms above a pub. The common consensus so – and I'm sorry to have to say this to you Macca – but the common consensus appears to be that you made the whole thing up!"

It made sense alright, whatever about the fact that it was that dweeb Bono who was breaking the news.

I'd always thought myself that the story was far-fetched.

"Rogan reached out to George Harrison also, he said" Bono went on.

"Who told him that the whole thing was just a major crock of shit. All's he said was that Macca was a bit of a nutter and that he'd had some sort of a breakdown in the 1980's and never came back. Too much acid back in the day, he said".

It definitely added up.

I mean there was no way that a story like this that had been doing the rounds for so long, would not have been followed up more earnestly by some journalist fucker or other that wanted to make a quick name for his or herself in the tabloids.

I'd heard of this Rogan character as well as it goes, and it was a well-known fact that he had a very notable reputation for knowing his stuff.

"IRRIS true, ye fuckehs!" retorted Macca, tearful once again.

"I'm no' makin' irrup abou' de songks!"

And with that he fucked his glass of red wine over Bono – no issues there - and went haring out of the place like a mad thing - but not before he'd overturned a few tables on his way, and knocked over a few of the other patrons' glasses as well.

"Yes indeedy" I said to the others, when I was sure that he was gone.

"Rearrange these words gents. His. Dude. Off. That. Head. Is. Fucking."

"I'm inclined to think that this Rogan character is correct" I continued.

"But anyhoo, on to more pressing matters. As in, there is a distinct lack of gargle on the counter before us dudes, to which as you are no doubt aware, any person with cash in hand can fashion a speedy resolution to said conundrum; if such an aspiration of course is strong in their heart. Or, to phrase it more succinctly - get the fucking scoops in Hewson, ye short-arsed prick! It's your fucking round!"

Bono duly obliged so, thankfully, after which the three of us talked of this and that for the next little while.

'He's not such a bad chap really, Bono' I was thinking, the more I got to speak with him.

A bit eccentric yes - what with his pet monkey and the using song lyrics for normal discourse type of thing – although he had at least been refraining from that bolloxology today – but his heart was definitely in the right place.

Sure hadn't he saved my life earlier on?

That had to count for something.

"But why were you here?" I asked of him then, remembering that that was something that I had wanted to know.

"You know; when I arrived earlier on with Macca and Billy from the Wirral here on my tail."

"Oh yeah, sorry, that was something and nothing really, to be honest" he replied.

"Paulie – you know, our manager? - told me that you were staying here so I just wanted to run this song by you that I thought might be a better option than 'Tomorrow'? It's off our new album that's coming out next year – a little number called 'Stay'? I thought that you might like it, you know?"

"Fair enough" I said.

"I appreciate the thought. Sure we can try it out tomorrow back in Abbey Road"

"You're going back to Abbey Road?" he answered, with a look of genuine surprise on his face.

"Are you sure that's wise?"

"Of course I'm going back to Abbey fucking Road!" I replied, with the look on *my* face conveying my belief that under the circumstances that this was the most natural thing in the world that I could possibly do.

"You don't think that I'm giving up that easily, do you?"

"But what about security?" he put forward.

"You do recall I assume that for a very large portion of today you were the target of a psychotic Liverpudlian Coleopteran and his - sitting here before you now - similarly murderous sidekick? Is it safe basically, I suppose I'm saying, for you to be wandering around the city on your own?"

He had a point.

It was a dangerous game, this Rock Star Demigod business.

Whatever about Macca and Billy from the Wirral, who knew what other lunatics might be looking to take a shot?

Sure wasn't Macca's own partner in crime John Lennon taken out similarly, for no apparent reason at all, by some nutjob on the streets of New York?

The solution to the problem anyway, was staring me in the face.

Billy from the Wirral!

Ok so he had been trying to take me out earlier on, fair enough; but isn't there an expression that says that you should make every effort always, to keep your enemies close?

And besides, if he was given a choice between having to look after Macca or myself, I was inclined to believe that he was way more likely to opt for yours truly than the scouse bawler, based solely on the fact that I was not - at least not yet anyway - for the birds.

"What do reckon Billy?" I put to him so.

"Are you ready to jump ship? I'll offer you the same daily rate as Macca, starting today. Right now, in fact. Are you up for it?"

He indicated then - fairly forcibly it has to be said - that he was.

"Too RICE I'm up forrih mace! Dah Macca lad izza fuckin' nusseh!"

I was in business so.

I could wander the streets of London now - or anywhere else even - safe in the knowledge that Billy from the Wirral had my back.

It was a load off my mind; I'm not going to deny it.

Another thing though was the disguises.

I was keen to know more about how that came about.

"Ahh dah waz nothin' mace!" said Billy.

"Juss me and Macca takin' two lads outce in Mayfair, likhe. Dey were juss walkin' daown de streece la'. We even cutce off der cerls as well likhe, and stuck 'em on. Juss te be authentic, likhe. Which remaainds me achtly, der still in de limo's boot! I muss sort darrou' layseh!"

Fair enough.

I was tired now anyway, so was thinking about calling it a night.

Billy got another round in then – fair play; never miss your round - but that would be it for me then after that, I was thinking, as soon as I'd lorried that last scoop back.

I lashed it in to me so, before making my excuses and rising to go.

"I'll bring ye te de room boss!" said Billy, to which I nodded OK.

"And I'll accompany you back to reception also." said Bono.

"I'm staying in Kensington, so I can get a cab from here."

That was K and the G as well, I indicated.

Arriving in reception so a few moments later, my eyes were opened then quite dramatically as to what lay ahead for me in the months - and probably years indeed - ahead.

That is I got a fairly definitive flavour as to what my life would be like as a Rock Star Demigod, if things continued on into the future as they had eventuated thus far.

More than a hundred fans had gathered in the foyer with U2 albums and a myriad of other band paraphernalia – concert programmes and what not – in their possession.

They had heard through the grapevine obviously that Bono was in situ, so were here now - as far as I could determine anyway - to meet with my diminutive new pal and get him to sign all of their crap.

Now after the day that I had had, and the hassle that I'd gone through already, I could think of nothing worse than having to stand there for the next however long, and make small talk with these bozos for as long as it might take.

I was very much of the mind in fact, that if it was me and I was presented with the same situation, that I'd be putting the old wayfarers on with a pretty decisive degree of exigency, and high-tailing it like a good thing to the lifts without delay.

And that is where folks, I really must attest, Bono and I are different in every way.

Rather than high-tailing it, as I have indicated already would have been my own preferred course of action, Bono stopped instead and started nattering with these dudes and dudettes as if they were his long lost pals!

It was like watching a master in action.

'Fair fucks te ye' I was thinking, as he worked the line slowly with patience and skill.

Every single thing that they said to him – and believe me we are talking about banalities here on a grand scale – he handled with benevolence and poise.

"Like, OH MY GOD!!" said one American oul one in her forties, who had a copy of 'Achtung Baby' clutched to her chest.

They were ALL Americans as far as I could see.

302

"We were like, in Tucson, like, five years ago" the oul one went on.

"And saw your show, and it was like, freaking awesome sir!" she babbled further.

"We were like, at the front and you – AAAAGGGGHHHH!!! (at this point she screamed) – you, like, grabbed my hand! Do you remember that sir? Bono, sir?"

This was just one story of I don't know how many stories that were of a bizarrely similar persuasion.

Bono just waded through them all though slowly, with a level of finesse and humility that I have never seen before, ever, with any other public figure.

'It's no wonder' I was thinking.

'That he is adored'

"I DO remember that show my love" he said to the American oul one.

"And I'm not gonna lie to you - your face looks strikingly familiar".

Which of course was total bullshit AND a total fucking lie.

But what did it matter?

He was giving the public what they wanted so what more could anyone ask?

It was a stark lesson for me; I don't mind admitting to it.

Was this the life for me?

Could I ever, when all was said and done, be like this?

Could I be - to put it even more definitively - could I be Bono?

I was inclined to think not.

Rather than wait there anyway for the fucker to finish, I tapped him on the shoulder and indicated to him that I was going to bed.

He said goodnight to me then, and added that he was looking forward to getting stuck into the recording tomorrow.

The gathered throng had a quick gander at me then as well, to see who I was; but went back to himself then when they realised that I was nobody important.

My star had not risen yet on the other side of the pond.

I headed for the lifts then with Billy from the Wirral at my side.

"I'll be going for the narky, uncommunicative type I think, young William" I said to him as we wandered across.

"Like Geldof maybe?" I suggested.

"Or John Lydon. You know - he of 'The Sex Pistols' fame – not my old pal from school"

He nodded to indicate that he understood.

Which of course he didn't.

But like; whatever.

"I mean, imagine having to be nice to morons like fucking that?" I continued.

It doesn't bear thinking about.

After which the lift arrived, and elevated us to the finest suite at the top of the hotel.

CHAPTER 22

There it is.

London town.

What a city?!

And it'd be even better if it wasn't so full of 'facking pommes' as the Aussies say.

The city of tiny lights.

Or is that LA?

Didn't Frank Zappa have a song about the lights in LA?

And a video too with that stop motion mutation shit going on, long before that mad fucker Peter Gabriel was arsing about with plasticine chickens and sledge-hammers.

It's some balcony anyway.

I can see the whole city from here, practically.

Although if you pay top dollar in a place like The Dorchester the very least that you can expect is a daycent sized balcony with which to survey the terrain.

Nice room too.

And to the rear, which is good.

Just Hyde Park at the front, so nothing much to see there bar greenery and shit.

There's St. Paul's to the west, with its' whispering gallery.

And Westminster too, with its' perennially obnoxious inhabitants.

Fucking Tories!

Is there anything more despicable than a Tory?

I consider it to be unlikely.

And yet the English electorate insist on voting them in over and over again.

Mad.

I'll have a smoke anyway and take in the view.

After the day I've had, a smoke will be good.

Nothing like the view of Dublin though, from Deer Park in Howth.

Now THAT's a view!

The Ringsend towers to the left, with the grand old medieval city in all of its glory nestled into the bay.

Portmarnock on the right there, with Malahide and Donabate further up,

304

meandering past other seaside stop offs; Loughshinny, Laytown and the like; all the way up the coast to Drogheda, Clogherhead and beyond.

DON'T go left on the second.

Left on the second is dead.

Head down and follow through.

DON'T duck hook it, for fuck sake!

Nice and easy.

Fuck it anyway.

I've only gone and duck hooked it left.

Twenty yards from the pin now.

An uphill chip.

Green sloping away from me too on the other side, so practically impossible to stop.

I'll open up the club face and hit across it.

Fucking commit to it though, Johnny boy; otherwise you're fucked.

Land the ball on the green like a butterfly with sore feet.

As that old dude Lee Trevino used to say.

BOOM!

A tap in!

Job done.

I can't see Prince in plus fours though, I'm not gonna lie.

That was one weird exchange between Bowie and himself.

Amazing really.

You think that you know a person from their public persona and it turns out then that you don't know them at all!

Like that short-arsed Bono fucker.

Although I should probably stop calling him short-arsed.

And giving him such a hard time, generally.

Sure didn't he save my fucking life?

And the way he was with those Seppos in the foyer as well?

Septic tanks by the way, in case you're wondering.

Yanks?

I mean that was admirable; very admirable; whatever which way you care to look at it.

He's actually a really nice dude, which is weird really, when you consider how much of a bonehead he is in public.

Macca though.

Macca, Macca, Macca!

Where did it all go wrong?

Someone's knocking on the door alright dude.

The men in the white fucking coats!

Poor old Billy from the Wirral as well.

He got the Macca treatment earlier on in the car.

"Oh yeah mace" he told me as we were coming up in the lift to the suite.

"I'm not fuckin' jokhin' mace, I nearly crashed de fuckin' thing on more dan one occasion, likhe."

"He juss kep' singin' deese, likhe, teddible bloody songks!"

I've been there before so know exactly what he means.

"Silly Love Songks, Pipes o' Peece, Mulla Kintiyeh – iwwaz dreadful mace, I'm not jokhin'! I honestly think darreye'm, likhe, scarred for life!"

Billy's alright I suppose, especially now that he's on my side.

I'll be keeping him an eye on him though.

He was, after all, trying to take me out earlier on.

Talking of which, I wonder how my unhinged mate Kate is getting on.

Probably skipping down Pall Mall by now I'd say, in her nip and pretending to be a fucking hummingbird.

She's odd in behaviour, there ain't no denying it.

And fucking 'Netherfeathers'?

What the fuck was all THAT about?

Off the charts lunacy to be fair.

She'd get on well with that Sting bollocks actually, now that I come to think of it.

If she could put up with the fucking stench.

And Grizzywarks?

What was that bolloxology?

More specifically, what in jaysus are these fuckers on?

I'm wondering actually if this is even the life for me.

On so many occasions since my near overnight meteoric rise, there have been bell ends to contend with on every front.

Are they all like this?

Will I become like this myself?

Not a happy prospect.

A simpler life methinks.

10am.

Summer 1980.

Or thereabouts.

Breakfast.

Cornflakes.

Milk.

Spúnóg.

Shovel it in.

Done.

Departure time - 10.15am.

Short stroll to field, jam jar in hand.

Kitchen knife jabbed into lid, twice.

To let air in, of course.

I'm not a TOTAL fucking maniac!

Wildflowers, daisies, buttercups - fuck them all in.

A third of the way up.

Bees.

Bees everywhere.

Bumbles.

Shuggies.

Red-arses.

No wasps.

Wasps are angry bastards.

And Red-arses are the toughest to catch.

See you coming a mile off.

Shuggies are idiots though.

Total fucking idiots.

Sluggish.

And bumbles are dopes too.

Too fat.

'How many have you got Paulie?'

My old mate Paulie is a master.

Like a lioness on the Serengeti, he is an artist at work.

Once in position, he pounces with guile.

A venus flytrap.

The tongue of a frog.

Not bad for a ten year old.

The trick of course is to ensure that the bees that are already within, do not escape whilst another is being caught.

The aperture between the lid and the rim of the jar must remain slight.

And yes, accidents will ensue.

Decapitations will occur.

But they're only bees and we're only kids, so, you know - shit happens.

People take life WAAY too seriously.

What's that Paulie?

Three and you're in?

Sounds like a plan.

But there are only two of us?

Here's Jimbo, striding across the field, ball under his arm.

Paulie must have seen him.

That's cool.

We can play with three defo.

Not two though.

I mean, how can you dribble past yourself?

Our bee jars will be our goalposts.

Fuck it anyway.

I draw the short blade.

I fucking HATE being in.

I'll let soft goals in though, so I'll be out soon enough.

"No letting soft goals in Johnser, or you'll be getting a kick in the bollocks from me!" says Jimbo.

I won't argue with Jimbo.

He's a lot bigger than me and likes throwing digs.

But he plays in goal for Stella Maris youths, so wouldn't you think that he'd want to be in?

They're evenly matched anyway - himself and Paulie - which is a right fucking pain.

I'll be in goal for fucking ages!

Will one o' yiz shoot for jaysus sake?

Paulie lets rip then, fair play.

An absolute corker from twenty yards out.

I'm not getting near that.

It hits the post though - aka bee jar - and off the lid flies.

Twenty plus bees released into our close proximity, with every single one of the oxygen starved little bastards pissed off with the world and looking for revenge.

Off we fuck so, with our legs and hearts pounding, screaming and laughing in equal measure.

Good times.

Simpler times.

A knock on the door so I head back inside.

"Hello?" I call out to whoever might be there.

"Room Service" a voice responds.

A familiar voice, female in inclination.

Belinda.

"What's up Belinda?" I say to her as I open the door.

"Have you had enough of Roger Water's big veined cock?"

"The fuck you talking about?" as she strolls into the room.

She throws her jacket onto a chaise longue type thingamajig next to the dressing table and heads across to the minibar to get herself a drink.

Good call that.

"Get me one while you're there, will you?" I say to her.

"What do you want?" she responds.

"A double JD with ice" I say, after which she brings said imbibe across.

"Cool suite dude" she says then whistling softly to herself as she takes a look around.

"SOMEONE'S coming up in the world!" she adds then, at which point I can see her mentally undressing me in her mind, as she tries to figure out, simultaneously, how much now and indeed in the future I might be worth.

She's some piece of fucking work, that Belinda.

She heads off to the bathroom then, for a bit of an old look see, and if anybody, right there and then, had asked me what the next words out of her mouth would be, I'd have bet a million fucking dollars that they would have been, verbatim, as follows.

"Oh my God, look at this tub! Wanna take a bath?!"

And this when she is a guest in my suite, having had, less than a couple of hours before, Roger Waters' cock rammed up her arse.

Probably.

As I said so before.

She's some piece of fucking work, that Belinda.

"What do you actually WANT from life Belinda?" I pose to her then when she returns; which I have to say is unusually circumspect for me.

"I mean is it all about cocks and being boned up the arse, or are there actual 'other' things that you see out there for yourself, at some other point down the line?"

"I dunno" she answers with a shrug, clearly not bothered either way by my fairly honest appraisal of what her life has represented – at least the parts of it that I've seen anyway - thus far.

"I'm just like, you know, havin' a laugh and that" she goes on.

"Sure life is so fucked up anyway, what's the point in taking any of it too seriously?"

She's right, I suppose.

Life IS fucked up.

But surely she must have at least some aspiration?

Something in life that she might want to achieve?

Judging by her present nonchalance though, it's clear to me that she's grand as she is.

We get locked so anyway, and shag once or twice, before I lay my head back and finally get some rest.

Belinda is asleep in no time, but I'm finding it difficult to nod off myself.

Adrenalin I suppose.

It's been such a fucked up day.

I like Tom Waits.

Although somebody told me once before that that old hobo routine is nothing more than a contrivance.

I find that hard to believe.

As in, if it is, he's one hell of a fucking actor.

As Axl Rose was rabbiting on about there also, earlier today.

Now THERE'S an unpleasant memory!

Axl Rose's John Thomas swinging around under his kilt at Slane?

I don't know how gay dudes do it to be honest.

I mean, other dudes' cocks are fairly grim.

Although each to their own as I always say.

Nothing to do with fucking me.

It's a funny old life, though, to be fair.

For Axl like.

Flying from place to place wearing kilts and no underwear?

He's a complex character is Axl.

Many layers.

Like on onion.

Belinda is snoring now like a bull fucking elephant!

I can't sleep now, not with THAT racket.

I'll go for a walk.

What time is it?

Fuck me, nearly 5am?

I thought it was midnight!

Perhaps I DID sleep?

A walk anyway might clear the head.

And early morning walks are good for the soul, I heard someone say before.

Should I be calling Billy from the Wirral though?

If I'm going out on my own?

Ahh no, sure I'll be grand.

The streets will be deserted at this hour.

I arrive to reception a few minutes later, and nod to the Tongan security dude on my way out.

"Morning sir" he remarks cheerily, doffing his cap to me as I make my way past.

Nice bloke.

But stay on his good side of course.

I'm thinking anyway that if I cut through the park it'll be a nicer walk than if I stay on the streets, especially at this hour.

I cross the road so, and scale a four or so foot high railing to get in.

There's no gate along here that I can see, so I might as well just enter here than anywhere else.

I make my way under some trees on the periphery, noisily disturbing scrub and dead leaves beneath my feet as I pass along.

Arriving at the interior of the park then, I note that it is deserted and that I am alone.

Heavy dew sits on the grass which moistens my shoes considerably as I continue along.

'I'll travel to the other side' I'm thinking.

'And decide where to go next, when I reach that junction on Bayswater Road'.

I exit there some minutes later, and cross at the point which leads to where I was yesterday, when I was on the run from Macca and Billy from the Wirral.

I head down a small road called Westbourne Terrace then, before encountering some tourists with suitcases, scuttling busily past; on their way to Paddington, presumably, which, from what I can gather from their words, is no more than a five minute journey from where we are now.

"Hurry, hurry, come ON!" says the Dad to the Mum and two young daughters that are scurrying in his wake.

"The train departs from Paddington at 6am and it's already five to!"

They do not look happy.

But why book a train that leaves at 6am?

That, it seems to me, is at the heart of why the whole shebang has gone so tits up.

'Book a train at a normal fucking time, dufus!!' I'm thinking, before realising then that I have actually – like Sting - said the words out loud.

The Dad looks back at me then with a scowl, and I swear that if he had the time and wasn't in so much of a rush, that he'd be stopping in his tracks and giving me a smack.

Which in fairness and under the circumstances, he'd have been well within his rights to do.

I would myself basically, if the shoe was on the other foot.

As it is anyway, he just bustles on down the road, with his badly set upon and singularly depressed looking family bringing up the rear.

I pop off then again anyway, taking a right on to Westbourne Terrace Road.

It all looks pretty familiar to be honest.

I'm almost certain that this is the route that I took yesterday evening, when the two lads were on my tail.

A couple of minutes later I am certain of it, when I spot the bridge at Little Venice where Kate Bush was shot.

I wonder how she's getting on?

Thank fuck for her ball of mustard wha'?

Which is not a sentence that I ever imagined I'd be saying before now.

These Rock Star Demigod types are mad fuckers!

Although maybe with the fame and the adulation and all that, you just become that way over time?

Look at Macca for example.

I mean that poor bastard has had people screaming at him since 1962!

Surely that has to have an adverse effect.

And on a related note, is that something that I really want for myself?

For the entire populace of the world to know my every coming and going, and what I had for fucking breakfast?

Imagine meeting that travelling family for instance, several years from now?

And the entire dynamic of the encounter being different as a result merely of the fact that I am famous and they think that they 'know' me.

Do I really want to lead a life that's as shallow as that?

I walk past the bridge anyway and take a left on to Delamere Terrace.

There's a canal of sorts to my right, so I'll just follow that along and see where it goes.

It's beautiful at this hour.

Bewitching.

Some badly needed serenity for the soul methinks.

Hardly a sound to be heard bar a soft rustling of leaves in the trees that line the canal bank and intermittent birdsong to accompany the dawn.

I stroll along further lost in my thoughts.

It is fully light now, with the city slowly but surely starting to wake from its slumber.

A milk float trundles by, and I wave to the driver as he carries on past.

"Mornin' squire!" he shouts in my direction, to which I respond cheerfully.

"And the top of the morning to your good self also!"

Everyone is in good form on sunny summer mornings.

And why not?

It's good to be alive!

Ironically enough then, I arrive at the entrance to Kensal Green Cemetery.

"I'll have a wee look inside" I'm thinking to myself, not put off at all by where I am arrived.

"And see if I can spot any famous graves."

I actually like graveyards as it goes.

I honestly can't see what all the fuss is about.

You know; how others find them creepy?

I see them as calm peaceful places, rather than environments that are ominous.

Time stands still in graveyards and gives one an opportunity to reflect.

I enter through tall iron wrought gates that are slightly ajar and carry on down a main thoroughfare that's directly before me.

To my left and right there are headstones and memorials of varying sizes and shape, with dense undergrowth prevalent everywhere in between.

I don't know if there are any groundsmen employed here, but if there are, they're a lacklustre lot.

Although in disorderliness often, I think, there is charm.

I move in off the main pathway then, with a view to exploring the headstones in further detail.

A light breeze is blowing but the sun is now up, with the temperature rising steadily.

As I carry on my way, I notice that the ground beneath my feet is unnervingly uneven.

Several of the headstones and crosses, particularly the older ones, are leaning over quite dramatically also, which I assume is as a result of a shifting of the soil over the years.

Antiquarian social status is very evident here also.

Does anything ever change?

Bog standard 'Joe Soaps' have bog standard headstones, with most of them so overrun with ivy and lichen now, that it's hard to determine with many of them who they actually were?

Alternatively, the more auspicious deceased have considerably more salubrious monuments to denouement erected in their memory.

Lord Dorchester, the Princess Sophia, King George the third – no expense spared there.

Actual FAMILY mausoleums no less!

Although when all is said and done, what exactly does it matter?

They're all as dead as fried chicken either way.

I spot some familiar names as I wander along.

Isambard Kingdom Brunel.

A famous engineer I believe.

And William Makepeace Thackeray, the great English novelist.

Anthony Trollope.

I think of Belinda then and smirk.

Now there's a trollop for ye lads, if yer looking for one!

I hear a noise from behind then, and turn to see from where it has come.

There is no-one afoot.

Probably a ghost I muse nonchalantly, before traipsing further on.

Next up, Mary Scott Hogarth; dead at just seventeen the headstone reads.

"Charles Dickens' sister-in-law, vat" says an old dude that I encounter at said grave.

"Really?" I answer, interested to know more.

"Oh yes" he answers.

"Died all ovva sudden vey say."

"'art attack, mose probly" he continues, before wandering off.

'Jaysus' I'm thinking, as the old dude shuffles away.

'The transience of life wha'?

Might as well grab it with both hands while you can.

Who knows what the fuck is around the corner?'

I wander off then again, spotting a large sepulchre next out of the corner of eye.

It's nestled into an 'off the beaten track' corner of the graveyard, and on its side is the inscription 'I WILL ARISE'.

Wishful thinking there Bubba, I'm thinking.

I'd say the chances of you rematerializing in corporeal form at any point in the near to distant future are remote.

When was it you died again?

The eighteenth century?

I rest my case.

I stroll further on until the pathway widens and I find myself before a large building, which upon further inspection I notice, is a crematorium.

'West London Crematorium' I see inscribed on a placard near the entrance.

It is an impressive edifice indeed, classical in design and imposing in nature.

Large metre thick granite columns adorn the entrance on either side.

I only mention these as mere seconds after I stop to inspect one of them - the one on the left - it appears to be, before my eyes, disintegrating.

A large two inch portion of it just above my head has fallen away.

Another portion of it then, this time to my right, at knee level, has fallen away also.

'What the deuce is going on?' as Kate Bush would say.

A figure emerges then from behind a large mausoleum no than twenty metres away from where I am at present located.

A figure in black brandishing a gun.

Hence the disintegrating column and not some supernatural anomaly.

Moving towards me slowly then the figure takes aim.

I run for cover but he has me in his sights.

A sharp pain in my left side stops me in my tracks and I fall to my knees.

I try to rise, but am caught once again, this time in the arm.

I fall further still and am face down now in the gravel, just to the right of the crematorium.

I turn over then so that I am facing upwards, just as my assailant arrives at my side.

The pistol he is using has a silencer attached, which is the primary reason I suppose, why no-one has come to my assistance.

It's hard to make out his face in the early morning sun.

But his voice, when I hear it, is unmistakeable.

"I'm soddy la'" he says.

"Burrye can't 'ave ye goin' te de press abarrar songks!"

Macca.

Fucking Macca!

So he IS mad enough to take me out.

I thought that that was all just bravado.

"Jesus Christ Macca!" I respond, struggling to catch my breath.

"I was only taking the piss, you fucking gobshite!"

"I couldn't give a flying fuck about your poxy songs!"

"Soddy mace, burrye can't take dah chance" he responds, as he points the pistol at me once again.

"At least wi' you arra de way, I can rest in peece once again."

'Yeah, nice choice of words Macca, ye PERRICK' I'm thinking, given my present circumstances.

'Rest in peace, bloody hell!'

And with that he pulls the trigger and everything goes black.

And then soon after a form of candescence.

Not light.

Bodily senses not applicable.

I drift upwards, weightlessly.

Buoyancy?

None.

Material definitions?

Meaningless.

Everything is clear.

I pass through clouds.

No.

I am AS ONE with clouds.

And all else.

Starlings gather.

Synchronous symmetry.

One, two, ten, twenty.

One hundred.

Two hundred.

Harmonious equilibrium.

One hovers nearby.

"I am a Glide Officer" it indicates.

"And I have been waiting for you for some time"

I indicate that I understand but am unsure how.

As it is and as I sense it, I appear to hold no physical form.

"Don't worry" the Glide Officer expresses.

"This form of existence will be familiar to you soon".

Another starling makes itself known.

"Story bud" it 'says' as it appears on my right.

"I'm a Hover Head."

His presence feels familiar.

"But you probably know me better as Phil Lynott"

"You know - the ex-Rock Star DemiGod?"

"Come on" he continues.

"Follow me over here"

We swoop downwards with ease and land on the bough of a tree – I'm getting the hang of this.

Hang on a second!

I am a bird!

"Indeed you are pal" says Phil, who has clearly 'heard' what I was thinking.

"And a starling, no less, fair play!" he proceeds further.

"Normally you have to go through one or two other transformations before you arrive here."

'Fuck me, Kate Bush was right!' I'm thinking.

"Indeed she was!" says Phil, which leads me to thinking that if he can hear everything that I'm thinking, then I'd better keep my thoughts to myself.

"Indeed you had!" he says with a chuckle/warble, after which I realise that he can 'hear' everything in my mind.

This will take some getting used to.

"Indeed it will!" he answers again, at which point I'm thinking that if I was human again I'd be giving him a knee in the stones.

"I saw ye in Slane dayer as well dayer pal, a few monts ago, an' you worr bleedin' deadly so ye wayer!" he 'says'.

"Oh an' tanks for sort'in' dah Burddin prick owras well" he goes on.

"I'm owndly soddy darrye didden doowih meself all dowez yeeyors ago."

"Not a problem dude" I answer with a coo.

"He defo had it coming".

"So like Phil, let me get this straight" I 'ask' him then, as I shuffle from side to side on the branch.

"Am I like, actually dead now? Like, you know, officially and that, as a person?"

"Oh yeah pal" he 'answers' with a whistle.

"Shore if ye dowent beleeyev me, we can go te yorr funeradoddle in a few dayez tiyem!"

"We can fly toowih like, ye know?" he goes on.

"Really?" I'm 'thinking', which upon reflection seems a bit weird.

And daunting.

As in, what if nobody turns the fuck up?

And then I get to thinking - what the fuck are you going on about, ye thick fuck?

OF COURSE they'll turn up!

INCLUDING all o' those mad Rock Star DemiGod types as well!

Sure why wouldn't they?

YOU WERE JOHNNY FUCKING FREAK SHOW FOR FUCK SAKE!!

Made in the USA
Columbia, SC
11 September 2019